A FINANCIAL COLLAPSE
CRY HAVOC

ANGERY AMERICAN

Cry Havoc
Copyright © 2016 by Angery America. All rights reserved.
First Edition: November 2016

No part of this book may be reproduced, scanned, or distributed in any printed or electronic form without permission. Please do not participate in or encourage piracy of copyrighted materials in violation of the author's rights. Thank you for respecting the hard work of this author.

This is a work of fiction. Names, characters, places, and incidents either are the product of the author's imagination or are used fictitiously, and any resemblance to locales, events, business establishments, or actual persons—living or dead—is entirely coincidental.

PROLOGUE

Election time in the United States of America is a long drawn-out expose of unrestrained spending and a non-stop bombardment of ads. There once was a time when the media *reported* on the election cycle. But in today's America, the media is simply another arm of the two parties. No longer are there unbiased reports on the good, the bad and the ugly of a candidate. Now, all those talking heads on the TV and radio are merely pundits of their preferred candidate.

The Presidential election of 2016 was no different. As had been the trend in recent elections, it was worse than the one before. The election of Obama saw a vicious competition that many thought witnessed the depth of depravity that candidates could sink to. But this election proved that wrong in a big way. Sadly, what it foreshadowed was the continuing trend of the nation being divided further and further.

Oh, each candidate always proclaimed they were the one to unite the country. But in every case they merely pandered to the most radical elements of their respective parties. No one, at least in recent memory, was about uniting the country. It was about winning power, seizing power for their party. It was in their minds to reward their supporters and punish their adversaries. And that was the real change in the mindset. *To punish those that opposed them.*

Obama was the first President to speak this out loud. But he didn't just talk the talk, he walked the walk as well. Using many federal agencies to serve up retribution on those he saw as enemies, he utilized the IRS, the Justice Department, and even the Department of Agriculture. All of these were viewed as useful tools or weapons to the new President and those in his administration. And they used them to their most utmost effectiveness.

So, the election of 2016 simply moved the nation further down the path of division, resentment and hate. It was no surprise then that successive administrations would be worse than the previous, though each time the current election was always called the worst one yet. And it was. It was as if there were some sick race to the bottom of human nature, like some abhorrent game those in power would continue to implement in order to see just how far they could manipulate the population of the richest nation in the world.

The real goal of all this was to push the country farther and farther to the left. Those on the right were always portrayed as extremists, not that the typical individual of a left-leaning mindset saw their neighbors with a right-leaning mindset as extremists; but they were very carefully herded in that direction.

America was formed on the concept of individual worth. And that simply could not be tolerated in what those in power foresaw for the country. In order to achieve their goals, they had to change this. It was started in the schools, to ensure that the next generations didn't hold onto archaic ideas. Anyone who held onto these out-of-date values was berated publicly. They were humiliated and accused of any and all crimes, real or not. The masses had to be brought into line.

Social conditioning is a very complex process, and social media plays a major role in that in this modern world. People can't hide from their accusers or their accusations, whether they are fabricated or not. And these *Social Justice Warriors* played a significant part. They were recruited to shout down any dissenting voices. In the new America, there could only be one line of thought; and that was whatever those in power wanted it to be.

Those Americans who were more independent, more self-reliant, stood to lose the most. And to ensure these people, as well as everyone else, came to heel, three things had to be controlled. First was the possession of firearms. An armed populace possesses the ability to resist, which is precisely what Thomas Jefferson and the other founding fathers intended when they crafted the 2nd Amendment. But that simply does not fit with the new narrative. Second was money, the medium of exchange. The ability of people to purchase what they need, when they need it, and from the source of their choice, had to be restricted. To that end, the removal of cash from circulation had to be carried out for the overall plan to be effective. But it was understood that simply couldn't happen overnight. The last point of manipulation in order to realize absolute domination of the population would be the total command over communications. People who can communicate and share ideas or plan and coordinate are not as easy to subjugate as those whose only source of information comes from those seeking power over them.

The election of 2020 was set to further all of these goals, just as those elections prior to it had done. But things were progressing too slowly for those at the helm, and something had to be implemented to speed it up. With this in mind, the triangle of freedom in the United States would become first leg of the assault. The top of the new President's agenda was to push the House and Senate to ratify the Small Arms treaty. Oh, there was great outrage from the reps on the right, lots of pulpit pounding and chest thumping; but in the end, it passed both chambers with a nearly ninety percent "yes" vote. This was gasoline on the fire. The second act of the new President was to capitulate to Iran and acknowledge their right to self-defense, and in that light, their right to nuclear weapons. This process had already been started by Obama; the new occupant of the Whitehouse just laid the capstone.

And with Iran firmly in Russia's pocket, things would certainly only get worse. When the US *accidentally* bombed elements of the Syrian Army, claiming they thought they were ISIS, the Russians moved in missile systems capable of shooting down American aircraft, as well as cruise missiles. The pieces were being set for a head-to-head confrontation with Russia. Russia was not going to allow Assad to fall, no matter how bad the new President of the United States wanted it.

Further emboldened by the perceived support of Russia, radicals in the Middle East pressed their campaigns of terror and fear throughout the world. Israel was under near constant attack from the West Bank. When ISIS was finally defeated, despite the best efforts of the Obama and Clinton administrations, Iran was even further empowered. Hezbollah began direct action operations against Israel. Of course, publicly they denied this. But with the full backing of the Russians, there was little the world could do to combat it, short of full-scale World War.

The trail to destruction was thus begun. Oh, there were other potholes along the way, but these events were to have such a profound effect on the country that it would be forever changed. When Obama knelt at the feet of the Persians, figuratively if not literally, it emboldened the Iranian leadership. When the President proposed a further reduction in nuclear arsenals with the Russians, the government of Putin eagerly agreed. A great victory in the name of humanity was made out of the decommissioning of upwards of sixty percent of the US & Russian arsenals. The Russians played up the plan in the media, and appearances between the two leaders were plastered all over the MSM. The Russians, however, were not decommissioning anything.

Under the Small Arms Treaty, it was announced to the nations of the world that the private ownership of military-grade weapons was now outlawed. Much was made that America, reputed to be the last Super Power, had the greatest number of such weapons in private hands. The fact that the US Administration ratified the treaty, then went even further by reducing its nuclear arsenal, heralded a new era in global peace, while at the same time continuing to bang the drums of war. The rest of the world may have bought this, but the owners of the more than 300 million guns in the US certainly didn't. And here, another wedge was driven into the nation.

There are many gun owners in the country that certainly believe military-grade hardware should be outlawed. They joined the applause of the Treaty. Those that believed that high capacity magazines should be outlawed joined into the orgy of praise as well; that is until it was revealed that supplemental wording was added that banned any weapon that was capable of mechanical self-loading. In the beginning, this caused some confusion and misconceptions. When it was revealed that any magazine-fed weapon, regardless of capacity, was banned, the cries of violating the Constitution grew louder. When it was further revealed that the term "magazine" also included tube-fed weapons, the cries reached a crescendo. Now there was no doubt what the intentions behind this Treaty were, the virtual total disarmament of the American People.

The events happening around the globe faded from the minds of most Americans. So caught up in their fading freedoms, they paid less and less attention to what was happening on a global scale. And while they wouldn't pay attention for now, a time was fast approaching when they would no longer be able to ignore it.

For many in the prepper community, the writing was on the wall. All across the country, people were making decisions. Some were headed to their BOLs, while others were trying to buy up whatever ammo was left out there; and prices were astronomical. There would be no more shipments, no more mags, no more parts, nothing. All those people that figured they would see "it" coming and head out and use their credit cards to prepare were caught with their pants down, and Big Brother was squeezing Astro Glide into his hand.

When the TSA started to set up roadblocks and search vehicles, the shit hit the fan. The Feds decided to go big. Many people were caught off guard by the TSA being the ones to man these road blocks. But the ice had already been broken on that issue years ago. Of course it was called training for terror operations back then. The Feds just didn't mention who those terrorists would be, we the people.

The first roadblocks were set up in Michigan. It was bait, and the Michigan Militia took it. When the militia heard that the TSA goons were searching people on the interstates, confiscating and arresting people for possession of firearms, even though the "grace period" wasn't up, they made their move. A unit of the militia planned a quick op when they heard of a roadblock nearby.

Using six vehicles, they approached the roadblock from both directions. This particular roadblock was on a frontage road that paralleled Hwy 96 outside of Lansing. The lead car had two militiamen in it. As they approached the roadblock, they were challenged by the TSA and asked if they had any weapons. When they replied they did, they were ordered from the car. Both of them were wearing body armor with plates, front and back. Most of the attention of those manning the roadblock was focused on the two "noncompliant" passengers.

It was then that the other twenty-five members emerged from the remaining five SUVs and opened fire on the TSA, DHS and State Patrol officers at the roadblock. The incident would forever be referred to as the "Lansing Incident". It would be a battle cry for the Patriots of the nation and the anvil against which all freedom-loving men and women of the US would be hammered. Four militiamen were killed, as well as two Troopers, two DHS personnel and four from the TSA. The firefight was intense and short. Almost all the vehicles at the scene belonging to any of the agencies involved were burned through the use of homemade thermite grenades.

The militia managed to escape from the scene, recovering their fallen comrades. Not all of them were caught, although the MSM would report otherwise. This was our Concord, the spark that started it all. America was now a police state. And to make matters worse, America was also about to go to war.

This was the moment the Administration was waiting for. Before the fires were even out in Lansing, the Attorney General was issuing decrees to local, state and federal law enforcement agencies. All weapons in private hands were to be seized immediately. To get around any Constitutional or legal loopholes, the President enacted several Executive Orders, not the least of which was 13603, section 501 that was to have a profound effect on the citizens of the nation. This particular section of the EO was headed by Employment of Personnel and allowed the establishment of the National Executive Defense Reserve or NEDR. It was created under the auspices of training civilians in executive level positions in the Federal Government. In reality, it was a cover to create a private, federal police force, answerable only to the President and the Attorney General.

KLB Inc was awarded an indefinite delivery contract to provide for detention and housing of "suspects and subversives" utilizing the guidelines established in the

NDAA. The National Defense Authorization Act allowed for the indefinite detention of American citizens without any Constitutional protections. The Council of Governors was instructed to assist the DHS with the activation of the Regional FEMA camps. These camps would be used to house persons arrested under provisions of the NDAA. Soon, American Citizens would be facing American troops on the streets of the nation. That is unless their attention gets focused elsewhere.

CHAPTER 1

Daniel Taylor lived in a four-story apartment on Century Cir, off of I-85 on the north side of Atlanta. He worked in the IT department of one of the banks in the upscale Buckhead area and attended the University of Phoenix DeKalb Learning Center across the street from his apartments. In his position, he was responsible for keeping the network secure from the constant, daily attacks on the bank. He was one of many who lived in cubicle land staring into computer monitors all day. Once he finishes his degree, he hopes to get promoted out of the gopher farm and upstairs; but for now, this was his life.

While cyber-attacks on banks were nothing new, things were really getting bad lately. He and the others tasked with securing the banks' servers from attacks were barely able to keep up. And it wasn't just them. In white-papers that circulated through the IT world, it was now openly acknowledged that the early stages of war were already in motion. Power plants, utility providers, banks, traffic networks, military and law enforcement networks across the nation were under constant and crippling attacks. While it wasn't stated publicly, those in the industry knew where the attacks were coming from.

The daily power outages occurring around the country were reported as brown-outs due to excessive demand. The summer was exceptionally hot and people were trying to stay cool. While that was the *official* story, the real reason was the number of cyber-attacks on the various utility providers; not only power companies and infrastructure, but water operations as well, and even internet and phone providers. The attacks were sufficiently widespread that most people didn't acknowledge them for what they were, a coordinated attack on the US. In the modern world, warfare extends into the cyber world.

Daniel's girlfriend Christy lived nearby in a different apartment. She had hinted several times at wanting to move in together, but so far he'd been successful in dodging that particular bullet. He wasn't ready for any sort of a commitment. He liked his freedom; and from the talks around the water cooler and the employee lounge, married life came with way too damn many restrictions for him. He enjoyed his weekends in north Georgia where he camped, hiked and fished. He liked his time in places like the Bowmans Island unit of the Chattahoochee River.

This is where he got away from the hustle and bustle of Atlanta. Up there it was quieter and there were fewer people. On the weekends, he would load his van up and head out of town with his camping gear and a cooler, not to return until sometime Sunday afternoon. Sometimes Christy would go with him. She wasn't much of a camper, but was learning to like it. Watching the sun set from the top of a ridge, or the sun rising over a secluded pond, made it worth the trip. Most of the time, however, he was alone; and that was how he liked it.

The van was something he could never have afforded. It was left to him by a friend of his father when he passed. Old Tom Maples used to love to run the woods with Daniel, and the two became great friends. Tom bought the Sportsmobile customized van late in life and the two used it extensively. It was a Ford van with a diesel engine and a Quigley 4x4 added to it. It was set up to sleep two people, and included an outside shower and an enclosed toilet inside. It was the ideal vehicle for Daniel's weekend forays into the mountains.

All through the election, things in Atlanta got progressively worse, culminating in riots. The National Guard was brought in to put them down after the police were overwhelmed. This caused even more riots and problems. Two Guardsmen were shot and killed and their weapons stolen. The result was for the Governor to authorize the Guard troops to shoot armed individuals and looters on sight. Seventeen people were killed, fourteen of them black, which just added fuel to the fire of racial inequality. The world was coming apart at the seams while the band played on.

Daniel let out an evil laugh as he jumped and slapped the sign that indicated the elevator. He packed into the first elevator that stopped on his floor. From the looks on the faces of the people already on it, they were not happy with one more person squeezing on. He simply smiled and edged his way in. When the doors opened in the lobby, he was first one off and made a mad dash for the parking garage.

Traffic was a nightmare, as is typical for any part of metro Atlanta, and especially in Buckhead. While he was ready to get home and load up, he wasn't letting it get to him. Where he was headed there wouldn't be any traffic. The one thing he did notice was all the police on the road. On his ride home, Daniel saw more Atlanta cops, State Troopers and Sheriff Deputies than he ever had. Several times, he saw these officers putting people in handcuffs and stuffing them in the back of their car. It seemed like the number of people being arrested was increasing.

Daniel flipped on the radio, looking for a distraction. He was scanning through the stations looking for something to listen to that wouldn't drive him nuts. The radio stopped on one of the local talk stations, and Rush Limbaugh was on. He was ranting and raving about how the Republicans had completely caved on Israel, how they were done, they would never be a viable party again. Well, this certainly wasn't helping his sanity, so he punched a key on the radio and smiled as Kid Rock's Cocky started.

His cell phone rang. Looking down at Christy's name on the screen, a smile came across his face.

He tapped the screen. "Hey, sexy". This was his standard answer.

"Hey, babe. Where are you?"

"Stuck on 85, sitting in traffic. Where are you?"

"At my apartment. What are you wanting to do this weekend? I was kinda hoping we could go to Buckhead tonight. You know, take me out to do what I want, and then we can do what you want." Christy's voice trailed off into a breathy, seductive tone.

Well, now that was an offer he had to think about. "I was hoping to head up north and check out that trail we found the last time we were up there." He didn't say anything more than that, not "do you wanna come" or anything. He was going to have to see what sort of mood she was in.

"Aw, come on, baby. We haven't gone out in like forever. I wanna go out. Take me out tonight, please," Christy cooed into the phone.

Daniel's hand fell into his lap, and he looked up through the sunroof of the van, his mouth hanging open. In his mind he was screaming *why, why, why*; but he knew he couldn't say that to her. He hated to "go out", bar hopping. Going to clubs and being dragged out onto the dance floor was simply not his thing. But he liked Christy, for a couple of reasons. That last thought brought him back around, and he put the phone back to his ear.

"Sure, babe. We can go out. I need to get home and get a shower and change. Just come over when you're ready," he finally said.

The conversation didn't last much longer than that. Christy was excited at the thought of spending the night in Buckhead, while Daniel was miserable at the same thought. Then he smiled, knowing the hours he would spend slogging through the bars and clubs would be worth it when they got back to his place.

He finally made it home and into his apartment on the second floor, closing the door with an audible sigh. His first order of business was to get out of the corporate monkey suit and into something more comfortable, so he headed for his bedroom and returned, wearing a t-shirt and shorts, and feeling far more relaxed. He knew Christy would be a couple, hell more than a couple, hours before she showed up, so he grabbed a beer and turned on the TV. Fox News and CNN were running talking heads from opposite sides of the gun debates, and MSNBC was interviewing some clown from the EU who was pontificating about the US's role in the global economy and how they weren't acting very responsibly.

None of this was doing anything to improve his mood though, and he flipped to the guide and found Jack Ass the Movie, which was exactly the sort of mind-numbing entertainment he wanted. Daniel decided to start getting ready, turning up the volume on Johnny Knoxville's antics as he headed for the shower.

He was sitting on the couch watching a piece about Rommel on the Military Channel when he heard that distinct knock on the door. He flipped off the TV and grabbed his keys and wallet before heading towards the door. Opening the door, he was greeted with an amazing sight. Christy had one arm resting on the door frame over her head. She was wearing what is often referred to as the *little black dress*, "little" being the key word; and she was smokin' hot in it. Adding in the black heels and the fact that the small dress barely contained her chest, he questioned in his mind the plan of going out, thinking that staying at his place would be better. But then, if he took her out and let her party it up, it would certainly pay off.

"Damn, you look fine," Daniel said as he stepped towards her.

Christy wrapped her arms around his neck and smiled, revealing her beautifully perfect white teeth. Then she pushed herself up on her toes and leaned in and kissed him. "You don't look so bad yourself," she said with a smile. Stepping back to check him out, "and all by yourself. I'm so proud."

Daniel did a little pirouette. "Not bad, huh?"

Christy reached out and grabbed his ass. "Not bad at all. So where we going?"

He had planned what he would say to this question. "I thought we would start at Churchill's." Before he even finished saying it, he started to smile, knowing how she felt about the British-style pub.

Christy spun and started to walk towards the stairs, tossing the little black purse over her shoulder. "I'll pretend I didn't hear that."

They started the night at Aria Restaurant off E. Paces Ferry Rd, a trendy upscale little place with great food and prices that reflect it. Daniel knew this night was going to cost him. But since he wasn't going to the woods this weekend, he was going to make it as enjoyable as possible; and keeping Christy in bed all weekend would certainly be enjoyable.

They enjoyed their dinner, he having Salmon and Christy a chicken something or other. Because of the difference in dishes, they had two different bottles of wine at the table as well. Neither of them wanted dessert, and Daniel quickly paid the bill and they were off to find some music and people.

Daniel was pulling out of the parking lot when he asked Christy where she wanted to go. Her reply was no help. "Surprise me." All he could do was roll his eyes as he pulled out onto the road. This scenario had entered his mind, and having been a Boy Scout, he was ready. He headed down Paces Ferry to Piedmont and made a left. The stars were lining up tonight and a car was pulling out of a spot in front of the Havana Club as he pulled in.

Looking over at Christy, he asked, "Feel like dancing tonight?" his eyebrows jumping up and down as he did.

Christy was obviously surprised. Being a typical guy, he tried to avoid dancing at all costs; and for him to suggest it was certainly a surprise. "You mean you're actually going to dance with me tonight?"

Daniel looked over at her as he put the van in park. The small silver chain she wore around her neck caught his eye, the little pendent resting in the top of her ample cleavage. He looked a little lower until his eyes settled on the little black dress covering his desires. He reached across to her seat and laid his hand on her thigh, running it slightly up her leg under the dress. "You look amazing tonight. Wanna dance?"

Christy took a deep breath, her mouth slightly open, and began to vigorously nod her head. "Yeah, oh yeah. Let's go."

Inside, the bar was packed with all the young and beautiful of Atlanta. Techno dance music filled the place and bodies on the floor writhed to the rhythm. As soon as Christy broke the plane of the door, her arms went up and she began to shake her ass to the music. They spent the next several hours dancing and drinking. Christy was having a great time, and he knew he would later. It was the only thing that kept him going.

Daniel needed a break from the dance floor and told Christy he was going to get them a drink. She nodded and turned back to the gyrating crowd. Daniel went to the bathroom to take a leak. Of course there was an "attendant" in there, an older black man sitting on a stool. Daniel saw him when he came in and rolled his eyes. After finishing his business at the urinal, he went to the sink. The soap dispenser was gone and the old man held out a bottle of liquid soap. Daniel stuck his hands out and the old guy pumped a few squirts in his palm.

As he washed his hands, he looked over to the paper towel dispenser, and just as he suspected, it was empty. A smirk ran across his face. When he finished, the old man tossed him a hand towel and he dried his hands. Sitting on the counter was a small basket full of bills. He handed the towel back to the old guy and he tossed it into a basket on the floor. It was now that he was expected to tip this guy for some soap and a towel.

The old man was smiling at him. Daniel looked at him, patting his pockets. "Sorry, man. Don't have any cash. I'm going to the bar for some drinks and I'll take care of you next time."

"Jus' don't forget about me," the old guy said with a wink.

Daniel left the restroom, shaking his head at the thought of having to pay to take a piss, and he fought his way to the bar. He was trying to get the attention of one of the hot bartenders, which appeared impossible, so he occupied his time with one of the huge TVs behind the bar. A local news anchor was on the screen. Behind her was a line of riot police forming a skirmish line. Daniel was absentmindedly watching when the scroll at the bottom of the screen said, *Riot at Tower Place turns violent.*

He immediately left the bar, headed for the dance floor to find Christy. He found her dancing with some Latin guy with no shirt. He wedged in between them and she threw her arms around his neck and kissed him.

Pulling away from her, he shouted over the music. "We gotta go!"

She was still smiling and dancing to the music. "What?" she shouted back.

"We gotta go!" he shouted again.

She simply smiled back at him, grabbing his hands and pulling him towards her. Daniel gripped her right hand and pulled her from the dance floor. She tried to protest, pulling away.

"What the hell?" Christy asked.

"Look, there's a riot starting over at Tower Place. We need to get the hell outta here before they bring in the National Guard and start shooting people."

"Why? That's blocks from here. Come on, come back out and dance with me."

"No, I'm leaving. I'm not getting caught in that shit. You coming?" Daniel asked.

The tone of his voice, or maybe his posture, drove the point home. "Fine."

Daniel led her out of the club and to the van. He was putting her in on the passenger side when she wrapped her arms around him again. Christy pulled him to her and started to kiss him, but the sounds of a police helicopter flying low overhead brought Daniel's attention back to more pressing concerns, even if they weren't enjoyable as what was happening.

Backing away from her, he said, "Hold that thought. Let's get out of here first."

She leaned back into her seat and smiled, closing her eyes. Daniel looked in the direction of Tower Place at the glow rising above the buildings. Sirens filled the air, as well as police and news helicopters. All he wanted to do was get back to his apartment as fast as he could. By the time he got around the van and into the driver's seat, Christy was passed out, her head slumped over on the door.

He pulled out of the parking lot and headed back towards the apartment. Traffic was building and police were beginning to shut down intersections. Daniel was forced to take several turns he didn't want to, and as a result, he was getting father and farther from his apartment.

What should have been a twenty-minute drive ended up taking over an hour and a half. Daniel never saw any trouble. He never got close enough to whatever was going on to see, and that was fine with him. Pulling into the parking garage, he managed to wake Christy up without too much trouble and helped her get to the elevator and into the apartment.

Once inside, Christy sat on the edge of his bed and he went into the bathroom. For a moment, he leaned on the sink looking into the mirror. He wanted to get out of town this weekend, out into the woods, and not let her talk him into staying here, especially now there was a frickin riot. He quickly washed his face and kicked his shoes off, trying to relax.

Opening the door, he saw her lying naked on the bed, propped up on her elbows. The light from the bathroom lit her side facing him, and a smile spread across his face. Maybe staying here wasn't such a bad idea, he thought as he stepped towards the bed.

Daniel woke up with light streaming through the blinds in the morning. Shielding his eyes with his hand, he sat up, and then he closed them again. Christy was lying there, sound asleep. She looked so good. Running a hand over her ass, he covered her with the sheet and headed for the kitchen. He needed his hangover remedy. Not that he drank that much, but the combination of the alcohol, the music and the stress of the ride home made him feel like he drank an entire liquor store.

After taking two Excedrin and drinking a huge glass of water, Daniel went to the fridge and dug out some cream cheese. From a paper bag on the counter, he pulled out a huge "everything" bagel, then looked inside and found a plain one. With his bagel fixed, he headed for the living room and dropped onto the couch, flipping on the TV.

He changed the channel to Fox News to see what was going on in the world. What he saw shocked him. On the screen was a view of Tower Place. Cars were on fire as well as some buildings in the distance. It looked as though there were hundreds of police, but unlike last night, these were not riot cops. The shields and clubs were gone, replaced with armored vehicles and rifles.

The reporter on the scene was saying something about 'an unknown number killed in the fighting'. He sat up on the sofa, leaning forward. In the background of the view, it appeared that a large section of the area was blocked off and there were bodies visible in a couple of places. The reporter came back into view again and he could see she was crouching behind the corner of a building as the cameraman leaned out to get shots of the action. Gunshots could be heard in the audio, the camera bounced and jerked with each report.

Daniel sat there shaking his head. *People are fucking nuts* he said to himself. Watching what was unfolding before him, he started to get a little nervous and got up, returning to the kitchen. He felt like he should be doing something, but what? The riot was still pretty far from his place and shouldn't be a problem, but better safe than sorry. Daniel went through the cabinets really quick to get an idea of what he had on hand. Being a bachelor, naturally they were pretty bare. Deciding it would be a good idea to have a little more on hand, he figured a trip to the store wouldn't hurt.

Back in the bedroom, he tried to wake Christy, but she was suffering from the mother of all hangovers and was in no shape to leave. She curled up into the comforter and mumbled something about chicken noodle soup. He leaned down and kissed her on the head and said he would be back shortly.

Changing into a pair of jeans and Polo shirt, he picked through the leather tray that sat on his dresser, looking for the right folder to take. Daniel had a thing for knives and had quite the collection. He settled on a carbon fiber ZT and clipped it into his pocket, then slipped a Leatherman Wave into his back pocket with a small Fenix flashlight. He so badly wanted to take his Glock, but in the current environment that was just out of the question.

Yes, guns were now outlawed. Daniel knew it. But he wasn't getting rid of his. He'd bought it at a gun show and there was no paper trail to him. No one knew he had it, not even Christy. Daniel didn't think of himself as one of those chest-thumping type of patriots. He didn't go into the military; it wasn't in his family. But he was a patriot. He loved his country and the freedoms it afforded him. Seeing them diminish pained him, and he'd decided to only be pushed so far.

Taking the stairs down to the parking garage, he quickly made his way to the van, heading to Wal-Mart. Traffic on this side of town was fairly light, though there was a huge police presence. It seemed that every intersection had an officer of some type sitting nearby. He made it to the store without incident.

Surprisingly, the place wasn't very crowded. Maybe everyone was staying inside to watch the news. The lack of crowds let him make his rounds quickly. He hadn't really thought about how much he was putting in the cart, and by the time he made it to the register, he had a cart mounded up with stuff. As the cashier rang it all up, he stood there thinking of all the trips up and down the elevator it would take to get all this into his apartment.

His haul filled a considerable amount of space in the floor of the van. On the ride back, he listened to the radio, trying to keep tabs on what was going on. Then he heard something that really shocked him. The mayor was considering a dusk to dawn curfew, though no official announcement had been made. 'Knowledgeable insiders' stated it was all but a certainty.

Suddenly, his trip started to make even more sense. If a curfew were started, there would be no way for him to get to the store during the week. Back in the garage, he grabbed up two handfuls of bags and headed for the elevator, it looked like he would have to make three or four more trips to get everything moved.

Back in the apartment, he set the first load down in the kitchen, then had an idea and went to the closet in the living room where he kept all his camping gear. Throwing equipment over his shoulder, he finally found what he was looking for, his pack hammock, and headed for the garage again.

Back at the van, he laid the hammock out on the ground beside the open door of the van and piled all the bags on top of it, then grabbed the ends and pulled them up, making what looked like a huge Santa bag. Daniel was grinning from ear to ear; this would save him a couple of trips. With great self-satisfaction, he went to throw the bundle over his shoulder and discovered it was far heavier than he had thought. With a grunt, he finally managed to get it over his shoulder; but he had to lean way forward to get the bundle into a position where he could walk under the weight.

Finally making it back to the apartment, he dropped the bundle on the floor in the kitchen. He stared down at the pile spread across the floor. With a sigh, he leaned over and started to put it all away. All the cabinet doors were open, as well as the pantry. Empty shopping bags were scattered all over the kitchen, covering nearly every horizontal surface visible. Taking a quick break, he turned on the TV, back to Fox News to see if there was any new information. What he heard couldn't be good. The Governor was going to have a press conference at 4:00 today. He figured that if a politician was going to get on TV on a Saturday, it had to be bad news.

With nothing to do for a couple of hours, he went to check on Christy. The bed was empty and the shower was running. Back in the kitchen, he made lunch, a couple of turkey sandwiches and a bowl of chicken noodle soup. He was sitting on the couch playing Battlefield on the Xbox when she came out, drying her hair with a towel.

"Oh, that looks good. I'm so hungry," Christy said as she sat on the couch.

"I thought you might want something to eat."

"Mmm, this is good. Now I see what you've been doing all morning. Boys and their video games."

"Shows what you know, I just started. I've been to the store already and bought groceries."

Through bites of her sandwich, Christie asked, "What's on the news?"

Daniel grabbed the remote and switched the TV back to cable. Fox was already on. "Riots, riots and more riots."

Christy wiped her mouth with a napkin. "What happened last night?"

"Seventeen dead, or at least that's what they are saying right now. The Governor is going to have a press conference later. Maybe we'll get a little more info."

"Let's watch a movie or something. It's the weekend and this is depressing."

"You're right," Daniel said as he leaned back and put his arm around her.

Finding a movie on pay-per-view, they spent the rest of the afternoon spooning on the couch. With Christy in his arms, he could smell her hair. While it didn't smell like the woods of north Georgia, it was an enchanting scent; and the woods will always be there. The movie was almost over when Daniel looked up at the clock. It was nearly four. He paused the movie and switched back to Fox News. Christy didn't complain. She was obviously interested in what was going on as well.

The screen displayed a podium with the seal of the

Governor. The talking heads were all guessing what he would say. As they waited, the screen split to show the riot that was still taking place near Tower Place. Christy shook her head. "That's just awful. I never imagined we'd see that sort of thing here. It's like watching some other country."

Daniel squeezed her a little tighter. "I know. Remember when Venezuela fell apart? Looks like that."

The Governor stepped up to the podium and the talking heads disappeared. He began to speak about the riots and the increasing level of lawlessness that seemed to be overtaking most of metro Atlanta. To combat the rise in violent crime sweeping the city, he'd activated the Georgia National Guard, and they would be assuming the lead role of law enforcement in the city. To make the job easier, he was instituting a dusk to dawn curfew, effective immediately. Anyone caught on the streets during the curfew would be arrested, no questions asked.

"This isn't going to end well," Christy said.

Daniel grunted. "Nope. Wish I were in the mountains."

She slapped his leg. "What is with you and the mountains?"

Daniel pointed at the TV. "You don't have this kind of crap up there. There's fewer people. Less trouble. Plus, it's probably ten or fifteen degrees cooler up there right now!"

Christy stretched. "I guess I should get going so I can get home before dark."

Letting her go, he sat up. "It's so weird we're even talking about a curfew here. I mean, this is ridiculous."

Christy kissed him. "It'll be alright. You going to walk me down to the garage?"

ANGERY AMERICAN

Standing up, Daniel slapped her ass. "I hate to see you go, but I love to watch you leave."

Christy rolled her eyes. "Pathetic."

The two had been together so long now that Christy had clothes at his place and he at hers. So she walked to the garage in a pair of sweats, the little black dress and heels over her shoulder in a bag. At her Honda, she tossed the bag in the seat and spun around to face him.

"I had a great time," she said as she wrapped her arms around his neck.

"Me too," Daniel replied as he leaned in and kissed her.

"Better than the mountains?" She asked with a wink. Daniel looked off as though he were mulling the question over. She slapped his shoulder. "It better have been!"

He laughed and kissed her again. "It was a great time. Wouldn't trade it for anything."

She smiled as she got in the Honda. "That's what I thought."

CHAPTER 2

It was Monday and back to the grind. Daniel was sitting in his cubicle monitoring what was becoming a never-ending series of concentrated, though ineffective, attacks against the network. It was ridiculous that in this day anyone would actually try a brute force attack against a network like the bank's. But for the last week, someone, or several as was probably the case, had been trying exactly that.

Daniel was shaking his head at the thought when Kilroy's head popped over the top of cubicle. Looking up at the shiny head brought a smile to his face.

"Dude, you seeing all this?" Tom asked.

Daniel looked back to his monitors. "Yeah, what kind of moron tries this kind of thing now-a-days?"

"Don' know. You track the IPs yet?"

"No. Why don't you? I'm locking down all the ports they probe. Let's see if we can find out where these fuckers are."

"Cool. I'll do it. Where'd you go this weekend?" Tom asked.

"Ended up staying home."

Tom's face screwed up. "Why? Thought you were headed north."

"Let's just say Christy can be persuasive."

Tom's head cocked to the side in confusion; then it hit him as his eyes drifted to that pic again. "Details?"

"In your dreams, brother. In your dreams," Daniel said as he swiveled around to his computer.

Even though Daniel couldn't see him, Tom nodded and his shiny head dipped below the cubicle wall. Daniel was busy trying to isolate ports in the network where the hackers were probing. It was not a very sophisticated attack, simply typing IPs into a browser window then using one of several black-market programs to try passwords until it finds one that works. The problem with that is that modern networks are protected by numerous layers of security. After only a few attempts, the firewalls and networks flag the port and lock it out. Then a human has to look at it and decide what was going on and take further action. Daniel was the human in this case.

Daniel was focused on his monitors. He loved this shit. Someone was trying to get in, and he was going to stop them. He was so busy, he didn't notice Amber, who was leaning on the edge of the cubicle wall that separated him and Tom. Tom, however, did notice her. Amber had a crush on Daniel. With the pics of all the cool places he went to pinned to the walls of his cubicle, and the fact that he had a hot girlfriend, he was an irresistible conquest for her.

Tom had completely stopped what he was doing. From where he sat, all he could see was Amber from the waist down. He was running his gaze up and down her legs. She was wearing the old fashioned stockings with the seam on the back of her legs. Amber finally tried to get Daniel's attention.

"Daniel, are you busy?" She cooed.

Daniel didn't bother to look up. He knew from the voice who it was and wasn't interested. As hot as she was, Amber had a reputation for sleeping her way to the top. "Kinda busy. What's up?"

She was holding a thumb drive, and naturally her hand was buried between her huge tits. "Oh, sorry. I found this thumb drive in the ladies' room earlier and I'm not sure who it belongs too."

"Sorry, Amber. I'm really busy right now. See if you can find out who it belongs to."

Amber's lips formed into a fashionable pout. "Okay. I'll come by later when you're not so busy". She straightened up and noticed Tom, who tried to appear like he was looking at something tacked to the wall of his cubicle. "What are you looking at, perv?" She barked and stomped off.

Tom was embarrassed, turning several different shades of red. To try and cover for it, he stood up, looking over the cubicle and asked, "Daniel, did you track those IPs?"

Daniel spun around in his chair. "What? You were supposed to track them down!"

Flustered once again, Tom replied. "Oh, right", and quickly sat down to his computer.

Amber was not happy with Daniel not noticing her and that creepy asshole Tom ogling her. She was pissed. Finding her way back to her cubicle, she threw the thumb drive onto her desk and flopped into her chair, making sure to cross her legs as she was wearing a really short skirt. She sat there for a moment thinking about the rejection. *One of these days I'll get him. I'll rock his world and he'll never go back to that skank,* she thought.

She sat there for a moment, then her eyes fell on the

drive. She picked it up and plugged it into her computer. It was against policy, but if it wrecked her machine, then Daniel would have to come by and fix it. A thin smile spread across her perfectly painted lips as she muttered. *I hope it's got the mother of all viruses on it.*

Daniel suddenly sat upright, running his hands through his hair. He sat there staring at the screens before him. All morning he fought off the probes of the network, but now they were suddenly gone. He stood up looking at the monitors, his left arm across his chest and chin in his right hand. He was interrupted by Tom.

"Dude, you stopped it. They're gone."

Daniel sat there for a moment before replying. He didn't bother to turn around. "Either that or they're in. Did you trace the IPs?"

"Working on it," was all Tom replied before disappearing into his cubicle again.

Whoever was probing the network was using a sophisticated program that bounced the connection all over the world. It successfully masked the originating IP, but would eventually turn up, requiring some time to sort through it. Daniel and Tom would spend the rest of the week working on the project.

While sifting through the trail of the IPs, Daniel kept a couple of windows open on one of the monitors. One was a local news station and the other alternated between Fox News and CNN. The local station was dominated by the riots. After the riot over the weekend and the deaths that went along with it, the tension was building in Atlanta. Fox and CNN were showing similar video from around the country, riots, protests and lots and lots of police.

A video of white armored vehicles caught Daniel's eye, and he turned the volume up to see what was going on. The video showed a number of vehicles that were assembling in a large parking lot. It took a few minutes to figure out where this was all taking place. Apparently, the mayor of Detroit had requested federal help to deal with the riots in that city. The number of shootings, which was already high, was climbing dramatically. Several police officers had been hit in shootouts erupting during riots in the city.

People were becoming agitated. Those on the right were mad about the usurpation of their second amendment-recognized right to own firearms. Those on the left were demanding more *entitlements*. Many had been energized by Bernie Sanders' campaign of socialist ideas, and they were demanding a *fair and equitable* distribution of the wealth of the nation. These two groups naturally clashed with one another. The police clashed with both.

In the beginning, the protests over the ownership of firearms were peaceful, if not loud. But as the realization became clear that the intent was the complete disarmament of the American people, they became more violent. As for those demanding *their fair share,* they did as they always did. Their protests consisted of riots, looting and arson. Typical moves from the leftist playbook. The country was ripe for revolution.

Daniel sat there chewing on the end of a pen, watching as more and more vehicles added to the mass already there. The view changed to an aerial shot where the full magnitude of the force descending on the city came into view. A line of the white vehicles stretched for blocks.

A phone rang and Daniel looked over at his. Not him, thankfully.

Tom came around the cubicle. "Hey, man. Wow, where's that?"

"Detroit."

"I wish they would come here. Things are getting out of hand 'round here."

Daniel swiveled in his chair. "I don't think that would be a good thing for anyone."

"Yeah. Well, if you're not out in the street, there's probably nothing to worry about. Anyway, Malcolm wants us in his office." Tom raised his eyebrows and stuffed his hands in his pockets.

"What for?" Daniel didn't like going to Malcolm's office. While his boss was a decent guy, he never called you over just to chat.

Tom shrugged his shoulders. Daniel levered himself out of his chair and the two headed off to see what the boss wanted. Tom stopped outside of the office while Daniel wedged himself past him inside and fell into one of the two chairs in front of the desk.

Malcolm was just a couple years older than Daniel and had hired him for his position. Every time Daniel came into the office, he remembered that interview. With his pressed shirt and stylish yet ridiculous suspenders, Malcolm reminded him of Irkle. Now, every time he sees him, that's all he can think of.

"Come in and have a seat, Tom," Malcolm said with a wave of his hand.

Tom quickly came when beckoned, taking a seat beside Daniel and folding his hands in his lap.

Malcolm turned his attention to the big flat monitor on his desk for a second before looking back and smiling.

"What have you got for me?"

Tom looked at Daniel. "Huh, well I'm still working on the IPs."

"There were several sources of the attack. It's weird that anyone would try a brute force attack on a network like ours. I think there is more to it," Daniel said, slumping back into the chair.

Malcolm looked at Daniel. He liked the guy for his work. He was good, but he couldn't stand his obvious lack of corporate decorum.

"I don't think there's more to it, really; just some stupid hacker group, probably. But find those IPs and get back to me on it. Did they ever get in?"

"No. I saw every port they tried and locked them out each time. There were a bunch, but Tom and I stopped 'em." Daniel knew Tom was always worried about his job, though he didn't need to be. He did a good job; and whenever the chance arose to give him credit, he would.

Malcolm looked at his watch. "It's close to quitting time. Make sure everything is secure and I'll see you guys tomorrow."

Daniel and Tom nodded and left the office. On the way back to their desks they stopped by the break room where Daniel got a Mountain Dew and Snickers bar.

"Hey, thanks for backing me up in there," Tom said as he stared into the vending machine.

As he opened the bottle of Dew, Daniel replied. "You don't need any back-up. Don't let him bother you, man. You do a good job and don't have shit to worry about."

"Yeah. Well, that's easy for you to say. You don't have a wife and kids." Tom replied as he pulled a Butterfinger from the little tray in the machine.

"No worries, man. I'll see you tomorrow."

Daniel quickly went to his desk and gathered his stuff, making his way to the elevator before Malcolm could change his mind. A light rain fell as he pulled out of the garage, low hanging clouds adding to the dismal afternoon. Rain anywhere near quitting time meant the already bad traffic was going to be even worse. Daniel let out a long breath, reached up and hit the button on the stereo for the CD and soon The Devil Went Down to Georgia filled the van.

Traffic was crawling along when Daniel noticed one of those big flashing construction signs on the side of the road, —-*BE PREPARED TO STOP*—-, flashed over and over. *Just freakin' great,* he thought as he slapped the wheel with both hands. Daniel leaned around to try and see the accident that must be ahead. There were certainly enough flashing lights up there.

As he inched forward, the lanes became separated by orange construction cones. Daniel craned his neck more, trying to see. Slapping himself on the forehead, he looked down at the Cobra CB hanging under the dash, then reached down and turned it on. Channel 19 was crowded with truckers talking about the jam. Then he heard one of them say it was a roadblock, that the police were stopping everyone and checking IDs. Another trucker said some people were being pulled off to the side of the road and dogs were going around the cars.

I don't know what them sum bitches is lookin' for, but they got traffic all fucked up.

Tell me about it. I got to be in Nashvill' by seven am and these assholes is got the whole damn city jacked up.

The talk continued along the same course. Daniel could finally see all the cops up ahead. They were standing between the lanes, yellow rain slickers, orange cones on their flashlights and all. Daniel finally made it to the first of the officers, who did not look happy. With rain dripping from the brim of his Smokey the Bear hat, he rolled his finger in the air. Daniel got the hint and rolled the window down about three inches.

"Roll it ALL the way down."

Daniel rolled it down some more, about half way. The officer took a step closer and shined the flashlight in, looking around. "Let me see your ID." The soaked officer practically spat.

"What's going on?" Daniel asked. He was actually curious.

"I said, give me your ID."

"No offense; and I'm not trying to be a hard ass, but do I have to? Have I done anything wrong?"

A look of disgust spilled across the cop's face as he slowly shook his head. Reaching inside his slicker, he pulled the mic for his radio out and keyed it. "Noncompliant in the number one, green van."

"Hey, I'm not lookin," he was quickly cut off. Daniel wasn't expecting this. He just asked the question. A ticket for reckless driving and several hundred dollars for an attorney had taught him a couple of things; well, he thought it had.

"Pull over there", the officer stated flatly, pointing with his flashlight.

"*Shit*" he muttered under his breath as he pulled out of the travel lane and onto the shoulder where several additional unhappy and wet cops were now waiting on him.

Before he even stopped, they were already on both sides of the van. Instead of talking to him through the window, the officer on the driver's side simply opened the door and ordered him out. At the same time, an officer on the passenger side opened that door.

"Shut the vehicle off and step out, sir," The officer now standing in the open door said.

"Easy, guys. I just asked if I had to give him my ID. I'm not doing anything wrong. Is there any reason to suspect that I have done anything wrong?"

"Sir, I asked you to step out. Are you going to step out and allow me to look in your vehicle?" Now, other officers were coming up.

"Do I have to? All I did was ask a question. Can you answer my question?"

"Sir, I asked you politely. Now I'm telling you to step out or I'm going to take you out."

From the other side of the van, other officers joined in. "Make it easy, buddy. Just step out and let us do our job. If everything is Ok, you'll be on your way."

"You still haven't answered my question. Can you answer my question? You say you're asking me to and if I don't, you're going to take me out. Am I under arrest?"

The situation was getting out of hand as additional officers had converged on the scene. Daniel was beginning to doubt even asking the damn question. He wasn't against the cops, but he knew he had rights. The officers now surrounding the van though had a completely different opinion of the situation.

"No. You are not under arrest, but you will be if you don't step out and give me your ID. Just make it easy. Just step out."

"Quit being an ass. Get out of the van!" another officer screamed.

"Are you ordering me out?" Daniel asked the officer in his door.

"Yes. I am ordering you out of the van."

"Okay. I'm going to undo the seatbelt, and I'll get out."

Daniel clicked the button and pulled the belt from around him and stepped out. He was immediately grabbed and shoved against the hood of the van. This surprised him, as he expected them to throw him on the ground, in the mud. The officers were talking amongst themselves as they patted him down and cuffed him. As he leaned over the hood he saw one of the officers on the passenger side lean in the open door, at the same time the officer cuffing him spun him around.

"I do not consent to a search of my van."

The cop shot him a look of pure annoyance. "Billy", the officer that was beginning to search the van straightened up, looking at the other officer who shook his head slightly.

As the officer was going through Daniel's wallet for his ID, he asked, "What are you trying to hide?"

"Nothing. I haven't done anything wrong and you can't just search me."

"If you haven't done anything wrong, what are you worried about?" The officer pulled out the license from the wallet, then took another card out and held it up for the other officer to see.

"You have a concealed handgun license? Do you have any weapons in the van?"

"No. I don't have any now; sold them all right before the last ban was passed." Technically, he wasn't lying. He didn't have any with him at the moment.

"If I had a dollar for every time I heard that recently? You know it is now illegal to possess most firearms?"

"I do, so I made a quick buck. Wasn't against the law at the time."

The officer wasn't amused. He had handed Daniel's ID off to another officer who had probably stepped away to run it. They stood in the rain for several minutes. While they waited, Daniel asked, "What's this all about?"

"It's just the brave new world. If I didn't have to deal with so many people like you, it would all go a lot faster."

Daniel shook his head to knock some of the rain off. "Would you consent to a search?"

With a smug smile, the officer replied. "That's not going to happen. See, I'm on the winning team."

Daniel didn't reply. The statement stunned him. He thought about conversations he'd had up in the woods before the old man died about the *us and them* mentality. And now he was staring it straight in the face. The officer returned and handed the ID back to the officer talking to Daniel. "He's clean."

"Turn around," he said. And then the officer started to unlock the cuffs. "Next time, it would be in your best interest to just go along with the program. Just think, you wouldn't be all wet now if you had just showed your ID to begin with."

Daniel turned to face the officer, rubbing his wrists. "Am I free to go?"

"Yes sir, you are free to go, for now."

Daniel didn't waste any time getting into the van and heading home. Though, for the remainder of the ride, all he could think about was the last two words the cop said, for now. His phone chimed. He saw it was Malcolm and did not feel like hearing from him. Malcolm was rather liberal and a, *I told you so* was not going to improve his mood.

Daniel made it home and fell into his sofa with a groan of relief. It had been a long day, and finally being home took a load off his mind. He craned his neck, looking back over his shoulder at the fridge. There was a six-pack of Woodchuck cider in there and he wanted it; just didn't feel like getting up. But it damn sure wasn't coming to him. With a grunt, Daniel heaved himself off the sofa and went to the fridge. His phone was sitting on the kitchen island vibrating. He ignored it.

He brought the whole six-pack back to the sofa, not wanting to have to get up again. He fell into the sofa finally. Flipping on the TV, he scanned the news networks. It was more of the same, more riots, more shooting and more of people getting pissed off. He stopped on MSNBC when he saw an update of the Lansing Incident, where even the crawler at the bottom of the screen called it that.

Another of the Michigan Troopers shot during the firefight had died. They were showing a tape from earlier in the day of the Governor of the state giving a press conference. He was ranting about the people involved and how they would be brought to justice, and about how what had occurred was an act of domestic terrorism. The Governor went on to say that he had been in talks with the President earlier in the day and that the Michigan Militia has been officially designated a terrorist organization. This designation allowed for the use of federal assets in tracking them down.

Daniel just shook his head. He wasn't a fan of what happened. No one in their right mind would be. But he could understand the mindset of those that thought that way. Opening his second cider, he flipped the TV over to the Xbox. A little time in the world of Battlefield would take his mind off this crap. Before the game even loaded, his phone started ringing. The caller ID showed it was Malcolm calling again. *Not tonight,* he thought as he returned the phone to its cradle.

Dinner never entered his mind as Daniel played video games, getting his ass handed to him by eight-year-old kids. He was taking a break to go dig around in the fridge, when he picked up his cell phone and saw all the messages. There were nineteen new emails, all of them with the little urgent sign attached. He was trying to decide if he was even going to look at them when the phone rang. Malcolm again. Shaking his head, he reluctantly answered the call.

"What's up, Malcolm?"

"Daniel, where the hell have you been? I've been trying for hours to get in touch with you!"

"Been busy, man. What's up?"

"I need you to come in. There's a serious problem on the network."

"Dude, it's dark. You know we can't travel after dark." A thin smile cut his lips.

"I know. Do you know Robert Thomas?"

"Yeah, I know Bob. Isn't he the head of physical security?"

Daniel could almost feel the agitation through the phone. "Yes, *Robert* is the head of physical security. He's going to be in touch with you and will send you a pass that will allow you to travel. We have the permission from the SEC to do what we need in order to deal with this situation."

"What the hell's going on? I thought we had it under control when I left."

"Well, it would appear we didn't. I need you to come in. Robert will be in touch shortly with the instructions. I'll see you soon." The line went dead and Daniel dropped the phone on the counter.

"This is bullshit!"

Daniel figured while he waited he could watch a little more news, and he started to scan the news channels. It was just more bad news. Most major cities were having almost nonstop riots of some sort or another. It was getting ugly. It was as if something major happened. Something nationwide. Cities all over the country were now in turmoil. Having seen enough of this in the last few days, he pulled up the guide to find something else to watch, deciding Big Bang Theory would make a nice distraction.

It wasn't long before the phone rang, and Daniel hoped it would be Malcolm telling him he didn't have to come in. The number displayed on the caller ID was from the bank, just not from Malcolm.

"Hello."

"Daniel, this is Bob Thomas. I just emailed you a form

you need to print out and keep with you on your way in. My cell number is with it. If you have any trouble, call me immediately." Bob's gravelly voice filled the speaker. Daniel could almost smell the cigarette smoke.

"Sure thing. What the hell's going up there?"

"I have no idea. That's why we need you. Malcolm is about to shit himself. Pack a bag, too. You may be here a while."

"What the hell do you mean, pack a bag? I'm not sleeping in my cubicle."

"You won't have to. We have facilities here. Things are getting shady around here and all over the metro, and it may be hard to get out once you get in. Better safe than sorry."

Daniel sat up on the edge of the couch. "Whadda'ya mean, *facilities?*"

"You'll see when you get here." Bob paused for a moment. "Have uh, have you got any guns?"

Daniel pulled the phone from his head. He did indeed have a couple left, but wasn't about to admit that to anyone, especially over the phone. "No, Bob. I sold all mine before the ban."

A chuckle came from the other end. "Yeah, me too. Damn shame, really. But if I had any, I'd bring 'em with me today. Just remember, if you get stopped at all, call me immediately. And call me when you get to the parking garage so I can let you in. See you soon."

"Alright, see you soon." The line went dead.

Daniel sat there for a moment looking at Sheldon on the TV, a hundred thoughts running through his head. Jumping up from the sofa, he headed for the closet where all his gear was. Standing in the open door, he looked at everything, trying to decide what he would take. In the end, he decided to take most of it. After all, he wasn't going to have to carry it. It would all be in the van.

He was nervous as he backed out of his parking spot in the garage at the apartments. It was dark now, officially a time that was prohibited for being on the road. As he pulled out, his headlights revealed an empty road for as far as he could see. It was weird and nice at the same time, no traffic. Daniel pulled up an old Creed album on his IPod and plugged it into the stereo.

Human Clay was playing when he approached his first APD roadblock. Without looking over, he reached into the passenger seat and patted the sheet of paper he had printed out just a short time ago. The officers waved him to a stop, making their point with the ARs they held to their shoulders. Daniel rolled to a stop, making sure to keep his hands on the steering wheel.

The officers shouted orders as they approached. They seemed particularly on edge, and Daniel wasn't about to mess around, knowing if he did, he would wind up in the morgue. The officers separated as they approached, one on either side. The officer that approached his side was a young guy around his age. The other one was older. If age were an indicator, he would be the more experienced, though the younger one was issuing all the commands.

"Keep your hands where I can see them and roll down your window!"

Daniel immediately rolled the glass down, keeping his other hand on the wheel. The younger officer stepped up. "What are you doing out here? You should know there's a curfew!" More of an accusation than a question.

"I work for one of the banks downtown and have been called in to assist with a problem. I have a pass here from your department that gives me permission."

The younger officer pulled the door open. "Get out!"

Daniel complied. As he climbed out, the older officer asked, "Where's the form?"

"On the passenger seat." He indicated with a nod of his head.

"Out. Hands on the hood!" The younger officer shouted as the older one went into the passenger side and retrieved the sheet lying there.

As Daniel put his hands on the hood, the young officer buried the muzzle of the carbine in his back. "Do not move. Understand me?"

Daniel simply nodded his head in reply. He was kicking himself in the ass for not calling Bob. It just slipped his mind, but he could suddenly very clearly remember him saying it.

"Hey, Jimmy. Get his ID." The older officer called out as he walked around the front of the van. He'd slung his rifle over his shoulder.

The younger officer pulled Daniel's wallet out and tossed it to the older one and continued to pat him down.

"Jim, this looks legit. I'm going to call it in and see," The older officer said.

"Whatever. I'll keep an eye on him here. What the hell do you do for the bank that makes you so special?"

Without looking up, Daniel answered. "I do network security."

"Oh, yeah. Big bad hackers gotta be stopped, huh? Give me a break. All the shit going on and you're worried about some kids trying to hack into your network." The younger officer taunted.

"I didn't want to come in. Believe me, not my choice."

"Leave him alone, Jim. He works for the bank that our paychecks are written on. He checks out. You must be damn important for the SEC to request you personally." The older officer said.

"I'm not. But I guess my boss knows someone," Daniel replied.

"Alright. Go on, don't make any pit stops and be careful. Things are getting a little hairy over the direction you're going," The older officer said.

Daniel quickly got back in the van and started it. The officers stepped apart and he pulled between them. The younger of the two still had a look of contempt on his face. He wanted to give the guy the finger but thought better of it.

The rest of the ride to the office was uneventful for the most part. The closer he got to the bank, the more people he started to see. Usually, only fleeting glances as they darted in and out of shadows. Once, he got a clear view of two men who were both wearing the mask from the movie V for Vendetta. Now he really wished his Glock were close enough to get to.

As he rounded the corner to the bank, he was surprised to see large roll-up doors closing off the entrance to the parking garage. He stopped in front of one of them, just staring at it. *Where in the hell did that come from?*

His cell phone suddenly rang, causing him to jump in his seat at the same time the door started to open. "Hello?"

"I told you to call me when you got here. I also told

you to call me if you had any trouble, neither of which you did." Bob growled into the phone. He then continued. "Pull through the gate to the underground lot and stop in front of the big roll-up door that will be in front of you as you come down the ramp. When the door opens, drive through it and wait for me."

"Okay." Daniel replied as the line went dead. He looked at his phone. "Asshole hung up on me again."

Normally, the drive to the lower, underground portion of the parking structure was blocked by one of those little arms that is raised up and down. Pulling through the gate, he saw the arm was up, and he hooked a right and drove through it as the gate began to lower behind him. He had never been down in this part of the building before. As with any large modern building, everyone had a prox card for the hundreds of readers located all over it. Access was controlled through permissions; and his certainly didn't have permission to access this part of the building.

The gate at the bottom of the ramp was already going up as he descended. By the time he got to it, there was enough room for him to pull through. It immediately began to lower as soon as he cleared it. A short, chunky man in a gray work shirt and charcoal-colored pants was standing in an open door waving at him. Daniel looked around at the massive machinery inhabiting the cavernous space under the building. Most people that work in office buildings have no idea of the myriad of systems required to support it. They go through their day completely oblivious to them until a door won't open or the air in their office is too cold, hot or in between.

Daniel got out of the van, slung his pack over his

shoulder and headed for the open door. Getting close enough to the man in the door to see him, Daniel read the name tag sewn to the breast of his shirt, Eugene. In the pocket on the other side protruded an amazing array of items, pens, pencils, screwdrivers and even a little thermometer.

"You Daniel?" The man asked in a nasally voice.

"Yep, that's me."

"Let's go up and see Bob before you head off to do whatever it is you're here to do."

Daniel followed Eugene into an enormous elevator.

"Not like the ones you're used to, huh?" Eugene asked. Before the doors closed, he pressed the button for fifteen.

Daniel looked around as the two big doors came together. From the diamond plate on the floor to what looked like moving blankets hanging on the walls, it certainly was not. "No, the ones in the lobby don't look anything like this" he said as the car started to lift.

"Guess not. Gopher farm folks wouldn't really like having to ride to work in one of these." Eugene replied.

Daniel watched him as he spoke, noticing he couldn't see the man's mouth that was hidden behind an enormous mustache, just the bristles moving as he spoke. He had to pretend to look around the car as the image of Wilfred Brimley came to mind. They could be brothers. Nothing more was said on the ride up. The car stopped, the doors opened and Daniel followed Eugene out into a nondescript hallway.

Unlike the parts of the building Daniel was familiar with, no pictures adorned the walls, no artwork occupied the corners, and there were no tables with flower arrangements. At the end of the hall was a single door. Eugene pulled his prox card down. It was attached to a small retractable reel clipped to the already overburdened pocket. As he waved it at the reader, a beep was followed by a green light, and the door clicked open. As Daniel passed the reader, he raised his right hip. He kept his card clipped there where it was tall enough to hit the readers. Instead of the chirpy beep, he got a lower grating sound and a red light, he didn't have permission to enter the door.

They entered a large dark room. To their right was a big console with the wall above it covered with flat-screen monitors. Each of the screens was subdivided into a grid with a different camera view in each one, sixteen views per monitor. A large monitor in the center of the wall had a 3D image of the building on one side and a floor plan of one of the floors to the right of it. Two operators sat at the console watching the screens. They didn't even look up as Eugene and Daniel entered.

Eugene continued through the room towards a glass-enclosed office, and Daniel followed him.

"Help yourself to the pot, Gene. It's fresh," The man sitting behind the desk said without looking away from the monitor on his desk. "You want some coffee, Daniel?"

"Thanks, Bob," Gene replied as he lifted the carafe from the heater.

Inside, Daniel let out a little sigh of relief, not having to rely on his few encounters with Bob to ensure it was him. "No, thanks, I'm good. What'cha need?"

Bob looked up from the monitor. "I just wanted to meet you. I know we've met a few times, but it's been awhile and we will probably be working together."

Daniel cocked his head to the side. "Working on what?"

"You've seen what's going on outside and it's only getting worse. You've got to get busy on the network stuff; and that's a real problem, by the way. And I have to protect this building. We've been lucky up to this point, but the riots are getting closer and larger, more violent. If they kick off around here, I'll need everyone's help."

"Yeah, sure." Daniel replied. Then the phone on Bob's desk rang.

Bob pressed the speaker button on the phone. "Yello."

"Robert, this is Malcolm. Has Daniel arrived yet? I thought he would be here by now."

"Yes, Malcolm. He's here in my office. We were just having a little talk. I'll send him down to you."

"Thank you. Tell him to hurry. There's no time to waste."

"You just told him yourself. Goodbye, Malcolm." Bob pressed the button again, ending the call, not waiting for Malcolm to respond. He looked up at Daniel. "What's up his ass? Is he always so wound up?"

Not sure what to say, whether it was a set up or not, he simply replied. "Yeah, he's a little intense."

Bob was busy typing away at his keyboard. Daniel just stood there for a moment, looking around. Gene was sitting in a chair in the corner soaking his whiskers in the edge of a coffee cup while he blew on the hot brew.

"I guess I'll head down. Good to see you again, Bob. Or do you like to be called Robert?"

Bob looked up. "My mother was the only person that called me Robert, and that only happened prior to a grade-ass whoopin from my ole man. No, do not call me Robert." Bob looked back at his monitor, then back to Daniel. "I just gave you access to the entire building. Your card will open every door on the campus. I also just added Gene's contact info to your contacts so you can reach him if you need to."

Daniel pulled his phone from his pocket. "How'd you get access to my contacts?"

Bob smiled. "It's my job to know about the people that work here. Don't worry. All I did was add Gene. If you need anything, you can call either of us. Oh yeah, I added mine too."

"Just do me one favor" Gene said from behind Daniel, who turned to look at him. "jus' don't need anything." Gene's face broke into what Daniel could only imagine was a smile as the ends of the whiskers turned up slightly.

"Don't worry about him, Daniel. Gene's not exactly a people person. He's more at home with the boilers than people."

"I understand boilers," Gene said.

Daniel said his goodbyes and left Bob's office. He looked at the wall of monitors as he passed them and was soon in the hall again. After shutting the door, he paused there for a moment. This all seemed a little weird. Without much more thought, he headed for the elevator. The doors slid open and he stepped into the big metal box.

Daniel found Malcolm in his office. He was sitting at his desk with his chin resting in his hands staring at his monitor. When Daniel came in, Malcolm didn't even look up. "I'm fucked," he said and shook his head. "We are so fucked."

The language caught Daniel off guard. He'd never before heard Malcolm swear; so to hear an F-bomb, two, no less, was a shock.

"It can't be that bad."

"Oh yeah?" Malcolm swiveled his monitor around to where Daniel could see it. The screen displayed numerous rows of numbers, big numbers; and they were counting down.

It took a moment for what he was seeing to register, Daniel stood there watching as the numbers rolled down. These were huge numbers, but they were not infinite. "Is that what I think it is?"

"Yep. I've tried everything and I can't stop it. We've already lost billions."

"I can stop it!" Daniel shouted as he bolted from the office.

He ran down the hall to the largest of the server rooms in the building. Slamming his hip into the card reader at the door, he rushed in. He headed for the rack that contained the switches that were the portal to the outside world. It took several minutes to disconnect all the fiber from the switches. Networks of this size are not like the ones at a typical home. It isn't just one line. There are lines that connect to the internet and others that connect to a myriad of banking networks.

When everything was disconnected, Daniel wiped the sweat from his brow. Even though the room was maintained at 68 degrees, he was sweating profusely. The room was loud on a normal day. From the fans on the servers, to the wall-mounted AC units that kept the room cool, there was a lot of noise. It was even louder now that all the servers were sounding their various alarms about loss of network connectivity. When he returned to Malcolm's office, he found him still sitting behind his desk; though now he looked even worse than he had previously.

"What the hell did you do?" Malcolm asked, obviously confused.

"I pulled all the fiber from the switches. The network's isolated now."

"You did what!"

Daniel reached over and spun the monitor around. The figures on the screen had stopped, and a curser blinking in the corner was the only thing active on the screen.

"Looks like it worked to me." Daniel spat back. "What the hell else were we gonna do?"

Malcolm jumped from his chair. "We can't take the bank off the network. You know what kind of shit storm this is going to cause? The SEC will crucify us!"

"Losing everything the bank has to some unknown hacker would be just as bad. Have you let anyone know about this yet?"

Malcolm slowly fell back into his chair, the fear that gripped him obvious on his face. "No." Looking at the phone sitting on his desk, he appeared to become physically ill. Taking a deep breath, he said. "I guess I need to."

"Yeah, I think so. I'm going to call Bob. He needs to know what's going on."

Daniel left Malcolm's office, heading for his cubicle where he flopped into his chair. He sat there for a moment then palmed the receiver from the phone and dialed Bob's extension.

"Yes." Was Bob's terse answer.

"Bob, do you know what's going here?"

"Not entirely, just that you guys had some trouble on the network. What's up?"

"Someone breached the network, and billions of dollars were siphoned off before I stopped it. At least, I think I stopped it."

There was a long pause before Bob replied. "Come up to my office."

"Sure." Daniel hung up the phone and headed for the elevator.

He was standing there waiting on the car when he remembered the little hallway that led to Bob's office. There was no other elevator, just the freight car. The ding indicating the arrival of the car sounded and the doors opened as Daniel turned to step in.

A sly smile cut Daniel's lips as he lifted his hip at the reader outside Bob's office. In the corporate culture he was a part of, something as trivial as having access to a door that others didn't was something to be coveted. Now, according to Bob, he had access to the entire building. Inside, the two men were still sitting before their monitors. Daniel glanced over at the wall of videos and stopped in his tracks. The view from the hundreds of cameras routed to this office showed a truly disturbing scene.

"So, what's going on?" Bob asked over Daniel's shoulder.

The question startled him and Daniel spun around. "What the hell's going on out there?" Daniel asked pointing to the bank of monitors.

"Looks like more of the same."

"Yeah, but it has spread around the metro, and increased exponentially around Tower Place here. What the hell's going on?"

Bob walked over to the console and manipulated a small joystick. A video feed that filled one entire monitor began to move. The image swung then zoomed in to a line of police. Daniel stepped toward the monitor. "Holly shit, those aren't riot cops. They've got shotguns."

"They probably have less-than-lethal rounds in them. Let's see what happens." Bob replied.

The crowd opposite the police was taunting them, throwing bottles, bricks and anything else they could find. The police used shields to block the missiles, maintaining their line. Though the observers in the bank couldn't hear it, they could see an officer using a loudspeaker, giving orders to the crowd. The crowd responded with more bottles. Then, from somewhere deep in the crowd, came a Molotov cocktail. On the video feed, Bob and Daniel watched as the flaming bottle arched towards the line of officers. Landing in front of them, a ball of flames erupted, followed by a large cloud of smoke.

The smoke obscured the crowd for a moment, but not the officers. They immediately replied with a volley of tear gas and mini beanbags fired from shotguns into the crowd. The crowd started to run, pushing and shoving to try and get away. Some people fell and were trampled by others trying to vacate the area as fast as possible.

"Oh, they're gonna be pissed now," Bob said, watching the crowd as it began to break up.

"Not nearly as mad they'll be tomorrow." Daniel replied.

Bob glanced over at him. "Why's that?"

"Do you know that we handle EBT card transactions?"

"Nope, but what's that got to do with this?" Bob asked, pointing at the monitor.

"I had to pull our network down. Right now there are millions of credit, debit and yes, EBT cards that don't work."

"That was how you stopped the problem with the network? Are you nuts? You know what kind of shit that's going to start. Look at what's already happening."

Daniel looked at the monitors for a moment. Shaking his head, he asked. "What is going on?"

"Ah. Now that's the question, isn't it?" Bob replied. "What's got all these people so stirred up? You notice how all of these riots seemed to start at the same time all over the country?"

Daniel shrugged. "Yeah, but there's a lot for people to be mad about. The election got a lot of them pissed off. Then the whole gun thing; that was bound to cause trouble."

Bob pointed at the monitors. "Look at those people. Do they look like the kind of people that are pissed the government's taking their guns?"

Daniel looked at the faces on the monitors. It was a diverse crowd. Men, women, black, white, old and young. "Looks like a little bit of everyone, really."

Bob manipulated the joystick, bringing a group of people into focus. "How about them?"

It was a group of young men, at least that's what they looked like. They all had their face covered with a bandana, except for two of them who were wearing the V mask. Daniel pointed at the screen. "I saw two people like that on my way in here."

Bob nodded. "Those, my friend, are professional agitators."

"Huh?" Daniel asked, confused.

"Look at them. Backpacks, that one has on elbow pads,"

Bob said, pointing at the screen. "And that one has a gas mask around his neck."

Daniel said, "That doesn't really mean much. You can get that stuff anywhere."

"Except that mask costs about three hundred fifty dollars." Bob looked at Daniel. "Not exactly the kind of thing you can find in the hood."

"So, who sent them here then?" Daniel asked.

Bob shrugged. "Don't know. You tell me."

"I'll give you a hint. It's the government," One of the guys manning the security monitors said.

Daniel looked down at the man who was still watching the cameras. "Why the hell would they do that?"

Bob rubbed his chin. "Do you remember what happened in Ukraine at Maidan?"

Daniel scratched his head. "Yeah. The people gathered there to protest the government or something."

"They were protesting the government's decision to side with the EU and not Russia."

"Oh, yeah. Then the protestors, the ones that wanted to side with Russia, started to get violent."

Bob waved a finger at Daniel. "That's what you were told." Pointing to the group of men on the monitor, Bob continued. "What really happened was the government sent in guys like these to start the trouble. The separatists, as they're now called, simply wanted the freedom to choose. But the Ukrainian government wasn't having that."

"What the hell does that have to do with us? With this?" Daniel asked, pointing at the monitors.

"The point is that governments, even ours, will do whatever it takes to get what they want. If that means killing a few cops, so be it," Bob said.

Daniel was shocked. "You think our government is behind this? You think they would sacrifice innocent people like that?"

"I know they would. Now, I'm not saying this is all their doing. But those guys you see outside are on some alphabet-soup agency payroll. I guarantee it."

Shaking his head, Daniel said, "I call BS."

Bob turned and headed for his office. "Guess we'll have to wait and see who is right. Let me get a cup of coffee and I'll show you where you can crash for the night."

Daniel followed Bob into his office. It was the picture of clutter and disorganization. The desk top was completely obscured by stacks of paper, unrecognizable pieces of dissected electronics and more Styrofoam coffee cups than should be acceptable. A large safe sat against one wall beside a well-worn couch. To Daniel, it reminded him of a dorm room.

Looking around, Daniel asked, "Damn. You live in here?"

Pouring a cup of coffee from a stained pot, Bob shrugged. "Sometimes."

"Why do we have a place to sleep here?"

Placing the pot back onto the crusty burner, Bob smiled and said. "Follow me." As he headed towards the elevator, he talked. "When this place was built, a small area was set aside as a shelter. We have the occasional winter storms and other things that can cause people to get stuck here. It was actually a good idea."

The elevator stopped and they were once again in the basement of the bank, in the mechanical space. Daniel looked out into the cavernous space filled with the noise of the many machines that keep such a large building functioning and asked. "Has it ever been used?"

Bob laughed. "Oh yeah. It's been used. But not as a shelter. More as a love shack."

"Love shack?" Daniel asked.

"Yeah. Some of the muckity mucks have used it a time or two to." Bob looked up and rubbed his chin. "How should I say it? Interview perspective young ladies."

Daniel was shocked. From what he knew of all the suits that worked in the bank, they were all stiff as a board and had no personality at all. "Really? You mean...." Daniel started to ask.

Bob smiled and said, "Wanna see the video?"

The image of the line of large oil paintings lining the lobby wall flashed into his mind. All those pasty-faced balding old men. Daniel's face contorted. "Hell no!"

Bob started to laugh. "Neither did I! But it keeps those fat asses in check."

Daniel followed Bob across the mechanical space to a door Bob unlocked with a physical key. Thinking that was odd, he asked Bob why the door didn't have a card reader.

"This space is designed for use during power outages and such. So a card reader wouldn't work."

Making sense, Daniel nodded and followed him in. Bob flipped a switch and fluorescent lights flickered and came to life, revealing a large room filled with evenly spaced cots.

"Oh, this is lovely," Daniel said sarcastically.

Bob chuckled and slapped him on the back. "Don't worry, Sport. You don't have to stay here." And he started across the large room.

Daniel shot him a look. "Sport?"

As he walked, Bob pointed out the bathroom facilities. "Over there are the shitters and showers."

Daniel looked over to see essentially a locker-room style shower arrangement. Sinks lined one wall, with mirrors over each. The only hint of privacy was the partitions separating the toilets.

"Nice and private. I like it."

Bob grunted. "Don't worry, Champ. You don't have to stay there."

The comment irked Daniel. "Champ?"

At the far end of the dormitory-style area was another door that they passed through. It led into a long hallway with doors off to either side. At the far end of the hall was an open door with light spilling into the dark corridor.

The two walked down the hall to the open door. Bob poked his head in and pronounced. "He's not here."

Daniel looked around Bob into the small room. These were very much like a college dorm room. A single bed sat against the wall with a small dresser and night stand. A flat screen TV was mounted to the wall. An open door led to the private bath. Daniel looked at the soiled bed. A large dark area roughly the size of a man took up most of the sheet. Empty fast food wrappers littered the floor beside the bed along with empty plastic two-liter Dr Pepper bottles. The room was a mess. Daniel looked at the TV to see the frozen image of a naked woman.

"What the hell? Is there some bum living in here?"

Bob shook his head. "Nah. Gene stays here from time to time."

"My early opinion of Gene is quickly changing."

Bob laughed, slapping Daniel on the back. "Don't worry

about Gene. He's a good guy. Pick any of these rooms. You and Gene are the only ones down here." "Here's the key to the door."

Daniel pocketed the key and glanced back into the room again. "I think I'll stay down there," he said as he headed back to the opposite end of the hall.

"It's here if you need it," Bob said.

The next day many of the employees of the bank were turned away at the door. As the network was still down and there was no certainty as to when it would be back up, many of them would have nothing to do. The exception was for customer service agents. In the coming days they would face an onslaught of angry, desperate customers. There were meetings galore at the bank, not only at the bank Daniel worked for, but many others.

While Daniel managed to disconnect his network from the world, the damage was already done. All those connections to the internet, other banks and, the most damaging of all, the Federal Reserve, served to spread the virus literally at the speed of light. All over the country and in some places around the world, banks were in full panic. In an effort to calm the panic, two days after the initial incident, the White House came out with a statement that all electronic financial transactions were going to be suspended.

The statement went on to assure people that their accounts were backed by the Federal Government, and order in the financial markets would soon be restored. What it didn't say was that the real reason for the "temporary halt" was to stop the slide of the US markets, which had already lost over twenty percent in the past two trading days.

Efforts were being made to determine who was behind the event, but at the moment it was almost a moot point, at least to most Americans.

It was these Americans, the ones that to this point that had maintained their lives in as normal a routine as they could, and now were added to the already disgruntled masses in the streets. Most people had no way of purchasing anything. If you didn't have cash or convince a merchant to take a check, there was no way to buy. For most people, it meant that within twenty-four hours they were for all intents and purposes broke. The frog started to notice the change in the water temp.

Much to Daniel's relief, he didn't have to stay at the bank. The other side of that coin was that, unlike most other bank employees, he had to come to work. The fact that his credit cards or his debit card didn't work didn't matter that much to him. After all, he worked for the bank. And while they didn't have unlimited amounts of cash, there was a substantial amount of it securely locked up in the basement of the bank. Arrangements were made for bank employees to receive cash from their accounts over the counter. The banks doors may have been closed to the public, but they were open for those inside the banking community.

CHAPTER 3

It was on the third day after what was now being called the "Financial Holiday" that Daniel started to have trouble. He was on his way to work when a crowd of people was blocking an intersection. They were accosting drivers as they tried to make it to their destinations. Daniel was third in line at the light when the crowd spilled out into the road. Like ants, they spread out in all directions, enveloping cars. Those unfortunate enough to be caught in the middle of the intersection suffered the worse.

When they started breaking out windows and pulling people out of their cars, Daniel quickly checked the mirrors, looking for an escape. He was in the right-hand lane, a large planter separating him from a parking lot. Daniel quickly backed the van as much as he could; those behind him were also looking for a way out. The van was big and powerful, with large bumpers on either end. Shifting into four-wheel drive, he was able to climb the planter into the parking lot.

The rest of the way to the office he never stopped again, bypassing traffic lights by using parking lots, or simply running them after slowing to make sure there was no cross traffic. The bank had taken on the appearance of a fortress. All first-story windows and doors were protected with the same kind of roll-down doors as the entrances to the parking garage. Pulling up to the garage entrance, he quickly swiped his card and waited nervously as the door rolled up.

This time, he didn't park under the building; he went to the top deck, waving at the uniformed, and now armed, security officer stationed on the first level. He parked in a spot on the edge, looking east. It was early, and as he leaned against the wall looking out across the area, he could see and smell acrid smoke. It was rising in several places. And the sirens, which had of late become omnipresent, seemed to be everywhere at once. The wails and warbles bounced off the buildings from all directions.

From his rooftop perspective, he could see a crowd that was just coming around a corner two blocks away. It was made up of people of all types, but was just what the movies always depicted. Shouts and the sounds of breaking bottles added to all the sirens to create a morbid symphony of noise. Daniel shook his head, looking at the crowd. Then he went to the van and grabbed the messenger bag. After closing the door, he noticed that the big square cap that sealed the end of the front bumper was jutting out. He stepped towards it and gave the cap a light kick. It didn't budge, and he smiled as he headed for the stairs.

A pedestrian bridge tied the building to the garage on the fourth level, he took the stairs in no real hurry and came out on the fourth deck, taking the bridge over the street below into the building. Another guard was stationed just inside the building, also uniformed and armed. At first, the appearance of uniformed men with pistols and shotguns had caused much concern amongst the mild-mannered folks working in the building. The complaints reached the point that some asked that they be kept out of sight; but as the rioting worsened around the building, the complaints disappeared.

Daniel went to the little concession stand located just past the bridge. It had the usual array of items any hip suburbanite would appreciate, Starbucks coffee, bagels and pastries and even a decent deli. He grabbed his morning Mountain Dew from the case by the register, paid using his employee ID, another nice feature of working for the bank, and headed for the elevators. According to what had become his new routine, the first stop was Bob's office.

There was no real reason for him to go up there every day; it had just become the routine. He would go up there and hang out with Bob for an hour or so, watching the monitors and talking about what was happening in the world. One of the biggest benefits of this new routine was that it really pissed off Malcolm, who tried to put a stop to it. But Bob pulled rank on him and the issue went away.

Daniel flopped into a chair across from Bob's desk. The ever-present ashtray was now overflowing with butts, a ring of fine ash surrounding the tray. The principle of maximum angle of repose had been exceeded. Numerous coffee cups littered the desk as well, some having been there so long a brown ring showed around the bottom where coffee was soaking through.

"Bob, you look like shit. When was the last time you actually slept?"

Bob held up an empty cup without looking up from the monitor. "I just finished another two hours."

"When was the last time you left this place?"

"And go where?" Bob asked as he picked up and shook the various cups.

"Home? To get some sleep?"

"I should have you over some day. You'd understand." Bob found a cup with liquid in it and swished it suspiciously.

"Guess I'll head downstairs and wallow in Malcolm's neurosis," Daniel said as he stood up to leave.

Bob looked up. "Before you go, shut the door real quick."

Daniel pushed the door closed and looked back at Bob.

"You remember when I asked if you had any guns?" Bob asked as he rocked back in his chair, putting his feet up on his desk.

"Yeah. Told you I sold 'em all."

"Yeah, bullshit, whatever, I would recommend you bring one if you've got it. Things are getting pretty shitty out there and it may become an issue."

Daniel wanted to tell him so bad that he still had his carbine and Glock, but he just couldn't bring himself to do it yet. "Yeah, well, I wish I did. You got any?"

Bob smiled and swung his feet off the desk with what seemed an excessive amount of enthusiasm. Standing up, he went over to the safe and dialed in the combination. Bob pulled the door open, then removed a padlock and opened an interior door. He then stepped aside to reveal the contents of the safe.

"Holy shit, Bob!"

Something resembling a smile cracked Bob's face. "You like?"

Wide – eyed, Daniel stepped towards the safe. "Who wouldn't? How – how in the hell do you still have these?" Looking back at Bob, "Aren't you worried about getting arrested?"

Bob crossed his arms over his chest and looked down at the floor. Sweeping the toe of his shoe, in desperate need of a shine, across the stained carpet, he replied, "Well, there's an exemption for law enforcement."

A little confused, Daniel asked, "You still a cop?"

"Retired." Bob replied before flashing another smile.

"And it applies to you as well?"

"Membership has its benefits, don' cha' know."

Turning back to the safe, Daniel began to take a closer look. "What kind of ARs are those?"

"There are three Patriot Ordnance Warhogs, two Mossberg 500s and a few Sigs, plus enough ammo to feed them for a while."

"Damn. That's a hell of a collection." Daniel replied, shaking his head.

"That's not my collection. My collection wouldn't fit in that safe."

Daniel stood there, stunned for a moment. Before he could say anything, a voice from the control room called out. "Hey, Bob. You need to come see this."

Daniel and Bob walked out to the dark room illuminated only by the wall of monitors. "What's up, Andy?" Bob asked as they came in.

One video feed suddenly filled the entire wall. It was a view of the street in front of the bank that was filling with people. It was obvious these people were pissed, the epitome of a riot in its infancy. The camera panned back and forth, taking in the whole street. Off in the distance, they could see fires, dumpster fires from the look of it. The crowd farther out was larger, and it looked as though it was moving to the business district.

"Damn, this isn't good," Bob said to no one in particular.

"What 'cha want to do?" Andy asked.

"Nothing. Just watch it. I'm gonna go talk to the brass," Bob said as he headed for the door. "Daniel, come with me."

The request caught him off guard. "Sure" was all he replied, taking one more look at the screen as he turned to follow Bob out of the office.

Waiting in front of the elevator, Daniel asked, "Where we going?"

"I'm going to talk to the execs. I want to shut the building down today, and call off the staff before any more of them get in."

"You think it's gonna get that bad?"

"I hope not. But I'd rather not have a couple hundred people here to worry about if it does."

"Why am I coming with you?"

That shady smile cracked Bob's face again. "Spread your social circle; meet some interesting people."

The ding announced the elevator and the door opened. Gene was standing in the car behind a cart eating a sandwich with his right hand, a rubber glove on his left.

Daniel noticed the cart was loaded with all manner of apparatus for unclogging toilets. Daniel took another look at Gene, the mustache moving up and down, then the sandwich.

"Hey, Gene. How you doin'?" Bob asked as they stepped in.

Swallowing a mouthful, he replied. "Same ole shit."

Bob laughed, looking down at the cart. "So it seems."

"I don't know why these prim and proper ladies insist

on flushing their damn harpoons down the toilet," Gene said as he stuffed the last bite of the sandwich in his mouth.

"Harpoons. Never heard 'em called that before," Bob replied with a laugh.

Gene just shrugged his shoulders, pulled a comb from his shirt pocket and ran it through his mustache. Replacing the comb in his pocket, he pulled the rubber glove back on his left hand. "What'r y'all up to?"

"Going up to talk to the brass. We may need to shut the building down. Looks like there's a riot brewing."

"Good. I hope they do. I could use a break."

The car stopped and Bob told Gene he would talk to him later. Daniel nodded at Gene as he stepped off the elevator. Once the door shut, Daniel looked over at Bob. "I can't believe he was eating a sandwich after plunging a toilet."

Bob laughed. "Yeah, that's Gene. He's a real piece of work."

Daniel's face turned sour. "That's just friggin' nasty."

Bob let out a loud laugh, slapping Daniel on the back. They came to a door at the end of the corridor and Bob went through it with Daniel following. They stepped out into an opulent sitting area, nothing like the part of the building he worked in.

"Holy shit. Where are we?" Daniel asked.

They were walking towards a large mahogany desk where a very attractive blonde was seated.

"Welcome to the den of the beast. You smell that?"

Daniel looked around. "Smell what?"

"Bullshit."

The blonde looked up and a brilliant smile flashed

across her face. "Why, hello, Bob." She stood and walked around the desk, wrapping her arms around Bob's neck. Once in the embrace, Bob turned slightly so Daniel could see him. He crossed his eyes and lolled his tongue from his mouth; and with his left hand, he patted her back, while with his right hand, he mimicked squeezing her ass.

Daniel stood there bug-eyed. "Tiffany, so good to see you." The girl stepped back, flashed the smile again and looked at Daniel. Bob caught on and introduced him. "Tiff, this is Daniel. Daniel, this is Tiffany."

"Nice to meet you." She replied, offering her hand, which he took, holding her eyes just a moment longer than business etiquette dictates.

Bob broke up the moment. "Tiff, is your boss in?"

She let out a huff of a breath before heading back around the desk. "Yeah, he's here. But he's busy with everything going on."

"I need to see him, and it's critically important I see him now."

"I'm guessing from your tone you're not bringing good news."

"No I'm not. But he needs to hear it, now," Bob said with a tone of finality.

"Go in and take a seat. I'll let him know you're waiting."

"Why, thank you, beautiful," Bob replied, as he flashed his own nicotine-stained smile.

Tiffany returned his with a coy, off-the-shoulder smile of her own. Bob moved for a door to the right of the desk and Daniel followed him. Looking at Tiffany, she gave him a smile as well. They entered another anteroom, a waiting area where the unwashed masses awaited their audience with the power brokers behind the doors on the opposite side of the room.

They each took a seat in the overstuffed leather chairs. Daniel ran his hand over the arm of his. This damn sure wasn't imitation. After a moment, Bob stood and walked across the room to a credenza and opened a lower door to reveal a mini fridge.

"Want a water or something?"

Daniel looked over. "Yeah. Sure, water's good."

Bob tossed a bottle to him. Daniel couldn't help but notice the Fiji label. Downstairs, they had stopped putting spring water in the water coolers and switched to "drinking water". He made a smirk and shook his head as he twisted the top off the bottle.

Bob flopped back into his seat, noticing Daniel's annoyance. "Nothing but the best up here, buddy."

"So I see. Hey, what's with Tiffany? You're fuckin' nuts by the way."

Bob laughed, blowing water out of his nose. With a grunt, he replied. "Yeah, hot as asphalt in July, huh?"

"Yeah, I'd say. You know there are cameras up there. Someone saw your little show."

"Pfft, yeah. Know who saw it? My guys. Andy's probably already deleted that little piece of evidence."

A digital tone sounded, filling the small space. "Bob, he'll see you now."

Bob rose from his chair. "We're on," and he headed for the door. Daniel followed him into a massive office. Opposite the door stood an impressively large and ornate antique desk. Behind it sat a man in his late fifties, Daniel estimated. He looked exactly like you would expect a banker to. He wore a business suit, the coat hanging behind him, sitting in only the vest. As they walked in, the man looked up but did not smile.

"Mornin', Byron." Bob offered.

The man simply dipped his chin. "Bob", just an acknowledgment, nothing more. "What's on your mind?" He asked, then diverted his attention to some papers on his desk.

"Have you seen what's going on outside?" Bob asked.

Byron motioned to one of several TVs hanging on the wall to his right, "Of course, it's all over the news. Looks like more of the same." When he finished speaking, he looked up as a tolerant father would at a child demanding his attention.

"You're wrong about that. It's not more of the same. This crowd is bigger and getting closer to the building. I think we should take some preemptive action." Bob returned, then crossed his arms over his chest. He was not about to be ignored.

Byron rocked back in his chair and let out a sigh. "And what would you have me do? It's a job for the APD."

"We need to call off the staff for the day, and close the building."

Byron practically leapt from his chair. "Are you out of your damn mind? You know what that would do to our business?"

"What business? Everything is shut down because of the attack. You don't need all those people here if this riot is THE riot. Call off the staff, I'll secure the building, and we can wait for this to all blow over."

Byron's face jerked into a sneer. "You don't have to tell

me about the damn attack! I have agents from the FBI and the SEC crawling up my ass with a damn magnifying glass." He looked at his watch. "As a matter of fact, they should be here any minute. Besides, security is your job. That's what I pay you for."

"All the more reason to shut the building and get everyone out of here. Security is my job and I'm telling you what needs to be done. If you choose to ignore it, that's on you." Then Bob had another thought. "Besides, if the building is empty for the most part, and the shit hits the fan around here, I'll be able to make sure you get out of here without trying to wade through a couple hundred people."

Byron stood there for a second, considering the last point. If the shit did indeed hit the fan, the only person he was worried about getting out of here was himself. He looked up at Bob, then at Daniel.

Jutting his chin in Daniel's direction, he asked, "Who's that?" As though Daniel weren't standing in front of him.

Bob looked over his shoulder at Daniel. "He works in IT and is my contact with them during this little incident."

Byron looked at Daniel. "You the one responsible for fucking my network up, making me the Judas of the entire banking world?"

Daniel stood there stunned, not knowing what to say. His mouth was dry and his voice refused to work. Finally, Bob came to his rescue. "No, he's the one that pulled the network down from the outside world. He's the one that saved whatever ass you have left."

Byron shot Bob a look. "Fine, we'll shut the building. Tiffany will take care of getting the emails out." He paused for a moment and pointed at Bob. "You do not leave this building, though, not until I do." Byron leaned over and pressed an intercom button on his desk and asked Tiffany to come in. "Now, if you gentlemen don't mind, I have shit to do."

Bob didn't reply. He simply turned and grabbed Daniel by the arm and headed for the door. They passed Tiffany in the anteroom. "Sorry," Bob said as he passed her. She looked at him, confused. "For what?" Bob smiled. "You'll see; and make sure you get out of here as soon as you can too."

Tiffany was still looking confused as the two men left the room. Daniel followed Bob to the elevators, not the freight elevator they took up, but the private car for the man in the big office. Bob waved his prox card at the reader by the button then pressed the now-illuminated call button. Daniel just stood there not saying a word. He was still choking on his tongue.

When the car arrived and the doors opened, they were greeted by four men in blue blazers with FBI emblazoned on them in big yellow letters. Bob stepped aside as the men exited, nodding at them as they passed; and he quickly ushered Daniel into the car. Once inside, Daniel let out a long breath, running his hands through his hair.

Spinning around to face Bob, he half shouted. "Dude, why in the hell did you take me up there with you?"

"What, you scared to swim with the sharks?"

Daniel just shook his head. Then his phone vibrated. "Nice, looks like I get to go home."

Bob leaned against the wall, watching the numbers tick by on the display over the door. "You're not going anywhere."

Daniel jerked his head up. "Why the hell not? I'm on

the list here. It says I don't need to come in. Since I'm here, I think I'll leave."

"Let's go to my office and take a look at things."

The mob on the monitor was not the same one he had seen earlier. Daniel was shocked at what he saw. There was a line of police in front of the bank, all decked out in riot gear, shields, helmets and gas masks. In the center of the road was a burning police car, several piles of burning tires and dumpsters full of flames. A figure erupted from the crowd of rioters wearing one of the masks from V, a flaming trashcan over his head. He ran towards the police in an effort to hurl the can of fire.

As soon as he crossed the center line of the road, marked by the piles of burning tires, the man crumpled and fell to the pavement. In the bottom right corner of the screen, a police officer was racking a shotgun, the spent shell of a less-than-lethal round bouncing on the pavement. At the same moment, a phalanx of officers rushed forward, the officers in the front holding shields up to deflect the bottles and rocks pelting them. Just as with the Roman Legions, the second row of officers held their shields over their heads, blocking the missiles landing on them.

They covered the man in the road as additional officers in the rear grabbed the stricken man and pulled him back to the police line. The line of rioters surged forward but were immediately turned back with streams of pepper spray from fire extinguisher-size canisters.

"Holy shit," Daniel said as he watched the scene unfold.

"That's nothing. Just wait till it's live rounds they're using," Bob replied.

"Bob, you want us to lock down the building?" Andy asked from his console.

Bob scanned the various cameras. "Yeah, everything on the ground level. Send out an email telling everyone to take the pedestrian bridge to the garage. We should never have opened it in the first place. Those idiots upstairs want everything to look normal." Bob gestured towards the screen. "Does that look normal to you?"

"Done." Andy replied.

On a couple of the monitors, the large gates began to lower on interior hallways of the first floor. If Bob had had his way, they would have remained down. But earlier in the day, Byron had insisted they be raised. Now, he wasn't even going to bother to ask. The building was getting locked down. Daniel's phone vibrated, and he pulled it off to check the message.

"Where are you!?" Malcolm's signature was under it.

***

Teague closed the phone and let it drop into his lap as his head fell back onto the couch. He let out a long breath that was half groan, half regret. Coming back to the moment, he pulled the cover off the back of the phone and removed the SIM card. Sitting up, he tossed it into a burn bucket with some fuel, lit it and watched as it disappeared in the flame. Crossing the room to where his pack sat beside the door, he reached into it and took another card out and inserted it into the phone.

He'd only been here for two days and it was time to move again. The ambush happened three weeks ago. He thinks it's been three weeks now; and since then, he hasn't spent more than four days in one spot. Everyone involved in the ambush had been on the move just as he had. The ambush had been a spur-of-the-moment mission, and while they had been looking for a chance to make a stand, the roadblock had just fallen in their lap. As soon as contact was broken at the scene, they immediately separated into smaller cells. These smaller cells continued to break up until every militiaman was on his own.

Each person was left to their own devices with one simple goal, don't get your ass caught. In this manner, no one knew what the other's plan was, unless of course you ran your mouth. The three militia members caught so far were members of the same cell. They made a group plan and discussed it in detail with one another. When the first of them was apprehended, the other two fell like dominos. In their plan, they all agreed not to be taken alive. "*From my cold dead hands!*" was the unanimous cadence shouted by the three. In the end, only one of them even fired a shot, for which he was immediately shot multiple times in return.

Teague's plan was a little more sophisticated. He actually had a network of people in place to help him, not that they knew why they were doing the things he asked. He'd known them all for so long, that when he called, they answered. The network he was relying on was so far removed from him that if the Feds ever did manage to put it together, he would already be long gone. So far, everything had worked out. He was already in Arkansas, and this next ride would get him into Alabama. Once in Alabama, it wouldn't take too long to make his way to Atlanta. He just hoped his cousin would let him crash at his place.

***

Daniel looked at the phone and grunted. Bob looked over and he showed him the message. Bob snorted and took the phone. Daniel watched as he typed a reply. *Been sent home. All nonessential personnel have been furloughed today.* He sent the message and handed the phone back. Daniel took it and snapped it back into the cradle, giving Bob a smile as he did. "What now?"

"Let's go get a coffee."

Daniel nodded and the two of them headed for the door. On the way out, Bob said, "Andy, call me if anything happens."

"Sure thing, boss."

They took the elevator down to the level with the pedestrian bridge. The little coffee shop was located inside the building where the bridge connected, and they ordered a coffee before the two ladies working there shut down. They took up a seat at one of the high tables where they could watch as all the employees left.

"How bad do you think it's going to get out there?" Daniel asked.

Bob took a sip of the coffee before replying. "Dunno. It may blow over or they may try and burn the damn city down. Either way, I didn't want the building full."

Daniel nodded and looked out across the small mezzanine area where the shop was located. It opened up onto the large foyer of the main lobby, and the open space there continued up for one more floor. From where Daniel sat, he could see the windows on the front of the building, though at the moment, all he could see was the back of the large security shutters covering them. The sound of Bob's Zippo popping open caught his attention, and he looked back just in time to see him light a smoke.

"Are you freakin nuts?"

Bob blew out the smoke. "What, who's going to complain?"

"Still, you're not supposed to smoke in the building."

Bob flicked some ash into an empty creamer cup. "Aw, come on. You're also supposed to pay your taxes on time, wait thirty minutes after eating before you swim or eat red meat. Come on, man; you can't be that big a pussy."

Daniel's back stiffened. "I'm no pussy."

"Calm down there, John Wayne. Just fuckin' with ya."

Daniel sipped his coffee. Who the hell did this guy think he was anyway?

Daniel's phone vibrated. Malcolm again. *I am leaving now. You need to be here in the morning.*

Daniel jumped up from the chair, startling Bob. "What?"

"Malcolm's headed down here now. I don't want him to see me. Let's go."

"I ain't worried about him. Let's finish our coffee." Bob shook his head and took another sip.

The elevator bank was only twenty or so feet away and he was able to hear the ding announcing the car's arrival. With nowhere to go, Daniel ran around the counter of the coffee shop and crouched down. Bob was laughing at him as he did. Malcolm came around the corner of the elevator bank and saw Bob, who was still laughing. He walked over and stood on the other side of the half wall that enclosed the café area.

Bob simply sipped his coffee, never acknowledging the other man's presence. After a minute or two, Malcolm got irritated. "Why are you still here, Bob. I thought everyone was told to leave."

"Actually, the email said all nonessential personnel were sent home. I'm essential," Bob replied with a smile.

"You know you aren't allowed to smoke in here." Malcolm replied in an attempt to get the upper hand.

Bob's response was to light another one up. He inhaled deeply while looking Malcolm in the eye then blew out three perfect rings into the air. When he finished, he smiled. "So sue me."

Malcolm walked off in a huff. Bob smiled at himself. It wasn't every day you got to piss someone off so easily. Daniel waited behind the counter, not wanting to chance a look and getting spotted by Malcolm. Bob left him there for a couple of minutes before he finally said, "Coast is clear."

Daniel peered over the counter with one eye, looking the café over. The only person he saw was Bob, sipping on his coffee and smoking. Cautiously, he stood up and walked around the counter, still looking for Malcolm. Finally making his way back to the table, he took a seat across from Bob.

"What'd he say?" Daniel asked.

"Who?"

Daniel lifted his hands off the table. "What'da you mean, who?"

Bob laughed. "Don't worry. He's got no idea you're here."

Byron suddenly appeared. Having come down his private elevator with Tiffany. He has two of the security guards with him. His briefcase at his side he looked at Bob and said, "These guys are escorting me home." He waved his hand in the air. "I'm not taking any chances with all this."

Bob smiled, "Sure thing Byron. I can understand."

As the two men talked the elevator dinged again. Daniel turned just in time to see Amber round the corner. He rolled his eyes and muttered under his breath, *shit*.

She walked up and smiled coyly, "Hi Daniel. I was hopng you could help me. I don't have my car today. Can you give me a ride home?"

Daniel shook his head, "No sorry. I'm not leaving. I have to stay here to work on the breach."

Byron shot Daniel a look. "Breach? Is that what you call it? A fucking breach?"

Bob put his hand on Byron's shoulder. "Give the kid a break. He's an IT guy. That's what they call it."

Amber's lips formed a pout. "Oh. I'll find some way."

Tiffany smiled. "I can give you a ride."

Byron was eyeing Amber up and down. Like a predator sizing up it's prey he said, "I'll give you ride. I have a car and driver." Nodding at the two security men he added, "Not to mention these fellas."

But just as Byron thought he was sizing Amber up, she too was like a cat with a mouse. She smiled, "That would be very kind of you," she replied. She never acknowledged Daniel again as a much more worthy conquest now presented itself.

The group quickly walked off as the two sized one another up like a starving man before a buffet. Daniel rubbed his head, "That was fucking weird."

Bob laughed. "Business as usual my friend."

***

Malcolm looked down at the crowd below the bridge as he

crossed. They looked pissed. One guy, young black kid in a gray hoodie looked up, locking eyes with him. The kid was shouting something, but no way he could hear it up here. Malcolm just stared back at him. His apparent indifference sent the kid into a rage. He tore the red bandanna from his face and began to scream. Then, in a final act of defiance, he gave Malcolm the finger. Malcolm just shook his head and continued to the garage where he took the elevator up to the next level where he was parked.

Malcolm was digging around in his pocket for his keys when he stopped in his tracks. He stood there for a moment. Certainly he wasn't seeing what he thought he was seeing. But there sat Daniel's van in his usual spot.

"Son of a bitch."

That little shit. Sure, he was good at his job, but he was the biggest pain in the ass. The thought passed through his mind that if he weren't so damn good, he could terminate him. But then he knew deep down that he couldn't do half of the stuff that Daniel could. The kid really was good. Malcolm located his car, hit the button and the locks popped open, and soon he was heading down to the exit.

When he got to the exit, he was forced to stop. There was a big gate blocking the exit. One of the security officers approached him on the driver's side. Malcolm was surprised as he had not seen the guy until he was almost at the window. Malcolm put the window down as the guy got there.

"Can I get out?" Malcolm asked.

"Hang on a sec." The security man keyed his radio. "Got one ready to exit. Is it clear?"

The radio crackled with a reply. "Uh, yeah. Looks alright. There's one guy out there, but he looks ok."

"Alright, open it up."

Malcolm and the security officer watched as the big steel gate rattled and groaned while rising. Once it was high enough for the car to clear, the security officer told him to go ahead. As Malcolm pulled out, he looked to his right checking for cars. Then his windshield exploded. Shocked is not the word for what he felt. Suddenly, someone was at his car door trying to get in. Malcolm was startled to see a young guy in a gray hoodie with a red bandanna over his face. He was pounding on the glass and screaming. Malcolm was stunned. He didn't know what to do. Shock prevented him from moving.

"Go go go!" The security officer was screaming. The kid at the car window ignored the screaming guard; or maybe he didn't even notice the man.

Malcolm looked in the rearview mirror at the security officer, who was frantically waving for him to go. Then he looked to his right out the passenger side window, and he gasped. A sea of people was pouring around the corner of the garage. It looked like those videos of the tsunami that struck Indonesia; but instead of water, it was people. Looking to his left again, the kid was still there, but he had dropped a pack off his back and pulled a metal bar out of it. He took a batter's stance at the window with the bar.

A series of pops went off in rapid succession and the kid fell to the floor of the garage. The security agent appeared at the window. "Dammit, man. Fucking go!" he shouted while holding his pistol on the stricken man. Finally, Malcolm floored the gas and took off. The security officer keyed his radio, calling for the gate to be closed immediately. The crowd on the street was still running towards the open gate. The gate began to lower and the security officer back-peddled into the garage, weapon still drawn, with an eye on the shrinking opening.

Bob looked at the message that was marked urgent. "Need you up here now. Andy."

"Come on. Let's go back to my office," Bob said as he stood up, dropping the butt of a cigarette into the empty cup.

"What's up?" Daniel asked.

"Don't know. But I bet it ain't good."

Bob watched the video for the third time. He simply couldn't believe what he was seeing. On the screen beside the one playing the recently recorded video was the live shot from the camera outside the garage. The crowd out there was still growing, and two cars parked on the other side of the street were already on fire. All types of objects were being thrown at the building. Several people were using the post of a street sign to batter the gate.

Bob reached for a radio sitting in a cradle beside Andy. "David, soon as you can, I need to see you up here."

The reply that came back was distorted by the sounds of banging on the metal gate. Mixed with shouts, it was almost inaudible. "You gonna send someone else down here to relieve me first?"

Bob thought about it for a moment. "Andy, pull up to the front of the building."

An exterior view of the front of the building filled the monitor before him. It looked like most of the people out there had moved around towards the garage. At the moment, things were quieter out there.

Bob keyed his radio. "S1, S4."

"Go for S4."

"Go relieve S3"

"Roger that. On my way."

Andy spun around in his seat. "Want me to call 911?"

"Not yet. Let's see what David has to say first. It's not like they'd come right now anyway."

Daniel pointed to the screen. "Looks like they're already on their way."

Bob looked up as Andy spun around. He quickly brought up a monitor to the center of the screen. In the bottom left corner of the screen, the top of the metal gate of the garage exit could be seen along with part of the crowd gathered there. On the top half of the screen, the Atlanta PD, in full riot gear was forming up. A skirmish line was already formed, and they were advancing one step at a time, banging their batons on the top of their shields. The crowd paid them little attention.

"Shit. Andy, call Carlos and tell him what's going on."

Daniel looked at Bob. "Who's Carlos?"

"He's a LT with the Atlanta PD, a good friend of mine. I need coffee. Anyone else?"

"Yeah, I could use some," Daniel said.

Daniel followed Bob into his office. "See if you can find a cup," Bob said as he blew stale ashes out of a cup on his desk.

Daniel was standing beside the coffee pot, going through the various cups scattered around it. His face appeared as ill as he felt, looking into some of the cups. He was certain some of these would be of interest to the CDC.

"Found lots of cups. You got a clean one anywhere?"

Bob was wiping his cup out with his tie. "Look under the counter. Should be some Styrofoam cups under there."

Much to his relief, Daniel found one cup still in the plastic sleeve and poured himself a brew. The liquid was dark, really dark, like it had been on the burner all day. Bob poured a cup without a second thought and took a long drink. He looked up to see the security guard from the garage standing outside his door.

"What the hell happened?" Bob asked.

David ran his hand across his face. "I'm sure you already saw the video. What was I supposed to do, let him beat the guy's brains in? If the dumb ass would have just driven off, it wouldn't have happened. But he just sat there looking all stupid."

"Yeah, we saw the video, but you gotta know that killing one of them is just going to make things a lot worse out there," Bob said, shaking his head.

"I know, sorry. But I couldn't let that dumb shit get beat. Who was that ass hat anyway?"

"His name's Malcolm, head of IT security," Daniel said.

David looked at him. "You mean that guy was in charge of the department that caused most of this shit? Those people are rioting out there because they can't get to their money or use their damn food stamps, and I saved his ass? Shit, if I'd a known that, I would've stepped back and watched. It's IT's fault this shit is getting worse."

"Careful there, David. Daniel here works for that man," Bob said.

"Don't worry. I think Malcolm's an ass hat too. And for the record, there were already riots before the whole bank holiday thing," Daniel said.

Andy stuck his head into Bob's office. "Bob, Carlos on two."

Bob walked around his desk and fell into his chair, paused for a moment looking at the phone, then picked it up, pressing the button for line two at the same time.

"How's business, Carlos?"

"Market's peaking. What'da need, Bob?"

"I guess you know things are a little hairy down here right now."

"Yeah, the riot guys are out. We should have the protesters cleaned out soon. They're bringing in a sound cannon right now; that should run 'em off."

"Good. It should make it easier for you guys to get to the crime scene." Bob shook out a smoke and lit it. There was a pause on the other end.

"What crime scene?" Carlos asked.

"We were evacuating the building earlier and one of our people was attacked by someone in the mob."

"I'm sorry about that, Bob, but right now we just don't have the time to deal with it." Carlos was getting irritated with this trivial situation considering what was going on throughout the city.

"That's not the issue. One of my guys shot him."

"Are you fuckin' serious?" Carlos shouted. "Dammit, Bob."

"Look, I got it all on video. It's a clean shoot."

"Where's the actor?" Carlos asked in exasperation.

"That's the real problem. He went down just outside

our security doors on the parking garage. The crowd down there is beating the shit out of the door, and we can't see the body now."

"Shit, what exit? I'll see if we can get it cleared out."

"It's the north exit. You've got a riot squad just down the street from them now. If your guys can push 'em down the block, we can get in there."

"You aren't getting in anywhere. Just stay out of it. I'll see what I can do about getting them cleared out, then get back to you. Keep your shooter onsite. He can't leave."

"10-4, Carlos. Let me know if we can help," Bob said.

"As if people weren't already mad enough at the banks, then you guys, one of the banks, whack one of the poor demonstrators," Carlos said with clear irritation.

"Poor demonstrators, my ass," Bob said with a snort.

"Well, that's how the media is describing them. They're going to have a field day with this when they find out about it. You're going to have cameras shoved so far up your ass you'll be able to taste them. I'll be in touch," Carlos said and hung up.

Bob hung up the phone and looked up at David. "How's it look?" David asked.

"He's pissed, but you should be alright. Go get a drink and take break."

David nodded and left the office. Daniel waited until he was gone to comment on how casual David acted after shooting someone. Bob told him David was a vet that had spent six tours in Iraq and Afghanistan. He'd killed before.

For the next several minutes, they watched as the APD tried to push the crowd back. Volley after volley of teargas was fired into the crowd, many of which were thrown back.

ANGERY AMERICAN

Riots and unrest have been going on for so long that many people were now coming out equipped with their own gas masks. While their numbers were low, they made up the front line troops in the gas war with the police.

The police would deploy gas and rush the mob. The rioters would fall back a bit, regroup and surge towards the officers, who would then deploy another round of gas as they fell back, before regrouping and charging the rioters again. It was essentially a stalemate. Neither side really had the upper hand. While both sides were constantly being reinforced, the police had the advantage in equipment.

"Holy shit. What the hell is that thing?" Daniel asked as a large hulking vehicle came into view.

"It's about to get really interesting," Andy said as he guided a camera on the behemoth, zooming in as he did.

Bob chuckled. "Yeah, unless they got some really good hearing protection, they aren't going to stand in front that thing very long."

The riot squad parted to let the truck pull through to the front of their line. The appearance of the thing sent the crowd into a renewed fervor, jumping up and down and throwing everything that they could break loose at the officers. Once the officers were reorganized, they began to move forward, keeping pace with the truck. Initially, the crowd began to fall back in anticipation of what the truck may do. When nothing happened, except for the officers gaining ground, they decided to stand their ground.

Once the crowd stopped falling back, the LRAD opened up on them. The effect was profound and immediate.

"Holy shit!" Daniel shouted as anyone in the direct path of the weapon fell to their knees and cupped their ears.

People began to run in every direction. It was an impressive sight on the cameras, watching the sea of bodies move as if one organism, enveloping everything in their path.

"Oh yeah, that got their attention," Bob said as he lit a cigarette.

The sound cannon was having the desired effect, and the crowd fell back farther down the block. The truck was finally in front of the exit of the parking garage. It pulled over towards the door and stopped parallel to it in the street. The doors on the rear opened and some officers quickly exited, running the couple of feet to the roll-up door. Other trucks pulled up as well, more backup for the officers on the ground.

"There's Carlos," Bob said.

Andy was already swinging the camera around so they could look down on the scene. What they saw was Carlos standing there looking around, but no corpse was in the frame. Carlos pulled a cell phone from his pocket and started to dial.

"Shit," Bob said as his phone started to ring.

"What'cha see down there, Carlos?"

"There's nothing here, no body, no blood, nothing. You sure he went down?" Carlos shouted into the phone over the chaos surrounding him.

"I've got it on video. He was down. Someone in the crowd probably carried him away."

Across the street from the bank's parking garage was another parking structure. This one served several businesses on the block and was open to the public, using those little kiosks to pay by entering your space number.

Shorter than the enormous garage across the street, it was only two stories.

Suddenly, the camera on the garage exit flickered and another view took its place. Bob looked at Andy, wondering what the hell he was doing. Seeing the video feed explained it in a flash. A group of people was running across the top deck of the garage towards the side bordering the street. Carlos was saying something to him on the phone when Bob cut him off.

"Carlos, on the roof behind you guys. People are moving in on you!"

"What?" Carlos shouted back.

"On the roof of the other garage!"

On the screen, they watched as the people made it to the edge of the parapet wall. They watched with horror as they lit Molotov cocktails.

"Behind you. Look up. You've got incoming!" Bob shouted back.

On a small image, they watched as Carlos finally caught on to what was happening. He was shouting at the other officers and pointing up at the garage just as the flaming missiles came over it in a slow arch. The officers began to run for cover, taking up positions behind the truck, between it and the bank's security door.

"Son of a bitch!" Bob shouted as he headed for his office.

Andy and Daniel were watching the camera feeds when Andy quickly zoomed in on a figure. He was moving in a low crouch to the wall, it wasn't until the camera had zoomed in enough that they were able to see the AK-47 he was carrying.

"Bob, one of 'em's got a gun!" Andy called out.

Bob came out of his office holding an AR in each hand, and an OD bag slung over his shoulder. Daniel was wide-eyed.

"What the hell are you doing?"

Bob thrust one of the Warhogs into his hands. "Follow me." Then he snatched a radio from the charger on Andy's console. "Keep me informed on what's happening."

"10-4, boss."

Bob headed for the door and paused just outside it, looking at Daniel. "You coming or not?"

Daniel simply nodded and followed him out the door. In the elevator, Bob told him what his plan was. They were going to go to the top of their parking garage which would overlook the one across the street. He would call Carlos and ask if they needed their help suppressing the group on the roof. Daniel didn't say anything, just nodded his head. Bob pulled two magazines from the bag and handed them to Daniel. He tucked one into the back pocket of his jeans and the other he inserted into the rifle, giving it a tap.

As soon as they exited the elevator and headed for the pedestrian bridge to garage, Bob was on his phone. "Dammit!" he shouted when Carlos's voicemail picked up. He tried two more times on the way to the top of the garage with the same result.

Making it to the edge of the garage roof, he was able to look down and see Carlos and some of the other officers taking cover behind the truck as Molotovs broke on the other side of it, sending thick clouds of black smoke swirling up, and forcing Daniel and Bob both to fall back.

"Bob, what do you want to do?"

Bob didn't answer. He tried his phone again. This time,

Carlos answered. "Carlos, there's a guy with an AK on top of that garage!" Bob made his way to the edge and looked down. This time, he could see Carlos. Looking down the street, he could see that the crowd was reforming, albeit farther away this time.

Daniel was looking down on the garage across the street and could see everyone there. The man with the AK was peering over the top of the wall at the officers. Then the officers launched teargas at them.

"You guys need to get the hell out of there!" Bob screamed into the phone.

"Were fucking trying. You see all the damn fire?" Carlos shouted back.

"Yeah I do. Look up."

"What?"

"Look up, dumbass."

Bob was looking down when Carlos leaned away from the building to see him.

"What the hell are you doing up there?"

"When I saw the guy with the AK, I came up here in case you guys needed some help."

"We don't need any help. I told you to stay out of it. Are you armed?"

"What fucking good would I be if I weren't?"

Daniel hit Bob. "Gun!"

Daniel's warning was immediately followed by a volley of shots, causing both men to jump. The riot police on the road began to scatter, looking for anywhere to take cover. At the same moment, almost as if it had been coordinated, a half dozen flaming tires came rolling down the road towards the besieged officers. From below, the AK was answered with return fire. Most, but not all of the crowd that had reformed farther down the street, began to scatter once again. Those that stayed began to rush the police.

Bob looked over to see Carlos firing a handgun. Daniel was looking at the shooter across the road. He could plainly see the man, and then he looked at Bob who was looking down at Carlos, and finally at the Warhog in his own hands. He charged the rifle.

"Carlos, you want us to take him out?"

Two officers were down in the street, Bob watched as Carlos looked at them, then at the shooter who saw him and switched his fire to the back of the truck.

"Carlos, dammit, we can take him out!"

"Take him out. Shoot, shoot!" Carlos shouted into the phone.

Bob looked up at Daniel as his rifle barked. Daniel fired round after round about a half second apart. Bob looked across the street to see the shooter sprawled on the ground. Another person tried to grab the AK and Bob dropped his phone and quickly engaged him, felling the man with two shots. The others began to try and take cover. A milk crate full of cocktails was sitting just far enough back that Bob was able to put rounds into it, spraying the flammable liquid in a wide area.

Bob ejected the mag in his rifle and dug through the bag, pulling out another with red tape around it, jammed it into the rifle and began firing at the spreading pool of gas. The tracers streaked across the street. On the third round, a ball of flames and thick black smoke erupted.

Both men stopped firing and watched the smoke rise. The others on the deck across from them were running for the exit, rounding the corner and heading down the ramp, out of sight. Bob was brought out of his trance by the sounds of shouting on the road below. Looking down, he could see officers helping their fallen to the truck. The crowd had fallen back farther down the block, probably as a result of the gun fire. Carlos looked up and gave Bob a wave. He waved back just as Carlos climbed into the back of the truck and shut the door. It quickly started to move, heading back the way it had come.

But the rioters on the street were trying to capitalize on the moment. They were rushing headlong at the retreating officers. The LRAD opened up again, to little effect. One of the other trucks that came up to provide support began to fire numerous rounds of CS gas in rapid succession. But this too had little effect. These were professional agitators; and they were wearing gas masks and hearing protection.

When the gas and LRAD had no effect, the truck changed tactics and quickly drove towards the approaching rioters. Once in range, it suddenly emitted a thick orange stream from a nozzle mounted to its roof. The sticky pepper spray worked and stopped them in their tracks. To make sure no one tried to assist them, an officer stepped from the truck with a handheld launcher and fired several canisters onto the road behind them before quickly getting back in the truck.

These weren't gas canisters. They emitted a small cloud of smoke but there just wasn't enough volume to gas. Some protestors were running to the aid of those stricken with the sticky foam. As they got to area where the canisters landed, they halted in their tracks, covering their mouths and noses; and then they retreated the way they had come.

Those still fighting the foam were stuck and had to endure the overpowering stink of the Skunk bombs. It also makes a very effective area denial weapon because, once deployed, it can linger for up to six weeks and only be neutralized with a proprietary soap.

Daniel and Bob soon discovered the power of the weapon from their rooftop position when the odor, carried by the urban wind currents created by tall buildings and narrow roadways, took it up to them.

Bob coughed and covered his face. "What the hell is that?"

Daniel buried his nose into the crook of his elbow. "Holy hell. What is that? Smells like a cross between something dead and shit." He was backing away from the edge of the wall, trying to find relief.

"That's just God awful!" Bob shouted as he ran for the opposite side of the parking deck. But Daniel took a minute to reflect on what had just happened.

Daniel stood there gawking at the scene across the street from him, at the man he had just killed. The man was sprawled out, like someone in the middle of making a snow angel, only the body was on fire. He was jarred back to reality by his phone ringing. At first, he didn't notice it. The vibrating is what finally got his attention. Plucking the phone from the clip, he looked at it and was confused. He shook his head and looked again. It was his home number on the screen.

"Hello?"

"Daniel?"

"Yeah. Who the hell is this?"

"It's Teague."

"Teague?"

"Yeah, your cousin."

"How the hell did you get in my house?"

"The door was open. Hope you don't mind that I let I myself in."

Daniel had to think about that for a minute. He was certain he had locked the door. It would be stupid to go out and not lock it.

"Uh, yeah, sure. What are you doing in town?"

"Just bumming around. Thought I'd drop in and see ya. When you coming home?"

"Don't know. Things are a little… weird at work today."

"I bet. Been watching the news. Looks like the shit's hit the fan downtown."

Daniel looked back across the street. "You have no idea. Just hang out. I'll call you when I'm ready to head home."

"Cool. I'll be here, drinking your beer."

Daniel ended the call, hoping there was somewhere he could buy some beer on the way home, because he damn sure was going to need a drink after today.

"Who was that?" Bob asked.

"My cousin. Just came into town."

"He sure picked a hell of a time for a visit."

"Yeah. Well, he has never been real bright. We grew up together. Spent all our summers together tear-assin' around the woods. Ya know, just being kids."

"Let's head back to my office."

Daniel slung the carbine over his shoulder and suddenly felt sick. He leaned on the edge of the parapet. His head spun and his stomach was in knots. Suddenly, he knew he was going to be sick and leaned forward and puked over the side. After emptying his stomach, he was wiping his mouth when Bob asked, "Feel better?"

Looking at Bob, Daniel replied. "Don't know what happened."

Bob lit another cigarette. "First time, huh? Happens to everyone the first time."

"First time?" Daniel asked, unsure exactly what Bob was talking about.

Gesturing with the cigarette towards the other side of the street, Bob replied. "Killing someone. Happens to everyone the first time. Well, almost everyone. Come on. Let's get back to my office so you can sit down."

When they walked in, Andy was replaying the video of the shooting. He had caught on to what was happening and had trained a camera on the top deck of the garage. Daniel glanced at the screen, then looked away. The scene playing over and over in his head was bad enough. He didn't need to see a live action replay. Bob walked by without noticing the video. He went straight to his office, and Daniel followed him. Bob leaned his rifle by the door in his office before sitting down behind his desk. Daniel leaned his rifle by the door as well, and sat in one of the office chairs.

Bob snatched a coffee cup from his desk and observed the bottom of it with dried, crusted coffee. He wiped it out with the tail of his tie, then set it down on the desk and repeated the process with another. Opening the bottom drawer of his desk, he pulled out a bottle of Johnny Walker blue label and poured two fingers in each cup, handing one to Daniel.

Daniel took the cup and looked at the little brown bits floating around in the amber whiskey. *Fuck it*, he thought, and tossed the Scotch back. He followed it with a hard exhale and looked at Bob.

"Damn, that's good. Thanks, I needed it."

Bob tossed his back and bared his teeth. He looked like a werewolf. Picking up the bottle, he poured another in each cup. "You need another."

Daniel didn't even hesitate this time, though he only downed half of it in the first swallow, actually taking a moment to savor it. He motioned with the cup at the bottle. "Must be nice having that in your desk."

"Conditions are what you make 'em."

"I guess. Couldn't pull that off downstairs."

Bob smiled as he lit a cigarette. "Who's going to search me?"

Daniel looked out towards Andy, sitting at his console. The video of the shooting was gone and he was panning the exterior cameras around.

"Wonder how things are going outside? I'd like to get the hell out of here if I could," Daniel said.

"Let's go see."

At the moment, the street was relatively clear. The mobs had dispersed. Fighting tear gas and clubs is one thing, but taking bullets was more than most of them bargained for. Once the powerful funk was added to the concrete canyon, they lost all desire to fight.

"How's it look, Andy?" Bob asked.

"Looks like the animals have returned to their cages for now."

With much effort, Daniel stood up. "Bob, I'm going to take off. I'm sure your cop buddy will want to talk to me. I'll come back tomorrow."

Bob stared at the monitor for a moment, rubbing his chin then looking at his watch.

"Go ahead. Go home. You too, Andy."

Andy spun around in his chair. "You sure, boss?"

"Yeah. You two get gone while the gettin's good."

"What about you?" Daniel asked.

"Me? Oh, I'll stay here and keep an eye on things. There are still guys in the building, so I'll be alright."

"Alright then, I'm outta here," Daniel said.

Andy leapt from his chair. "Me too."

"Before you go, Daniel, come in here," Bob said as he walked into his office.

Bob opened the top drawer of his desk and took out a business card and handed it to Daniel. "If you have any trouble, I mean any with the cops, give them this card and call me. Call me before they get to you if you can. This time, don't forget."

Daniel looked at the card, Lt. Carlos Delgado, Atlanta Police Department. Complete with office, fax and best of all, cell phone numbers. He stuck the card in his pocket and headed for the door.

"Hey, when you coming back?" Bob asked.

Daniel stopped at the door and scratched his head. "Dunno. Do I even need to come back?"

That caught Bob off guard. He shrugged his shoulders before replying. "Well, ya got me there. Just keep your phone handy in case I need to get in touch with you."

Andy and Daniel left the office and walked down to the garage together. Andy was parked on the first floor of the garage and Daniel's van was on the top floor.

"Be safe," Daniel said as they headed for the stairs.

"You too, man."

Andy headed down and Daniel went up, taking the stairs two at a time. When he came out of the stairs on the top deck, he went over to the wall and looked over the side at the street. It was empty, like creepy empty. Looking down, he pushed empty shell casings around with his foot. It was surreal, shooting at someone in downtown Atlanta and no cops showing up to slap cuffs on him.

Daniel hopped into the van and headed for the exit, tires squealing as he wound his way down through the decks. Andy was already gone and the security door was closed when he got to it. As he approached it, the door began to open. He knew Bob was up there watching the cameras. He stuck his arm out and waved at the camera as he pulled through and onto the street.

Daniel was very nervous as he drove towards home, remembering his last ride through town. To try and calm his nerves, he turned on the radio. The radio blared news, telling about the riots around the area. The shooting was not mentioned at all. He thought that was a little odd; but then without the media being able to move around the streets, it wasn't too surprising. He couldn't take the constant talk of riots, looting, shootings and general mayhem. Those depressed him, so he switched to the MP3 player connected to the stereo.

He wasn't in the mood for rock, and settled on Mumford and Sons instead. Before the first song was finished, he saw the entrance to his apartment complex ahead and relief washed over him. Pulling into his spot in front of his building, he shut off the van and sat there for a moment, looking around and listening. He was nervous as all hell, not that there was any obvious danger at the moment. It was simply becoming a way of life it seemed.

Before getting out, he dug around in his bag and found his flashlight. With the light in one hand and his pocket knife in the other, he got out and headed for his apartment. As he went up the stairs, he had the key ready and stuck it in the deadbolt as soon as he reached it. Daniel quickly opened the door and froze in his tracks. He was staring into a giant black hole; at least it looked giant from where he stood.

"Oh, sorry dude. Didn't know it was you," Teague said as he lowered the pistol.

"Asshole, you scared the shit outta me!" Daniel shouted.

"Sorry, cous. It's a little scary out there right now." Teague replied as Daniel stepped past him into his apartment. Teague stepped out of the door and looked around before closing it.

Daniel went straight for the fridge. He needed a beer. He opened one and took a long drink, downing half the bottle. When he lowered the bottle, Teague was just standing there. Daniel set the bottle on the counter and looked at Teague.

"What the fuck, man?" Daniel asked.

"Sorry, dude. You been out there? It's scary."

"If you only knew."

From the back of the apartment a voice called out. "Is it safe?"

"Who the hell is that?" Daniel asked.

"Shit, forgot. Yeah, come on out." Teague called out.

Daniel leaned forward to see who was coming and saw Christy as she rounded the corner.

Her face lit up when she saw Daniel, and she quickly moved towards him. "Hey, babe. I'm so glad you're here!" She shouted as she wrapped her arms around him.

With a beer in one hand and Christy's arms around his neck, Daniel looked at Teague with raised eyebrows.

"She jus' showed up, cous."

Christy pulled back, then quickly leaned in and kissed him.

"I was worried about you. The news is saying there was shooting near your office. Is everything ok?" Christy asked as she looked him over.

"Yeah, I'm fine. Let's go sit down. I'm beat."

The three of them went into the living room. Daniel sat on the couch and Christy fell into it beside him. Teague flopped into the chair, putting his feet up on the coffee table. While he wasn't bothered by Teague's feet on the table, the number of empty beer bottles on it did get his attention. The TV was on and a local news anchor was going on and on about the violence around town as well as around the country. Atlanta wasn't the only place falling deeper into chaos.

Daniel squeezed Christy's thigh. She looked up and smiled. "I see you've met my cousin Teague."

She smiled back at him, then looked at Teague. "Yeah, I came by and surprised him. He scared the crap out of me."

Teague shrugged. "Sorry, didn't expect anyone." Pointing at Daniel, he added, "He said he was going to call when he was headed this way. Lucky I was here."

"Yeah, I was really lucky he dropped by since I left the door unlocked." Daniel replied. Then he looked over at Teague as he took another pull off the beer.

"What? You really need to pay more attention, especially right now." Christy replied.

Teague just smiled. "Indeed."

"Well, what brought you out to Atlanta?" Daniel asked Teague.

"He's wandering." Christy replied.

"Wandering, huh?"

"Yeah, just wanted to get out of Michigan for a while. Figured I'd better do it now before there's nothing left to see."

"That shouldn't take long considering the way things are going right now." Daniel replied. Then he asked, "How's everyone doing up there?"

Teague looked at the floor. "Good, everyone's good."

"Hmm." Daniel replied as he finished his beer.

"I'm starving. You got any food?" Christy asked.

"Don't you remember the epic grocery haul from the other day? Take a look and see what you can find."

Christy jumped up. "You guys hungry?"

Teague rolled his head on the back of the chair. "Starved."

"I could eat something." Daniel replied.

Christy headed for the kitchen. Daniel watched her leave and once she was out of earshot, he sat up on the couch. "What are you really doing here?"

"Dude, I told ya. Just wanted to travel a little."

"Really?" Daniel said in disbelief. "That shit up there didn't have anything to do with you it, did it?"

"What shit?"

"Dude, don't even try to play with me. You know what I'm talking about." Daniel fired back.

Teague quickly sat up in the chair. "I didn't have

anything to do with it. Sure, some of my friends did, but I wasn't there."

"Mmm, hmm. I figured it was something like that, all that anti-government crap you used to spout off."

"You guys want a burger and some onion rings?" Christy called out.

"Hell yeah!" Teague called out.

"Sounds good, babe."

Teague leaned towards Daniel and tried to whisper. "Dude, she is hawt!"

"I heard that." Christy shouted, her back to them at the stove.

Daniel smiled. "The problem is she knows it too."

"Hey, I heard that too! Watch it, mister!" Daniel looked over to see her pointing a spatula at him.

Daniel smiled and Teague let out a loud laugh.

"You know I love ya, babe," Daniel said.

Christy's back was to him, watching the burgers on the stove. "Whatever!"

"So, you really didn't have anything to do with it?" Daniel asked.

"No, I told you. I'm just on vacation."

"Cool. Let's find something to watch. How are those burgers, babe?" Daniel shouted.

"Burned, if you keep it up."

CHAPTER 4

Carlos sat at his desk with his head in his hands. All the riots lately have taken a lot out of everyone. Now things were going to a whole new level. Southerland and Andrews were in the hospital with gunshot wounds. Things were definitely getting serious. The fact that all weapons were now outlawed made no difference. Most people had not turned them in, and certainly not the typical gang banger. Hell, even he didn't put all of his weapons on the forms he had to fill out as a law enforcement officer. They said he could keep his, but Carlos didn't trust the government any more than the people currently burning down the city. The only difference between him and the rioters was that he wasn't ready to start lighting fires, yet.

Another officer walked by him and paused. "Hey, Carlos. They're gonna be alright. Word from the ER is neither of them had serious wounds."

Carlos looked up. "Thanks, man. That's good, real good."

The other officer quickly moved off and Carlos looked at his desk. It was mounded with paperwork that needed to be completed, but he just didn't have the energy or give a shit about doing it. Under the new laws, the use of the rifle in the riot changed the entire dynamic of how the city would deal with them from now on. The first thing the APD did was to call the FBI and tell them about the shooting of two of their officers. Now, in addition to the state investigation into the shooting, there would be a federal one as well. But that was above his pay grade, and other people had to worry about that. He knew though that at some point he would probably be interviewed by the FBI and the GBI, the Georgia Bureau of Investigation.

His phone rang and Carlos picked it up without even thinking. "Carlos".

"Carlos, this is Richard Folsom with the FBI. I'm on my way down. Can you hang out till I get there?"

Carlos rocked back in his chair and looked at the ceiling, shaking his head. "Yeah, sure. How long till you get here?"

"My team will be there in about fifteen minutes."

Rubbing a hand through his hair, he replied. "I'll be right here. Got nothing better to do right now."

"Thanks", came the terse reply before the line went dead.

Carlos hung up the phone then stomped on the floor. "Well, shit!"

"What's wrong?" A female voice asked from behind him.

Carlos spun around to see detective Nora Fitz from the vice squad. "Some dick from the FBI is on his way down here, to interview me I assume."

"Dick? That's a little harsh, isn't it?" She asked with a smile.

"No, he's a real Dick, some guy named Richard Folsom."

"Dick," Nora said, shaking her head. "That's damn funny," She added as she walked away.

***

Daniel, Christy and Teague sat and ate the hamburgers and the onion rings. Teague was stuffing a couple in his mouth, his head slightly back, looking at her. Not only was she hot, but the girl could cook. The TV was on CNN, and footage of riots from all over the country flashed across the screen. The ticker at the bottom slowly crawled across the screen with other news facts. The NYSE had been shut down at 1:00 PM when the circuit breakers kicked in due to excessive losses. In California, police were looking for whoever attacked a Girl Scout campout, killing three young girls.

"What's going on at work? It must be crazy down there." Christy asked between bites of her burger.

The question caught Daniel off guard and he almost choked on a mouthful of burger. Recovering, he looked up. "Ah, yeah. You might say that."

Christy and Teague both sat there looking at him, waiting for more. When he didn't continue, Teague said, "And?"

"And, what?" Daniel replied.

"What happened?" Christy asked.

"Nothing, nothing really. Just the same stuff you see there," Daniel said pointing at the TV.

Teague looked at the big screen. "More than I'd want to deal with. That's part of the reason I left Michigan."

"Me too. I haven't been anywhere near the business district. But I was told today I may have to go to the ER to help out," Christy said. She was a pediatric nurse that worked in the neonatal unit.

Daniel looked over at Teague. "Yeah. Some bad shit up there, huh."

Teague stared at the screen. "Yeah."

"How long is Teague staying here?" Christy asked.

"I don't know. How long are you staying here?" Daniel asked.

Teague just shrugged his shoulders. "I guess till you kick me out."

"So, you're leaving tomorrow then?"

"Daniel, that's not very nice." Christy fired back.

Teague just laughed and Daniel followed suit. "He can stick around. I don't care." Looking at Christy, he asked, "Why are they sending you to the ER?"

She shrugged. "I guess things are getting really bad in there. I walked through, and it was just lined with people. I don't want to go down there."

"I don't think you should. If they say you have to go there, you shouldn't go back to work." Daniel replied.

"I wouldn't go." Teague added.

Christy was shocked. "How could I do that? If the ER is so swamped they're pulling nurses from other departments, then they really need help. I'd have to go. I couldn't not go."

"You could also get stuck at the hospital. You know the bank has a dorm in the basement? There are even private rooms for the more important people," Daniel said.

Teague took a drink of beer. "Figures. Rich ass fat cats with their own little bunker in the bank."

"What's it for?" Christy asked.

Daniel shrugged. "I don't know. I just found out about it."

After finishing their burgers, Daniel said he was tired

and wanted to go to bed. Christy said she'd go with him and Teague said he was going to stay up and watch TV for a while. Daniel went to a closet and got out extra blankets for Teague and threw them at him before heading to bed.

Teague was sleeping with his face wedged into the joint between the arm and the back of the sofa, sound asleep. He opened his eyes. Was it a noise? Lying there seeing only the fabric of the couch, he listened. Knock, knock, knock, resonated from the door, very loudly and with force. Teague bolted upright, his blanket covering half of his head. The knock came again. He jumped up, looking around, not sure what to do.

Looking back at the door, he called out. "Who is it?"

After a brief pause came the reply. "Agent Richard Folsom with the FBI."

Teague's mouth fell open and it took a conscious effort on his part not to piss on himself. For a moment, he didn't know what to do. Quickly crossing the room, he pulled his pistol from his bag and checked the action. Moving back to the door, he looked through the peep, there were two men outside. That struck him as odd. If the FBI knew he was there, they would send the same SRT team to kick in the door as they did in other takedowns.

"What do you need?" Teague called out.

"Is Daniel here?"

Teague jerked his head back, looking at the door. Daniel? They wanted Daniel. "Uh, yeah. Let me get him."

Teague headed for Daniel's room. Stopping by the bathroom, he shoved his pistol into the center of a stack of towels on a shelf over the toilet, then went to Daniel's door and opened it. Daniel and Christy were lying there, and Christy was sleeping commando.

"Dude, the FBI's here."

Daniel was asleep when the door opened. All he heard was *FBI* and *here*. Sitting up in the bed rubbing his eyes, he asked, "What, who?"

Teague was half leaning into the dark room holding onto the doorknob. "The FBI is at the door asking for you."

"What, the FBI? For what?" Daniel asked as he got out of bed.

"How the hell would I know."

"What's going on?" Christy asked as she sat up, covering herself with a sheet.

"The FBI's here, babe," Daniel said.

"The FBI, for what? What's going on?"

"I don't know."

The knock sounded from the door again. Teague looked over his shoulder. "Dude, you better go find out what they want."

"Yeah, I'm going, I'm going," Daniel said as he pulled on a pair of shorts.

"I'm gonna grab a shower," Teague said as he headed for the bathroom.

Daniel walked past him and headed for the living room as Teague went into the bathroom. Closing the door, Teague leaned against the door trying not to lose it. Looking at the stack of towels, he reached in and pulled the pistol out. Its mere presence reassured him. Looking around the bathroom, he knew he had to find a better place to hide it, but still have it handy. The obvious places would be searched; and he was about to just stick it under the sink when his eyes fell on the toilet.

Gently taking the cover off the tank, he laid his Rock River 1911 into the bottom and replaced the cover. It would probably be searched as well, but at least it was out of sight. He quickly turned on the water, making it exceptionally hot, and got into the shower. He was so nervous, all he could do was stand there and stare at the curtain in the direction of the door.

Daniel turned on a lamp by the sofa as he headed for the door, then looked through the peep. Two men in blue windbreakers with FBI in yellow letters were standing there, obviously annoyed. They looked up simultaneously as he opened the door.

"Sorry, I was asleep," Daniel said.

"I'm Richard Folsom. This is Chris Collins. May we come in?"

Daniel rubbed the back of his neck. "What's this about?"

"What happened at the bank yesterday."

"Oh, that. Yeah, come on in."

The two men followed him in. Daniel flopped onto the sofa, threw his feet out on the coffee table and crossed his arms over his chest. Agent Folsom took a seat in the chair, and the other one just stood there looking around.

"Who else is here?" Agent Collins asked.

Daniel looked back over the sofa. "My girlfriend and my cousin."

Agent Collins looked back towards the bedroom. "Where are they?"

"She's back there in the bedroom, and I think he's in the shower. So, what can I help you guys with?"

Agent Folsom set out a notepad on the table and flipped through some pages for a moment, looking at the notes intently. Looking up, he asked Daniel to tell him what happened.

"I guess you're asking about the shooting?"

"That'd be a good place to start," Folsom said with a nod.

Before Daniel could start, Christy came out and sat down on the sofa, moving away the blankets Teague had left scattered around. Daniel looked at her, then back to the agents.

"This is my girlfriend, Christy."

The two agents nodded, and she smiled and looked at Daniel. "What's going on?"

"Daniel's about to tell us," Collins said. Everyone in the room looked at Daniel.

He went on to describe the events on the roof of the garage, the Molotov cocktails, the man with the rifle, the shooting of the two officers and finally of the LT with the APD asking for their help. When he finished, he was leaning forward on his elbows looking at the table. Agent Folsom took notes as he spoke and flipped through the notebook as he relayed the story.

"You shot someone?" Christy asked with a little shock.

Without looking up from the notebook, Folsom asked, "Who fired first?"

The question caught Daniel off guard. "Uh, the guy with the AK."

Looking up, Folsom asked, "No, you or Bob?"

Daniel fell back into the sofa, letting out a huff. "Um, I think I did. Bob was on the phone with the cop."

Folsom nodded his head, flipped through the notebook,

made a note on another page then closed the book. "Well, your story lines up with Bob's."

"Am I in trouble or something?" Daniel asked.

"I don't see any problems right now. You guys were backing up the police at their request, so you're good for now."

"He's taking an awful long shower, isn't he?" Agent Collins said, stepping towards the hallway to the bathroom.

Daniel and Christy both looked back towards him. "I guess," Daniel said.

"Why don't you check on him," Collins said.

Daniel shrugged and stood up and headed for the bathroom. He rapped on the door. "Hey man, you still alive in there?"

The door jerked open. Daniel jumped back a bit, bumping into Collins who was standing very close behind him. Teague stood there with a towel wrapped around his waist, drying his hair with another.

"What's up?" Teague asked.

"Ah, nuthin'. Just wanted to make sure you didn't drown," Daniel said as he headed back to the sofa.

Teague followed him into the living room with agent Collins right behind him. Teague went to his bag in the corner and bent over, opening it up. When he bent over his towel fell to the floor. Christy let out a little giggle. Teague looked back at the agents who were not the least bit amused to be staring at his bare ass and ball sack. Teague picked the towel up and wrapped it back around himself, collected his clothes from the bag and straightened up. He held the clothes up and smiled, then headed for the bathroom to get dressed.

"I'll be in touch if we need anything else," Folsom said as he headed for the door with Collins in tow.

Daniel followed them to the door, thanked them for coming and said he would cooperate in any way he could. After shutting the door, he could hear Collins say "That kid's a smartass."

Teague was in the bathroom with his back against the door, leaning on the vanity for support. He was laughing so hard tears were running down his face. The only thing keeping the sound in was his hand clasped over his mouth.

***

With the building empty, Gene took up his preferred post while at work, in his small office in the bowels of the building. He felt at home in the engineering spaces of the giant place. Sure, it wasn't like being onboard ship, but it was as close as he could get. Asleep with his feet up on the desk when the phone rang, he nearly fell out of the chair. What was left of his tuna sandwich resting on his chest, fell on the floor. After flailing about for moment to regain his balance, he answered the phone.

"Engineering."

"You awake, Gene?"

"Am now, Bob. Thanks. What's up?"

"I knew you'd still be here. You plan on going home any time soon? Things are quiet outside right now if you want to bail out."

"Nah, I'll just stay here. No reason to go home."

"Well, come on up to my office. We'll have a drink."

"Sounds good to me. On my way."

"Say, Gene. You still hiding that illegal .45 in your desk?"

Gene replied with a chuckle. "He, he. Of course I am."

"Bring it with you then."

Gene found Bob at his desk, one foot propped on it. In hand was the omnipresent cigarette. In the other, he cradled a glass of scotch. Only this time it was in a clear tumbler. Gene fell into a chair across from him. Bob leaned forward and slid the bottle and another glass across the desk. Gene quickly poured himself a little more than two fingers of whiskey.

Taking a sip of his whiskey, Gene asked, "Why you still here. Why not go home?"

"Same reason you're still here. Nothing to go home to. Already have two ex-wives. Just an empty house, my friend."

Gene laughed to himself. "Amen to ex-wives. Mine divorced me as soon as I retired. So long as I was in the Navy and stayed gone a year at a time, we were happily married."

"Hung around to get half of that Navy retirement, huh?"

"Yeah, damn bitch." Gene replied laughing. "So what the hell's going on around here?"

Bob laughed, filled his glass and gave Gene a rundown on what had happened, telling him about the riot and the shooting. When Bob wrapped it up, he dropped his butt into an empty cup on the desk and refilled his glass.

"Damn, you killed him?" Gene asked as he leaned out for the bottle.

"I guess. He wasn't moving and was on fire last time I saw him."

"Where's Daniel? Getting' drunk someplace?"

With a chuckle, Bob replied. "Yeah, probably. I am."

The phone on his desk rang. Bob looked over at it, then drained his glass.

***

Daniel hung up the phone and looked at Teague and Christy. "I have to go back to the office."

"What, why?" Christy asked.

"That was the FBI agent. He said I needed to go back there and go over what happened again."

"Dude, you want to go out in that?" Teague said pointing at the TV.

They were watching the news and things all over the metro area were getting out of hand again. News of the shooting had found its way to the media who were now reporting on it, though they had it wrong. The story the news media was putting out was that the police had shot two rioters in Buckhead. There was no mention of the two officers that were wounded. This news pissed off the already unsettled masses in the streets.

Atlanta wasn't the only city having trouble. Cities across the nation were in the same shape, having exactly the same troubles. Several reports of exchanges of gunfire between the police and rioters were all over the news. The incidents of shootings of both police and rioters were increasing. Both sides were escalating the use of violence. The fact that the banks were still closed, EBT and debit cards were not working and no one had access to cash unless they had it on hand was combining with the rise in violence to create the perfect storm.

The federal government's response was heavy handed. As a result of the Lansing Incident, the President invoked the Insurrection Act of 1807. The act was amended in the 2007 Defense Authorization Act and provided to the President more power than the original Act. Section 1076 subsection 333 was changed to read; *When the President determines that the authorities of the state are incapable of maintaining public order.* This was the end run on the Posse Comitatus Act that allowed federal troops to be used domestically. This section, along with section 334, which provides; *The President has authority to order the dispersal of either insurgents or "those obstructing the enforcement of the laws".* These were the tools used to justify the violent reaction.

Protestors were listed under section 334. When the various governors failed to gain control of the spreading riots, the feds stepped in. Section 333 was used against those refusing to hand over their firearms. It was as if the demise of the country was being orchestrated and everyone was playing their part in tune. While the White House focused on the issue of guns, one they've salivated over for years, the economy was circling the drain. Commerce in the nation was essentially halted. Cash was king and no one had any. That is until the markets started to tank. A week's worth of double digit percentage point losses signaled the end of the dollar. Trading was permanently halted a week later.

"I don't want to stay here. Can I come with you?" Christy asked.

Daniel looked away from the TV. "You guys wanna come with me? It's certainly safer than it is here."

"I do. Teague, you coming?" Christy asked.

"Sure, why not. Let's go see what the belly of the beast looks like."

Unlike his last trip to the bank, this time Daniel wasn't stopped by the police. There weren't any.

"Where are all the cops?" Teague asked.

Daniel's head was on a swivel. He was watching the people running through the streets. Every business they passed was being looted. It gave him an eerie feeling seeing the people of the city tear it apart with absolutely no concern about being caught.

"This is really messed up," Daniel said.

"It's scary. Hurry up," Christy said.

Teague was looking out the back window. "These people are like animals. Look at them."

Daniel called Bob and told him he was on his way in and that he was told by the FBI agent to come back.

"Yeah, I talked to the Dick too. I'll be waiting on you. When you come in, pull into the underground section. I'll open the gates for you as you pull up."

"Thanks, Bob. By the way, I've got my girlfriend and cousin with me. They didn't want to stay at my place."

"The more, the merrier."

Daniel was sitting at the entrance to the garage as the gate rolled up when Teague shouted. "Holy shit!"

Daniel looked out the window to see a squad of riot police running before a massive crowd of rioters. The officers were in full-on, every-man-for-himself retreat. The three of them sat there transfixed on the scene. They watched as one of the officers was dragged down by the crowd, like the slowest Zebra in the herd. He was set upon by the swirling mass of people. It wasn't long before one person held his helmet aloft, then other pieces of the riot gear began to appear, hoisted like trophies.

"Get your ass in gear!" Bob's voice blared from an intercom mounted on a pedestal at the gate. Daniel's head snapped around to see the gate was open. He floored the van and was in the garage in a flash. The gate immediately began to close. The rioters were more than a block away, but Bob wasn't taking any chances.

Daniel shut the van off, though he couldn't tell as the engineering space he was parked in was so loud, it didn't miss the sound of the diesel engine. He was looking back at Christy in the mirror when there was a knock on his window. The sudden knock caused him to jump in his seat. Looking out, he saw Gene standing there, the broad smile on his face hidden with those whiskers.

Daniel stepped out as Teague got out of the passenger side and opened the rear door for Christy.

"Scare easy?" Gene asked.

"Not usually. Thanks for the effort though."

"Bob was afraid you'd get lost. Sent me down here to make sure you didn't get eaten by the hogs."

"There are hogs in the building?" Christy shouted over the din around her.

Teague started to laugh. "No. It's just an old saying, went to shit and the hogs eat 'im."

The explanation didn't clear the issue for her. "So there are no hogs?" she asked, looking around.

Gene let out a laugh and led the trio through a door and to a freight elevator. On the tenth floor, they changed to one of the public elevators to get to Bob's office. They found Bob where Daniel had left him, sitting at his desk, cigarette in hand. Daniel looked around the office, looking for the agent.

"The Dick's not here yet," Bob said.

"What do they want? What are we supposed to do?" Daniel asked.

Christy and Teague stepped into the office, interrupting Bob's answer. He looked Christy up and down with raised eyebrows. He quickly stood up and offered her his hand. "Hi, I'm Bob."

Christy smiled and introduced herself, then looked around the dark, cluttered office. She was just about to sit down when the lights went out for a brief instant before coming back on. Bob looked up at Gene, who nodded and left the office.

"What was that?" Daniel asked.

"Andy, what's up?" Bob called through the open door.

Andy shouted his reply. "Power's out, We're on generator power now."

Bob excused himself to Christy and stepped out. "See anything out there?"

Soon, everyone was in the outer office looking at the monitors. In full HD, they were watching the chaos on the streets outside the bank. In the short time since they had arrived, the mob on the street had moved up the block, past the bank and were constructing barricades in the streets. More fires were now burning, piles of tires that threw up huge clouds of thick black smoke. Across the street from the bank, buildings were being looted. Andy was panning the cameras around and the view on all sides of the bank was the same. They were completely surrounded.

"Hmm, this doesn't look good," Bob said. Then he turned to face everyone. "We may be here awhile."

"What do you mean by that?" Christy asked.

Bob pointed to the monitor. "You want to go out there?"

"Don't worry. We'll be fine here. They'll get the

power back on soon and the police will push them back," Daniel said.

"How long will the generator run the building?" Teague asked.

"I don't know. When Gene gets back he can answer that." Bob replied.

The phone in Bob's office rang. He stepped into the office and answered it, and after a few moments, he returned.

"Was that Gene?" Daniel asked.

"No. That was one of the security guys. He said the folks outside are raising hell on the security shutters."

"They can't get in here can they?" Daniel asked.

"Well, I mean, it's possible, but not likely."

Bob picked up the phone again and called Gene, asking him to come up to his office. While not happy about the request, Gene said he was on his way. While waiting for Gene, they watched the cameras. The crowd outside was getting bigger and more riled up by the minute. The protesters on the street woefully outnumbered the police forces. They simply could not field enough officers in any one part of the city to make a meaningful difference.

"What's that?" Christy asked, pointing at one of the monitors.

Everyone turned to look at the monitor she was pointing at to see a Humvee sitting far down the block. On top of the truck was a large square object. Bob told Andy to zoom in on it so they could get a better look. As the truck grew in size on the screen, the object mounted to the top became clearer.

"It's an LRAD," Bob said.

Christy looked over at him. "What the hell is an LRAD?"

"It's a sound cannon used for crowd control" Bob said.

"What the hell is a sound cannon going to do?" Christy asked.

"Oh, it works. They used one earlier to great effect," Bob said with a grin.

Gene came to the door looking none too pleased to be back in Bob's office. He announced his arrival with a loud sigh, making it obvious he did not want to be there. Bob looked up at him with amusement.

"Sorry to call you back so quick," Bob said.

Gene didn't even crack a smile. He was not amused. "What do you need, Bob?"

"How long will generators run the building?" Bob asked.

Gene rubbed his whiskers for a moment, thinking. "I think it will run the building for about 36 hours under full load." Bob rocked back in his chair, putting his hands behind his head. Now he was thinking.

"What can we do to extend that time, just in case it's needed?" Bob said.

Gene shrugged his shoulders, holding his palms out as if the answer were obvious. "Reduce the damn load."

"Well, there's nobody in the building right now but us. What's the biggest load we have?" Bob asked.

Gene thought about that for a minute. "I would have to say lighting and AC are the biggest loads."

Bob let out a sigh. "Damn, turning off all the lights would take forever to do in this building."

Gene laughed. "You want the lights turned off? Is that all?"

Bob swiveled his head around to look at Gene. "Yeah, that's all."

"Andy, move your ass," Gene said.

Andy swiveled around the chair and stepped out of the way. Gene flopped his ass in the chair and pulled the keyboard out from under the desk. Using a side monitor, he opened up a program. Once the program loaded, he swiveled around to look at Bob. "You want them all off?"

"We should probably keep some minimal lighting on in the building, but I would like to have everything visible from the exterior turned off."

"Okay, all exterior lights and all exterior office lights. That do it for you?"

"How will the cameras really see what's happening outside once it gets dark?" Daniel asked.

Without looking from the monitors, Bob replied. "We have both thermal and IR cameras." Bob looked over at Daniel and grinned. "We can see in the dark."

"Go ahead and turn the lights out, Gene."

Once all the lights were shut off, Gene suggested they shut down two of the generators. With no more load than they had running, one generator should carry it, though he would have to check the load to ensure they could also run the cooling towers and chiller plant. Bob agreed and asked him to go take a look and see what they could do to conserve fuel for the generators. There was no telling how long the power would be off.

"Worst case, we could shut down the chiller too. Might get a little warm in here, but it would save on fuel," Gene said.

Bob nodded. "Shed as much of the AC as you can. See if we can buy ourselves some time."

Gene nodded and spun back around in the chair and

began pecking away at the keyboard. Graphics of the building appeared, showing various systems as he shut them down.

"Where's that FBI guy?" Christy asked.

"From the looks of things outside, I don't think he's coming," Teague said.

All this time, Teague had been standing in the corner staying quiet and keeping to himself. He was a little nervous at the thought of being in such close proximity to an FBI agent. Daniel and his hot-ass girlfriend had no idea what he'd been up to, and he wanted to keep it that way. Getting his family involved in his troubles was the last thing he wanted to do. But the war on the streets below them would surely keep the feds away.

"Yeah, don't think Dick's coming," Bob said.

Christy leaned over to Daniel and whispered into his ear, "Who's Dick?"

Daniel turned his head slightly and whispered back, "The FBI agent. Bob calls him Dick."

"Hey, Bob. The largest load running in the building right now would have to be the servers and their cooling equipment. You think we should shut them down too since the bank is off-line?" Daniel asked.

Before Bob could answer, the phone rang. Bob palmed the phone. "Yello".

"Bob, you need to pull up the camera facing the east exit of the parking garage, now," The voice on the other end said.

Bob told Andy which camera to pull up. "Why? What's going on?"

"You'll see in a sec."

When the video popped up, they could see the large security gate on the screen. Bob leaned in toward the screen and said out loud, more to himself than anyone else. "What the hell is that?"

The voice on the other end of the phone answered the question. "They're using a saw to cut through the gate. It's some kind of chop saw."

"Holy shit."

"Are they cutting their way in?" Daniel asked.

"Sure as shit looks like it," Teague said.

Bob directed his attention back to the phone. "We cannot let them get through the gate."

"Well what the hell do you want me to do about it?"

"I don't know. But we have to stop them somehow."

"Shoot the fuckers," Teague said.

Everyone in the room turned and looked at Teague. He simply shrugged his shoulders and stared back at them. "What else are you going to do? If they get into the garage, they can get into the building."

Bob looked back to the monitor. "Go down and bang on the door. See if it scares them away. We're watching you on the camera."

"All right. I'll give it a shot. But if I get shot at, I'm shooting back."

They all watched the figure on the screen move towards the security gate as a steady stream of sparks spilled from it. There was no audio, just the sight of the figure moving towards the gate. He held a 12-gauge shotgun up at low ready. When he got to the gate, he banged on it with a balled fist and the sparks stopped. They watched as the man kicked the gate and it appeared he was shouting at it. Suddenly, the security guard jumped ducking his head and pressed himself against the wall beside the security gate. From his actions, they could only guess what was happening. He was being shot at.

Bob still had the phone. He could hear the man yelling. He could hear what sounded like small pops. Then he heard and saw on the monitor the phone falling to the floor. The security man took half a step away from the wall and began to fire his shotgun into the security gate. In what seemed to be too short of a time span, he was reloading the tube on the weapon.

"Andy. Give me an outside view of the door, now."

When the camera view popped up, the screen showed a body sprawled on the ground with something lying by its right hand. Bob told Andy to zoom in on it, and the object rapidly grew in size. A Glock handgun soon filled the screen. Andy backed the camera view out to take in the crowd. They could see the guy with the chop saw. He was yelling and gesturing wildly. People were running in all directions. Several of them were being helped, as it appeared they were wounded.

Inside the garage, the camera there showed the security man pick his phone up. Then Bob heard him scream into the phone. "They're fucking shooting at me!"

"Smitty. Get yer ass out of there. We'll secure all the gates behind you." Bob replied.

"Oh, my god. Is that guy dead?" Christy asked no one in particular.

"Sure looks that way." Gene replied.

Bob was still watching the cameras. The crowd outside

was getting their act together, rolling a dumpster down the road to use as cover to renew their assault on the gate.

"Gene. You got anything we could reinforce that gate with? They're going to get through the gate with that saw." Bob stated.

Gene thought for a moment, sucking on his whiskers as he did. "I've got a couple of package chillers in the basement that came in last week. With all this crazy crap going on, we haven't been able to install them yet. They're almost as wide as the gate, though they are only about five feet tall."

"It will slow em down. Let's do it. How many do you have?"

"Three."

"Take two of them and stack them against that gate and put one in front of the other. When they get through this one and see the crates, they may try the other. And when they see another crate there, maybe they'll give up."

"Why are they trying to get in here anyway? We haven't done anything to them." Christy stated.

"They're pissed at the world right now. No one can get to any money. Those food stamp cards don't work, and this is a bank, the epitome of evil from their point of view," Teague said.

"That, and Bob and Daniel did shoot one or two of 'em earlier." Gene added.

"We need to try and push 'em back from the building somehow," Bob said.

"Aren't the police coming?" Christy asked.

"I doubt it from the looks of things out there right now," Bob said.

"Hey, Bob. When we were on the roof, I saw a pipe for

a fire hose. If we had a hose, we could turn it on 'em, hose 'em down, and maybe they would pull back," Daniel said.

"That's a good idea." Bob replied. "Gene, you got some hoses?"

"Yeah. We got 'em. How many you need?"

"Alright. Here's what we're gonna do. Gene, you and cousin here go move the crates into place. Daniel and I will get the hoses up on the top of the garage and put some serious water on the unwashed masses down there. Andy, you stay here and keep me up to date," Bob said.

"What about me?" Christy asked.

Bob looked at Daniel. "You stay here and give Andy a hand for now."

"Fuck that. This isn't some stupid movie where the girl is useless and is the first to get killed. I'm going to help one way or another." The use of profanity surprised Daniel. He'd never heard it come out of her before.

Bob raised his eyebrows at her, looked at Daniel and said, "Feisty little thing."

"More than you can handle," Christy replied as she folded her arms across her chest.

"Bob, let me and Christy go up on the garage. You need to find your security guys and get them set up. Plus, you can keep an eye on things here and let us know what's going on." Daniel said.

"Alright, let's get going," Bob said. He handed Gene and Daniel each a handheld radio.

"Come on, Daniel. I'll show you where the hoses are," Gene said as he headed for the door.

Gene, Teague, Daniel and Christy took the elevator down to the bowels of the building where Gene was more comfortable. He showed Daniel where the hoses were stacked, then went to get his forklift.

"Be careful up there on the roof," Teague said.

"Sorry for all the trouble, man. Guess you picked a shitty time to visit."

"Hey, no worries. It's a shitty time in general right now."

Christy pushed a Rubbermaid cart over and Teague and Daniel loaded up four lengths of fire hose on it, then Daniel and Christy headed for the elevator. Somewhere back in the mechanical space, Gene tooted the horn on the forklift. Teague looked over his shoulder and turned to go find the fat man.

Daniel looked over his shoulder as he pushed the cart. "Sounds like your date's waiting."

Teague gave him the finger.

Once inside the elevator, Christy leaned against the wall. She was biting her fingernails, a nervous habit.

"Quit, you'll ruin your manicure," Daniel said.

She paused to spit out a piece of nail or something. "Right now, that's the least of my worries." She looked at the stack of hoses on the cart and gestured with her chin. "Is this gonna work?"

Daniel looked at the cart and shrugged. "Dunno. But we need to do something."

The elevator opened and Christy screamed. Daniel was leaning over the cart about to push it, and he jerked his head up to see Bob standing there with a cigarette clenched in his teeth and a Cheshire-Cat grin on his face.

"Damn it, Bob. You scared the shit outta me!" Christy shouted.

"Sorry, Christy. Didn't mean to. I wanted to give

Daniel this." Bob picked up a rifle that was leaning beside the elevator door and laid it on the cart.

Christy looked at it, then at Daniel. "Are we really going to need that?"

"I hope not," Daniel answered.

"Better safe than sorry," Bob said with a nod. "Get up to the roof and see if you can push those idiots back."

Daniel nodded, "We'll try."

***

Bobby Milsaps and Amy Snapp had been partners on the Atlanta PD for nearly two years. In the beginning, some of his male colleagues gave him a lot of crap about having a *chick* for a partner. But she'd proved herself to be just as good, and in many cases, a hell of a lot better than many of the men he worked with. They'd become good friends, spending off times with each other's families a couple times a month.

Looking at Amy, Bobby said, "This is getting to be some real bullshit."

Amy adjusted the riot helmet on her head that was just a little too large. "I know. They keep pulling us back. Why don't they just let us go in there and end this once and for all?"

A call came out. *On line!*

"Shit. Here we go again," Amy said.

"Don't worry. I got your back," Bobby said.

Amy looked at him as she dropped her face shield. "And I got yours."

They marched up the road, yet again, towards the line of protestors. It was the same, one step, bang your shield, take another step. It was meant to intimidate the protestors, but it really didn't have much effect on them. As they closed on the crowd, the second echelon of officers began firing teargas at the crowd. It had little effect on those protestors that were prepared for it.

"I'm getting sick of this shit!" Bobby shouted.

The line of officers continued up the street. As they came in range of the protestors, rocks, bottles, bricks and Molotov cocktails began to rain down on them. An officer in front of Amy was splashed with fire. Bobby grabbed her and pulled her to the rear of the formation. Officers there were waiting with CO_2 extinguishers, and they quickly doused the flames.

Bobby was checking her over. "Are you alright? You okay?"

She pulled the helmet off her head and dropped it on the street. "I'm ok, but this is just insane."

Bobby looked at the line of officers still advancing. "It is. We're never going to win."

Amy brushed hair from her face. "I don't live in this Godforsaken city."

Bobby looked at her. "Neither do I." He stood up and held his hand out. She took it and he pulled her to her feet.

"Let them keep it," Amy said.

Bobby nodded. "You going to be alright?"

She nodded. "You?"

"I'll be a hell of a lot better at home with Sandy."

Amy leaned in and hugged him. "Let's get the hell out of here."

They would be the first of many, many officers across the country to abandon their posts to take care of their families.

CHAPTER 5

Daniel and Christy dragged the hoses across the top deck of the parking garage to the standpipe on the corner. Christy grunted under the weight of the canvas hose. "These things are heavy!"

"Come on. Let's just get it over there." Daniel groaned in reply.

Once there, Daniel started to screw the hose onto the pipe. Christy grabbed the nozzle and started to stretch the hose out. As soon as she had it laid out across the deck, she shouted to Daniel to turn it on. Looking over his shoulder he nodded and spun the large knob, sending water ripping into the hose.

Christy wasn't expecting the force of the water charging the line and it quickly got away from her. The nozzle was open and air was escaping with a loud hiss as the water surged in. When it hit the nozzle the hose began to whip around. She jumped on the hose but was about ten feet from the nozzle. As the nozzle whipped around spraying water, she screamed at Daniel. "Turn it off! Turn it off!"

Daniel looked back to see a scene out of a Road Runner cartoon as Christy tried to control the hose. Laughing to himself, he turned the water off. Christy got to her feet, brushed the wet hair from her face and walked back towards Daniel.

"You get on that end. *I* will turn the water on."

Daniel smiled. "You looked good out there, hanging onto that thing." He grabbed the bottom of her t-shirt and tugged on it. "Look at you, all wet. You look fine."

Christy grabbed his wrist and tossed it away from her. "I am not in the mood." She pointed towards the nozzle. "Get your ass over there."

Daniel laughed as he headed for the red nozzle lying on the deck. Picking it up, he dragged it over to the edge of the garage and looked down at the crowd below. They were at it again with the saw, trying to cut through the gate. Daniel jerked the nozzle, pulling a little slack and hung it over the wall. Looking back over his shoulder, he nodded at Christy. She nodded back and opened the nozzle, sending another surge of water to the nozzle. This time though, it went down onto the crowd.

Christy ran over and grabbed onto the hose behind Daniel, taking some of the strain off him and allowing him to adjust the stream. In a moment, there was a solid stream of water cutting into the crowd below. Daniel laughed like a maniac, seeing the effect it had on the people in the crowd. They ran from the water as if it were acid.

Laughing. Daniel screamed. "Look at 'em run!"

Christy looked over the edge, and a smile spread over her face as she watched the stream of water chase people around on the street.

***

Gene set the second packaged chiller unit on top of the first one. The two covered the door and would make it very hard to get past if they managed to breach the door. He was backing the forklift away when a thought came to him and he started to laugh.

He looked at Teague. "Wait here a second. I have an idea."

Going back into the mechanical space, he picked up a pallet and pulled it around to his shop. There, he pulled a small air compressor out and put it on the pallet. Then he tossed an extension cord on and, lastly he hefted a small drum with a gun attached onto the pallet. Then he dropped a long-handled scrub brush on and headed back to the parking garage.

Gene went to the door he had just blocked and set the pallet down. Plugging in the air compressor, he gave it a minute to build up some pressure before picking up the gun. With a smile on his face, he squeezed the handle and started squirting grease on the deck. After squirting a heavy pattern out, he grabbed the scrub brush and made sure the grease was spread out nice and thick. He laughed to himself as he unplugged the air compressor. If these people managed to get through, this may not stop them, but it sure as hell would be funny to watch on the cameras.

As Gene walked around the forklift, Teague was shaking his head. "You are one weird ass old dude."

Gene grunted as he wedged himself into the seat of the lift. "You should have seen me when I was in the Navy. Come on, let's go do the same thing to the other gate."

Teague looked down at the greased floor and rubbed the toe of his boot through it. There was no resistance. He laughed. "Anyone who steps on that is going to bust their ass."

Starting the forklift, Gene barked. "That's the idea!"

***

Bob was back in the control room watching the soaking Daniel was putting on the crowd in front of the garage gate. They weren't liking it and were running from the building. While the hose put out a pretty powerful stream, it wasn't strong enough to knock anyone over. The people simply didn't want to get wet. It was kind of odd really. After all, it's only water.

Andy was laughing as he watched. "Looks like they don't care for the bath."

Bob lit a cigarette. "From the looks of them, they could use a shower."

Andy was also keeping an eye on the news. A report flashed across the screen and he picked up the remote to unmute the TV. "Hey, Bob. Check this out."

A female reporter came on the screen and began talking.

We have breaking news that is very concerning. A Georgia National Guard infantry armory in Lawrenceville has been looted. This means military grade weapons are now on the streets.

A male anchor joined the conversation.

That's right, Denise. With the riots currently going on in the city, things can only get worse if these types of weapons make it into the city.

What's the National Guard saying, Bob?

They have secured the location now and reinforcements are on their way. But they say a considerable amount of their weapons were looted and are unaccounted for.

"That can't be good," Andy said.

Bob was shaking his head. "Nope."

Andy picked up the remote and switched to CNN to see what was happening on the national level. The ticker scrolling across the bottom of screen was reporting the same event in other parts of the country. The talking heads were discussing the consequences.

...cannot help the situation. Weapons of this kind making it onto the streets will only make things worse.

Do we have any idea right now who is responsible for looting these armories?

While it is still early in the investigation, initial reports point to right-wing pro-gun extremists being responsible.

"Bullshit!" Andy shouted at the TV. He pointed to one of the monitors showing the crowds on the street outside the bank. "Those aren't right-wingers! Look at those animals!"

Bob chuckled and patted Andy on the shoulder. "Calm down, Andy. They're just playing their part, my friend. Just doing what they're told."

"News, my ass!"

They continued to watch the report that went on to reveal the looting of several armories across the country. All of the armories in major cities were experiencing heavy rioting. As they listened, Andy asked. "Don't you think it's kind of odd that all these armories were looted at nearly the same time?"

Bob let out a long breath. "Sadly, I don't. I think this was all planned and not by any right-wing extremists."

"That's what I was thinking."

Bob went to his office and poured a cup of coffee and walked back out into the control room. "Personally, I think we're watching the beginning of a revolution."

***

Christy was laughing hysterically. The people on the ground were running from the stream of water as Daniel chased them around the street. They'd managed to push them back from the building and the mass was now standing just out of range of the hose, shouting and shaking their fists. In the opposite direction on the street stood a line of riot police. They were banging their shields with their batons and shouting nearly as loud as the protestors. Daniel looked towards the police line, where one of the officers raised his shield in a salute. Daniel waved back.

"Look at those cops. They're pretty happy," Daniel said with a nod of his chin.

Christy wiped hair out of her eyes. "They may be." She pointed to the protestors on the other side of the street. "But those people sure aren't!"

Daniel looked across at the rioters. A heavy set woman stepped out of the crowd and gave Daniel the finger as she cussed at him. Daniel laughed and waved at her which only agitated her even more.

Daniel slapped Christy on the ass. "Come on, let's go back to Bob's office."

She laughed, grabbed him and kissed him. "This is so much fun!"

He grabbed her. "I had no idea you had this side."

She leaned in close. "Careful what you wish for."

Everyone met back at Bob's office. Just as Daniel and Christy came in, the lights flickered. Gene looked up and pronounced. "Power's back on."

"Good," Bob replied.

Teague was sitting in the other chair at the console and swiveled around. "I think we should start thinking about getting out of here."

"Why?" Christy asked.

"How long do you think we can hole up in here?" He pointed off in the direction of the street. "You think they're just going to go away?"

"We're safe in here." she replied.

"For now," Gene added.

Christy looked surprised. "You think they could get in here?"

Gene laughed. "They will, eventually. There's no doubt that they will ultimately get in. That is unless the cops get a handle on things."

"I think Cousin is right." Bob said.

Bob's statement surprised everyone. Daniel asked, "What?" Bob told everyone about the armory lootings.

"That's several miles northeast of here. I doubt that it's going to bother us," Daniel said.

"It's not the fact they were looted. It's the way the news reported it," Bob said. "They're already saying it was right-wing extremists that did it."

Christy fell into a chair. "So, what's that mean?"

"I doubt a bunch of right-wingers planned all these lootings to happen at the same time. It took a lot of coordination."

"Oh, they could do it," Teague said. Everyone turned to look at him. He shrugged it off. "I mean, look at the thing in Lansing. They can coordinate operations if they want."

Bob sipped his coffee as he studied Teague. "Where'd you say you came from?"

Teague tried to play the question off. "I've been traveling for a while. Just out seeing the country."

"He's from Michigan, Bob," Daniel said.

Bob chuckled. "Out seeing the country, my ass." Teague ignored the comment.

"I don't get it. What's the big deal with them saying it's right-wing people looting the armories?" Christy asked.

Coffee cup in hand, Bob pointed to one of the monitors. "Look at those people. Do they look like members of the GOP to you?"

Christy pursed her lips. "Sounds kind of racist, Bob."

Bob laughed out loud. "It's got nothing to do with racism." Pointing to one of the monitors, he asked Andy to zoom in. "Look at that sign. *Give us our money. EBT is a right. I want my fair share.* Does that sound like something you'd hear out of a Republican, a Conservative?"

Gene grunted. "Fucking Republicans aren't conservative anymore. They're pandering to the same crowd the damn Democrats are."

"I don't see why it matters what those people on the street think. They're all acting like animals," Christy said.

Just then, the TV with CNN on it changed. The multi-color screen of the emergency alert system came up and the all-too-familiar tone followed. In the center of the screen was a black box that read:

THIS IS NOT A TEST

A state of emergency is in effect. Remain where you are and await further instructions.

THIS IS NOT A TEST

At the same time, everyone's cell phone began to issue the same tone and scroll the same message. As each checked their phone, Bob said, "Well, this sucks."

Christy was looking at her phone. "What is going on?"

"I think the shit has just hit the fan," Gene said.

"I can't text," Andy said. "I'm trying to text my Mom and it says communications are restricted as a result of a national emergency."

Bob picked up the phone on the desk beside Andy and pressed nine for an outside line. He immediately heard the rapid busy signal. Not the usual one you hear when a line is in use, but the fast one that lets you know something is wrong with the line.

"Land line is down too," Bob said as he dropped it back into the cradle.

"What?" Christy asked.

Bob leaned back on the desk and shook out a smoke. He lit it and took a deep drag, letting it dangle from his lips as he spoke. "You know, the powers that be have been prepping this country for a long time for a civil war, revolution, whatever you want to call it. I think we've just witnessed the kickoff."

Andy swung around in his chair. "I need to get the fuck out of here. My Mom isn't well. I need to get home to take care of her."

The lights flickered again and dimmed. Gene announced. "We're on generator again."

Bob pointed at the monitors. "Let's take a look around the area, Andy."

It was getting late in the day. The clock on the wall to

the right of the monitors indicated it was nearly 8:45 PM, dusk outside. The streets were filled with throngs of people. But more striking than the number of people on the street was the absence of light. The streets were already getting dim. The only lights the cameras could find were from the fires started by protestors, and there were many. Columns of smoke could be seen rising around the city.

"Change to the roof top pole camera, Andy," Bob said.

The big screen on the wall flickered to a new view. This one was high above the city and had a three-hundred-sixty-degree view of Buckhead and greater metro Atlanta. As the camera panned around, Christy whispered. "Oh my God."

"Look at all those fires," Daniel said quietly.

Bob sipped his coffee. "And some of them are huge too."

From the high vantage point of a camera mounted to a pole on the roof of the bank, the real situation in Buckhead and greater Atlanta could be seen. Smoke rose from numerous places around Buckhead. There was also smoke rising from the areas outside Buckhead, showing the chaos was spreading in midtown and downtown Atlanta.

"I think we need to get the hell out of here," Christy said.

"And go where?" Bob asked.

Christy looked at him. "It's not safe here. With the power out, we can't last long here."

"It's not just here. The power is off everywhere, at least everything in the areas we can see from here," Andy said.

"This is a problem. I agree we need to move. But before we do, we need to have a plan in place. Somewhere to go. We can't just run into the street with the rest of these morons," Bob said.

Teague was sitting in a chair, leaning back with the

front legs off the floor. "You know, they're about to send troops into the area, don't you?" Everyone looked at him. Dropping the chair to the floor with a thud, he continued. "This is the first phase of the operation. They've taken away the ability of people to communicate. No comms, no organization. They killed the TV, so the news can't show it either. Shit's about to get real."

Bob looked into his cup and swirled the grounds in the bottom of it. "What makes you so sure?"

"They've been planning for this for years." Teague replied.

"You one of those conspiracy whack jobs?" Andy asked.

Teague shot him a look of disgust. "You one of those idiots that believes everything the media tells you?" With a sweep of his arm, Teague added. "Have you seen this shit? Are you aware they've outlawed the ownership of guns? I've seen firsthand how far they will go."

Bob set his cup down and crossed his arms. "Why'd you leave Michigan? Really?"

Daniel started to wag a finger at Teague. "Were you still messing with those militia groups up there?"

Teague grunted. "It's not called Militiagan for nothing."

Andy rose from his chair. "Holy shit! You're one of those guys from that shooting aren't you?"

Christy looked at him. "What? They caught all those guys!"

With a sneer, Teague replied. "That's what they told you. They didn't catch all of us."

"Why'd you do it?" Daniel asked.

Teague stood up. "The real question is why didn't you? How far are you going to let them push you? Some of us can only take so much shit. At some point, someone needs to stand up." Pounding his chest, he added. "On that day in Lansing, I *was someone!*"

"None of this shit matters right now. We have to deal with the situation at hand," Bob said.

As Bob was talking, Gene came through the door. He'd slipped out without notice when the TV went out. He was pushing a cart with a large black piece of equipment on it. "Make room," he said as he wheeled it into the security office.

"What's this?" Bob asked as Gene passed him.

Gene pushed the cart over into the far corner of the room and replied. "Remember when I ran the coax for that camera up there on the pole?" Bob nodded. Gene squatted down and started digging around behind the turret the monitors were mounted in. "Well, I ran another one with it." He pulled a cable out and stood up, connecting it to the box.

Gene stood and patted the box. "This is a Kenwood TS 990S. It's a HAM radio. I keep it in my office and play around with it."

Christy wrinkled her nose. "What's it for?"

Gene smiled as he turned the large console on. "This has no government off switch. With this, we can listen to what's going on around the country, the world even." Gene turned to the radio and continued to connect cables and other boxes together.

"I'm hungry," Daniel said.

"There's food in the café downstairs. We can get what we need from there. Make sandwiches," Bob said as he looked at Christy.

Her eyes narrowed. "I'm not here to make sandwiches and do the laundry."

Gene looked up. "I'm hungry too. I'll go make them."

Daniel leapt to his feet. "No, no. I'll go make them." Looking at Christy, he asked, "You wanna come help?" Gene shrugged and turned back to the radio, pulling a chair over to it and sitting down.

In a huff, Christy replied. "Fine."

Daniel ushered her out the door. Once in the hall, Daniel said, "I just didn't want him handling my food. I've seen him do some nasty stuff."

"Like what?"

The elevator door opened and they stepped in. "Don't worry about it. Let's go see what we can find down there. I'm starving."

Down in the café, they wasted no time in going through the small shop and seeing what there was to be had. As it turned out, the little café had been recently stocked. There was still a considerable number of boxes with the Sysco label on them sitting in the corner of the small kitchen waiting to be put away.

"Hey, look at this," Christy said.

Daniel looked over to see her holding the metal door of a small walk-in cooler open. He poked his head through the door. "Wow. There's a lot in here." Stepping in, he started handing packages out to her. "Let's put together a nice meal."

Once everything was prepared, they cleaned the utensils they used for prep and hung them back in their place. After all, they would probably have to use them again. Using a cart found in the storeroom, the food was loaded on and they wheeled it towards the elevator.

Pushing the cart, Christy said, "They must cater for the building here. There's a lot of food in there."

"Yeah. We're lucky. I have a feeling we're going to need it."

Christy stopped. "How long do you think we'll be here? Why can't we just leave?"

"We'll leave just a soon as we can. You've seen what's going on out there. I don't want to get caught in that. The power is out, and the phones are out. We need to wait and see what's going on before we try and leave."

Christy nodded. "But we will leave?"

Daniel leaned in and kissed her. "Just as soon as we can."

They pushed the cart through the door of the security office where a tinny voice was coming over Gene's radio. Bob held a finger to his lips. Daniel pushed the cart off to the side and sat on the counter beside Andy's position to listen to what was being said. The voice had a thick drawl and Gene was smiling as he talked into the mic.

"It's good to talk to you, Sam. Been too many years."

"You too, Slim. Like I said, if you can make your way here, we're in good shape. The Governor told the President she could stick her Emergency Decree where the sun don't shine. I don't like that bitch no way. Our power is still on and should stay on. They broke the circuits where they leave the state."

"Any trouble anywhere?" Gene asked.

"Awe, there's some shit in Austin, the bastion of liberal bullshit in our great state. There's a little trouble in Dallas and Houston, but I think the Guard will take care of that pretty quick."

"What's the Army out your way doing?"

The voice on the radio cackled. "You won't believe it. The commander of Fort Hood called up the Governor and put the base under his command!" The man laughed uproariously. "Can you believe that? I bet that bitch in Washington is screaming her lungs out. From what I've heard, the other Texas bases did the same. Know what the best part is? She's got two planes, them big-ass ones. Whatever one she's on is called Air Force One. Well, Air Force Two is sitting at Lackland! We've got her damn plane!"

Gene laughed and keyed the mic. "That's pretty damn funny, Sam. Let me think about things. We're kind of bottled up here in Atlanta right now. I don't know how I'd even get out."

"Well, Slim, you better make up your mind quick. They're talking about closing the border and not letting anyone in."

"Alright, Sam. Thanks. You going to be monitoring this frequency?"

"If I'm awake, I'm on here."

"Alright then, Sam. I'll talk to you later, buddy." Gene dropped the mic and looked at Bob.

"What the hell was that all about?" Daniel asked.

"Things aren't looking too good out there," Bob said. "Gene talked to a few people around the country, and a lot the big cities are looking just like Atlanta. The lone exception is Texas. They still have power and things are pretty normal there."

Teague sat back and put his hands behind his head. "You may all go to hell. I will go to Texas."

Bob chuckled. "Davey Crockett, nice one."

"I'm serious, though. From what I just heard here, I'm going to Texas. There's nothing here." He pointed at the monitor. "Look at those people out there. You think things are going to get better here soon?"

"How the hell do you plan to get to Texas?" Andy asked.

Teague shrugged. "Same way I got here. Where there's a will, there's a way."

Gene stood up and walked over to the cart of food. "While we debate, I'm going to eat."

"Sounds good," Bob said. "Quite the spread, Daniel."

"I helped!" Christy said.

Picking up slices of cold cuts, Bob glanced up and with a smile said, "Thought you weren't here to make food and do laundry."

Christy picked up a deviled egg. "I like to eat too."

The group chatted as they ate, keeping one eye on the monitors. The talk was light hearted, until the TV began to emit the emergency alert tones again. The screen switched to a podium with the seal of Homeland Security on it.

"What's this shit?" Teague asked. Bob shushed him.

The Secretary stepped up to the podium. She was a short woman that belied her hotly contested appointment to the post. The President wanted to make a statement. She wanted to show she was supportive of women and, like her predecessor, was sympathetic to the *plight* of Muslims in America. With her hijab in place, she looked directly into the camera and began to speak.

ANGERY AMERICAN

As you are now all aware, a state of emergency has been declared as a result of the financial crisis. We are working diligently on discovering the source of the problem and, rest assured, we will find those responsible.

As a result of the inability for families to secure food and other necessary items, the President has ordered the implementation of several executive orders. Firstly, these orders will allow the government to set wages and control the flow of money. It will also allow the control of prices. This is to prevent price gouging. As this is a financial issue, we will work diligently to make sure all Americans have access to the funds they need.

Additionally, these orders will allow the government to take control of critical stockpiles, such as food and fuel, to oversee the proper allocation of resources. Healthcare will also be controlled to ensure it is available to all in need.

To deal with the growing lawlessness in some of our cities, the United States armed forces are now wholly responsible for ensuring the peace. As a result, a dusk to dawn curfew has been established. Let me make myself very clear. We will not tolerate the lawlessness consuming some cities. The armed forces have been authorized to use lethal force. This is no trivial matter and I urge you to heed this warning.

In a continuing effort to prevent further penetration into our nation's critical systems, all forms of communication will continue to be restricted. We cannot allow those that wish us harm continued access. All phones, both cellular and land line, will continue to be interrupted with the exception of 911 lines which can still be used. Likewise, the internet will also be limited until we have a better understanding of the situation.

Continue to monitor your local television and radio stations for updates, as this will be the only way you will be able to receive current information. We ask that everyone remain calm and give the authorities time to sort the situation out.

With that, the screen returned to the color pattern with the text. Daniel looked around the room. Everyone was still staring at the TV, except Gene. He'd pulled a chair up to the cart and was shoveling potato salad into his mouth as though it was a job. Daniel got a shiver and continued to survey the room. When he got to Teague, he was staring back at him.

Teague rocked his chair back onto the back legs again and loudly said, "Bullshit!"

Everyone's attention was on Teague. After a moment, Bob asked, "Care to elaborate?"

Teague pointed at the TV. "That bullshit. It's all bullshit."

Rolling his hand in front of him with a look of expectation, Bob said, "And?"

Teague jumped up. "You guys believe they've killed all forms of communication because someone hacked a bank?" He looked around the room. "I mean, come on. The only reason they'd do that is to keep us in the dark about what they're up to."

"Let me guess. You think they're going to start rounding people up and putting them in FEMA camps?" Daniel asked.

"If you think they're not going to use this opportunity to do just that to some people, you've been drinking the Kool Aid too long."

Bob started to reply but was interrupted by Andy. "You ought to see this."

Tapping a few keys, Andy combined all the monitors on the wall into one large view. It was an image from one of the thermal cameras. It clearly showed the rioters' positions, marked by large white spots of bonfires. The camera scanned the crowd that was, for the moment at least, rather calm. There were many small fires with groups gathered around them. There was almost a festival air to the scene of people gathered around and socializing.

The camera panned up the street. This is what Andy wanted everyone to see. On either side of the street, close to the faces of the businesses lining either side were lines of soldiers. Even in the fuzzy view of the thermal camera, it was obvious they were in full battle rattle.

Bob leaned back against the wall. "Oh, this is about to get real interesting."

"What are they going to do?" Christy asked.

"Whatever it is, it ain't going to be good."

Teague rose and pointed at the monitor. "Now you're about to see why they've cut all the communications. Shit's about to get real."

The bank sat at the intersection of Peachtree and Piedmont in Buckhead. From that location, they could see the surrounding financial district, as well as the full length of either road. Just to the southeast across Peachtree was a large subdivision, Peachtree Park. Atlanta is one of those rare cities where suburbia reaches right into urban districts. High-rises sit in close proximity to homes, grocery stores and gas stations.

While the riots focused on the financial district, it was inevitable that it would spill out into the surrounding area. Many of the local businesses had already been looted and several of them burned. And many of the homes in Peachtree Park were looted, and some burned as well.

It was through the scorched businesses on Peachtree Rd that the troops approached from the southwest. As they closed in on the first line of the rioters, the soldiers seemed to fade away. They disappeared into the many buildings along the street. Some would reappear on the rooftops, taking up positions to cover the final assault.

"What are they doing? Where'd they all go?" Christy asked.

Teague sucked his teeth and lowered himself into a chair. "You might as well sit down. They're going to wait. I imagine it will be after two AM before they make their move."

"Why so late?" Andy asked.

"Because people sleep the hardest at that hour. It's the witching hour for violence."

Gene mopped his mustache with a napkin. Leaning back, he patted his stomach. "I guess we'll see what's going to happen in a few hours. I'm going to see what else I can hear on the ether."

Christy looked at Daniel. "I'm tired. Can we go sleep for a while?"

"I think everyone should get some rest," Bob said.

Gene was staring intently at the radio as he worked the dial. "I'll sleep when I'm dead."

Daniel stood up and took Christy's hand. "Come on, I've got a place we can crash for a while."

Bob pulled a handheld radio from a multiple-radio charger. "Here, take this with you. I'll call you if anything starts to happen."

"Thanks," Daniel said as he took the radio. Then he headed to the door with Christy in tow.

Christy leaned against the wall beside the elevator and ran her hands through her hair. "I'm so tired. What are we going to do? We're stuck down here."

The elevator dinged and they stepped in. "For now, we'll wait. There's nothing else we can do. But I need a little sleep."

Daniel took her down to the room Bob had showed him earlier. The bed was a little small, but they would fit if they spooned, and that was fine with him. He lay on the bed with his face in Christy's hair. It smelled incredible and relaxed him some. His mind was reeling from the day's events. After a while, Christy seemed to sense it.

"You asleep?" She asked.

"No."

She reached back and ran her hand over his leg. "You alright?"

Daniel thought for a moment. "I can't stop thinking about the man I shot."

"On the roof?"

"Yeah. I don't know if I did, but I must have. It's kind of strange. I can see the shooting in my mind but I don't know if I killed him or not."

"I can't believe this is going on. I mean, there was a shooting and no cops came. What are we going to do? If the police can't get here, how are we going to get out?"

Daniel let out a sigh. Shaking his head, he replied. "I don't know. Things are getting out of hand. Maybe we should go to Texas. Maybe Teague has a good idea to go out there."

Christy sat up on her elbow. "You want to leave Atlanta? What's in Texas? Do you know anyone out there? Where would we go?"

He patted her leg. "I don't know what to do, babe. I'm just thinking."

Christy lay back down and draped her arm over him. "Let's see what's happening in the morning."

CHAPTER 6

DANIEL WAS LOOKING FOR THE next handhold. He reached back and chalked his hand as he surveyed the rock face. The breeze picked up and he looked back over his shoulder. The wind felt good on his face. Turning back to the rock face, he reached for the small bulge in the rock and his foot slipped.

Daniel! Daniel, you there?

He bolted upright in the bed, scaring Christy. She sat up, rubbing her face. "What's wrong? What is it?"

Daniel picked up the radio. "Yeah, I'm here." And he rubbed his eyes. He was sweating from the dream and felt disoriented.

Come back up, the show is about to start.

"On our way." he replied. Looking at Christy, he said, "You coming, or do you want to sleep?"

She jumped from the bed. "Oh, I'm coming."

Back in the security office, Bob was sitting in a swivel chair looking at the monitor. Once again, Andy combined the screens into one large view. Bob alternated between sipping coffee and smoking a cigarette. As Daniel and Christy came in, he saluted them with the cup.

"Perfect timing. Looks like they're about to kick this thing off."

Teague was sitting in a chair with his chin on his chest, asleep. Daniel looked around and asked. "Where's Gene?"

"He went down to get some sleep."

Daniel looked at the monitor. "What's going on?"

Bob motioned at the screen with his cup. "They're moving now. Let's see how they handle these guys."

Christy went to Bob's office for a cup of coffee. This was easier said than done. While there was coffee, a cup was another issue all together. She tried several cups, one or two of which made her physically ill at the sight. She went back out to where everyone else was and found the cup she had used when they ate earlier and took it back.

After fixing her cup, she came out and offered Daniel a sip as she sat down beside him. Daniel took it, swilling down a large gulp. Smiling, he thanked her and turned his attention to the monitor.

Andy pointed at the screen. "The guys on the roof are moving."

Daniel looked at the time in the corner of the screen and it showed 2:20.

Teague sat up and stretched, his face turning red as he did. "I told you it would be around 2:30 or 3:00."

They watched as several men on the rooftops moved into their final positions, what certainly looked like firing positions. At the same time, the men on the ground began moving up Peachtree Rd. The protestors were oblivious and there was no movement inside their position. The men on the street stopped advancing, taking up positions behind cars and against buildings.

They watched in silence. There were no microphones for the cameras. As it was early and still dark, it was like watching an old black and white movie. They could see the flashes and streamers of smoke racing towards the protestors' positions. While they couldn't see the other side of the rioter's position, they could see additional smoke canisters arcing in from the other side of Peachtree, and there were many.

As the smoke landed, the troops moved in. These weren't normal riot control troops. There were no bump helmets with visors, batons and plastic shields. These people were in full battle rattle as they began to run towards the rioters' position. They'd piled up all manner of obstacles, but they weren't very effective. As the troops swarmed in on foot, armored vehicles rounded the corner, spotlights blazing. They drove straight into the barricades, easily breaching them.

Christy held her hand to her mouth as she watched people being gunned down in the road. "Oh my God. They're killing them."

"Those ain't rubber bullets," Teague said.

Pointing at the monitor, Daniel said, "They're handcuffing some of them."

"They might be better off being shot right here," Teague said.

The group watched for over an hour as people were marched out, their hands cuffed and chained at the waist, leg irons restricting their ability to walk. The men on the ground were dragging bodies out and placing them in body bags, which were quickly loaded onto trucks and hauled away.

"They're not leaving any evidence," Bob said.

Teague wagged a finger at the monitor. "They're not leaving anyone behind."

Christy looked at Daniel. "Where are they taking them?"

"Nowhere good." Bob replied.

"How can they do this? I mean, those people weren't doing anything," Christy said.

Teague stood up. "There's a dusk to dawn curfew. They were on the street, so in the eyes of the government, they are criminals."

"But we have rights. How can they do this?"

Teague looked at Christy and shook his head. "Shit. You've only got the rights they allow you to have. The government has a monopoly on murder."

About an hour and a half after it all started, it was over. The trucks were gone and not a single person could be seen on the street below.

"Looks like they wanted them gone before the sun came up," Daniel said.

Teague stretched again. "No bodies, no crime. I'm going to get some sleep somewhere." He left the office to find a place to grab a couple hours sleep.

Daniel rubbed his temples. "I'm tired too. I'm going back downstairs." Looking at Christy, he asked, "You coming?" She nodded and followed him out of the office.

Daniel woke up when Christy got out of the bed. She looked over her shoulder. "I have to pee."

Daniel sat up and looked at his watch. "What time is it?" They were in the basement of the building with no natural light coming in, so he had no idea if it was day or night. "Holy shit. It's like nine in the morning!"

Christy came out of the bathroom. "Good, we needed the sleep. Let's go up and see what's going on."

"Yeah, let's get some coffee too."

They went up to the café for some coffee. It had to be better than the swill Bob made in his office. At the café, they had to figure out how to get the big machine working. But between the two of them, they'd ordered enough cups and watched them being made that they muddled through it. It wasn't long before the wonderful aroma of coffee filled the café.

While the coffee brewed, Daniel went in the back and found something for them to eat. He came out with a couple of croissants and egg salad. Christy was sitting at a table cradling a cup of coffee, another sitting on the table for Daniel. He set a plate down in front of her and pulled up a chair.

"Ooh, I love egg salad," Christy said as she picked up her sandwich.

Daniel picked up his cup. "I need this."

As they talked, Teague showed up. He looked like a toddler that just woke up from a nap. His hair was a mess and he had a red line on the side of his face. He bobbled up and looked at Christy, then Daniel. Then he looked at the sandwich lying in front of Daniel. Reaching out, he mashed a finger into Daniel's croissant. "You gonna eat that?"

Daniel slapped his hand away. "Yes, get off it, dick."

Teague smiled and headed for the coffee maker. He returned with a cup of coffee and the tub with the remainder of the egg salad. Taking a seat, he dug into the egg salad with a spoon. After shoveling a couple of spoonsfulls into his mouth, he looked at Daniel and asked, "What's going on outside?"

Daniel shrugged as he took a sip of coffee. "No idea. We haven't been upstairs yet."

"Where did you sleep?" Christy asked.

Teague worked his neck. "On, I found a couch in some office. It sucked. Hard."

Holding her coffee under her nose, Christy said, "You should have come down to the little rooms. The beds are pretty comfortable."

Daniel stuffed the last bite of his sandwich in his mouth and stood up. "I'm ready to go up and see what's going on. You guys coming?"

"Yeah. I'm curious to see what's happening," Christy said as she got up.

Teague waved them off. "You guys go on. I'm going to find something else to eat. I'll be up in a bit."

Bob was sitting in Andy's chair when they got up to the office. Naturally, there was a coffee cup in front of him and another cup full of ashes. Bob looked up and smiled as they came in.

"You guys get some decent sleep?"

"We did." Daniel replied. "What's going on up here?"

Bob pointed at the monitors. "See for yourself."

They looked at the big screen. It was focused on the area of the assault the previous night. There were no people in the frame. Several small wisps of smoke rose from various places, but there were no more fires.

"Everyone's gone," Christy said.

Reaching for the camera controller, Bob added. "From there at least." He pulled up another view. Farther down

Piedmont, they could see a large crowd gathered, a very large crowd. "Looks like they are grouping up into bigger crowds, maybe to try and defend themselves from what happened last night."

"What's the rest of the area look like?" Daniel asked.

Bob pulled up the camera on the roof and swung it around. As the camera passed the 400 expressway, Daniel yelled. "Stop!" Bob stopped the camera and Daniel pointed at the monitor. "Look at all the cars on the expressway."

Bob nodded. "Looks like people are trying to get the hell out of town."

"I think we should soon as well." Daniel replied.

The camera started to move again, turning to the southeast. "There's been a lot of helicopter activity over at the dome in downtown Atlanta," Bob said.

As the top of the dome came into view, all they could see, even with the maximum zoom on the camera, was a Blackhawk helicopter dropping below the roof line.

"Is that the military?" Christy asked.

Bob nodded. "Yeah. They've been flying in all morning. Plus, I've seen several other choppers flying around too. State police, sheriff's department and some with no markings, but they have to be feds."

"I really believe we need to start thinking about getting the hell out of here," Daniel said.

Bob let out a sigh and reached into his shirt pocket for his cigarette pack. It was empty. He shook it with exasperation, crumpled it and threw it across the room. Getting up, he walked back into his office and took a carton out of the freezer of the small fridge. There were two other cartons there. Bob didn't like running out of smokes.

Taking a pack out, he tossed the carton on his desk and went back out to join Daniel and Christy.

Bob lit a cigarette and took a deep drag. Blowing out the smoke, he said, "I'm waiting on Gene. I asked him to check the fuel levels of the generators."

Daniel stood up. "While you wait on him, I'm going out to the parking garage. I need some air."

Christy jumped up. "I'll come with you."

They went to the top of the garage. The morning was clear and warm, but not yet too hot. Daniel leaned over the edge of the parapet wall and looked down. The fire hose they had used the day before was still there. Christy came up beside him.

"What are you thinking about, babe?" She asked.

"It just seems like the world is coming apart and we don't have any idea what the hell is going on. No phones, no internet, no news. Nothing."

"I know. It's scary. I want to leave but I don't know where to go."

Daniel hung his head. "I know. Without info, we don't know what's safe and what's not."

Christy took his hand. "Let's go back and see what Gene says."

Gene and Teague were there when they got back to the office. But the look on everyone's face told them the news wasn't good. "What's the word?" Daniel asked.

"There's enough fuel for maybe another eight hours." Gene replied.

Daniel was surprised. "So we'll run out of fuel today."

"Without a doubt." Bob replied.

"So what do we do?" Christy asked.

Teague grunted. "Get the fuck out of Dodge."

"I agree," Bob said. "With the curfew in place, we need to get on the road early." He pointed at the monitor that was now showing the 400 once again, and said, "There's plenty of people moving around out there. We need to take advantage of it and get the hell out of here."

"To where?" Daniel asked.

"Texas!" Teague shouted.

"Where in Texas? You know anyone there?" Daniel asked.

"I've got a friend in Nacogdoches," Gene said.

Daniel was shaking his head. When Teague had previously said Texas, he hadn't really thought much about it. But now that it was actually being discussed, he couldn't believe it. "You realize Texas is like six hundred miles from here, right?"

"Closer to seven hundred," Gene said.

"That presents the first obstacle," Bob said. "That's a lot of fuel."

Daniel sat down in a chair. "That's not a problem. My van has an aftermarket tank, a Titan. It holds sixty-eight gallons. I could easily make it to Texas on a full tank." It was just a natural reply. The van *could* make it. Not that he was actually considering it.

Christy looked at him. "You actually want to go to Texas?"

"But do you have a full tank?" Teague asked.

Daniel shrugged. "No, only about a half tank."

Gene rubbed his whiskers. "Then we need to think about this. If we're actually going to try and make a run for Texas, we have the fuel on hand."

Bob nodded. "We could take it from the generators' tanks. Good idea, Gene."

Daniel stood up. "Wait a minute. What are we talking about here? Why the hell would we go to Texas? I mean, first, it's seven hundred miles. Fuel aside, do you actually think we'd make it? And if we did, where exactly would we go?"

"We can't drive at night. There's a curfew. It would take forever to get there," Christy said.

"Not to mention all the roadblocks we'd probably encounter," Teague said.

Bob shook out a cigarette and lit it. Taking a long drag, he thought for a minute. Looking at the smoke between his fingers, he said, "Well, the way I see it, Texas might be the safest place to go. I think things in this country have changed in a major way. I think it will be a long time before they go back to the way they were. You all saw what the government did to those people down below. They went in shooting. Those they didn't kill, they hauled off to God knows where. I don't want to end up in either of those situations."

"I don't do FEMA camps," Teague said.

"What other option do you have?" Gene asked. "Go home, where there's no power, no communications? Sit in the dark and wait to see what happens?"

Staring at the floor, Daniel shook his head. "I don't know. It just seems a bit rash to run off to Texas. I don't know."

Pulling the comb from his pocket, Gene combed out his mustache. "You better hurry up and figure it out. We'll run out of fuel in a few hours, and then this place goes dark. Then there won't be any fuel to put in the van. You'll be down to only one option, sitting in the dark at home."

Christy grabbed Daniel's arm. "Babe, I'm with you. Whatever you want to do."

Daniel looked at her. She was an amazing woman. Maybe he'd been wrong about keeping a little distance between them. He smiled and said, "I know you are." Looking at Gene, he said, "Let's go fill the van. That way, we have an option."

"We need to start a plan for getting out of here then. We can't just pile out into the street," Bob said.

Daniel nodded. "Alright. You guys work on that while Gene and I go down and fill up the van."

It took a little maneuvering to get the van close enough to the diesel tank to transfer the fuel. Gene was an interesting guy and obviously took a lot of liberty with his position in the building. He'd acquired all manner of stuff that would be hard to justify as being needed, but was handy to have. One of those was the transfer pump they were using to move the fuel into the van.

Both men were wearing earmuffs to protect against the roar of the generators. They were loud as hell and hot. While Daniel watched the van, Gene disappeared and came back riding the forklift. A pallet sat on the forks with four small drums on it. He climbed off the machine and opened the bungs on them, setting the lids on top of each drum. Daniel wasn't certain what he was doing, but figured it out when the tank on the van was full.

The two couldn't communicate due to the level of noise, but when Gene moved the nozzle of the pump into one of the drums, Daniel knew what Gene was up to. The drums were small, fifteen gallons. These would be easier to handle on the road should they need them.

Gene leaned in close and shouted. "Where do you want to put it?"

Daniel looked at the van and pointed to the large rack on the roof. "Let's put them up there. That way we save space inside."

After filling the small drums, Gene nodded and hopped back on the forklift, raising the load up. Daniel climbed up the ladder on the rear of the van and got on top. He rolled the barrels onto the rack and laid them down. The rack was large enough to hold them and still had more space. Gene waved at him and tossed up a couple of ratchet straps. Daniel strapped the drums down and hopped off. It was nice knowing they now had over one hundred and twenty gallons of fuel onboard.

Once the fuel was on the van, Gene waved for him to follow and the two went to Gene's office. Stepping in, Daniel took the muffs off his ears and wiped sweat from his forehead.

"Damn, it's hot out there."

Gene tossed his muffs onto his already cluttered desk. "Yeah. Most people have no idea what these buildings are really like. They only know when the elevator stops or the shitter won't flush."

Daniel nodded. "I guess I was guilty of that too."

Gene smiled, the ends of his mustache turning up. "Yeah. But you're learning."

Daniel laughed. "Better late than never. You ready to head back upstairs?"

Gene held up a finger. "Not yet. While we're down here, I'd like to load some other things we may find useful."

Curious, Daniel asked, "Like what?"

Gene rubbed his hands together, "Oh just some party favors. Follow me."

***

Bob, Christy and Teague leaned over Bob's desk. A large map of greater Atlanta was spread out. Bob laid a finger on the map and traced it across the paper.

Picking up an atlas, Bob opened it. "I think we should take I-20 west. It'll be the fastest way,"

Teague nodded. "But we can only travel during the day and need to find decent places to spend the night."

"You think with the curfew we could get in trouble if someone finds us at night?" Christy asked.

Bob shrugged. "Right now, who knows?"

"The object will be to not to be seen at night. Daniel's van is a dark olive drab, the perfect color to hide. We'll find places to pull off in the evening, giving us plenty of time to find a good place to hide. Once we find that place, we'll have to take care of things like food and whatnot before it gets dark. Once it's dark, there's no lights, no sound. We have to just maintain a stealth mode. Sleep in shifts so there's always someone awake to serve as a lookout."

Christy looked at Teague. "You think it's that dangerous?"

Bob chuckled. "We don't know. And I, for one, don't want to find out the hard way. He's right. Good thinking, Cousin."

Teague pointed at the map again. "We also need alternative routes around all major cities. I'd prefer we didn't drive through any of them, personally."

"That would add a lot of time. I agree we need alternate routes, at least two. But I say we drive through them if there isn't anything major going on. It will all depend on what the roads are like." Bob replied.

Teague nodded. "Agreed. You got a highlighter?"

The three got to work mapping their routes around larger cities like Birmingham and Tuscaloosa in Alabama. The next major obstacle would be Jackson, Mississippi. Once they cleared those, they'd face Monroe and Shreveport in Louisiana. But there would be countless smaller cities between that they'd have to deal with as well.

They also mapped out a route that would keep them off the interstate entirely. The thought was that the interstate could either become locked with traffic or simply unsafe. The route off the interstate would take considerably longer. But it was better to have a plan than to go forward blindly and have to adapt on the fly.

"We need to think about food," Christy said.

Shaking out another smoke, Bob replied. "Yes we do."

Christy looked at Teague. "Come on. Let's go down to that little café and see what we can scavenge from there. There's a lot of stuff there."

"Good idea," Bob said with a wink.

"We can also raid all the vending machines too," Teague added.

Christy wrinkled her nose. "I don't want to live on candy bars and chips."

Bob pointed at her with his cigarette. "Yeah, but it'd be better than being hungry."

Christy shrugged, "I guess."

Teague headed for the door. "Come on. Let's see what we can find."

As they opened the door, Bob said, "I'm going to stay

here and watch the cameras. We need to know what's going on outside." And he turned his attention to the monitors.

He shook out yet another smoke and put his feet up on the desk and leaned back in the chair. Smoking with one hand, he used the other to manipulate the camera controller. Bringing up the multi-camera view, he examined each for any movement. One view caught his eye and he expanded it to full screen.

This was a view of Piedmont Road. A block or so down the road was the Piedmont Peachtree Crossing shopping center. It was home to a Kroger, World Market, Starbucks and other trendy shops, all of which were now looted out. The Starbucks had burned and was now a pile of charred ashes. But the plaza had a large parking lot that was filling with people, spilling out onto Piedmont.

Bob zoomed the camera in. There were no police or any form of crowd control present. As Bob moved the camera around, he began noticing several of the people in the crowd were armed and many of them were wearing masks. He watched as the crowd spilled out onto Piedmont and began making their way both directions, a large portion moving towards Peachtree. *This can't be good,* Bob thought as he watched what was growing into a sea of people spread out onto the streets.

They seemed to come from everywhere and swell in numbers as they filled the streets. While Bob couldn't hear them, they were chanting and shouting as they moved through the trash-strewn canyons. At intersections, the crowd would break into groups, some staying at the intersection, others moving on. Those that stayed began throwing up barricades, using everything at their disposal from park benches and garbage cans to blocks and tires. This was going to make getting out of the area a real issue.

***

Daniel and Gene finished loading Gene's *party favors* into the van. Daniel stepped back, rubbing his head. "You think this is safe having this stuff in here?"

Gene shrugged. "Eh, just don't mix 'em."

Daniel shook his head. "I'm going outside to get some air."

"I'm headed back up to Bob's office," Gene said as he turned away.

Daniel wanted to be alone for a minute. He took the stairs up to the top level of the garage and looked out across the area. His nostrils were assaulted by numerous smells. Burning rubber, garbage and an odd odor he couldn't quite put his finger on. It gave the area an overriding pungent smell that wasn't pleasant. Daniel looked down over the edge of the wall and was surprised to see so many people on the street.

How the hell are we going to get out of here? He asked himself.

The enormous mass of people on the road below him were spread out all along Peachtree. Most concerning, they were building barricades at the intersection with Piedmont, their way out. This worried him and he quickly headed back for Bob's office.

Daniel was a little excited when he came through the door to the office, and he started talking without looking at the monitors.

"We're in trouble. There's no way we can get out of here

with that crowd out there! You should see all the people on the street!"

Cigarette in hand, Bob pointed at the wall of monitors. "You mean them?"

Daniel looked over and felt a little silly. "Yeah. Them. They're building barricades out there."

The view on the screen swung around. Again, Bob pointed at the monitor. "You mean those?"

"Yeah, Bob. Those. What are we going to do?"

Bob got up and walked towards his office. "We're going to wait on Gene."

Daniel looked around. "Where's Gene? He said he was coming up here."

"He left, saying he would take care of this," Teague said.

"What the hell does that mean?" Daniel asked.

Teague shrugged. "Hell if I know."

Christy stood up. "Sit down and have something to eat, babe. We found a lot of food we can take with us. But you should eat something now."

"But, what's Gene doing? We can't get out of here with that mob out there."

Christy pulled him into a chair and said, "Sit down. Gene said he had it. He was actually laughing as he left. Said he'd be back when it was all ready." She set a large bowl of soup in front of him and some crackers.

He started to protest but Christy cut him off, telling him to eat. Daniel didn't understand why no one was concerned. Didn't they realize what it was like out there? He looked up at the monitor, at the growing crowd on the street in front of the bank. *Where are the police or National Guard?*

The day was spent hanging out, watching the growing

mobs on the street. Teague disappeared to, as he put it, *search the building for anything useful.* Daniel took that to mean he wanted to be nosy and probably break into things. He remembered his cousin from his youth having an uncontrollable temptation for locks. If something was locked, be it a door, a gate or, God forbid, a box, he had to get into it. Even now, Daniel could see him prying open file cabinets all over the building.

After being gone several hours, Gene reappeared. He was dirty and looked tired. Coming into the office, he slumped into a chair and announced. "It's done."

Daniel looked at him. "What's done?"

Too tired to smile, Gene replied abruptly. "You'll see."

Not long after Gene's arrival, Teague showed up as well. He dropped into a chair beside Gene. Bob lit another cigarette. He seemed to have an unending supply. Looking around the room, he cleared his throat.

"Now that everyone is here. I think we need to talk." He paused and looked around the room. "We know we can't stay here. We have to leave." He pointed at the monitors. "From the look of things outside, we need to get the hell out of the area."

Daniel leaned forward in his chair. "But is setting out to Texas the right choice?"

"And that is the question." Bob replied.

"What are our choices?" Teague asked. "Stay in a place that's burning down around us?"

Bob shrugged, leaned back in his chair and threw his feet up on the counter. He was wearing two different socks of a loud pattern, both bunched up around his ankles.

Christy noticed and giggled. Bob looked at the inch of exposed flesh between the sock and the pants and smiled.

"We could just try to go upstate. I know a bunch of places up there," Daniel said.

Bob nodded. "We could. But Gene here isn't much of a camper."

"I don't shit in the woods," Gene replied.

"Besides. Every place you know of there, so do another couple thousand people. It could get crowded," Bob said.

"Not to mention the fact that Texas has held it together. They told the Feds to go pound sand. They have electricity and things there are normal still," Teague said.

"I think we should go to Texas, Daniel. I mean, sure this is home, but if it's too dangerous, I'd rather just leave. Together," Christy said.

Daniel looked at her. He was so unsure. There were so many things to consider. So many unknowns. Should he toss in his lot with this group of people he hardly knew? Sure, he really liked Christy, maybe even loved her; that was yet to be answered. But he didn't know Gene hardly at all, only seeing him around the building. Same for Bob, who he had a little more than a passing familiarity with. As for Teague, when they were kids, they played together often on summer breaks. The two would run the woods together and get into the typical trouble boys left unsupervised in the woods would get into. But that was a long time ago and both, now men, had changed a lot.

Daniel looked around the room. It seemed everyone's mind was made up and they all were waiting on him. He threw his hands up. "Let's go to Texas."

Christy clapped and jumped up, wrapping her arms

around his neck. "I'm so excited. This is going to be so much fun!"

Teague snorted. "That remains to be seen."

Gene levered himself from his chair. "Now that it's decided, we need to get ready. The generators won't last more than a couple of hours. I suggest if anyone wants a shower, you get it now."

Christy spun around. "That's me. I'm going down to get one." Then she had a thought. "Are we going by our places to get stuff?"

"We'll have to see what it's like out there. If it's safe enough, yes. If not, then we'll just have to keep moving," Bob said.

Daniel stood up. "I guess I'll go take a quick shower too. Might be the last chance."

Christy, Gene and Daniel left the office and headed for the shelter in the basement. As they came out into the mechanical space from the elevator, Daniel stopped in his tracks and shouted. "What the fuck did you do to my van?"

The van had been pulled up closer to Gene's work area. It was now adorned with expanded metal mounted to pipe frames and welded to the body of the van over all the windows. The front bumper now sported pieces of pipe welded to it at six inch intervals and very sharp. It had a quite a Mad Max look to it.

Gene smiled. "You like it?"

"Like it! Look at my paint! You ruined it!"

Gene rubbed his mustache and nodded. "I guess you're right. All those rocks, bottles and other shit that's going to be thrown at this thing wouldn't leave any marks on it." He looked at Daniel and smiled. "Sorry."

Daniel walked over to the van. The new screens were very well made. The welds were nearly perfect and didn't look as though they'd been rushed. Gene was obviously skilled when it came to fabrication. All the welds had been ground and brushed clean and covered with a layer of gray primer. The more he looked at it, the more it made sense. Gene was right. They were sure to run into trouble somewhere, and these would prevent them from having things hurled into the van.

Christy was looking at the short pipes welded to the front bumper. She looked back at Gene and asked. "What are these for?"

Gene walked up and turned sideways in front of the van. "Crowds sometimes will try to stop vehicles by simply standing in front of them. These will keep folks from doing that. No one's going to want to take this stabbing into them long."

Daniel came around after inspecting the van. Looking at Gene, he smiled. "Damn good idea, Gene. I'm glad we have you with us." Gene smiled.

Christy leaned over and shouted at Daniel. "I'm going to take a shower. You coming?"

Daniel nodded and took her hand. Looking at Gene, he said, "Thanks, Gene."

Gene wiped his mustache and glanced at Christy. Feeling she couldn't hear him, he asked, "Can I come?" Daniel laughed and followed Christy towards the little door leading to the shelter.

CHAPTER 7

THE VAN SAT IDLING, ITS Powerstroke diesel engine running smoothly, nearly imperceptibly. An air of nervousness settled over the group. While everyone was certainly ready to begin this expedition, trepidation at what awaited them consumed each and every one.

"Everyone know what they're supposed to do?" Bob asked, getting a nod from each of them.

Gene looked at Teague. "You sure you understand what you have to do when you get up there?"

Teague waved him off. "Gene, this ain't my first rodeo with this kind of thing. This is kid stuff."

Christy wrinkled her nose. "What kind of kid were you?"

Teague smiled and pointed at Daniel. "Ask him. We did it all together."

Christy looked at Daniel. He held his hands up. "Not all of it."

Teague laughed. "My ass!"

"It's time," Bob said as he looked at Teague. "Get your ass up the stairs, cousin."

Teague pointed at Daniel. "Don't you fucking leave without me."

"Don't worry, buddy. I won't. You just hurry up and get your ass down the stairs as fast as you can."

They climbed into the van and took their seats and Gene took up his position. Bob was riding shotgun up front. He had one of the twelve-gauge Mossbergs in his hand, and two carbines sat on the floor between the seats. Gene had moved the two crates blocking the roll-up door, so Bob and Daniel sat staring at the gray metal as they waited.

Teague sprinted up the stairs to the top level and ran over to the side where the bottles waited. A couple dozen small plastic water bottles sat lined up against the wall. Each one had a wad of aluminum foil shredded into the bottom. Two gallons of muriatic acid sat with them.

Teague pulled the nitrile gloves from his pocket and put them on, along with the safety glasses hanging around his neck. Bob insisted on the safety equipment. Teague protested, but was actually very happy to have it on. Opening both of the jugs, he picked up the first one and started pouring acid into the bottles. It was a quick and messy job, spilling quite a bit of acid on the concrete. As soon as all the bottles had acid in them, some considerably more than others, Teague started capping the bottles and tossing them over the side of the building.

He tried to make sure there were some close to the building and others farther out in the street. They wanted to create a bit of a path out into the road. When there were still three bottles left to throw over, the first one on the ground detonated with a surprisingly loud pop and a shout from the crowd below. He quickly capped the other three and threw them over before turning and running as fast as he could for the stairs.

He took the stairs in great leaps, covering four and five in a jump. On one landing he twisted his ankle slightly and had to slow down a bit. But as he came out onto the ground floor, he started shouting. Hearing him coming, Gene hit the button and the security gate started to rise. The side door was open on the van and Teague dashed for it, diving in, out of breath. As soon as there was room, Daniel pulled the van through. The fuel barrels on the roof scraping along the bottom of the door. once the van was through, Gene ran for the side door as well. Once he was in, Christy slid the door shut.

Bob's eyes darted left and right. The bottles had the desired effect and cleared people away from the immediate area. They were running in every direction thinking it was some sort of poison gas.

"Go left!" Bob shouted, and Daniel gunned the van onto Piedmont Rd.

The road was cluttered with broken pieces of bricks, wood, glass and spent tear-gas canisters. The crowd, temporarily dispersed by Gene's impromptu chemical bombs, saw the van when it rolled out of the garage and were now focused on it. Rocks, bottles and other debris now started flying towards the van, though not many of them actually hit it.

Christy shouted "Oh my God!" as a bottle smashed against the screen on the rear window. "They're so many of them!"

Gene casually looked out the window. "Let me see if we can thin 'em out a bit." He reached down and picked up a hose with a funnel connected to it, then took a gallon jug and started spinning the lid off with two fingers.

"What's that?" Christy asked.

Gene smiled. "You'll see."

Once the lid was off, he started to trickle the oil into the funnel. Almost immediately, a thick cloud of smoke started to billow from the rear of the van. Daniel looked in the rearview mirror and saw the smoke. "Oh shit! The van's smoking!"

Bob looked over his shoulder and added. "Oh shit."

Gene was laughing. He stopped pouring the oil in and held the jug between his legs as he held the hose up to allow the oil left in it to drain into the exhaust. "Don't worry! It's just a little something I added to the van!"

Daniel looked in the mirror again. "You did this to my van? What the hell did you do?"

Gene shouted over his shoulder. "It ain't going to hurt it." Then he looked out the rear window. All he could see was the cloud of thick white smoke. "They ain't coming through that!"

And they weren't. The street was thick with the smoke. It billowed up between the buildings that prevented it from dissipating too quickly.

Daniel was racing towards the incomplete barricade at the intersection of Piedmont and Peachtree. "Brace yourself!" He shouted just before they crashed into the pile of tires, pallets and other crap the protestors had piled up. It was no match for the van, which easily crashed through it.

Christy's apartment was the closest and was the first destination. It was a straight shot down Piedmont for a mile or so, then a right on Lindbergh Dr. This route would take them past the Havana Club where Daniel and Christy had been dancing when the riot news broke, as well as a number of high-end luxury car dealerships, including Jaguar, Rolls-Royce, Land Rover, Mercedes Benz, and one that carried both Ferrari and Lamborghini.

The smoke did its job and they got away from the bank with no damage and no real conflict. But things quickly changed as they passed by the luxury car dealerships. Those who viewed themselves as underprivileged had apparently decided to get themselves a fine automobile. They witnessed someone breaking the showroom window at the Ferrari dealership on their left, and they sped along to avoid the melee there. But then it got even worse. As they came up to the Rolls Royce and Land Rover dealerships on their right, folks had already broken out all the glass and were driving out with the ride of their dreams. Guess it had not occurred to them that these vehicles were maintained with very little gas in them, and the likelihood of getting more gas during this nightmare with virtually all businesses shut down would be next to zero. And with the attention these cars draw on the road, their journey would probably be a very short one, and end quite badly.

Teague commented on the scene. "Hey, maybe they figured it was worth it to go out in style; but that's giving them the benefit of the doubt that they were thinking at all."

Daniel managed to quickly drive on past the car thieves without too many issues, but they weren't out of the woods yet.

"There's trouble ahead. I see smoke," Daniel announced.

Bob shifted the shotgun, "Just keep driving. Look for a weak spot and push through it. No matter what." He looked at Daniel. "Do not stop this van."

Daniel nodded and gripped the wheel a little tighter. People filled the street ahead of them. Debris from the businesses along Piedmont littered the road and several small fires burned in the road as well. A couple of the businesses were even on fire. As they approached, Daniel stared in amazement as two men carried a commercial espresso machine across the road in front of them. *What the hell do they think they're going to do with that?* He thought.

But the looting wasn't limited to coffee makers. He saw many items being carried away. Flat screen TVs seemed high on the list. As well as clothes. One man ran across the road with a stack of shoe boxes, presumably with heisted pairs of sneakers in them. Daniel started to accelerate. He wanted anyone considering coming at the van to think twice about it.

The van swerved between piles of burning tires, flaming dumpsters and other obstacles. Bob put his window down and poked the muzzle of the Mossberg out. Gene had the foresight to add shooting ports through the screens. They were holes cut through the expanded metal, reinforced with pipe around their edges. This would allow them to deploy weapons from inside the van, a critical addition to the van's defenses.

"Call out any threats you see!" Teague shouted. He was in the back of the van. Gene had taken the glass out of the rear doors to allow for the same thing. This was Teague's position. He had one of the Patriot Warhogs poked out the rear. He was very familiar with the AR platform and was happy to have it in his hands. If anyone approached the back of the van, he was going to shoot them in the face.

People of every class and station swarmed the area like

ants picking at a carcass. Only, these were people picking at the corpse of civilization and the body wasn't even cold yet. If the rest of the country was in the same shape as here, the nation was in a world of shit.

The van started drawing more and more attention. Not that cars were uncommon, but driving one right into a crowd of looters was. People began pointing at the van and running towards it. Others shoved shopping carts out into the road. Daniel slammed into these, sending them flying through the air. Others rolled small dumpsters out or tossed trash cans in his path. All of these he plowed through.

"Hurry up!" Teague shouted.

"I'm trying!" Daniel shouted back.

"Everyone, settle down. Just keep your eyes open," Bob said in a calm voice.

But the people on the street were moving. The sight of the van on the move was like a flame to a moth. Whether it was because their cars were out of fuel or they were simply caught up in the looting, people were rushing towards it. Lindberg was just ahead and people were filling the intersection.

"Find a hole and steer for it," Bob said. "They'll move."

"Do you see a hole, Bob? I damn sure don't!" Daniel shouted back.

"Oh my God! Look at all of them!" Christy shouted.

Teague came forward and stuck his head between the front seats. "Get off me, asshole!" Christy shouted. He ignored her and checked out the crowd.

"Where do I go, Bob? Where do I go?" Daniel shouted.

Bob pointed to the right side of the road. "Get up on the sidewalk."

"Fuck this," Teague said as he disappeared back to his seat.

Daniel was steering the truck for the sidewalk, but it was crowded with people. A sudden burst of gunfire caused him to duck, and the van jerked as he did.

"What the hell was that? Who's shooting at us?" Daniel shouted.

Bob was looking for the shooter. Teague shouted over everyone in the van. "Just drive! It's me. I'm clearing the street!"

And it was working. When the shots rang out, people scattered in all directions. Mainly out from in front of the van, which opened a lane for Daniel.

Bob pointed to the opening. "Punch it! Go!"

Daniel floored the van, and the Powerstroke belched a cloud of smoke as they bounced over the beginnings of yet another barricade. They made it through the intersection as a hail of shit landed on the van. Teague, sitting in the back of the van, was laughing hysterically. Daniel made a mental note to thank him properly.

They finally made it to Christy's apartment complex, Post Peachtree Hills Apartments. A trendy complex that tried to offer the feel of a mountain retreat. Lots of stone columns and varied exterior color schemes. It sported everything a young woman would want in upscale multi-family living. It had two pools, a fitness center and a clubhouse that hosted events encouraging the residents to feel they are part of a community.

But there wasn't much of a sense of community there today. It was clear there'd been trouble. Broken windows and debris littered the usually attractive landscape. Christy stuck her head between Bob and Daniel.

"Oh my God! What's going on here?" She asked.

"Where's your apartment?" Bob asked.

"I know." Daniel replied as he wheeled past the clubhouse.

He threaded his way back to the rear of the complex. Christy had a second floor apartment. As an attractive single woman, she didn't want a ground floor apartment that would be easier for someone to break into.

"Daniel, you and cousin go with Christy. Gene and I will stay with the van. But you need to be Ricky Tick. We've got no time to waste here," Bob said. "Gene, get that other shotgun and cover the rear of the van." Bob shouted over his shoulder.

Gene nodded and pulled the Mossberg over, racking a shell into the chamber. When Daniel stopped, Bob said, "Leave it running and hurry the hell up!"

Teague was already out the back doors and shouted, "On you!"

Gene opened the side door and stepped out, and Christy followed. Daniel quickly got out, looking at the people who were watching them from balconies and those milling about the complex. Bob shouted at him as he looked back in the truck.

"You forget something?" Bob asked. Then he tossed the Warhog to him. It surprised Daniel. Guns were outlawed and he wasn't comfortable having one in public. But it had the desired effect. People disappeared from the balconies, and those in the parking lot decided they weren't all that interested in the van now.

Daniel led the way up the stairs towards Christy's apartment, with her following and Teague bringing up the rear. The news wasn't good when they got to the second floor. Christy's door was open, the frame of the door smashed in. Christy let out an audible gasp as she went to step through the door.

Teague grabbed her and pulled her aside. "You don't know if there's anyone in there! We need to check first." He looked at Daniel. "You follow me and watch my back. I'll clear the place. Just stay with me."

Daniel nodded as Teague shouldered his weapon and stepped through the door. The living room and kitchen were a mess. Everything was tossed. The smell of rotting food mixed with the general odor of a space that's been closed up with no air circulating. Seeing no one thus far, Teague moved towards the hallway with Daniel in tow. The first door was the bathroom. It was empty. The second door was her small office. As Teague was about to kick the door open, it suddenly swung inwards. A young guy stood there with a bandana over his face and pack slung from one shoulder. Teague immediately stepped forward and delivered a devastating butt stroke to the kid's chin, crumpling him to the floor. Teague stepped over him and cleared the room.

Looking over his shoulder at Daniel, he said, "Check the bedroom!"

Daniel nodded and went to the bedroom, the door already open. It was empty and, just like the rest of the house, had been tossed. Christy was standing in the living room looking at her life scattered and smashed on the floor. Daniel called out to her and she made her way down the hall. When she saw the man on the floor with Teague standing over him, she stopped.

"Why'd you do this? Why'd you wreck my house!" She shouted. The kid was on the floor, rocking back and forth as he held his jaw. Seriously pissed off, she delivered a savage kick to his stomach.

Teague grabbed her by the arm. "Go get your shit. We don't have time for this. What's done is done."

Teague was pushing her away as she took another shot at him, a glancing blow that added insult to the injury. She went to the bedroom where Daniel had already pulled out a duffle bag and laid it out on the bed. Her clothes were scattered all over the room. All the drawers of the dresser were pulled out and dumped. The little musical jewelry box her dad had bought her on a family trip to France when she was twelve lay smashed on the floor. She started to cry.

Daniel came to her. "Come on, babe. I know this sucks. But we have to hurry. Let's find your clothes and get out of here."

She wiped her eyes and nodded. After all, these were just things. They could always be replaced. Well, most of them could. They could hear Teague in the hallway screaming at the kid, but they had to focus on what they were doing. It didn't take them long to get what she would need from what was left.

Christy went into her bathroom. "Let me grab one more thing." Once in, she screamed. "They destroyed my makeup! What the F…, man!" In a whiney voice, she added. "Why'd they do that?" She came out with a few things and tossed them into the duffle. Looking at Daniel, she said, "Let's go." She sounded defeated. As they passed Teague and his captive, Christy kicked him in the ass. "Why'd you break my makeup, you sorry prick?" She kicked him again. "Asshole!"

He flinched and she reached down and snatched the bandana from his face. "I know you! What are you doing here? You sick asshole! What'd you come here for?"

He held his hands up. "I'm just looking for food! That's all!"

Teague kicked him. "In the apartment's office and bedroom?" He looked at Daniel and Christy and told them to take off.

They headed out and Daniel suggested they check her kitchen to see if there was any food they could use. But that turned out to be a useless endeavor, as it had all been cleaned out. Not even the spices remained. Teague watched as they headed for the door.

Daniel paused as they stepped out and looked back. "You coming?"

"Yeah, I'll catch up in a minute. Just want to make sure this asshole doesn't try anything." Daniel nodded and he and Christy headed down the stairs.

He looked down at the kid and asked, "What the fuck were you doing? Did you think you were going to break in here and try to take her ass? Is that what you thought?"

Holding his hands up, the kid replied. "No, no. I was just looking for food."

Teague snarled. "You lying fuck!" He stood up and delivered several savage blows with the butt of the rifle to the kid's head, leaving him unconscious. With his adrenaline pumping, Teague straightened up and looked around. Wiping sweat from his brow, he quickly headed for the door.

Teague ran down the stairs, taking them in big leaps and landing on the sidewalk in moments. Bob was standing beside the van with the door open while scanning the area for trouble. As Teague passed him, Bob asked, "Everything okay up there?"

Teague looked back over his shoulder. "Yeah, there was a guy in there, but he wasn't any trouble."

Bob looked towards the apartment. "Where is he?"

"Sleeping." Teague answered as he climbed into the back of the van.

"Where are we going now?" Christy asked.

Bob climbed in the van, placing the butt of his rifle on the floor between his feet. He rubbed his temples in frustration. "I think after this we need to get the hell out of town."

"I agree," Teague said.

Christy looked at Daniel. "Don't you need to go to your apartment?"

He shrugged. "Not really. I mean, there's lots of food there, but I don't think it's worth the risk. We'd have to go back north, and that's just too dangerous in my opinion."

From the front seat, Bob asked, "What about you, Gene?"

"I'd like to go by and get some tools. But there's nothing there I can't live without." Gene answered.

Christy looked at him. "What about clothes? You're still wearing your work uniform."

Gene held up a bag. "I have others here."

"Work uniforms? Don't you want something else to wear?"

Gene laughed. "Sweetheart, I've been wearing a uniform

of one kind or another for so long, it's all I own. I don't need other clothes."

Christy looked him up and down. She couldn't understand why anyone would want to wear that sort of get-up. But the decision was made and they were getting out of the area as fast as possible.

"Alright then. Let's head to my house. It's south of here and will be a good place to stay under the radar for a couple of days," Bob said.

Daniel started the van. "Alright, navigator. Which way?"

Bob leaned back and thought about it. "My place is about thirty miles from here. I usually take I-85, but I'd rather not be on the interstate for this trip."

"Where is your place, exactly?" Daniel asked.

Bob pointed off to the southeast. "It's down southeast of the metro area, near the Chattahoochee River. Pretty rural out there."

Daniel drummed his thumbs on the steering wheel. "That means we have to get through some densely populated areas of Atlanta."

"And we have to do that without getting on the interstate if we can avoid it." Bob added.

There was no good way. In the end, they started working their way south on surface streets. For the most part, they drove through sprawling bedroom communities of suburban Atlanta. The route took them through Druid Hills and down to Gresham Park. It was not an easy trip. Everywhere, people hustled about, bent on their own personal mission.

But the real threat was the number of people they saw with guns. For something that was outlawed, there was certainly a proliferation of firearms on the street. Conversely, there was the obvious absence of any kind of law enforcement. They were simply gone. No APD, no National Guard, no LEOs of any kind. That vacuum had to be filled somehow. Both the good and the bad were doing their best to plug the breach.

Residents of the nicer suburbs were doing what they could to keep riff raff out of their neighborhoods. Most of those neighborhoods had cars pulled up to their entrances, blocking the road. Armed men would watch the van with suspicion as it passed them by. Nothing says creeper louder than a van. Back in the day, there was the joke of "hey kid, you want some candy?" Or asking a child to help you find your pet to lure them into a van. The modern version of that is a creepy-ass van with 'free Wi-Fi' on the side of it. And with Gene's modifications, it now resembled something out of a Mad Max fiction. The van naturally drew everyone's attention.

"How far away are we?" Christy asked as she watched a truck slowly roll past them on the other side of the street.

"We've got a long way to go. Keep your eyes open," Bob said.

To stay away from the interstate, Bob was guiding Daniel down Moreland Avenue, a fairly large thoroughfare common to the US. Numerous streets intersected with it, and its sides were lined with small commercial centers and entrances to housing developments. This was urban sprawl. It's what kept America growing for so long. But what it did was put resources farther and farther from the very people these areas were developed for.

Farmers and ranchers were pushed farther and farther

from the city center. Waterways were *managed*, a benign term for redirecting, damming, polluting or in many cases, removing them all together. In other places, they were artificially dug in locations water was never meant to stand, all in the name of progress of course. But it seems the modern vision of *progress* is to remove people as far away from any form of independence as possible. Progress is synonymous with dependence, dependence on the government, on the system, on others to fulfil your daily needs. And now, with the great system of progress brought to a grinding halt, people were left to fend for themselves.

The whole modern idea of *progress* is that there will always be more progress. The idea that we, as a nation, should prepare ourselves for the day when not only do we stop progressing but actually to start to regress was simply unfathomable. How could that happen? We're America, the land of perpetual opportunity! But all that opportunity was based on perpetual consumption. And when that stopped, the nation stopped.

As they approached I-20, they came to the intersection with Memorial Drive. Gene started to chuckle and pointed out the window of the van. "Check those guys out."

Daniel looked out the window. A Valero gas station sat on the corner opposite a pay-day loan store. This neighborhood could be considered the *other side of the tracks*. The parking lot was crowded with armed men, some standing on the edge of the road. Those at the side of the road were waving at cars as they passed. The real shock was the military armored vehicles sitting in the parking lot.

The two MRAPs filled most of the parking lot. The men swarming around them seemed excited. They were very animated as they whooped and shouted. Not only did they have the two trucks, they also had M4s and SAWs. They were shooting these wildly into the air. Not the best way to entice people in to buy gas.

"What are they doing?" Christy asked.

Bob looked at the station as they rolled over Memorial. "They're selling gas. See that generator there? It has a small pump set up and they're pumping gas out of the underground tanks. They obviously took over the station and are selling what's now their fuel."

Christy took in the scene. "They commandeered the station," She said. More of a statement than a question. She turned back to the front, looking out through the expanded metal that covered the windshield. "We need to get away from people."

"Amen, sister." Bob replied.

As they came abreast of the station, Daniel looked out at a young kid sitting in the turret of one of the MRAPs. He was sitting behind a SAW and had a bead on Daniel as they passed. Whether it was ignorance, stupidity or sheer bravery, he wasn't afraid. It was as if he knew the kid wasn't going to shoot. It was more of an intimidation move.

"There's your armory stash," Teague said as he made his way up to the front of the van. "Do they look like the type of people that could take down a National Guard Armory?"

Bob flicked a butt out the window. "Nope. And it's scary that those kinds of people have that kind of hardware. But you have to wonder how they got it."

Gene snorted. "You know how they got it."

Christy looked at Gene. With genuine curiosity, she asked, "How?"

Gene started to laugh. "The government gave it to them!"

Confused, she asked, "Why would they do that?"

"To cause chaos. Having people like that on the street will make normal folks scared. And scared people are much easier to control," Bob said.

Christy looked back towards the gas station. "How do you know? I mean, I don't believe it."

Gene shrugged. "Can't prove it. But how else do you think they got that stuff? There's no way a bunch of hood rats stole that from an armory. It would take more force than they can muster."

On the south side of I-20, the neighborhood changed yet again. Ormewood and most of the land on this side of Atlanta once belonged to the Creek Nation, before they too were forced out in the name of *progress*. Now, fast food restaurants and check cashing stores were the dominant businesses. In normal times, the neighborhood had its share of crime. If you left an IPod on the seat of your car, you could expect someone to knock out a window and take it. Shades were kept drawn to prevent anyone from seeing the new flat screen. It was a place where residents had to be proactive. Not that it was a crime-ridden hell-hole, but vigilance was the word of the day.

Now, things were different. Both the Shell and Citgo stations on this side were also being looted of their fuel. And from the numbers of cars lining up, cash was king and no one was asking any questions. Just as they passed Delia's Chicken Sausage Stand, two men ran out in the road in front of them. Both had pistols and were firing back in the direction of the old Smooth Ahslar Grand Lodge.

The old building was one of the original black Masonic lodges on this side of Atlanta. Now it sat defunct and graffiti-covered. Daniel slammed on the brakes as the two men, holding their pistols sideways and higher than their heads fired round after round back in the direction of the old lodge.

"Oh shit!" Christy shouted. "What do we do?"

Bob had his carbine up to his shoulder. "This ain't our fight and we don't know who's who."

The two men continued to fire as they made for the other side of the street. One of the men suddenly collapsed onto the road. His fellow shooter looked down at his stricken comrade, turned and took off running around the side of the First Iconium Baptist Church. Three other men spilled onto the street. They approached the downed man, still alive but badly hurt. They circled around him, shouting and kicking him. After a moment, one of them raised a pistol and shot him in the face as he pleaded for his life.

After the shot, the three continued to shout at the body. Then one of them noticed the van. Using his pistol, he swatted his partners and motioned at the van.

"Oh shit." Bob muttered.

The three stood in the road, looking at the van and talking, though it was unintelligible. They appeared to come to a consensus and started to walk towards the van.

"What do I do?" Daniel asked.

"When they get a little closer, run their asses over," Bob said.

"Screw that!" Teague shouted from the rear of the van as the back door burst open. Teague jumped out and rounded the corner of the van with the Warhog to his shoulder. He stepped wide, to draw fire from the vehicle should they start shooting. But seeing Teague and the rifle evaporated their resolve, and all three took off at a dead run in the opposite direction.

Teague glanced at the body in the road for a moment, then quickly got back in the van and slammed the rear doors. Bob turned in his seat and shouted. "Would you stop doing shit like that!"

Teague looked at him quizzically. "Like what?"

"Getting out of the van!"

Teague looked down as he positioned the butt of his weapon between his feet. Looking up, he quietly asked. "What was your plan? How were you going to get us out of here?"

Bob shook his head and pointed at Teague. "You're reckless and you're going to get yourself killed."

Daniel wasn't waiting around. As far as he was concerned, this conversation could happen later. He floored the van, producing a cloud of black smoke, getting Bob's attention again. When the old man looked over, Daniel asked, "Where we going Bob?"

Bob fell back into his seat. "Turn around. Let's get on I-20 west. We just don't have any other good alternate at this point. It'll just save time. We'll only have to be on it for a short distance."

Daniel slowed and glanced over at Bob. "Thought you wanted to stay off the interstate. You said we shouldn't be on it."

"I did say that. But we also just saw a man executed on

the road in front of us. We've still got about twenty miles to get to my place."

Gene shouted. "Turn this thing around."

Daniel cranked the wheel around, causing Gene to lose his balance. He laughed as he fought to keep his seat and shouted. "Yee haw!"

From his seat in the back of the van, Teague laughed manically. To him, this was all fun and games. He was already neck deep as it was. So he had no compunction about pointing a weapon at someone, or pulling the trigger for that matter.

Daniel took the on-ramp, and headed west on I-20. There were other cars on the interstate, and all of them were driving fast, very fast.

Christy leaned forward and looked between the seats. "This isn't so bad. There's other cars out here." She looked at Bob. "I think you were wrong about the interstate, Bob."

Bob was watching the other cars, his eyes constantly scanning. "Maybe. We'll see."

It wasn't long before they were approaching the I-75 interchange just at the edge of Turner Field and the south side of downtown Atlanta. Considering their location, they were making really good time. While there was some traffic on the road, it was nothing like the normal daily rush-hour traffic. As they approached the interchange, Bob fidgeted. At the last moment, he shouted. "Take seventy-five south!" He had intended to take them on out I-20 to the I-285 west side perimeter and then turn south; but even though this route down I-75/85 would take them closer to the airport, it could be a better route, and might answer some questions.

Daniel quickly changed lanes, putting them on a southern track out of Atlanta. As Daniel was scanning the road, he was surprised just how easy it was to travel on the highway. Then that very thought struck him. Why wouldn't it be? Sure, the downtown area was going to hell, but it wasn't the end of the world. He started to relax as he raced down the right-hand lane of the interstate.

Suddenly, Bob pointed to the right. "Take the ramp."

Daniel took the long sweeping ramp off the interstate onto the Arthur Langford Jr. Parkway, or the 166. Just as they got to the end of the off ramp from I-75 onto 166, Bob shouted for Daniel to pull over to the side and stop.

"I think I spotted the edge of a military blockade just past the 166 interchange, where I-85 splits to the west side of the airport and I-75 to the east side. You guys hang tight here while I walk over to the other side of 166 so I can look beyond to see if I was right." Bob exited the van and quickly ran over to the far side of the four-lane road, where he hid in the bushes while checking out the I-75/85 split beyond. "I'll be damned. Those cock-sucking feds have both interstates blocked." He could see people being handcuffed. And one guy with a gun that he didn't want to give up, who started running. The turret gunner on one of the up-armored Humvees cut him to ribbons with his 50-cal. That was all Bob needed to see. He ran like a scalded cat back to the van. "Hit it, Daniel. I'll explain as we drive; and I mean, drive fast!"

Just as they pulled off, a pair of Apache Attack helicopters flew overhead, escorting a pair of Blackhawks towards downtown Atlanta. Everyone in the van was suddenly aware of just how close they had come to a most unpleasant end to their journey.

After a few minutes of driving westward on 166, and everyone calming down a bit, Bob started explaining. "Guys, when I made that last minute decision to come down I-75 instead of continuing on I-20 to the perimeter, I was hoping we could safely sneak by the airport on the I-85 side, and on to the south side of the perimeter and then connect with South Fulton Parkway to get to my place. It wouldn't have been any quicker than the route we're now going to take, just the way I sometimes travel home as an alternate route and a change of scenery. To be completely honest, I guess I just needed to satisfy my curiosity as to what might be happening at the airport.

Well, now we know. You all saw the military choppers that flew over us. That was scary enough. What you heard but didn't see just before that was the turret gunner on an up-armored HUMVEE mowing down a guy who had a gun. There were at least a dozen military vehicles, including MRAPs, blocking both I-75 and I-85 southbound directions. They had lots of folks handcuffed and standing in a holding pen off to the side. Apparently, the feds are using the airport as a staging area, and don't want civilians to see it and figure out what's really happening. Now that I think about it, that makes perfect sense; it's the most logical place to operate from.

I'm really sorry that I put us in danger going this way. My curiosity nearly killed the cat."

The 166 wound its way through residential areas and light industrial tracts. The road was a wide four lane boulevard that would eventually narrow into a two lane route as it got farther from Atlanta proper. Where the road narrowed, houses came right up to it, with driveways connecting directly to it. At these houses, the ones they could easily see from the road as they drove by, they started to see a difference.

In many of these driveways, a car or truck sat at the edge of the road, preventing anyone from pulling in. At others, they witnessed people frantically loading their most treasured belongings into a car or truck in what looked for all the world to be a hasty escape. But even with that, the feel to the air was far less tense out here than in the city.

Christy leaned forward and looked at Daniel. "I have to pee."

Bob looked over at her. "Hold it."

She slumped back into her seat, her arms crossed over her chest. Daniel looked at her in the mirror, then he asked Bob. "How far away are we?"

"If it stays like this, twenty minutes."

Daniel looked back at Christy. "Twenty minutes, babe. Can you wait?"

Dismissively, she replied. "Fine."

"There's a toilet in the back," Gene said.

Christy shook her head. "No thanks. I'll wait."

Daniel smiled to himself. He remembered the first time she used the small stool in the van. It hadn't helped that he'd laughed at her until he couldn't breathe. They'd been up in the mountains of north Georgia camping for the weekend. In the middle of the night Christy had to use the bathroom. He told her she could just go outside because they weren't in a campground, or she could use the toilet in the van. She chose the one in the van.

The bathroom on the van is in what is essentially a very small closet. He never did get the full story from her about exactly what happened in there. But when she came out with her pants around her ankles and the blue toilet chemicals covering her from nearly the waist down, he burst into laughter. She was already crying, and him laughing only made it worse. But he couldn't help himself. He couldn't for the life of him understand how something like that could even happen. He'd used it many times. He knew how it worked. It was a simple device. And yet, somehow, Christy had managed to not only make the thing malfunction, but at the same time cover herself in that blue chemical agent. He knew that for her, that was an absolute last resort.

As they approached County Line Rd, Daniel had to slow down. The Dollar Store was being looted. People were streaming in and out of the shattered doors in a surprisingly orderly manner. Across the street, sat a Chevron station, and on the other side of County Line was a Shell. Both of these stores had armed men in the parking lot. But unlike the ones they passed in Atlanta, these men weren't waving people into the parking lots. They seemed more intent on keeping people out.

It seemed that the crowd was more interested in gutting the Dollar Store than the van. It was quite the contrary actually. Some people, upon coming out of the store and seeing the van slowly rolling by quickly ducked back in. It made Daniel smile. He was upset when he first saw what Gene had done to the van. But now, seeing how people reacted to it, he was glad he had, and it made him feel a little like a character out of a Mad Max flick.

As is all too common and seems only to confuse, the road they were driving changed names, not only the road name, but even the route number. It was now Campbellton Rd, route 154.

Daniel looked at Bob. "Are we on the same road? The name and highway number changed."

Bob lit a cigarette and snapped his Zippo closed. Blowing out a cloud of smoke, he asked, "Have you turned?"

Daniel shrugged. "No. Just wanted to make sure we were going the right way."

Bob nodded. "Just keep driving."

Christy was waving the smoke away from her face. "Do you have to smoke in here?"

Bob laughed and replied. "Yes, I do. The balcony is closed." Getting a chuckle out of Gene.

Teague crawled forward, obviously annoying Christy. "Hey, Bob. Can I have a smoke?"

Bob looked at him sideways. Taking the pack out, he shook a smoke from it and offered it to Teague. "Don't make a habit of it."

Teague clenched the cigarette in his teeth and smiled. "I won't." As he moved back to the rear of the van, he paused and looked at Christy. "Don't worry. I'll blow it out the back window."

She didn't reply, and he made his way to his spot by the rear doors. He enjoyed his smoke as he looked out through the expanded metal covering the window holes. The air swirling around him felt cool as he watched the trees rush by. As they were now even further from Atlanta, the landscape was becoming more inviting to a boy from Michigan. The large hardwoods grew right up to the edge of the road and the grass was still thick, though it wouldn't be for much longer.

At route 70, Cascade Palmetto Highway, Bob told Daniel to make a left. They hadn't passed many cars. It seemed people out here just weren't moving around. It was as if they were the only ones on the road. A housing development appeared on the left. It was occupied by large homes with a fake sense of wealth. While they were large two-story structures, they sat on small lots and were of mediocre construction. Stucco over OSB, cheap at best.

But it was someone's dream, many someone's from the size of the place. As they approached the entrance of Legacy something-or-other, they were closely scrutinized by a number of men manning a makeshift roadblock. They carried an assortment of weapons and watched the van closely as it rumbled past them.

"Looks like people out here are a little worried too," Daniel said.

"It's only a matter of time before the people in the cities are forced to leave. That's what those guys are waiting on." Bob replied.

But they didn't make it far before the road was completely blocked. Daniel slowed the van as the line of trucks and construction vehicles came into view. It was yet another large pre-planned housing development with a name to instill confidence, pride and possibly a little envy, Legacy at Palmetto Farms. This was kind of laughable when you considered the absurdity of someone farming palmettos.

The men at this roadblock were pretty serious. They'd commandeered construction equipment from the areas still under construction and moved it out onto the road, completely blocking it. They were all fairly well armed, with a number of ARs and AKs visible. Someone with some tactical experience was obviously overseeing the operations, as there were men placed on both sides of the road and there were two pickups turned into technicals with mounted men, possibly as chase vehicles or maybe as a quick reaction force.

A man stepped out from the roadblock and raised his hand, motioning for Daniel to stop. Daniel slowed the van as he muttered. "Oh shit."

Teague's head appeared between Bob and Daniel. "What sort of bullshit is this?"

Bob sat up. "I don't know. Get your ass to the back of the bus and keep your eyes open."

"What should I do?" Daniel asked.

"I suggest you slow down," Bob said.

Daniel slowed the van as they approached the man in the road. As he slowed, several other men came around the barricade to join the first one in the road. Daniel put both the front windows down as the armed man walked up to his side of the van and another approached Bob's side.

The man on Daniel's side was a big guy. He wore an olive drab plate carrier with several magazine pouches and a pistol in a drop-leg holster. With his bald head and ear rings, he was an intimidating sight. The man looked the van over as he approached, then looked at Daniel.

"Where are you going?" He asked.

Before Daniel could reply, Teague shouted. "None of your damn business!"

Bob turned in his seat. "You need to shut the hell up."

"Fuck him. Who's he to stop us and ask where we're going? It's none of his damn business." Teague shot back.

The bald man leaned in to look in the van. "Is there a problem in here?"

Gene spun around in his seat to face Teague. "Look kid, I like you." Gene paused and racked the shotgun in his lap. "But before I let you talk us into a gun fight, I'll cut you in half. Understand? Just keep your mouth shut. There's a time to fight and a time to talk. You need to figure those two out. You feelin' what I'm sayin'?"

Teague studied him briefly. Gene sat patiently, tapping his finger on the side of the shotgun. After a moment, Teague nodded. "Got it."

Gene looked back over Daniel's shoulder. "No problem here, bud."

Bob leaned forward. "We're heading to my house. I live over off North Cut Lane."

The bald man looked the van over again. With a nod at the windshield he asked, "What's with all this?"

Bob jabbed a finger over his shoulder. "Old Gene back there did that. We were in the Buckhead business district. It was rough. Good thing he did it too because there were a couple of times people were throwing shit at us."

"What's it like up there?"

"It's nuts. You don't want to go there," Daniel said.

"Riots?" The man asked.

"Oh yeah. We watched the Feds raid one of the protester encampments. They just executed people, right in the street. You want to stay away from the Feds, man. They're bad news," Daniel said.

The man reached into his plate carrier and pulled out

a small leather case. He held it up to show a badge. It was a shield with an eagle, and above it, Department of Justice. On the shield was a large US with Drug Enforcement Agency arching over the top of it. Daniel registered what he was seeing and swallowed hard.

The man looked at the badge, then at Daniel. "I am the Feds. And you're right. You want to stay as far from them as you can."

Trying not to give away the fact he was about to shit himself, Daniel nodded. "Yeah."

"Is the power on out here?" Bob asked.

"It comes and goes. What about in Atlanta?" The bald man asked.

"it went off yesterday. We were in a bank building and running on the generator. But fuel was getting low and the riots were getting worse. There was a lot of shooting between the cops and the people. We had to get out." Pointing to Christy, "we went to her apartment, but it was already looted. We decided it was a bad idea to try and go to anyone's place in town. Since I live out here far from town, I figured this would be the safest place for now."

The man nodded. "You got ID that verifies you live out here?"

Bob nodded as he reached for his wallet. "Sure."

Taking the ID, the man examined it briefly and handed it back. With a nod of his head, he said, "There's another road block up the road there. I'll radio them and let them know you're coming through. We're just trying to protect our homes is all."

Gene scooted forward. "Have you heard about Texas?"

The man shook his head. "No, what's up out there?"

"They told the Feds to stuff their martial law up their ass. They severed the power grid where it left the state and have mobilized the Texas National Guard to protect the state. The commander of Fort Hood even placed the base under the control of the Governor."

The man nodded, obviously thinking. "Interesting. How'd you hear that?"

"HAM radio. You guys have any here?" Gene asked.

He shook his head. "No. Wish we did."

Gene smiled. "No kill switch on those."

The man took an iPhone from a pouch on his vest. "Yeah. I remember when they came up with all that shit. They told us it was to prevent terrorism and to fight drug traffickers. We figured it was all BS."

As the man was talking, the phone suddenly began to emit the emergency alert tone, as did everyone's in the van. As they went for their phones, the man said, "It's a text. Says there's going to be an address by the Secretary of Homeland Security today at five."

Daniel leaned out the open window, and the man turned the phone so he could see it. "Looks like the phones are one-way now," Daniel said.

"What do you want to bet the power comes back on sometime before five?" Bob asked.

The man nodded and said, "I bet you're right. You guys go ahead." He turned and waved to the men behind him, and one of them climbed up onto a Case front-end loader that sat in the middle of the barricade and backed it out of the way, allowing them to pass.

Bob waved at the man. "Thanks. You guys take care of yourselves."

The man nodded. "We are. You do the same."

"That was scary," Christy said.

Bob snorted. "It could have gone a lot worse."

Gene smiled and looked at Teague. "You did good. I know you're young and think you're ten feet tall and bulletproof, and that your pecker is bigger than everyone else's. Hell, maybe it is. But you need to learn there's a time to fight and a time to listen. When you're running your face hole like you were, you leave nothing to the imagination of those you're talking to. They already know you're a problem, and they are then more likely to deal with it quickly. If you're quiet and just listening, they don't know what to think." Gene tapped his head with his finger. "Use it for more than just a hat rack."

Teague seemed to take the advice to heart, much to Gene's surprise. "I need to learn to think before I start running my mouth. Thanks for keeping me in line. I promise, it won't happen again."

Gene sat back and slapped his knees. "Then you and me will get on fine, just fine." He lifted the Mossberg and added. "And I won't have to shoot your ass with this thing."

Teague laughed. "I appreciate that, Gene. Really and truly."

The rest of the drive to Bob's went without issue. At the turnoff to North Cut Lane, they stopped for the two tractors blocking the way. Bob quickly waved at the two men and greeted them.

"Hey, Bill, Dale. How's it going?"

Dale stepped up to the van, cradling an AK. He looked in and surveyed the people inside. "I see you've got some refugees."

Annoyed, Christy shot back. "We're not refugees."

Bob ignored her comment. "Glad to see you guys out here. We've passed a couple other roadblocks, people doing the same thing."

Dale shrugged. "We gotta look out for our homes." He looked at the van and added. "Going all Mad Max?"

"We took precautions to get out of town."

"How was the trip out of Atlanta?" Dale asked.

Bob lit a smoke before answering. "It was rough, but not as bad as it could have been. Have you seen any trouble out here?"

Dale slowly shook his head and replied in a thick, slow southern drawl. "Naw. Ain't no trouble out here. Just being careful is all."

Bob nodded. "That's good. Is the power on?"

Dale shrugged. "Comes and goes. But your generator is running. We moved a couple fridges into your garage so we didn't lose all our food."

"No problem. Glad it was there for you." Bob wagged a finger at Dale. "I told you it would come in handy."

Dale dropped his head. "I know. You was right and I was wrong."

"It's alright, old buddy. Just glad we have it. At least as long as the natural gas keeps flowing."

Dale nodded. "When that runs out, I won't be able to cook anymore."

Bob laughed. "When the gas runs out, we'll have a lot more to worry about, old friend." Dale nodded and Bob added. "We're going to the house. I need to rest and maybe get a shower."

Dale slapped the side of the van. "Glad to see you made it out of Atlanta. Good to have you home, ole buddy."

Bob waved and guided Daniel to his house. The driveway cut through a stand of trees and curved towards the house. It wasn't visible from the road. The house was a simple wood-framed affair with several outbuildings. It was just the kind of thing you'd expect to find in the Georgia countryside. Where the driveway turned into the parking area at the house, sat a garden plot, long ago gone fallow.

Gene grunted. "Didn't figure you for the gardener type."

Bob looked at the small patch of ground where he'd had great aspirations. But like many would-be gardeners, it just didn't work out. "Yeah. Well, as you can see, I'm not. I tried it for a bit, just looking for a way to get out of the house, something to help lower the blood pressure. But work kept me too busy."

Daniel pulled up in front of a two-car garage door and shut the van off. He dropped his head to the steering wheel and let out a long breath. Bob got out of the van and stretched. He pointed at the house and said, "It ain't much, but me casa is your casa."

Teague climbed out of the van and stretched as well. Everyone was stiff and tired. Not that it was a long ride, but the tension of it all had left them weary. And this was only a thirty-odd-mile trip. If they were going to Texas, they'd spend days in the van.

Christy rolled out of the van and found Daniel on the driver's side. She wrapped him up in a hug, burying her face in his neck. He pulled her tight and buried his face in her hair. He was glad to have her, and was coming more and more to the realization just how much he needed her.

She pulled away from him. With a squint, she said, "I really have to pee!" He couldn't help but smile as she trotted towards the house with her knees locked together.

Bob and Gene were already in the house. Teague came around to the front of the van and reached in, grabbing Bob's carton of smokes off the dash. Taking a pack, he shook out a smoke and lit it up and leaned against the fender.

After taking a long drag, he looked at Daniel. "You really think that old fucker would've shot me?"

Daniel leaned against the fender beside him. Taking the cigarette from Teague, he took a quick drag and handed it back. Blowing out the smoke, he said, "You know, I think he would have. Old Gene doesn't seem to have much of a sense of humor."

"Yeah. That's what I thought."

Taking the cigarette again, Daniel said, "You really do need to calm down. I think he's right. There's a time for confrontation, but it isn't every time."

Teague nodded. "I know. Things will be different from now on. This shit is for keeps. There is no re-spawn."

Daniel smiled and slapped Teague on the back. "No, there's not. Come on. Let's go inside and check out the house."

The two men walked into the house. Bob's place was much like his office, at least in places. In the living room sat a recliner with an end table beside it. The table was covered with old newspapers and overflowing ashtrays. Ashes covered the floor around the chair and the table. Numerous coffee cups sat atop the papers and filled every inch not occupied by ashtrays.

The rest of the house stood in stark contrast to the

recliner. It was neat and orderly. The kitchen was orderly, not a dish in the sink. The exception was the coffee pot. It looked like Bob's coffee pot at work. Grounds were spilled on the counter around it. The burner, black from spilled coffee and the pot itself looked like some sort of science experiment, but not to Bob. He referred to it as *seasoning*. The rest of the house was furnished in the trappings of a country home. Simple, functional and comfortable. These things stood in contrast to Bob.

Christy came out of the bathroom and found Bob at the coffee pot in the kitchen. "Is there enough for me to have a cup?"

As he poured a cup, he looked over his shoulder. "Sure. How do you like it?"

"Black is fine." She replied and looked around the kitchen. "This isn't what I'd expect for your house."

Bob smiled. "Yeah. Doesn't fit the mold, does it? This was to be my escape. I wanted out of the city, something totally different. I was hoping to retire here and spend my days gardening, of all things." He laughed at himself.

Christy took her cup and held it to her mouth, smelling the thick elixir. "It's never too late to reinvent yourself." She looked around for a moment and asked, "There's no wife?"

Bob laughed as he swirled his coffee. "No. Some men just aren't meant to be domesticated. Guess I'm one of them. Oh, I tried. But I poured myself into my work. It's a fault I guess. But it's just what I am." He smiled.

Christy took a sip of her coffee. Looking over the top of the cup, she said, "At least you're living your life. On your terms."

Bob thought about that for a moment. "I guess that's true." He looked at her. "But it sure is lonely."

Christy perked up, almost bouncing. "Well, you're not alone anymore. You have us!"

Bob laughed, doubling over. Straightening up, he said, "Yeah. I've got Gene's weird ass. Crazy cousin and Daniel, who I just can't put my finger on."

Christy rocked back and forth. "There's me too."

Bob smiled. "Indeed there is. You're a beautiful young woman. Thankfully, I'm not a creeper and see you more as a daughter than a conquest."

Surprising Bob, Christy leaned in and hugged him. "Well, I like having you around. There's something about you that gives me confidence."

Bob looked down at the ground. After a moment, he looked up. "Christy. You're a sweet girl. But trust me, I am the last man you should put your trust in. There's a number of people that will attest to that."

Christy leaned and kissed him on the cheek. "You may have given up on yourself. But I haven't."

With her cup in hand, she exited the kitchen, leaving Bob to think about what she'd said. It had been a long time since anyone, outside of work, put their faith in him. It made him uncomfortable. He knew he'd let so many people down in the past. And yet, something about her words filled him with confidence.

Bob came out to the living room to find everyone there. He looked at the people he'd committed his future with. "The house is fully backed up by the generator. The water comes from a well. So you can take a shower if you want. So long as the natural gas holds out, the house will have power."

Christy spun around to face Bob. "In that case, I'm taking a shower!"

Daniel stepped over to her and put his hands on her hips. "Mind if I join you?"

Christy smiled a seductive smile. "I guess you do need to get cleaned up. If you're up to it."

"Oh, I'm *UP* to it." he replied.

Christy glanced down and smiled. "I guess you are, big boy!" Everyone got a good laugh out of that as she took him by the hand and led him down the hall to the bathroom.

As they left the living room, Bob said, "Have her home by midnight!" Daniel looked over his shoulder and smiled at Bob, who saluted him with a coffee cup.

CHAPTER 8

AFTER SHOWERING, AND SPENDING SOME quality time with Christy, Daniel was sitting on Bob's back porch. It was quiet. And, unlike Atlanta, there was no gunfire or smoke hanging in the air. From here, you would never know anything was going on. Bob came out onto the porch and handed Daniel a cup of coffee, then took a seat beside him.

Looking around, Bob asked, "Where's Christy?"

Daniel sipped the coffee. "She's asleep. I guess today was a little stressful on her. She's out of it."

Bob put his feet up on the handrail that surrounded the porch. "I know the feeling. I'm just glad to be out of Atlanta."

With a snort, Daniel replied. "No shit." He looked around at the quiet scene surrounding him. "You can't even tell anything is wrong out here."

"That's why I moved out here. After my last divorce, I wanted out of the rat race. The ex was all about image, and we had to have a big house and expensive cars. When we separated, I went the opposite direction. I wanted less."

With a sideways smile, Daniel asked, "How much did she take you for?"

Bob choked on his coffee so hard it came out of his

nose. He was laughing as he wiped his chin. "Not a dime! Like I said, my *last* divorce. I was educated this time. There was a pre-nup. Oh, she was pissed when we had to sell that big house. The only thing she got to keep was her car. Everything else was liquidated and we split it all up the middle. I didn't care if I got anything. I just didn't' want her to have any of it."

Gene joined Bob and Daniel on the porch with his own cup in hand. Shortly after, Teague came out too, carrying a small AM/FM radio. He extended the antenna and placed it on the handrail.

"There's supposed to be that broadcast any minute. Thought it would be interesting to hear what they have to say."

Bob leaned forward and grabbed the radio, setting in on a local station, and placed it back on the rail. The radio was for the moment still dead, nothing coming from its speakers until the feds wanted to use the airwaves to broadcast their propaganda. "Let's see what they have to say."

It wasn't long before the radio screeched with a carrier wave, then the emergency alert tone began to sound. After going through the series of tones, a computerized voice told them to stand by for an official announcement from the Secretary of Homeland Security.

"Here we go," Teague said.

This broadcast will serve as official notice of the conditions of Martial Law. Ignorance is no excuse to violate the rules. Due to the rising level of violence in major cities, and the local authorities' inability to control the situation, I have authorized the deployment of US troops to quell the violence.

With this in mind, any member of the armed forces that deserts their post will be arrested. Any members of the armed forces attempting to desert, may be shot. Desertions will be handled swiftly and harshly. To that end, I have requested assistance from the UN Security Council to provide additional peacekeepers to augment our forces.

In an effort to quell the violence, lethal force has been authorized for looters, groups of more than three people that refuse to disperse, and anyone found armed. The dusk-to-dawn curfew remains in effect, and any vehicle caught moving at night will be fired on.

We understand people need to move about to fulfill their daily needs. But it is imperative that you take these warnings seriously. There will be no other warnings. This is the only warning that will be issued. Additionally, the transmission from amateur radios, also known as HAM radios, is now, and until further notice, prohibited. These devices are being used to arrange riots and mass lootings, and we cannot allow that to continue. If you are caught with a radio, you will be arrested. A registry of licensed operators is being reviewed and everyone on that list will be contacted. You are hereby ordered to dismantle all antennas and render all radios inoperative.

There will be zero tolerance in dealing with illegal radio transmissions. Anyone caught with one will be detained under articles of NDAA, and can be held indefinitely.

With that, the radio went dead. The four men stared at it, waiting for more. But nothing further was said.

"What the hell?" Daniel asked.

"Is that all?" Teague asked.

Bob picked up the radio and turned it off. "I guess so."

"They're scared. Notice how she didn't mention anything about Texas? And they're trying to keep people from using radios. They're definitely scared," Gene said.

"There's a lot she didn't mention. All she said was we're going to start killing people," Teague said.

"We've already seen that," Daniel said.

Bob lit a smoke. "What bothers me more than anything is what she said about military members. I think they're having a hard time getting them to tow the line."

"Makes sense," Gene said. "That's why they're bringing in UN troops."

Teague was shaking his head. "Do they have any idea the kind of shit storm this is going to start?"

"They didn't mention anything at all about what caused all this. Nothing. Just told us they were going to start shooting soldiers and civilians alike. It's like they're not even trying to fix things anymore," Daniel said.

"Oh, they're fixing things, all right," Teague replied. "They're just working on a different problem. Us."

"Well, then what are we going to do?" Daniel asked.

Bob quickly stood up. "I say we eat. Who's hungry?"

"Stellar idea!" Gene said.

"What are we having?" Teague asked.

Bob rubbed his chin. "I was thinking I'd force-thaw some steaks. Maybe have some baked potatoes and broccoli. How's that sound?"

Teague clapped his hands. "Hell yeah!"

Bob turned to the house with Gene in tow, leaving Teague and Daniel on the porch. The two sat quietly for a moment, then Daniel asked, "You really wanting to go to Texas?"

Teague leaned back, rocking his chair off the floor. "I do. I think this is just the beginning. And I really don't think it's got shit to do with the banks."

"What do you think it's about then?"

Teague looked at him, stone faced. "A fundamental transformation of the nation."

Daniel shook his head. "That was Obama. This is Clinton."

With a sneer, Teague replied. "And she's worse than he ever was. While there was a lot he wanted to do, he was somehow restrained. Maybe out of fear, maybe because the timing wasn't right, but Clinton, she's not so restrained. She and her husband are a couple of Arkansas hustlers, and they have a body count the Marine Corps envies. She's going to get even."

Daniel was shaking his head. "I know you conspiracy-theory guys always think the government is out to get you, but to what end? They already have power and money. What's the aim of this kind of thing?"

Teague snorted. "Have you been asleep? Living in a cave or something? I know you like to go hike in the woods, but you have to have seen some of the news in the world. The goal is the same as it's always been. Sure, they have money and power, but they want more. More is the goal. These people see themselves as elites and the rest of us as commoners. They want to reinstall the royal ruling class who are above the law. Above reproach."

Again, Daniel shook his head. "I don't know. I don't buy it."

Teague shrugged. "What's it going to take? What do you need to see to make you believe?"

Bob came out the back door carrying a large platter. He set it on the table and pulled the cover off a gas grill sitting against the rail. In a moment, he had the grill lit and heating up.

"Those are some damn good-looking steaks," Daniel said. Then he looked around. "Where's Gene?"

Bob was scrubbing the grill when he replied. "He's out at the van getting his radio. He's pretty spun up about the whole ban on HAM."

"That was kind of strange," Daniel said.

"Why?" Teague asked. "It's the only form of communications they can't control. There's no off switch, no kill switch. HAM radio isn't like the internet or cellphones."

"Can't they just jam the signal?"

Bob dropped a steak onto the grill with a hiss as the meat seared against the hot metal. "It's not that easy. It's a big country and they can't jam it all. There just isn't the equipment to do it. So they can only do small areas, maybe regional."

"But they can hear what's going on and tell where it's coming from can't they?" Daniel asked.

Gene came out onto the porch with a plastic tub full of radio gear and deposited it on the floor. "Sure, they can listen and they can even get an idea where it's coming from. But there's only so much of that equipment around, though it is easy to make."

Bob looked up from the grill. "Hey, cousin. Run in the kitchen and grab those beers from the fridge."

Teague leapt to his feet. "Hot damn! Why didn't you say you had beer?"

Stabbing a steak and turning it over, Bob replied. "Because I wanted them for dinner!"

Daniel hopped up. "I'm going to wake up Christy. I'm sure she's hungry."

After a meal that belied the reality of the situation, the group sat on Bob's back porch watching the sky go from blue to orange.

Christy took a long drink of her beer, then asked, "Now what?"

Bob lit a smoke and threw his feet back up on the rail. "Now, I say we get a good night's sleep and worry about tomorrow, tomorrow."

"That works for me." Teague replied as he opened another beer.

With some effort, Gene rose from his chair. "Well, I'm going to set up the radio and see what's going on."

Daniel looked over at Christy. "I don't know about you, but I'm ready for bed."

Christy smiled. "Me too. I say we call it a night."

Teague snorted. "Yeah, like that's what you two are going to do."

Christy stood up and Daniel wrapped an arm around her waist. He smiled at Teague. "What else would we do?" He asked with a smile.

Teague snorted and took a pull off his beer as they went in the house. He knew what they were up to, just wished he had someone around too. Bob had sat silently through the exchange. After a moment, he looked over at Teague and asked, "You need some hand lotion or something?"

Teague stood up. "Fuck you, Bob." And he stomped off the porch.

Bob chuckled as he flipped the ash off his smoke and reached for the last beer. He was happy to be home and felt relaxed. Gene went out into the yard where Bob had a flag pole. He lowered Bob's flag and took a moment to fold it before carrying it back to the porch and placing it on the rail.

"Turning my flag pole into an antenna?" Bob asked.

Gene nodded. "Yeah, I'm going to run two wires up and stake them out to the side. Not perfect, but it should work well enough."

Gene went out and connected the splitter to the rope with a heavy rubber band and pulled it up. He then pulled the two ends of the antenna out and staked them into the ground using a couple of wood stakes he made from fallen limbs in the yard. He then ran the center point of the antenna back to the porch where the radio sat and connected it to the antenna tuner.

Once the antenna was connected, Gene pulled a chair up to the small plastic table and sat down. After a few minutes to configure the radio, voices began to appear out of the ether.

"Guess those old HAMs don't much give a shit about the ban on transmitting," Bob said.

Gene was focused on the radio. "Nope. The Feds can kiss my ass. Who the hell do they think they are to tell us we can't use radios. The bastards already killed all the other forms of communication. They're just pissed they can't turn this one off."

Flipping a butt off the porch, a bad habit, but it was his place, Bob said, "Yeah. You'd think during their little broadcasts they'd give out useful info. Maybe places to get food or water, medical care. Something that would help people. But all they do is issue threats."

"Government is violence, my friend. That's the only thing they know. Anyone or anything that doesn't go with the program will be dealt with violently."

Bob grunted. "They do have a monopoly on murder."

Gene looked at him. "No. But they want one. They're afraid when they don't have total control. And right now, they're really afraid."

Gene slowly went through the bands. Whenever he heard someone, he'd pause for a moment and listen. Most of what they heard was the same. People were talking about the location of things like food and fuel. It seemed everyone was looking for these two things. There was also a lot of talk about cash, or the lack of it.

Gene listened for a while to a group talking about the lack of currency. These guys were pissed that they had so much money in the bank and couldn't access it. They were indignant about the fact the government had the nerve to prevent them from accessing their money. After listening to the exchange, Gene chuckled and picked up his mic.

Keying the mic, he said, "That's because when you put money in the bank it no longer belongs to you. It belongs to the bank." Gene laughed as he released the PTT.

An operator on the other end jumped in immediately. "Bullshit, it does! It's my money! I earned it, and they have no right to take it from me!"

Laughing, Gene said, "If it's yours, go get it. Do you see what I mean?"

There was a long pause, then came a reply in a solemn voice. "It's not right. It's just not right."

Gene keyed his mic. "Didn't say it was right, just the way it is. Some of us have been saying this for years. They told us what they were going to do each and every time. But nothing happened. I hate to say it, but we allowed this to happen."

Bob looked over at Gene. "Little harsh there, Gene."

Gene dropped the mic. "Reality is a mother, Bob."

Bob sat there for a moment, then lit another smoke. "I guess you're right. We were just too docile as a nation. Look at what the Greeks did when their banks started screwing around. They took to the streets. They let the politicians know they were pissed."

"That's nothing. Look at what Iceland did in '09. They actually put some bankers in jail. You know, I've thought a lot about how these people see us, and the best analogy I could come up with is bees."

Bob was confused. "Bees? How so?"

Gene leaned back in his chair. "Well, beekeepers keep their bees in a hive. They make sure they have a place to live, and in the winter months, they even feed them. But the only reason they're there is to produce honey, which the beekeeper then harvests. The bees work hard to produce honey, only to have someone come take it. We are much the same, except the harvest we're producing is cash. We work hard to produce money and the bankers come along and take it. It's the same thing."

Bob mulled that over. The more he thought about it, the more he realized Gene was right. Humans all over the planet, no matter the nation, were simply being farmed for cash. After a bit, Bob said, "You know, Gene, I've never thought about it that way. But you're absolutely correct. That's exactly what they're doing to us."

Gene nodded. "It sucks when the realization comes to you. But it's the truth."

Bob shook his head. "Then why this?" He asked, waving his hands over his head. "Why all this shit that's happening now? I mean, they can't be making money off this situation."

Gene nodded his head. "What do you think the beekeeper does with a hive that's not producing? Or one that gets invaded by some parasite?" Bob shrugged, so Gene continued. "They burn it. Especially the ones that get invaded by parasites. They burn the whole hive. If a hive becomes unproductive, they may add brood or a new queen. But an unproductive hive isn't left to its own devices."

Not feeling too good about where this line of thought was going, Bob replied. "I see what you mean."

***

Christy lay wrapped in Daniel's arms. Her body was moist with sweat and their skin stuck together. But Daniel didn't care. It was worth it, for both of them. He ran his hand through her hair and thought back to a conversation they'd had several months ago. She was pestering him about *where their relationship was going.* He'd done his best to deflect the subject at the time. But now, when it seemed everything was falling apart, it was clear to him what mattered most. And he had it in his arms.

"I love you," he said quietly.

Christy didn't reply. He felt her move ever so slightly in his arms. Burying his face in her hair, he kissed the back of her head. After a moment she said, "So it takes the end of the world to get you to say it?"

He smiled with more than a little shame. "No. It's not that. It's just, I realize what's important now."

She rolled over to face him. The sheet slipping down to expose her bare shoulder and breast. "And what is important? What we just did, or me?"

Daniel looked at her for a moment. "You're what's important to me. More than anything." Smiling, he added. "Of course, what we just did is a fine bonus."

Christy studied his face for a moment. "Do you really mean it? Or is this just some passing thing, and when the lights come back on, we'll go back to the way it was."

Daniel ran his hand over her face. "No. This is for real. I'm all in. For now, and forever."

Christy moved in and kissed him, deeply. He replied in kind as she pulled the sheet over their heads. Looks like she wasn't quite ready to sleep just yet.

***

Teague sat on the porch. While he didn't have a watch, he knew it was late. A high pressure front had moved in and the skies were clear and the half-moon was bright. The radio sat quietly on the table, Bob and Gene having gone to bed. Off in the distance, he heard a coyote call, to be answered by several others. Some things never change, things that aren't dependent on technology or the modern world. Listening to the yaps and yips of the excited dogs made Teague think. He needed to be like the coyote. They all need to.

The coyote worked in a group. They chose their fights

and avoided the ones they couldn't win. They scavenged as a practice, but would fight to kill when necessary. And they mainly came out at night. Teague nodded his head. *Be the coyote,* he thought. If they were going to Texas, and he for one really wanted to, they would need to be more like the coyote. Looking at the rail, he saw Bob's smokes sitting there and snatched the pack up. He never was much of one to smoke, but enjoyed the occasional cigarette. Shaking one out, he lit it up. Inhaling deeply, he sat back with a sense of satisfaction.

***

Bob was dreaming of bacon and black coffee. He smiled as his eyes opened. It wasn't a dream. He could certainly smell bacon and coffee. Sitting up, he scratched his head. And as is the habit of a lifelong chain smoker, he started to cough. Once the fit passed, he quickly lit a smoke as he headed to the bathroom, scratching his ass as he went. After taking a long and very satisfying piss, he dressed and headed for the kitchen.

Coming into the kitchen, he was greeted by Daniel. "Morning, Bob. Hope you don't mind us taking liberties with your kitchen."

Bob smiled. "Not at all. Been a long time since I've had a beauty in the kitchen."

Christy smiled. "Thanks, Bob."

Bob bounced his eyebrows. "I was referring to Daniel."

Daniel gave him the finger as he slid an omelet out of a pan onto a plate. Christy laughed. "That's just mean, Bob." She looked at Daniel and added. "He's all man. Trust me on that."

"Take a seat, Bob. I'll have you a plate in just a second," Daniel said.

Gene came shuffling into the kitchen as well and fell into a chair. "Any chance I could get a cup of that coffee I smell?"

"Sure thing," Christy said as she poured two cups and carried them over to the table.

Picking up his cup, Bob asked, "How'd you guys sleep?"

"I'm a Navy man. When I sleep, I sleep." Gene replied.

Looking at Daniel, Christy replied. "We slept *really* well, thank you."

Bob nodded and sipped his coffee. Daniel set a plate with an omelet, bacon and toast in front of him. Bob smiled. "That looks fantastic. I didn't know you were a cook."

Returning to the stove, Daniel replied. "Actually, I'm not bad at all. I'm better on the trail though. I like cooking over an open fire."

"He's a great cook." Christy added.

Once Teague showed up, everyone was there. Over a hearty breakfast, they discussed their options. The choices were to stay at Bob's, as it was far enough from the city the group felt they would be safe. Or, head for Texas. Both had their uncertainties.

"But we know what's here. I mean, kind of," Christy said.

Bob nodded as he mopped his plate with a piece of toast. "That's true to a degree. It seems safe enough here at the moment. But we have no idea what's coming or how long this thing will last."

Teague rocked back in his chair. "I can tell you this isn't a short term deal. We saw the military on the streets already. We saw what they did to that camp. I say we head to Texas. It just seems safer."

"I'm with cousin on this one," Gene said. "The government has blockaded all communications. They don't want us to use HAM radio. They've instituted a curfew. To paraphrase Winston Churchill, this isn't the end, but it could be the end of the beginning. What I mean is, I think this is just getting started."

"It's a long way to Texas. How would we even do it? We've looked at the maps. We'd have to stay off the interstate and that would add time and miles to the trip. It just seems that there's a shit ton of risk," Daniel said.

Bob lit a smoke and blew a cloud out over the table. Christy scrunched her nose and waved the smoke away. Bob smiled. "Sorry, sweetheart, my house." She didn't say anything but was clearly annoyed. Bob continued. "It is a risk, a huge risk, really. But if the authorities in Texas are bucking the Feds, I think that's a better place to be. Sitting here, we'll run out of food pretty soon. I would imagine that eventually they'll turn off the gas, and that means no generator. So we'll be sitting around here in the dark with no food, no water, and possibly no way out because we waited too long."

Daniel dropped a crust of toast onto his plate. "I agree there are risks with both choices. I just think we need more information. I'm really worried about the drive and getting stuck, or losing the van. I mean, there are bound to be desperate people on the road, and that van will be very tempting."

"There are ways to deal with that," Teague said.

"Like what?" Daniel shot back.

Teague's chair banged onto the floor. "I was up late last night, sitting on the porch. I heard a pack of coyotes and started thinking about them. We need to be more like the coyote."

Daniel was shaking his head. "What the hell does that mean?"

"Well, the coyote lives in a pack. It works for the benefit of the pack. They scavenge as a way of life, which we would need to do as well. They choose their fights and only take on the ones they think they can win and avoid the ones they know they can't. And most importantly, they work primarily at night, which we would also have to do."

Nodding his head, Bob started to laugh. Pointing his smoke at Teague, he said, "You know, cousin, I think I may have underestimated you." He looked around the table. "I think he's right. If we're going to make a run to Texas, this is exactly how we need to do it."

Daniel protested. "But moving at night will be dangerous. We won't be able to see much and everyone will be able to see our headlights. We may as well play music through a loud speaker."

Raising a finger, Gene said, "There are things we can do to mitigate some of that."

"Like what?" Daniel asked.

Gene looked at Bob. "You got a laptop around here?"

Bob nodded. "Of course."

"Good. Then I can fix it so you can drive the van in the dark with no lights on." Gene replied.

"How in the hell are you going to do that?" Daniel asked.

Gene smiled, the ends of his mustache turning up. "Leave that to me."

Bob stubbed his cigarette out on his plate. "I think," he said with a pause, "we need to listen to the radio today." He nodded at Gene and continued, "Let MacGyver here work on the van. We'll go through the house here and see what we should take with us. That way, we'll have a little more info on what's going on and we'll be better prepared if we decide to leave."

Christy cleared her throat. "I think Bob is right. I think we need to be ready to move, but we should get as much info as we can."

"But if Gene is going to be working on the van, who's going to man the radio?" Daniel asked.

"I will." Teague replied. "I know how to use it."

Smiling, Bob said, "I had a feeling you did."

Daniel was thinking about the discussion. After a moment, he spoke. "I think Gene's little project is a good idea. But it's probably best if we move during the day. At night, the government has tools to see in the dark too. We'll be the only thing moving, and that will draw attention. If we move during the day, we'll just blend in with everyone else."

Bob nodded. "You're probably right. But the ability to travel at night if necessary will be a good resource."

Christy stood up. "I'll start going through the kitchen to see what food we can take with us." She looked around the table. "And since I," she caught herself and looked at Daniel, "we, fixed breakfast, you guys can clean it up." She picked up her plate and laid it in the sink before turning her attention to the pantry.

Bob looked at Teague. "Looks like you're on KP."

Teague snorted. "My ass. Looks like *we* are. You wash. I'll dry."

Bob resigned himself to his fate and joined Teague at the sink. Daniel went to help Christy as they began a thorough inventory of Bob's kitchen. Gene disappeared to the garage, a space he felt more comfortable in. He was always more comfortable around tools, machines and the inorganic than he was with people.

Once the dishes were done, Teague and Bob headed to the porch and turned on the radio. Bob lit a smoke and Teague pulled the pack he'd pinched off the rail the night before and lit one for himself. Bob looked at him and asked, "Where did you get those?"

Taking a drag, Teague replied. "You left them on the porch last night." Smiling, he added. "It's a scavenger's world now."

Bob grunted. "Maybe, but don't you be scavenging in my stash."

Teague laughed. "Don't leave them lying around."

They scanned the bands looking for voices. When they found one, Teague would pause to listen. They were hearing conversations from people in the southeast region. Most were the same. *How is it where you are? Here's what's going on around us.* They were able to glean some info from these conversations. Mainly, that the closer you were to an urban area, the worse your situation was. The farther from the city centers you were, the better you faired. But that depended on how well prepared you were.

They listened as one man bragged about how much food he had. He crowed about being able to survive without leaving his house for years. When the other end of the conversation told him maybe he shouldn't be saying that over the radio, the man laughed.

I've got enough guns and ammo here to stop anyone! The man practically shouted back. *Besides, no one knows where I am.*

The other side of the conversation came back with a reply. *Maybe not. But I know you're on a heading of 271 degrees from me. Anyone can track your signal.*

That was the end of the conversation. The other man never came back on the radio. Maybe he realized he was vulnerable and had said too much. Maybe he knew the other man was right and someone could find him.

Teague snorted. "He's a dumbass. Anyone could find him with the right antenna."

Bob cocked his head to the side. "How?"

"It's not that hard. You just make a directional antenna, hold it close to your body and turn in a circle. You'll be able to tell when the signal gets stronger. Then you just move in that direction."

Bob flicked the ash from his cigarette. "Huh. Didn't know that."

They continued to go through the frequencies, looking for more conversations. Meanwhile, Daniel and Christy wrapped up their inventory of the kitchen and came out onto the porch. Christy fell into a chair beside Bob and folded her arms over her chest.

Perturbed, she asked, "How do you live in a house with so little food?"

"And eat that crap?" Daniel added.

Bob laughed and shrugged. "It's just me and I don't need much."

"Kind of fond of sardines aren't you?" Daniel asked.

Smiling, Bob said, "They're easy and I like 'em."

"Well, I think we have all the sardines we'll need," Christy said.

Bob wagged his eyebrows. "I do, anyway."

Gene came out on the porch, wiping his hands on a rag. "Hey, Bob. Can I get that laptop?"

Rising to his feet, Bob replied. "Sure thing, Gene." And he headed into the house with Gene following.

Daniel looked at Teague. "What'd you hear on the radio?"

Teague told them what they'd heard, making sure to impress on them the information they'd gleaned about what it was like in the cities and how important it was to stay away from large population centers. The three discussed their options. Christy wanted to wait a while. Teague wanted to leave right away. Daniel was on the fence. He wasn't sure what to do.

Teague ran his hands through his hair. "Yeah. Well, we have to make a decision soon."

"Why?" Daniel asked. "What's the hurry? We're safe here. We've got food, water and even power. There's no trouble out here. What's the rush?"

Teague didn't have an immediate response. "I guess we really don't. But I would like to get on the road."

Daniel leaned forward and rubbed his face. "I just wish we had some damn information! The worst thing is the not knowing what's going on."

"I feel the same way. I just wish we knew what was happening around the country," Christy said.

Bob appeared in the door and said, "Hey guys, you gotta check this out."

They followed Bob through the house and out into the garage. It was dark with the big door closed. But there was light coming from inside the van. Gene was sitting in the driver's seat with the laptop on the dash in front of him. As they got closer, it became clear what was on the screen. It was an image of the wall in front of the van. There was a bright, nearly washed-out circle on the screen. But the tool bench that ran along the wall was clearly visible.

"What the hell is that?" Daniel asked.

Gene stepped out of the van and walked around to the front. "Look at the screen." Everyone moved around until they could see the screen. "Before we left the bank, I loaded a few things into the van. While this wasn't what I was thinking at the time, it's a perfect use for the camera and infrared light I took." Pointing at the top of the van, he said, "I mounted the camera and the light on the front of that rack up there. Using the monitor, we can drive this thing in the dark."

Teague clapped his hands. "That's genius!"

Daniel pushed his way towards the driver's seat. "Let me see what it's like." He climbed in and settled behind the wheel, as if he were driving. The view on the screen was good, though there was only a short distance to the wall in front of him. "I'd like to see what it's like outside."

Gene nodded. "Already thought of that. We'll try it after dark tonight. Take it for a spin and see how it works."

Daniel adjusted himself in the seat and pretended to be driving. "The angle is a little strange. It just doesn't feel normal to be looking to the right like this. But I think it will work."

"We'll find out after dark tonight," Bob said as Daniel got out of the van.

After Gene turned everything off, the group went back out onto the porch. They spent the rest of the day listening to the radio. Gene was a master at manipulating the controls and was able to find far more conversations than Teague. Using Gene's considerable skill, they were able to gather quite a bit more intel.

Gene stopped on one conversation that caught his ear, so they could listen for a while.

…completely shut down.

The whole city? How the hell do you close off a city the size of Birmingham?

With lots of tanks and machineguns. That's how. You don't dare get caught out after the curfew.

Are they shooting people?

Are they shooting people? It sounds like the Thunder Run into Baghdad!

Holy shit.

I'm serious. I've heard tank main-gun rounds being fired. They ain't playing. Plus, you can hear Strykers and Bradleys working in the city. But you know what the really weird thing is?

What's that?

There are signs directing people to aid centers in the city. I mean, they're bringing people into the city and there's all kinds of shooting going on.

Damn, how far out of town are you?

I live in Forestdale, on the northeast side. But we made a trip towards the city, during the day of course. I'm not about to be out after the curfew. That's when you hear most of the shooting.

I hear there's lots of strange stuff going on at the airports. You seen anything strange over there?

The airport is on the other side of town. No way I'm going over there. But we have seen a lot of aircraft, military stuff.

If there's a curfew, how was you out driving around?

They don't seem to bother with you during the day. Of course there are checkpoints on the highway. You don't want to get caught with a gun. But, other than that, they let you go where you need to. I guess they figure some folks still need to work.

Good talking to you. I'm getting off here before someone kicks my door in. Stay safe out there, bud.

You too, friend.

Gene looked over at Bob. "Well, that's interesting. Sounds like we need to stay away from the interstate and large cities."

"Any town. I say anything with more than one traffic signal, we go around," Teague said.

Bob flipped the ash from his ever-present cigarette. "Sounds like we need to travel during the day on secondary roads and try to avoid checkpoints. Stay away from any towns. And if it comes to it, we can travel at night as well."

Daniel stood up and leaned against the rail. "If they're not messing with you during the day, we should give that a shot. With the curfew in place, any movement at night will get us in trouble."

Teague rocked his chair back. "So, we're rolling up to a roadblock with a truckload of guns. That will end badly for everyone, because they aren't taking me anywhere."

"We need to make sure that doesn't happen." Daniel replied.

"So, it's settled then? We're heading to Texas?" Bob asked.

The group shared looks around. It was Gene who spoke first. "I've got nothing else to do. Let's go."

Bob looked at Daniel. After all, it was his van. Finally, Daniel nodded. "I guess so." Looking at the group, he asked, "Leave in the morning?"

Teague jumped up. "Hell yeah, guys! Let's go to Texas!"

The rest of the evening was spent ensuring the van was packed with everything they would possibly need. Gene spent time going through Bob's collection of tools. He wanted to take it all, but space was at a premium, so he was restricted to a small bag and what it could hold. Not that the additional tools were even needed; he'd already pinched tools from the bank before they left.

Daniel and Christy were adding the food from the kitchen to the van, trying to find room for it all. Christy pulled a short cardboard box out from under one of the seats. Holding up a jar full of a dark, thick liquid, she asked, "What the hell is in these?"

Daniel took the jar and placed it back in the box. "Oh, that's something Gene made up, just in case."

"Just in case of what?"

Daniel shrugged. "Whatever. It's napalm."

"Napalm! What could we possibly need that for?"

"Never know when you might need to burn something."

Christy looked at the box. "How did you make it?"

Daniel smiled like a kid recounting some forbidden chemistry experiment. "It was the coolest thing. We took Styrofoam cups and added them one at a time to the jars. They were about half full of gas and we kept dropping the cups in until they wouldn't dissolve anymore. It's really thick and sticky and even when it's burning, it will stick to stuff. It's really cool."

"Is it safe having it in the van?"

"Oh sure. I mean, as long as there's no flame around it."

Christy shook her head. "Oh, that makes me feel better."

Teague and Bob went through Bob's guns. Bob lamented having to leave them. But with the guns from the bank there was no sense in taking them all. Bob did add two though. A Ruger 10-22 and a beautiful brand new Ruger Mark IV Hunter pistol. They reasoned if they needed to hunt, the combination that used the same ammo could come in handy. Ammo, cleaning kits and spare parts were loaded into the van. They added a few other things as well, like a spotting scope, binoculars and a tripod.

Gene also took the time to go over the van. He checked all the fluids and even greased the undercarriage. And he checked all the tires and added a tire plug kit and small 12-volt compressor he'd found when rummaging around in the garage. He also added a couple jugs of motor oil, power steering fluid and anti-freeze to the van, stuffing the jugs into any small space he could find. A couple of rolls of duct tape and electrical tape finished his preparations. As he was wrapping things up, the smell of cooking meat caught his nose, and he wandered out to the back porch.

Bob was at the grill, cigarette in his teeth, a beer in

one hand and a BBQ fork in the other. "Thought we'd have another steak before we hit the road," he said as Gene came out.

Gene plucked a beer from a small tin tub full of ice sitting on the table. It was the last eighteen-pack from the garage. No sense wasting it. "Sounds good to me. I think the van is as ready as I can make it."

Daniel looked up. "What do you mean? There's nothing wrong with the van."

Taking a tug on his beer, Gene smiled. "No, there's not. And now I know there isn't."

Christy came out the door with a large bowl in her hands and set it on the table. "I made a salad, sort of. Bob, you really should eat more vegetables."

Bob snorted. "Lions and tigers don't eat vegetables. Vegetables are what my food eats!"

Taking a beer for herself, Christy replied. "Lions and tigers don't have high blood pressure or cholesterol. You should take better care of yourself."

"Christy, my dear. None of us gets out of this thing we call life alive. We're all going to die. I'd rather die with a belly full of meat than kale."

Gene saluted the statement with his beer. "Amen, brother!"

When the steaks were done, Bob piled them on a plate and set them on the table. Then he disappeared into the house. He came back out with an atlas in hand and sat down. He laid the map book on the table and opened it.

"Let's get the first part of our route planned out here," he said.

Teague took a plate and stabbed a steak with a fork. "You do that. I'm going to eat."

Without looking up, Bob said, "You should let the steak rest."

Teague snorted. "It can rest in my gut." And he sat down to get to work. "I gotta say one thing, Bob. You have fine taste in meat. These ribeyes are awesome."

The group, except for Teague who was too busy eating, gathered around the atlas. Several options were discussed as they traced the red lines on the page.

"We need to stay away from heavily traveled roads. The smaller, the better. No interstates for sure. Here's what I'm thinking." Bob traced his finger over the map. "We'll take 154 here down to highway 29. A couple of miles down is a power line right-of-way. I've ridden it before on ATVs. It will take us over here to twenty-seven, south of Whitesburg. Then we'll go up towards Georgia five and head west."

As Bob was talking, his cell phone began to issue the emergency alert tone. It had become the norm to have at least one cell phone available in case the government issued any statements. The phone issued the undulating tone while vibrating on the table. Bob picked it up, anxiously awaiting to learn about whatever new shit the government was planning to lay on the public.

After a moment of reading, he shook his head. "Listen to this shit. Due to the rising levels of violence and unrest in some of the major cities, the Department of Homeland Security issues the following statement. As the private ownership and possession of firearms is now outlawed, we are stepping up the program. If You See Something, Say Something. If you see anyone with a firearm, of any type, text 99999 with the information on the individual breaking the law.

"This also applies to illegal radio transmitters. If you know of someone using such a device, text 99999 with the whereabouts of the equipment and the individual. For participating in the preservation of law and order, you will be rewarded with cash and commodities. These unlawful acts are adding to the violence and must be stopped. Only by working together can we return our cities to a peaceful state"

Teague pointed across the table with his fork. "Now they want us to rat on each other. And for what? Some money?"

"What did they mean by commodities?" Christy asked.

Bob dropped the phone onto the table. "I would assume that means food, maybe fuel. Who knows. But it shows they know people can't get what they need on a daily basis and they're using it as a tool to clamp down."

Christy shook her head. "Clamp down on what? The people looting the cities? Then, good."

Daniel ran his palms cross the table. "Babe, we're the ones they're talking about here. We have guns and a radio. We're the people they want turned in."

"But we haven't done anything wrong."

Gene ran a comb through his mustache. "This isn't about right or wrong. This is about control. I worked for the government long enough to know that the number one thing they want to protect is their power."

Stuffing a piece of steak in his mouth, Teague said, "This doesn't change shit for us as I see it. We still need to hit the road and try to get to Texas, where there is some sanity."

"Indeed," Bob said. "But we'll need to keep all the guns out of sight."

"The radio too." Gene added.

"I'll keep my gun out of sight, but close. If I need it, I want to have it handy," Teague said.

The conversation died down while everyone ate their steaks. The trip weighed on each of them as the night wore on. Christy and Daniel turned in early, looking to spend some quiet time before they hit the road in the morning.

CHAPTER 9

Bob woke up early and sat on the edge of his bed in the glow of his alarm clock. It was 5:35 as he shook a cigarette out and lit it. Rising to his feet, his knees popped loudly and he flinched. Shaking his head, he stretched and walked to the bathroom on stiff legs. After his morning constitutionals, he came back out scratching his crotch.

Wandering around his bedroom, he picked through the clothes draped on the footboard of the bed, giving each a once-over and the all-important smell test. Finally, deciding on the least funky of the lot, he got dressed and headed for the kitchen. As he went down the hall, he could swear he smelled coffee. He was surprised when he rounded the corner and saw Teague sitting at the table, drinking a cup.

"I thought I was the first one up," Bob said as he took a cup from the cabinet and topped it off.

"I'm always up early when there's shit to do."

Pulling out a chair, Bob sat down at the table. "Well, there's plenty to do."

The only sound in the kitchen was the ticking of a clock over the microwave. The two men sat quietly for a moment before Teague spoke.

"You think we'll make it?"

Bob sat back in his chair. "Hell if I know. But we're about to find out."

At precisely six o'clock, Gene came into the kitchen. "Morning, fellers," He said as he poured himself a cup and pulled out another chair. "We ready to start this goat rope?"

"As ready as we're going to be, I guess." Bob replied.

"I guess I'll go wake up Romeo and Juliette. I want to get started as soon as we can," Teague said as he stood up.

He went back to the room Daniel and Christy were using. He quietly opened the door and crept into the room. It was dark, but the sky outside was beginning to lighten and filter through the blinds. He slinked up beside Daniel and knelt down, mere inches from his face. Smiling, he reached out and ran his hand through Daniel's hair. When the sleeping man didn't move, he ran his hand over his face, caressing it lightly.

Daniel smiled and, in the fog of sleep, said, "Morning, babe."

Teague was trying not to laugh, a tough task. He reached out and patted Daniel on the ass. Daniel smiled again. "Mmmm, you ready? It's early."

Stifling a laugh, in the deepest voice he could muster, Teague said, "Yeah, baby. I'm ready."

Daniel's eyes flew open as Christy shot upright in the bed. Her hair was a mess and in her face. She was brushing it away as Daniel bolted up in the bed. "What the fuck, man! What are you doing in here?"

"Wakey, wakey," Teague said as he stood up.

Christy looked at Teague. "What are you doing?"

Teague smiled. "Nice tits, Christy."

She looked down to see her bare chest and quickly pulled the sheet up. "Screw you, Teague. Get out of here!"

Daniel swung his feet out of the bed and stood up, pushing Teague towards the door. "Get out of here, asshole." Then he thought for a moment. "Did you grab my ass?"

By now, Teague was laughing. "Oh yeah. I grabbed it. Be glad that's all I grabbed."

Daniel shoved him out the door and slammed it shut. Christy shook her head. "What the hell is wrong with him?"

Daniel gave a slight chuckle. "That's nothing. You should have seen us when we were younger."

After dressing and grabbing a bag with the little they were taking with them, Christy and Daniel went out to the kitchen. Gene was at the stove cooking up some eggs, sausage and bacon. In the oven was a pan of biscuits.

"Wow, it smells awesome in here!" Christy said.

Bob snuffed out a cigarette on a plate on the table. Christy wrinkled her nose at it. "I figured we should eat as much of what I have as we possibly can before we go."

Gene looked over his shoulder. "Have a seat. It will be ready soon."

The coffee pot, now on its second brew, sat on the table. Both Christy and Daniel poured themselves a cup and waited on the food. Daniel looked across the table at Teague.

"Don't' do that shit again."

With mock indignation, Teague asked, "Whatever are you talking about?"

Holding his cup to his mouth, Daniel replied, "Whatever. Don't do it again."

Teague laughed and looked at Christy. She glared back.

Being not a complete fool, Teague kept his mouth shut. It wasn't long before Gene was setting plates on the table mounded with bacon, sausage and scrambled eggs.

Christy scooped up a spoon of the eggs and dumped them on her plate. "Gene, how did you get these so fluffy? I've never seen eggs like this before."

The ends of Gene's mustache rose up. "Learned to cook in the Navy. If there is one thing the Navy does right, it's cook."

There was little talk as they ate, each left to their own thoughts on the trip they were about to embark upon. When everyone was done, Christy rose to her feet and said she'd do the dishes.

Bob waved her off. "Leave them." He looked around the kitchen. "I have a feeling I'll never see this place again."

Christy looked at him for a moment as she thought it over. Sitting back down and picking up the last piece of bacon on the plate, she said, "I guess you're right. We're either going to make it to Texas, or we're not. But either way, we're probably not coming back here."

It was time to leave. There was nothing left to do. But the small group milled about the house, looking for any reason, real or imagined, not to leave. Except for Gene. He paced the driveway, checking his watch often. After nearly forty-five minutes, Gene started the van and walked back into the house.

Opening the door, he shouted. "The van's running! Let's go!"

Daniel and Christy shouldered their small packs and headed for the van. Bob waited for Teague to leave and made one last round through his house. He wasn't a sentimental man by any means, but he did feel a slight tug at the thought of leaving and never coming back to it. It was home. He'd had others, but this was the place he had decided to spend the rest of his life. It was a physical manifestation of his life's work. It represented everything he'd achieved, despite the efforts of two ex-wives.

The generator still hummed away outside, providing all important power that brought life to home. Bob didn't bother to turn off lights as he left, leaving everything as it was. Opening the door of the van, he took one last look before getting in.

"You alright?" Christy asked.

Slamming the door shut, Bob replied. "Yep. Let's go to Texas."

Daniel pulled out the drive and headed down the road. Where North Cut Lane hit the Palmetto Highway, Bob's neighbor was there once again. He and another man were keeping an eye on the intersection, as they put it. Daniel rolled up beside Dale and stopped.

Bob stuck his hand out the gun port. "Been good knowing you, Dale."

Dale shook it and asked, "Where you headed?"

"Texas."

With a look of surprise, Dale asked, "What in the hell for?"

"Things sound a little better over there, so we're going."

"Good luck with that. I think you are nuttier'an squirrel shit though."

Bob smiled and handed Dale a key. "Here's the key to my place. It's open right now. Help yourself to anything there. I don't plan on coming back. The generator is still running right now. Don't know how long it will hold out though."

Dale looked at the key. "I appreciate it, really do. We'll take care of your place for you. It'll be here for you."

Bob smiled. "One way or another, I'm not coming back here."

Dale stuck his hand in the window and smiled. "Well, I hope y'all make it to Texas."

Bob shook his hand and smiled back. "Me too, Dale. Me too."

Bob looked at Daniel and nodded, and he pulled out onto Hwy 70 and headed south, and then turning off onto Hwy 154 that melded into Hwy 29. It was smooth sailing until they reached the small town of Palmetto. As they approached Main Street, the road was blocked by several large trucks and armed men. Daniel looked at Bob. "What do we do?"

"Just slow down and do whatever they say." Bob then swiveled in his seat and pointed at Teague. "And you better keep your shit together. No shooting. Got it?"

Teague nodded. "Got it."

As they approached the barricade, a large man in camouflage stepped out. He was cradling an AR-type rifle in the crook of one arm and holding the other up in a *stop* gesture. Daniel slowed to a stop and the man approached the van. Others, behind the barricade kept rifle barrels trained on them.

In a thick southern drawl, the man asked, "What's yer business?" He was wearing a hunting pattern, and had what could only be a very large wad of chewing tobacco stretching his right cheek.

Bob leaned forward. Pointing, he replied. "We're just headed south on Roosevelt."

"Where to?" The man asked.

Bob shrugged. "Does it really matter? We're not looking to stop here. We just need to get by."

The man swapped the tobacco to the other side of his mouth as he leaned forward and looked into the van. He then inspected the modifications Gene had made and asked, "What's all this about?"

"We were in Atlanta. It was hell there. We did this so we could get out."

The man nodded. "I damn sure wouldn't want to be in Atlanta right now. We've heard there's all kinds of craziness going on there."

Bob huffed. "You have no idea, friend."

The man produced a small radio from a pocket. One of those FRMS types you get at Wal-Mart. Keying it, he said, "Let 'em through. Billy, you got a big van coming your way."

Ten four. Came the reply.

The man stepped back. "Y'all go on. Just don't stop nowhere."

Daniel nodded. "Thanks. We won't."

Bob waved, and the man nodded back at him as Daniel pulled forward and made the right onto Main Street. The men at the roadblock eyed them as they passed. Looking to their left, they saw several people milling about the Bojangles' and Subway shops. But it was obvious that the power was off in the whole town.

They passed a few people on the way out of town. They seemed to congregate in the business areas, where fast food joints and other such enterprises were located. People would stop in their tracks or pause their conversations to watch the van go by, not that a moving car was an anomaly. They passed several. Maybe it was just the look of thing.

Just past Tommy Lee Cook Road, Bob told Daniel to slow down. The power line right-of-way was just ahead and Daniel pulled off the paved road onto the dirt two track that ran through it. It was obviously well used by the locals.

Holding onto the *oh shit handle* on the passenger side as the van bounced down the dirt road, Bob said, "This thing is thirteen miles long."

Daniel nodded as he focused on the road ahead. The route was intersected by other roads crossing it. The occasional ditch required them to slow and cross it. As they passed a small pond, two young boys there fishing waved at them. Coming to an area that was an obvious track for off roaders, they saw several motorbikes and four wheelers racing around the track.

Bob shook his head. "Wasting gas. They'll regret that soon enough."

Christy leaned forward to see. "Looks like fun."

Further down the road, Bob laughed and pointed. "Check that shit out!"

Daniel looked over to see a decent-sized airplane sitting on the right-of-way. "How in the hell did they get that thing in here?"

Bob looked up at the power lines. "I have no idea. Must be one hell of a pilot."

Slowly creeping over a section of the route that appeared to be terraced, possibly for planting, Bob pointed to the right side. "See that little road?" Daniel nodded. "We have to get off here. There's a little creek up ahead that we can't cross in this."

Daniel took the small road and followed Bob's directions as he guided them through the small back roads, eventually bringing them back onto the track under the power lines. For the short leg to highway sixteen. It was clear sailing to the highway just ahead.

"Bob? Bob, do you see them?" Daniel asked in a shaky voice.

Christy immediately poked her head between the front seats. "What? What is it?"

Bob started bringing his rifle up with one hand and palmed Christy's face with the other, pushing her back. "If you want to help, you better get a gun. Just keep going, Daniel." As he brought his carbine to his shoulder, he shouted. "Teague, you have permission to shoot anyone who comes up behind us."

"Copy!" Teague shouted as he poked his carbine through the rear window of the van.

Gene picked up the shotgun and racked a shell into it. Casually looking up, he asked, "What seems to be the trouble, Bob?"

"Bunch of guys on ATVs, Gene. And they've all got guns."

Ahead of them was nearly a dozen or so men hanging out around a large bon fire. They were sitting on their machines drinking beer from the looks of it. All of them, even the motorcycles had either a rack or a scabbard to hold a long gun. While this wasn't anything unusual in the rural south, the fact they were all wearing a balaclava type mask with a skull print on it was. Just as those in the city that were bent on violence, a mask is the calling card of men with ill intentions.

The group suddenly noticed the van and immediately sprang to their machines. Gene picked up a carbine and tapped Christy on the shoulder. "You know how to use this?" He asked. She shook her head, indicating she didn't. He laid the rifle on the floor and pulled a Glock 17 pistol from the duffle bag that all of Bob's guns had been piled into. "Know how to use this?"

Christy nodded affirmatively and snatched the pistol from him. "Yes, I do." She dropped the mag from the weapon. Seeing it was loaded, she quickly reinserted it and racked the slide. She looked at Gene and replied. "Daniel taught me."

Gene nodded and had to grab onto the table to steady himself. "This ain't no game, Christy. You may have to use it. If you do, make it count." Christy nodded.

"Speed up," Bob said. Then he added, "Don't stop for anything."

The ATVs quickly split into three groups. One ran down the side of the right-of-way as though they were getting the hell out of Dodge. The other two headed straight for them. Two of the four-wheelers had two men onboard. The rear passengers stood up and raised shotguns. There was a thunderous explosion in the van as the windshield shattered and glass flew around the interior.

It was only the first shot from Bob's rifle, the first of many. The van was bouncing, as were the ATVs. The shots had the desired effect of causing the machines to take evasive actions. They were quickly closing on the road. Pavement would be their ally. Allowing the big diesel engine to put all that horsepower to work.

"Which way, Bob?" Daniel shouted.

"Right!" Bob shouted, pausing his firing just long enough to answer.

The carbine firing in the van was deafening. The thunderous explosions inside the enclosed cab were tremendous. But it got even louder when Teague began to fire from the back. Gene looked back to see the machines that at first appeared to be fleeing now coming up behind them. He stuck a finger in his ear and shook his head.

Digging into his bulging shirt pocket, he pulled out a set of foam earplugs on a plastic cord. Rolling them between his fingers, he stuffed them into his ears. As the foam expanded and sealed out the incredible racket around him, he smiled. He was ready now.

Pulling the box out from under the seat, he took one of the glass jars out. Using his pocket knife, he stabbed a hole into the top and stuffed a piece of a t-shirt he'd cut into strips and put with the jars. He repeated the process two more times. With the three jars in hand, he tapped Christy and motioned for her to move. She pressed herself to the side of the van and he scooted past her.

Teague was still shooting, but the machines pursuing them had split up and were now shooting back. Once he was beside Teague, he told him what he wanted to do. Teague looked at him like he was insane. "What?"

"Just grab the rope handle." He replied, pointing to the loop of rope he'd attached beside each of the rear doors.

Teague grabbed the rope and looked at Gene. "You sure you can hit it?"

Teague smiled and sprayed the cloth with a can of bar-b-que lighter fluid. "You just throw it!" With that, he handed one of the jars to Teague. Then he flipped open a Zippo lighter and lit the cloth. The size of the flame scared Teague as he tried to keep it away from him.

Gene sat on the floor of van and pressed against the wall to the side of the left door. He reached up and threw both doors open. A four-wheeler was rushing towards them since Teague had stopped firing. When the door came open, Teague immediately hurled the jar out the door like a baseball. Gene already had shouldered the 870 and brought the front bead up and pulled the trigger.

Teague's throw was almost directly at the machine racing up to them not thirty feet away. When Gene fired, not only did the shot shatter the jar and send the flaming napalm all over the riders, it killed the driver. The ATV cartwheeled wildly throwing both men off like flaming missiles. While the driver was killed, his passenger was not. Teague watched, transfixed as the man hit the ground tumbling in a flaming ball. He got to his feet and pawed at the flames.

Seeing their comrades die such a terrible death only enraged the others, and they raced even faster towards the van as it skidded onto the paved road. Daniel swerved wildly to avoid two cars sitting in the traffic lanes. And while he missed them, he couldn't avoid the body of a naked woman and bounced over her. If Teague hadn't been holding onto the rope handle, he would have launched from the van. As it was, Gene had to help pull him back inside as incoming rounds pinged off the thin metal body.

A rider on a motorcycle came racing up alongside.

He had some kind of cheap Tec 9-looking pistol he was firing wildly. As he came up beside them, Daniel saw him in the mirror and swerved into him. With only one hand on the handlebars, he wasn't able to avoid the collision and suddenly found himself pressed against the side of the van, dropping his weapon. Christy was looking out the side window when the black mask with the skull suddenly banged into the expanded metal. The man's eyes were wide and wild. She raised the Glock and began to fire, sending not only bullets, but broken glass and shards of metal from the protective screen into the side of his head. He and the bike crashed into the pavement, the bike ending up on top of him as he skidded down the asphalt.

Now that they were on the paved road, the ride became smoother. Teague went back to work with his carbine and managed to knock down another rider. Gene lit the other two jars and threw them out the back door. They shattered on the road in a thick cloud of black smoke. An ATV trailing them ran through it, leaving a rolling vortex in the smoke. But the rider didn't know it wasn't just gas. This stuff stuck.

The machine came out the other side of the burning mess with all four wheels on fire. He looked down at the wheels to see only flaming masses as globs of it flew up and onto him. He skidded to a stop and bailed off the machine, ripping his clothes off. But the rest of the group had had enough. They stopped to aid him, although they kept firing at the van as the fire engulfed the machine.

Gene leaned out and pulled the rear door shut. Bob was turned in his seat, looking back and shouting. "Is everyone alright? Is anyone hurt?"

Christy was stunned. She sat still, looking out the window, one arm braced against the door. Gene and Teague both answered with a thumbs up. Bob grabbed Christy's shoulder and shook her. "Are you ok? Are you alright?"

She looked at him and nodded. Then she saw blood on his hand. She stared at it for a moment before coming to her senses. "Bob! You're bleeding!"

Daniel looked over. "What?"

Bob looked at his hand. "It's my leg. I need something, a rag or something."

Christy looked around trying to find something. Then she snatched up her purse and dumped it on the floor of the van. She was looking for that pad she knew was in there somewhere. Grabbing the Kotex pad, she tore it from the wrapper and handed it to Bob. "Put this on it! Where is it? Is it bleeding a lot?"

Bob took the pad and looked down. He didn't like what he saw. His lap was very bloody, but it didn't hurt that bad. And thankfully the pain was in his legs and not in his crotch. He took the pad and pressed it onto his thigh. Daniel slowed, saying. "We need to stop!"

Bob shook his head and pointed out the shattered windshield. "No, drive! Keep going!"

Daniel kept looking at Bob until he admonished him and told him that if he wrecked the van they'd all be in trouble. Christy, likewise was very concerned and came up between the seats to try and help. But Bob wasn't in the mood for help.

"Christy, I'm fine for now. There's nothing we can do in here. When we get up to Whitesburg shortly, we'll stop and check it out. I'm fine right now though," Bob said, finishing with the thought, *I hope.*

Daniel was pushing the van as they screamed across the Chattahoochee River. As Whitesburg came into view, Daniel's heart sank. "Oh, shit."

Bob looked up as they approached the town. "It's alright." He looked back at Christy and Gene. "See if you can find something white we can hang out the window."

"How do you know these people are alright?" Daniel asked, his eyes darting back and forth between Bob and the approaching roadblock on the outskirts of the small hamlet.

Christy handed Bob a white t-shirt and he looked at Daniel. "Easy. They're not wearing masks. And some of them are in uniform."

Then Daniel noticed it too, and it struck him. When he saw the men on the ATVs, what had scared him the most was the fact they were all wearing the mask. It added an immediate air of uncertainty to them. The people just ahead of them now wore no masks. Bob pushed the shirt out the gun port and held onto it.

"Just slow down and ease up to them," he said, as the men manning the barricade moved to take cover behind the dump truck blocking the road.

Daniel did as he said and let the van roll very slowly forward as Bob tried to wag the shirt hanging out the side. When they were within shouting range, one of the men in uniform yelled for them to stop. Daniel did as ordered.

Grabbing the door handle, Bob said, "Here's goes nothing."

Before he could open the door, Daniel shouted at him. "What the hell are you doing?"

Bob opened the door. "Well, I can't lean out and talk to them." And he swung the door open and stepped out, t-shirt in hand. Holding the shirt up, he called out. "Is there a doctor? I need help!"

The man in uniform shouted back. "Tell everyone to get out!"

"Oh shit." Daniel muttered.

Bob looked back and jerked his head. "Come on, everyone out. Leave the guns in the truck."

"This is bullshit, Bob!" Teague called back.

"Just get out!"

The group did as ordered, and stepped out, Daniel and Christy both holding their hands up. Gene walked up beside Bob and folded his arms over his chest. Teague, not wanting to get far from his rifle, stayed at the back of the van. Once everyone was out, three men came out from behind the truck, weapons shouldered and began to advance towards them.

As they came close enough, one of them called out. "What happened to you?"

Bob looked down at his blood-covered pants and called back. "We had some trouble on the other side of the river."

"Where you coming from?"

"Atlanta."

The man questioning them exchanged words with his companions, then looked back over his shoulder. "Jason! Bring your bag and come out here!"

A young man came trotting out of the Dollar Store parking lot on the side of the road. A fire truck sat there with a couple of police cars. After conferring with the man giving orders, the group began to approach the van.

"Everyone just stay where we can see you!"

The young man with the bag came up to Bob and asked, "What happened?"

Bob shrugged. "Bunch of guys on ATVs came after us. I guess it's a bullet."

Jason looked back at the uniformed man, who nodded. Taking Bob by the arm, he said, "Sit down. Let's have a look."

Christy stepped forward. "I'm a nurse. Let me help."

Jason nodded, and she came up to help Bob get to the ground. The tension seemed to ease a bit and the uniformed man came closer, lowering his weapon to a low ready. He looked at Daniel. "You say it was guys on ATVs?"

With his hands still up, Daniel nodded and replied. "Yeah. There was a bunch of them."

"We've been having trouble with them too."

Teague came up to the front of the van. "Well, there's fewer of them now."

The uniformed man looked up, surprised. "You take some of them out?"

Teague nodded. "A few."

The uniformed man now slung his rifle. "Good. We saw the smoke and could hear the shooting. They've been ambushing people on the road."

The body of the woman flashed back into Daniel's mind. "We saw. There was a naked woman lying in the road. She was dead." At least, he really hoped she was before he ran her over. She was surely dead now though.

"Who are they?" Teague asked.

The man shrugged. "Hell if I know. Could be the damn high school football team for all we know."

Jutting his chin towards the man, Teague asked, "Who are you?"

"Chief of Police, Amos Southerland."

Daniel relaxed and lowered his hands. "Thanks for the help." He looked at Bob. "We were really worried about him."

Christy looked up and smiled. "It's not bad. A bullet grazed the top of his thigh."

A bullet had come in through the door of the truck and cut a diagonal path from Bob's hip to three inches above his knee. It was a nasty looking wound, but certainly not fatal if managed to prevent infection.

"Looks bad," Daniel said.

Bob looked up at him. "Thanks, buddy."

Jason, a paramedic with the volunteer fire department didn't look up from his work bandaging the wound. "It's not bad. Might be a little uncomfortable for a while, but you'll live. You're lucky. If that round had hit your pelvis, you'd probably already be dead. Or at least wish you were."

"You're a cheerful bunch." Bob replied, grimacing as Jason worked.

"What's your plan?" The Chief asked.

"We're headed to Texas. They still have power and have told the Feds to pound sand," Teague said.

Daniel didn't like him saying so much. Not that what they were doing was a secret, but to the wrong people it could create a problem. Fortunately, from the Chief's response, it wasn't an issue.

Chief Southerland snorted and spat at the ground. "Screw the Feds. This is all their mess anyhow. And then they go and shut off the power too."

"I think this is just the tip of the iceberg," Bob said.

The Chief looked at him. "I think you're right. I think it's going to get a whole lot worse before it even starts to get better. What's your plan now?"

Bob looked around, then at the van. His seat and the floor around it was covered in blood. "I'd like to clean that thing up before we leave."

"You should stay here for the night," Jason said. "You need to give this wound dressing and medication some time to set up, otherwise you'll be bleeding all the time."

"He's right," Christy said.

Bob ran a hand through his hair. "I'd like to get back on the road. We have a long way to go and only just got started."

"Another day won't hurt, Bob," Daniel said. Then he looked at the Chief. "We'd like to stay the night if that's alright with you."

Southerland nodded. "I don't mind a bit. Not sure where you'll stay though."

"We can stay in the van," Daniel said. "It's a camper and I also have a tent."

Jason finished bandaging Bob and stood up. "Drive down to the fire department. There's a grassy spot around back you guys could use."

Southerland nodded. "That's a good idea. You'll be close so Jason can keep an eye on that leg, and check it again before you head out."

The group got back in the van and followed Jason's directions to the fire station just down the road. Whitesburg was a small town, so the fire department and police utilized the same property. Daniel drove the van around behind the station and parked it under the shade of a pecan tree. Since it was a Sportsmobile, and set up to camp, it had an awning. Gene helped Daniel pull it out. A couple of camp chairs were pulled out, and they set up home for the night.

As Daniel was setting up, Christy went to find Jason. She caught up with him inside the fire station restocking the bag he'd used to treat Bob. He looked up as she came through the open bay door and smiled. "Hi."

She smiled back. "Hey." She pointed at his bag. "Restocking?"

He nodded as he dropped some bandages into the bag. "Yeah."

"That's what I wanted to talk to you about. You saw what I used for a bandage."

Jason smiled. "Good idea, really. Never thought of it."

"It's all I had. I was hoping I could get some stuff from you so I could take care of his wounds."

The corners of his mouth pulled down and he turned to face her. "I'd like to, but we don't keep that much here."

Christy's shoulders slumped. "Oh. Well, I'll figure something out."

Jason looked off and wagged a finger. "I have an idea. The Dollar Store sells stuff like that."

"I don't have much cash."

He shook his head. "Oh, you couldn't buy it anyway. Southerland closed the store. But if you talk to him, he'll probably let you get some stuff. But do it before I talk to him, because I'm going to clean the place out now that I've thought of it."

"He's back up at the roadblock, right?"

"Yeah. Hey, I'm going back if you want a ride. You can

get what you need, help me get the rest, and then I'll bring you back."

Christy smiled. "That would be great. Let me go tell Daniel where I'm going."

Jason nodded and said, "Just meet me at the truck."

Christy left to go tell Daniel. When he heard, he leaned in and kissed her. "That's why I love you. You're so smart. I would have never thought of that."

She smiled back. "Will you still love me if I tell you it wasn't my idea? It was that paramedic's. He's going to give me a ride back after we clean all the medical stuff out."

Daniel smiled and pulled her in. "I'd still love you, no matter what." And he kissed her.

She left to go find Jason and Daniel pulled a chair up and sat down. "What's going on?" Bob asked.

Daniel threw his feet up on a cooler they had packed to bring as much of Bob's remaining food as they could. "She's going to get some bandages and stuff to take care of your leg."

Bob nodded. "She's a smart girl."

Daniel smiled in agreement. "Yes she is."

Gene sat slumped in a chair. "What's for dinner? I'm hungry."

Bob looked at him and chuckled. "Gene, my old friend. You're going to have to get used to being hungry."

"Not tonight." Gene replied.

And they wouldn't tonight. Daniel went out and collected a bunch of fallen limbs from the many pecan trees scattered around Whitesburg. Using those, he built a fire and opened his fold-out grill he kept in the van for those trips to the mountains he loved so much. While he worked on getting a good bed of coals to cook over, Gene rubbed potatoes with oil and wrapped them in foil. The shit may have hit the fan, but for now, they could still eat well.

***

Christy held her hand out the window of Jason's truck as they rode through town. Just as she did when she was a kid, she let her hand surf on the air current rushing past the window. At least for the moment, she was removed from her situation, taken back to a simpler time.

"You guys really going to try and get to Texas?" Jason asked.

Coming back to the moment, she looked at him. "Looks that way. It was a snap decision. Gene talked to some guy out there and we decided to go."

Jason jerked his head. "That's a hell of a decision to make."

Christy shrugged. "It's a chance. It looks like the rest of the country is in trouble. You should have seen Atlanta. It was crazy. We saw the military come in and just shoot people." She shivered. "It was horrible." Looking as Jason, she asked, "What are you guys going to do?"

Jason had one hand on the wheel and thought about the question for a minute. "I don't know. We live here. This is home. We're going to do our best to help our neighbors."

"I just hope we don't come across anymore of those guys like earlier." Christy got quiet and picked at her hand. "I killed one of them."

Jason was surprised and looked over. "What?"

She nodded. "This guy on a motorcycle came up beside the van with some kind of a machinegun. He was looking right at me with that scary mask. I just pointed the pistol and shot it. I know I hit him."

"Hmm. They were wearing masks?"

She nodded. "Yeah, with that skull thing on it." She looked at him. "It was really scary."

Jason drummed him thumb on the wheel. "I know. We've seen them. We've been trying to keep them away from town. So far, we've been lucky."

They reached the Dollar Store and Jason parked in a handicap spot close to the entrance. There was a man in camo clothes sitting on a milk crate by the front door. He stood up as they got out of the truck.

"Hey, Jason. What's up?" The man asked, cradling a shotgun in the crook of his arm.

"Hey, Jim. I'm going to take all the medical stuff out of there and move it to the fire station."

Jim nodded. "That's probably a good idea." He pushed the door open as they approached to let them in.

Christy and Jason both grabbed carts as they went in and headed to the isle of first aid items. They cleaned the shelves of bandages and tape, alcohol, hydrogen peroxide, Band-Aids and antibiotic ointments. Anything that could be used to treat a wound was taken. They also took all the over-the-counter medications and piled them into a cart.

As they were collecting things, Christy tossed a couple of tubes of toothpaste and some sticks of deodorant into her cart. She was with all these guys and knew at some point some of them would start to stink. With that in mind, she added a few bars of soap. She also took the opportunity to grab a few other things like wash cloths and a couple of bath towels, things they hadn't thought about before. She also found the aisle with charcoal and like items and grabbed another can of lighter fluid. She remembered Gene's fire bombs and wanted to make sure he had what he needed. When she returned and dropped it in the cart, Jason raised an eyebrow.

Christy smiled. "In case I need to start a fire to boil anything."

He half laughed, "Yeah. Ok," but he said nothing more.

The last item she added to her cart was a couple of boxes of tampons and maxi-pads. They'd already proven their usefulness, aside from the obvious. And she certainly didn't want to need them and not have them. With the carts loaded, they pushed them out to the truck. Jason grabbed a stack of the plastic bags from the register on their way out.

At the truck, they bagged the items up with Jim's help, keeping them sorted. Christy made sure to bag her stuff up separately. When they finished, the bed of the truck was full of the yellow bags, their tops tied off. When they were finished, Jason told Jim to let Southerland know what he'd done. Jim nodded and waved as they got back in the truck.

Christy helped Jason unload everything into the fire station before picking up her bags. "Thank you for the help, Jason. I really appreciate it."

He pointed at the bags. "With that stuff, you should be able to take care of him."

She looked at the bags. "I think I've got everything I need."

"Thanks for the help, too. Now that I have all this stuff here, it won't disappear."

Christy smiled and headed for the door. "No problem. If I can help with anything else, just let me know."

She went back out behind the station. The smell of cooking meat greeted her as she rounded the corner and a smile spread across her face. She was hungry. At the van, she set the bags down and pulled up a chair. "Those steaks look so good! I'm starving."

"You ain't the only one, sister," Gene replied.

Daniel looked up from the small grill, a steak suspended from a fork. "They'll be ready in a sec." He flipped the steak and it landed with a satisfying hiss as fat dripped from the cuts, causing little flares in the coals below. As he watched the meat cook, Daniel smiled.

"You know how much food there is at my place?" He shook his head. "When all this first started, I made a run to the store and took a van-load home. What a waste."

Teague kicked his feet out towards the fire. "It won't go to waste. Someone will break in there and make a nice score."

Christy unfolded one of the camp chairs and sat down. "I guess this is what it's come to."

"It hasn't even gotten bad yet. It's still pretty early. If today is any indication, it's going to be a long ride to Texas," Bob said.

"But we've made it through it this far. We're all alive," Teague.

Bob took a deep breath. "We were really lucky." He lifted his leg. "Real lucky."

"Are those steaks done yet?" Gene asked, causing Bob to laugh.

Daniel poked one with a fork and inspected it. "Yeah, I think they are."

Plates were produced, each getting a slab of meat. Gene

raked the taters out of the coals and put one on each plate as well. From the cooler came butter, and salt and pepper shakers were set out as well. As everyone ate, Gene lamented the short future for butter.

Mixing his potato with the melted butter on his plate, he said, "Man, what are we going to do when there's no more butter?" Taking up a scoop of the mash, he said, "How are we going to eat potatoes with no butter?"

Bob laughed. "Don't worry, Gene. Potatoes won't last long either."

"Once the food we have runs out, we'll be down to eating whatever we can find," Teague said as he chewed on a bite of steak.

"Hopefully, we'll be in Texas by then," Daniel replied.

Bob nodded. "Hopefully."

When dinner was done, Teague volunteered to clean up the plates and forks. Daniel left the grill in the fire to burn off whatever might be on it. Then, the sleeping arrangements were discussed. It was decided Bob should sleep in the van because of his injury. Daniel said he and Christy would set up his tent and sleep in that. Teague, being Teague, decided to sleep on the roof of the van. Gene would recline in the passenger seat and sleep in that.

Daniel set the small Northface tent up quickly, having done so countless times before. Christy inflated the sleeping pads and unrolled the bags on top. With the light fading and little else to do, she bid everyone a goodnight and went into the tent. Daniel and Gene helped Bob into the van and onto the small bed that folded down.

Teague and Daniel sat by the low glow of the coals of the fire for a while. Daniel was still a little shaken up and tense from the ride. Teague was relaxed and acted as though it was nothing unusual. Maybe it wasn't for him, but this lifestyle was going to take some time for Daniel to get used to. Daniel stretched out a foot and pushed the end of a limb into the fire.

"You ok?" Teague asked.

He shrugged. "I guess so. This just seems so, I don't know, weird I guess. Hard to imagine something like today happening and there are no police or anything, or that people would actually do something like that in the first place."

"The only thing that held the animals in check was the thought there was a limit, that they could get caught and caged for a while. Now they know that's gone, people are going to do the things they've always wanted to. Others, just more of what they've always done."

Daniel shook his head. "You sure have a shitty outlook."

Teague leaned forward, resting on his elbows, and spat into the fire. "It's realistic. Even you. Why did you drive the speed limit? It's an arbitrarily imposed limit on your actions. Why do it? Because you didn't want a speeding ticket. This is the same thing, just on a more violent scale. Someone wants something, they'll just take it. See a pretty girl, no sense trying to get a date. Just knock that bitch down and take it. That's how they'll think."

"I guess I hoped for more from people."

Teague cocked his head to the side and looked down his nose at Daniel. "You, my friend, lived in a fantasy world. That whole, let's all just get along, only worked for those that obey the law in the first place. If you're inclined not to follow the law, then none of that means shit to you. So now you have to decide how you're going to deal with people."

Daniel leaned forward and picked up a small twig with several dry leaves on it, tossing it into the fire. After a brief moment, it flared it into a bright flame. "I guess we established that today."

Teague snorted and sat back. "I don't think you have yet. I've known you for your whole life. You're a decent guy. You don't have that mean streak in you." Looking Daniel in the eye, he said, "But you'd better develop it." He pointed to the tent where Christy was sleeping. "You've got to protect her. I mean, she did a good job today, but you know what men would do to her. She's beautiful."

Daniel looked at the tent and nodded. "You know, I took her for granted for a long time, but this," he waved his hands in the air, "whatever this is, woke me up. I know now what she means to me, and I'll do everything in my power to protect her."

Teague nodded, a thin smile cutting his lips. "She's a prissy little thing, but I will to."

Christy's muffled voice came from the tent, "I heard that, Teague."

Daniel shook his head and Teague laughed, saying, "You were supposed to! No go to sleep, Miss Priss!"

"Screw you, Teague," came the muffled replied.

"Love you, too," Teague replied.

Daniel's head was hanging and he was shaking it. "How much you think she heard?" He asked.

"All of it," Christy replied as her sleeping bag rustled inside the tent. "Come to bed."

Teague laughed. "Sounds like the boss has spoken. You better get going."

Daniel looked at the tent. "Yeah, she has."

CHAPTER 10

THE NEXT MORNING, EVERYONE WAS up early. Christy insisted they eat breakfast before leaving, and she prepared a pot of oatmeal from the large cardboard container they had brought with them. As they ate, Bob commented on the flavor, asking what she did to it.

"I added a little salt. No one thinks of it, but it really sets it off. Plus, I made it with milk and not water. Add a pinch of sugar and you're good to go."

"Salt. Really? Never thought of it. I only ate this stuff because my doctor told me to. Said it would help my cholesterol, but this," he held up a spoonful, "this is really good."

Christy smiled. "Thanks, Bob. It'll stick with you for a while."

Once breakfast was done, they quickly rinsed the bowls and loaded up in the van. Gene had cleaned the passenger seat before going to bed the night before. He started a pot of coffee on Daniel's gas stove and took the time to make the seat presentable. With everything ready, they loaded into the van and drove around the station and headed back the way they came into town.

Southerland was at the roadblock when they pulled up.

Daniel stopped beside him. "Thanks for letting us stay here last night. We appreciate it."

Southerland nodded. "No problem. Good luck to you folks."

Bob leaned forward and asked, "Where's that paramedic?"

Southerland looked back towards town. "He's probably getting some sleep. We had someone get burned last night, so he was up pretty late."

"Pass along to him my appreciation for his help yesterday. You guys went out of your way for us."

Southerland waved him off. "It's what we do. We're here to help."

"Best of luck to you, Chief," Daniel said as he started to pull away.

As they left Whitesburg in the rearview mirror, Christy scooted up between the front seats. "How far down here are we going? I don't want to get near those guys again."

Daniel pointed up the road. "This isn't the road we came in on. This one heads kind of west. We came in from the south."

Her relief obvious, Christy sat back in her seat. They were on the GA 5. A rural route that ran through lightly populated areas. The idea was to stay away from interstates and cities. Daniel pushed the van up to about sixty-five as farm fields and pastures rushed by. The air coming through the many broken windows was cool and refreshing.

Roopville was the first settlement of any size they came to. But they cruised over South Park without incident. Bob was navigating and told Daniel to make a left when Hwy 5 dead ended into GA 100, which was also Hwy 5 until it crossed the Alabama line and changed to Hwy 48.

They passed through many small hamlets in Alabama like Graham, Hawk and Morrison Crossroad. The road was empty for the most part, though they occasionally passed another car or truck. There seemed to be many more tractors moving around than cars.

Passing fields and farms, they saw many tractors out working. From the newest GPS-guided industrial machines to turn-of-the-century Farmalls. For their part, farmers were still going to work every day.

After a few hours of driving, Bob asked Daniel to pull over. They were between Lineville and Ashland. Christy seconded Bob's request. It was time for a pee break. Daniel picked one of the few places where the trees came right up to the road, as most of the area was farm fields. As soon as he stopped, Teague was out the rear door with his carbine at the ready. Gene and Christy helped Bob out, since he was stiff from sitting. As soon as he was on his feet, he waved his helpers off. "I can walk."

Christy retrieved a roll of toilet paper from the van and grabbed Daniel's arm. "I'm going behind the van. Keep everyone over here, please."

Bob laughed at her modesty. "You ain't got nothing I haven't seen before."

TP in hand as she rounded the van, Christy replied, "Maybe not. But you haven't seen this one, and you're not going to!"

Bob laughed as he shook a cigarette from his pack and lit it. He leaned against the van and asked Daniel to get the atlas. Daniel grabbed it and opened it up on the hood. "Where are we?"

With the cigarette pinched between his fingers, Bob

pointed at the map. "We're about right here on Hwy 9." He ran his finger along the road. "The problem is up here. We're not too far from Talladega and Birmingham to the north. I don't want to go anywhere near those two. We can go south down here to Sylacauga, but we'll need to cross the Coosa River at some point. We need a bridge on a secondary road."

Daniel studied the map. "If we go south towards Rockford, we can pick up twenty-two there and cross the river. Doesn't look like a major road. Better than going north and running the risk of having trouble and being forced farther north towards Talladega."

Bob finished his cigarette and flipped it into the road. "I like that. It keeps us to the south and away from any craziness around these bigger cities."

Hearing a noise on the roof of the van, Daniel looked up to see Gene. "What are you doing?" He asked.

Gene was struggling with one of the drums of fuel they'd tied up there. "Since we're stopped, let's top off the fuel. Better to have it in the tank than up here. Plus, we never know when we'll really need to be able to outrun someone."

"Good idea. Let me help," Daniel said.

Christy was finished with her task and came around the van with a camp chair, telling Bob to sit down. He protested until her hands landed on her hips and she cocked her head to the side. He knew he was beat, and sat as instructed. As much as he hated it, Christy insisted he wear shorts to make it easier to clean his wounds. The pants he'd been wearing were lost to the shears of Jason.

Bob plopped into the chair and Christy went to work cleaning the wound. She removed the dressing and inspected the gouges the bullet had torn into his leg. She took a bottle of contact lens saline from a bag and a small bottle of betadine solution. Using a Styrofoam cup, she poured a couple of fingers of saline and added the betadine, mixing the two.

Bob watched what she was doing and asked, "Is that safe to use on an open wound? Isn't that for your eyes?"

Christy didn't stop her work and replied. "It's just sterile saline. Same thing they give you in an IV. This is great for irrigating wounds. Now that the bottle isn't full, I'll add the betadine directly to it and be able to squirt it right into the wounds."

Christy took a couple of four by four gauze pads and soaked them in the solution. She used these to clean Bob's legs, removing dead tissue and dried blood. Bob tolerated the discomfort without complaint. Once the wound was clean, she placed a couple non-adherent pads on the canal the bullet cut and wrapped them with gauze. When she finished, she looked up at Bob and smiled. "All clean now."

Bob smiled back at her as she knelt in front of him, packing up her supplies. Bob took her arm. "Thank you, Christy." It was a simple statement, but she could tell from his eyes he really meant it, and probably didn't know how exactly to express himself. She patted him on the leg. "No problem, Bob. Someone's got to take care of you."

Through two failed marriages, Bob never managed to have any kids. Mainly because of what he'd always thought of as prudent planning on his part. But looking at Christy, if he had a daughter, she was what he imagined. Maybe he should have had some kids. But then he thought about those two evil bitches. No, he was far better off. And, considering the current situation, he wouldn't want to be worrying about kids who could be God knows where.

Gene finished transferring the fuel and asked Daniel to help get the drum back on the roof of the van. No reason to leave it behind, they might need it again down the road. Once the drum was secure and the chairs were loaded back up, everyone returned to their places in the van and Daniel pulled back out onto the road.

They drove into Ashland without issue. It was as if nothing out of the ordinary was going on. Bob laughed as they passed the post office and a man was mowing the lawn of the house across the street. At the Mapco convenience store caddy corner from the courthouse, the parking lot was crowded with cars and trucks. It appeared some method had been devised to pump fuel from the underground tanks. The residents of Ashland were lined up and patiently waiting their turn for fuel.

The van drew several looks from those waiting in line, but nothing more than a long stare. Here at least, things seemed normal. The parking places in front of the courthouse had a number of police and sheriff cars occupying them, the officers and deputies milling about with little show of ambition. They too turned to watch the van as it rolled by. Daniel worried they would see the bullet holes, or maybe the screens over the windows would draw their curiosity. Bob waved at them and a couple of the officers waved back.

Highway 9 had become 1st Ave in Ashland, and it became Hwy 77 that continued west, while Hwy 9 broke off and turned south just past the courthouse square. Daniel made a left onto 9 South. They hadn't even made it to the NAPA half a block down when a country sheriff suddenly rounded the corner behind them with his lights and siren going.

"Oh shit," Daniel said, looking in the rearview mirror.

Teague quickly shifted his position at the rear of the van. "Should I take him out?" He shouted.

Bob spun around in his chair and screamed, "Hell no! Just pull to the side, Daniel."

Daniel did as Bob said, hoping the patrol car would pass them. But it pulled in behind them and stopped. Bob lowered his weapon to the floor between his feet as the deputy got out of this car in a rather casual manner. Daniel watched as the deputy adjusted his gun belt while he walked up. The deputy gave the van a thorough look as he approached. Coming up to Daniel's window, he looked in at the occupants.

In a thick southern Alabama drawl, he asked, "Where you guys headed?"

"To a friend's place southwest of here," Bob replied.

The deputy had a thick pinch of snuff bulging his cheek. He adjusted it with his tongue. Christy had a full body shiver at the disgusting habit. The deputy nodded down the road in the direction they were traveling. "You folks are headed into a pretty rough area. There's some boys out there, waylaying travelers. They're looking for cars, fuel, food, guns an," he paused, looking at Christy, "women." Tipping his hat, he added, "Sorry, ma'am."

Bob looked down the road. "That's unfortunate. We need to get through here. We don't want to go north. The big cities are probably a pretty rough place."

With a quick snap of his head, the deputy spat a brown

slug into the dirt. "Well, we've had several folks come in here after running into them. Some of them didn't live long. If you continue out there, we're not going to come help you."

Bob nodded. "We understand, and wouldn't ask you to."

The deputy rapped a knuckle on the expanded metal covering Daniel's window. "Some pretty serious hardware you folks have on here. Where'd you come from?"

"Atlanta. We were downtown when it all happened. Had to take precautions."

Looking the van over, he replied, "Can't say I blame you. Just be careful. From what we hear, they're dropping trees over the road making people stop, and then they ambush them." He stepped back and tipped his hat. "Good luck to you folks."

Bob waved at him. "Thanks for the info." Then he nodded at Daniel to proceed.

As they pulled off, Christy climbed up between the front seats. "Is this a good idea? Maybe we should find another way."

Bob shook out a smoke and lit it, causing Christy to wave the smoke away. "It's the only way, Christy. We certainly don't want to go north. Just keep your gun handy."

The reply didn't give her any comfort, but she sat back in her chair, checking her Glock to make sure it was there. She had a bad feeling about this, but there wasn't anything she could do.

It was about halfway between Harkins Crossroad and Millerville, where the trees grew within feet of the road, that a large tree came crashing down onto their path. Daniel instinctively hit the brakes, putting the van into a slide. Bob shouted to get off the brake and speed up, actually reaching over and pushing the wheel to steer the van towards the canopy of the tree that reached all the way to the other side of the road.

Daniel did as instructed, mashing the accelerator to the floor. The van belched black smoke as diesel poured into the cylinders. They were nearly to the tree when men appeared from either side of the road carrying rifles. But the van was now going in excess of sixty and they didn't get too close. The big Ford crashed into the canopy of the tree and, for a moment, Daniel couldn't see anything but leaves and limbs as they scraped over the metal screen.

"Keep going! Keep going!" Bob shouted as limbs scraped and scratched down the side of the van.

Forward momentum suddenly stopped as the van strained against a large limb. Daniel paused long enough to shift the van into four-wheel drive and got back on the gas. The van began to creep forward when a shot rang out. Bob looked over his shoulder to see Teague shooting from the rear windows. Whoever had sprung the trap obviously thought the van was hung up and this was the time to hit it. But they didn't count on the people inside being ready for it.

Teague caught the first man in the chest, toppling him instantly. These guys weren't very well equipped, relying on surprise to give them the advantage. The two men with him quickly moved to take cover in the trees to the side of the road. Teague fired a quick shot at one of them, getting a yelp as the round slammed into the target's ass.

The van was struggling against the tree when a sudden lurch forward announced it had broken free. The van roared through what was left of the tree, headed for the opposite shoulder of the road. Daniel quickly corrected to maintain the road and they were quickly out of the ambush. What seemed to last an hour to Daniel had only lasted about three minutes.

"Wooo! That was a rush!" Teague shouted from the back of the van. He dropped the mag from his rifle, replacing it with a full one.

Christy brushed hair from her face and breathed a sigh of relief. She wasn't particularly enjoying this new world. But she was thankful to be with Daniel, Bob and the guys. The thought of trying to manage this on her own filled her with dread. She thought back about her apartment and what it looked like, not to mention the man that was there. She could only imagine what he wanted, not that it was that hard to figure it out.

But she wasn't about to let it beat her. She was ready to take on anything that came her way. With that thought, she looked at the Glock in her lap. It gave her a sense of strength, security, that she didn't just have to be a victim. Anyone coming after her would have to work for it.

"Look at this," Daniel said.

Christy looked up to see another downed tree in the road, its leaves already turning brown and limply hanging down towards the road. A car sat on the other side of it, burned to the frame. "Must have been what they were talking about," Bob said.

"That could have been us," Christy added.

"But it wasn't," Gene said.

Christy gripped her Glock, "And it's not going to be."

A short distance past Harkins Crossroads, they made

a right turn off Hwy 9 onto Hwy 148 that would take them through the southern part of the Talladega National Forest and into Sylacauga. This was a larger town than the last one, and as a result, the people weren't quite as well organized. There was no barricade on the edge of town, no obvious organization anywhere. With that said though, there also wasn't any real sense of chaos or danger. While there was no power in town, people moved about freely and calmly to fulfill their needs.

Other cars and trucks were on the roads and people treated intersections like four-way stops. There was no trouble, at least that they could see. Passing a gas station, they saw vehicles cued up, waiting for fuel. A large diesel generator was tied into the station to provide power. One of the highlights was the large ice dispenser in the parking lot. It was one of those do-it-yourself deals where you put in two bucks and could get a bag or ice in bulk to dump into a cooler. The line for ice was longer than the one for fuel. But here too, it was orderly as people waited with coolers for their turn.

But maybe it was the presence of the several sheriff deputies that was keeping everyone in line. Here at least, the veil of civil society seemed intact. As the van rolled by the station it naturally drew looks from the civilians and deputies alike. Daniel was always nervous when he saw cops of any fashion. Some of his previous encounters hadn't gone well, and he wasn't eager to relive those.

As they left town, Bob called out the turns to get them headed in the right direction.

"We have to cross the Coosa River. Take US 235 north towards Childersburg. We can cross there." Bob said as he studied the map. "I know I had agreed earlier with your suggestion for heading down to Rockford and crossing the river on Hwy 22, but I've changed my mind. Heading north from here just a bit and cutting across from Childersburg looks like it may be a bit shorter route overall. So, trust me on this."

Recognizing that Bob had done a really good job navigating thus far, Daniel didn't argue the point with him.

Headed towards Childersburg, they passed a couple of stalled cars on the side of the road. Shortly afterwards, they came across what looked like a family walking down the side of the road. Hearing the van, the man turned and waved, sticking his thumb out.

Daniel looked at Bob. "Should we stop?"

Bob looked up, but before he could answer, Christy did. "Of course we should. We can give them a ride."

Bob shook his head. "No. Not a good idea. Just keep going."

Christy was shocked. "What? They've got kids. We should help them."

Bob dropped the atlas into his lap. "The fact they have kids makes them even more dangerous. Their car probably ran out of gas, so they're walking. They're desperate. Not for themselves, but for their kids. Desperate people do desperate things. We can't risk this."

Christy was pissed. "That's a really fucked-up view, Bob."

He turned in his seat. "It's not the way I want to be. But this van is our life right now. Without it," he turned and pointed at the people they were now nearly on top of, "we're them. You think anyone is going to stop and pick us up?"

From the back of the van, Teague shouted, "I'm with Bob. They're not in the circle of trust!" Then he laughed at his own joke.

Gene looked at him and smiled. "That was really bad, but funny." Teague gave a thumbs up and turned to watch the rear.

Christy folded her arms and sat back in her seat. She was fuming inside. She knew there was nothing she could say to change the situation. But the next time they stopped, she was going to talk to Daniel. It was his van after all. He can decide whether or not to pick people up. Things may be bad, but she wasn't about to let it change her. No matter how bad it gets, you should still help those you can.

Childersburg was much like the last town, but with a minor difference. This time, they saw a pharmacy being looted. No one was trying to stop it either, which was more concerning than the actual looting. But they made it through town and over the Coosa without any trouble.

They turned south and worked their way westward across the state, trying to avoid getting any closer to the southern reaches of the Birmingham area than they had to. Their route would take them through more rural areas. Farm fields and woods were more preferable than built-up urban areas. However, those were not without issues. The south is crisscrossed with rivers, creeks and canals. All of these need to be crossed via a bridge, a natural choke point. Not to mention the real obstacle, the Mississippi River, that would need to be crossed at some point as well. And that river wouldn't have many secondary roads with bridges. At some point, they would have to use a major highway to cross it. This was the one issue that worried Bob more than anything.

It was in the afternoon that Bob said he needed a piss break. Christy immediately spoke up to say she wanted to change Bob's dressing as well. They were approaching the Black Warrior River on Underwood Bridge road. Daniel started looking for a place to stop, but both sides of the road were bordered by a large water-filled ditch.

"Right there," Bob said, pointing to the right side where a small bridge crossed over the ditch.

Daniel eyed the rickety structure with suspicion. "You think it'll hold us?"

Bob was shaking a smoke out of a pack and absent-mindedly answered, "Sure."

Daniel scowled, but turned towards the little bridge. It held, and soon they were in a small clearing bordered by trees. Bob pointed to the back of the small field and said, "Pull back there so we can't be seen from the road."

Daniel drove around a point created by the trees to where the clearing narrowed and was shielded from the road. It created a shady spot for them to stop and rest for a while. Teague was out the back door of the van before it was even in park, pecker in hand and pissing like a race horse.

"Woooo! Damn that feels good! I was seeing yella!" He shouted.

Daniel got out and stretched as Christy tried to help Bob, who wasn't interested in any assistance. "I'm fine, Christy. I need to stretch and then you can pester me."

"Whatever, old man. But you're not getting back in that van before I change your dressings."

Lighting his smoke, Bob dropped his lighter back in his pocket as he replied, "Yes, Nurse Ratchet."

She shook her head and reached in for a roll of TP. She was walking around the van when Teague nearly ran into her. He looked at the TP and, with a devilish smile, he asked, "You need any help?"

Christy was always a proper woman that didn't use profanity or vulgar language, except in extreme situations. Teague was an extreme situation. She gave him the finger. "In your dreams, asshole."

Teague laughed. He enjoyed messing with her. Pointing at the roll again, he said, "Hurry up with that stuff. I got a shit on deck that would choke a midget to death."

Christy shook her head. "Do you even realize what a shithead you are?" She didn't wait for an answer and headed off into the woods to find a spot to take care of her business.

Daniel had taught her the finer points of relieving oneself in the woods. Not so much by choice though. When they first met, she wasn't into the whole camping thing. But he went so often that she gave in and started to go with him. When she realized he didn't camp in the tidy campgrounds with air-conditioned bath houses, and that he wouldn't leave when she had to go, she was forced to learn.

After attempting several variations, she had settled on a method that involved finding a suitably small diameter tree, grabbing it with both hands and squatting down, using the tree for support. Unlike men, she didn't need to linger during the act, something she never could figure out. She was horrified when he tried to get to her to sit with one cheek on a folding shovel. This was certainly more dignified. She quickly took care of business and was headed back to the van.

Back at the van, Daniel smiled at her and patted a folding chair he was setting up. "Here, babe. This one's for you."

She smiled and sat down. "Thank you."

Teague walked back and snatched the roll from her hand and said, "I was serious about choking that midget." He then quickly disappeared into the woods.

She shook her head as she watched him leave. "I wish he wasn't here."

Daniel sat down in a chair beside her and looked over his shoulder. "He's not all bad. If you let him think he's getting to you, it only makes it worse. Just ignore him and he'll quit."

Gene unfolded a chair and plopped into it. "He's right. Onboard ship pranks and such were a common thing, but if you didn't let it get to you or didn't react, they just gave up. It was the ones that reacted that got screwed with. The better the reaction, the more they got targeted."

Christy shook her head. "I just don't understand you guys. I mean, why?" Before she could continue, Gene, Bob and Daniel answered in unison, "Because it's fun!"

She threw her hands up. "See, that's what I mean. How is making your friends unhappy fun? We women, we don't do that to one another."

Bob choked on a breath of smoke and started to cough. "Whatever! You just use passive-aggressive catty bullshit on one another!"

Gene held a finger up. "And us."

Still coughing, Bob nodded. "Especially us!"

Daniel didn't want in on this discussion, so when Christy looked at him, he just shrugged, getting a roar of laughter from Gene. Trying to find an out, Daniel stood up and asked, "Who's hungry? We have stuff to make sandwiches."

"Smashing idea, old sport!" Gene shouted.

Daniel went to the van and came back with a small aluminum folding table and set it up. Then, from the fridge, he returned with the sandwich fixings. Christy stood and offered to help. He smiled. "Just sit down, babe. I got it. Take a break."

They all relaxed and had a sandwich. As soon as Bob was done, Christy went to work on his wounds. They still looked nasty but were clean, and the bleeding had completely stopped, an improvement. As she worked, a sound drifted through the trees to them. It was a deep rumbling sound. Teague rose to his feet looking back towards the road.

"What the hell is that?" He asked.

Gene stood up and said, "It's diesel engines, a lot of them."

"Let's go take a look," Teague said.

"I'll go too," Daniel said as he got up.

Teague looked at him. "Get your gun, man. Don't go anywhere without your gun."

"Oh, yeah," Daniel said as he went around the driver's side of the van and grabbed his weapon. Teague and Gene were waiting at the front of the van for him. Teague pointed at the rifle. "That thing should never be more than an arm's reach from you, buddy." Daniel nodded. "I'm serious, dude. When you need it, you won't have time to go get it."

Slightly annoyed, Daniel said, "Okay, okay. I got it."

The three of them walked back towards the point that

blocked them from the road. They stopped where a few trees would block them from being directly observed from the road. As the trees thinned and they could see through them, they were able to make out large armored vehicles moving down the road. Emblazoned on the side of each one were three large letters, DHS, with the seal of the Department of Homeland Security.

They watched as armored vehicle after armored vehicle passed by. Daniel quietly asked, "What the hell are those?"

"They're MRAPs," Gene replied.

"Aren't those an Army thing?"

Taking the comb from his pocket, Gene ran it through his mustache. "Yeah, they are. But back in 2013, the government started buying them. I think they have over two thousand of them now."

"What in the hell do they need those things for?" Daniel asked.

"For this. For right now," Teague said. "They've been planning and waiting for this for a long time."

"How in the hell can people fight against those things?" Daniel asked.

"With IEDs." Gene snorted.

"I don't think you made any of those, Gene."

Gene rubbed his mustache. "Maybe not. But I can."

Daniel looked at him. "You really think that's necessary? They haven't done anything to us, so why should we assume they're our enemy?"

Teague pointed towards the road where the last of the MRAPs was passing by. "Run your ass out there and wave 'em down then."

Daniel watched as the last truck disappeared. Slowly

shaking his head, he said, "No, I don't think so." Then he smiled and looked at Teague. "Besides, they're gone now."

The three men walked back towards the van. Gene pulled out his comb and ran it through his mustache again. Daniel was beginning to understand this tale, Gene was thinking. "What's on your mind, Gene?" Daniel asked.

Gene blew the comb off and pocketed it. "Just thinking about those trucks. They may be an issue in the future."

Daniel was looking at the ground as he walked and asked, "What the hell were they doing out here?" Holding his arms out, he turned in a circle. "We're in the middle of nowhere!"

"Out looking to fuck someone up," Teague said.

Gene nodded. "That was a lot of hardware. I think we should stay here tonight. I don't want to get back out on the road too close behind them. Better to let them get on down the road a ways."

"I agree, good idea," Daniel said.

Back at the van, they shared what they saw with Christy and Bob while Bob's dressings were being tended to. Without looking up from her work, Christy asked, "What's that mean?"

"It means we're staying here tonight," Gene replied.

Christy looked up. "But it's so early. We could still go a long way today."

"No. Gene's right," Bob said. "We need to let those guys get on down the road."

Christy shook her head. "Why? As long as we're not on the road past the curfew, we're not doing anything wrong."

"That may be true. But why even take the chance if we don't need to?" Bob asked.

Christy looked around the small clearing they were parked in. Shrugging, she said, "Whatever, I guess. It's nice here."

They started to set up camp for the night, deploying the awning from the van and setting up the small tent. Gene was inside the van, rummaging around in the groceries. As always seemed to be the case, he was hungry. He came out with an armload, announcing he would take care of dinner.

"Since we're so far off the road, I think I'll build a fire tonight," he said as he placed a package of chicken breasts on the small folding table.

"A fire would be nice," Christy said. "It just doesn't seem the same to be camping and not have a fire."

Teague stood up. "I'll prepare a fire pit. We need to be able to put it out real fast if we have to."

After dinner, the group sat around the fire. It was kept small, but fed often to maintain a comfortable flame. Everyone had their chairs pulled up close with their feet outstretched toward the warmth, except Christy. She was curled up in the chair with her feet tucked in a small fleece blanket covering her, in a way it seems only women can do.

Gene had strung a wire antenna for the radio and had it set up on the small table beside him as he scanned through the bands looking for traffic. Daniel was nearly asleep, his chin resting on his chest. Bob and Teague both stared into the fire. It was a quiet time, with only the murmurs from the radio and the crackling of the fire breaking the silence.

Teague had his carbine lying across his lap. He leaned it against the chair as he reached out to toss another piece of wood on the fire. Just as it landed in the flames, sending up a shower of embers, a voice broke the silence.

"You keep them hands out there where we can see 'em." Teague looked up as two men walked out of the blackness that closed in from all sides around the small fire. Both were armed with shotguns, leveled right at him.

Gene looked up from the radio, then glanced at the 870 leaning against the table. "Don't even think about it," one of the men said.

Daniel woke up in confusion for a moment, until his head cleared and he comprehended what was going on. Christy's eyes darted back and forth between the men and Daniel. He looked at her and she could tell not only was he scared, he didn't know what to do.

Bob had a cigarette in his hand and continued to smoke it. The two men moved in closer. One of them had a large key ring hanging from his hip that jingled as he walked. Teague went to sit back, but one of the men shouldered his shotgun and shouted for him to stay just as he was. Leaning forward over the carbine, there was no way he could bring it up before they shot him. Feeling they had the situation under control, one of them flipped his weapon up onto his shoulder and began to strut around the group, the keys playing their song as he did.

"Well now. What do we have here? Trespassers, that's what we've got. Y'all are trespassing."

Calmly, Bob replied. "We didn't mean to. We just needed to be off the road by the curfew so…" the man cut him off. Spinning towards Bob, he pointed an accusatory finger at him.

"Ignorance is no excuse! It's no excuse for the law, and it's no excuse to me."

"We didn't mean any harm. We haven't harmed your land in any way." Bob replied.

"So you say!" The man shouted. He kicked dirt at the fire. "You've dug a hole, and you're burning my wood!"

"Looks like they've done harm to me, Tony," the other man added.

Tony looked at his partner. "I think you're right, Jeff." He looked around at the group. "The question is, what do we do with them?"

"I can think of a few things," Jeff replied. Then he looked at Christy and smiled.

Tony smiled back. "I guess some of them do have a use. But the rest of em, I just don't know."

"We meant no harm. We're leaving first thing in the morning. We can offer you some cash if you feel we've caused you damage," Bob said.

Tony spun around to face Bob again. "You ain't going nowhere!" He walked around the fire to Christy. Standing in front of her, he rubbed his chin. "Stand up. Let's have a look at you."

She trembled and looked at Daniel. "Don't look at him." Tony spat. "He ain't going to help you." Then, with a sinister change in tone, he demanded. "Now get your ass up!"

The shot was slightly muffled. The little felt blanket dampened the report of the Glock as it puffed up and blew shreds of the material into the air. The bullet caught Tony just to the left of his sternum and toppled him backwards, into the fire. Hearing the shot, Teague launched himself from his chair, crashing into Jeff, who was caught off guard by the shot. But he recovered quickly and was putting up a solid fight.

Gene rose to his feet, casually picking up the 870 as he did. The man Christy shot was rolling out of the fire. As Gene passed him he lowered the barrel of the shotgun to near pointblank range and, without stopping, fired a shot into the smoking man. He racked the shotgun as he walked to where Teague and Jeff were fighting for control of Jeff's shotgun.

The two men were tied up pretty tight and Gene couldn't get a clear shot without possibly hitting Teague. He stepped back as Teague mounted the man. He had the shotgun pushed down on the guy's chest, but couldn't get control of it from the stronger man. Gene side-stepped, lowered the barrel again and fired another shot. This one took Jeff's right foot off.

Jeff screeched in pain as he released his grip on the gun. Teague quickly pulled it away, sat up and pointed the muzzle at his face and pulled the trigger. The shot left a smoking crater in Jeff's face. Then it was again silent. Christy jumped up from her chair, Glock still in her hand. Her free hand was on her head as she paced back and forth saying. "Oh shit, oh shit, oh shit."

Daniel jumped up and grabbed her. She turned to him and started to cry. Gene racked his 870 again and replaced the two spent shells in the tube with fresh ones from the side saddle shell holder as he walked back to his chair. Leaning the shotgun up against the table again, he sat back down.

Bob was still in his chair, cigarette in hand. He hadn't moved. Looking at Gene, he said, "Well, damn." Gene looked back and shrugged before turning his attention to the radio.

"Didn't see that coming," Bob said.

"What?" Daniel asked.

Bob waved a hand out over the scene before him. "Any of it."

Teague searched the two bodies and collected their firearms. The two shotguns, a Buck sheath knife and a pocket knife were the sum of his search. He put the items into the van before returning to the fire where he looked down at the two bodies. "Daniel, help me drag these two pieces of shit out of here."

Daniel looked at Christy. "You alright?"

She wiped her cheeks and nodded. "Yeah."

He walked her over to her chair. "Just sit down for a minute. I'll be right back."

Teague grabbed Jeff by the hands. With a nod, he said, "Grab his feet." Daniel looked down at the mangled right leg. Teague followed his gaze and chuckled. "Or foot."

Daniel grabbed both pant legs and they lifted the body, half dragging it away from the camp. They didn't carry it far before dumping it in the brush. They returned and did the same with Tony. The smell of singed hair and burnt clothing stung Daniel's nose. He tried to hold his breath as they deposited Tony beside his friend. He stood there for a moment looking at the two men. Thankfully, Jeff's head was turned to the side, so he didn't have to look into the crater in his face.

He wondered what made these men do this, why they would even attempt such an act, and more importantly, just what they were planning. He paused there for a moment before turning away. With the unsavory task done, Daniel went back to Christy.

She was sitting in the chair with her hands between her

knees, the Glock still in her grasp. Daniel knelt down and looked at her. "You ok, babe?"

She didn't reply, just nodded her head. He lifted her chin up to look in her eyes. "You did good. Who knows what those guys would have done. They had us." With a slight nod of his head, he added, "But you acted at exactly the right moment. I had no idea you had this in you."

She rubbed her nose. "I don't have it in me. I was scared shitless. I just shot. I didn't even think I'd hit him, let alone kill him."

Bob's Zippo snapped open for a second, then closed. Christy looked up as he took a drag on the cigarette, then offered it to her. She shook her head but he insisted. "You need it. Don't need to smoke the whole thing. Just take a drag. It'll calm your nerves."

She hesitated for a moment, then accepted it and took a hesitant puff. Blowing the smoke out, she took a longer drag, then handed it back to Bob. "Thanks."

Bob smiled as he took it. "Like a pro. Thought you didn't smoke."

She half smiled. "Cigarettes. Everyone smokes something in college."

"That's my girl!" Teague said.

She ignored him and looked at Daniel. "That's two people. I've killed two people."

Daniel ran his hands back and forth on her legs. "It's a different time now. You've defended yourself. Nothing more, nothing less."

"How far are we from Texas?"

Bob blew out a cloud of smoke. "Depends. We could be there tomorrow if we pushed all day and didn't have any trouble."

Christy looked back down at the ground. "So a couple of days then."

"Probably," Bob replied.

"But we'll get there," Daniel said. Looking around, he asked, "You want to go to bed?"

Christy shook her head. "No. Can we build the fire up?"

"Sure," Daniel said as he got up to add some wood to it.

Teague was tapping his foot and looking at Gene. After a moment, he said, "Gene, you don't look like the kind of guy that did shooting and looting in the Navy."

Gene looked up. "What does that look like?"

Teague shrugged. "Hell if I know. But you're a badass in my book."

Bob snorted. "Gene's not a guy you want to cross. He's, how should I say it, devious."

Gene smiled. "Thanks, Bob," and he turned his attention back to the radio.

Bob motioned with his chin. "You getting anything out of that box?"

His attention still on the radio, he replied, "Some. Sounds like we're not the only ones with the idea to head to Texas."

"You hear other people talking about it?" Teague asked.

Gene nodded. "Uh huh. There are a couple of convoys that have been organized. They're grouping up for protection, trying to push through."

"Maybe we should join one," Daniel said.

Gene shook his head. "I don't think so. You remember that military convoy we saw earlier? Might explain what they're slinking around for." Gene pointed at the radio. "All these civilian convoys talking on the radio, giving their positions. They're telling the Feds where to find them. I have a feeling they'll be getting dealt with soon enough."

"I agree with Gene. We need to remain as small a target as possible," Bob said. "They might actually draw some attention off us when the time comes."

"I hope the time doesn't come," Christy said, getting everyone's attention. "Killing rednecks is one thing. Killing police or soldiers is something else entirely."

"Let's just hope it doesn't come to that," Bob said.

Teague didn't say anything. But he, for one, was hoping to have the chance to kill some Feds. He'd done it once, and he was ready to do it again. But he wasn't the only one thinking about it. The rest of the group was mulling it over in their minds as well. Well, everyone except Gene. He was occupied with the radio. He was always in the now, seldom looked to the future, and even less often dwelled on the past.

Around midnight, Christy said she was tired. Bob breathed a sigh of relief as he'd wanted to turn in for some time but was going to sit with her as long as she wanted.

"I'm bushed too. Think I'll turn in as well," Bob said.

"I'll keep watch," Gene said.

"Wake me up in a few hours and I'll relieve you," Teague said.

Daniel and Christy crawled into the tent and into their bags. Christy pressed a little closer to him on this night. He kept his arm over her, with his hand on his rifle lying beside her. He wasn't going to let her go. He'd learned so much about her, more than he ever imagined. And the more he learned, the more he loved her. He waited for her to fall asleep. Knowing she had drifted off when her breathing changed, he finally closed his eyes.

CHAPTER 11

Before Daniel opened his eyes, he could smell her hair. He held off opening his eyes, instead staying in the moment. It brought him back to so many mornings when he'd woken this way, in this very tent. For a moment, this was just a camping trip. Then the smell of coffee drifted through the fine mesh screen of the small tent. As much as he savored the scent of Christy, he simply couldn't resist the aroma of coffee.

Christy woke up when he pulled on the zipper of his sleeping bag. She bolted upright, wrapped tightly in her bag with the muzzle of the Glock poking out. "What? What is it?" she asked half awake.

Daniel put a hand on her shoulder. "It's okay. It's only coffee."

Her hair was in her face. She managed to free her arms and brushed it away, taking a deep breath. "Mmm, I need some." She then kicked off the bag as Daniel unzipped the tent.

Gene was fireside, tending a pot sitting in the coals. For all his oddities, one thing he was meticulous about was coffee. Gene approached the coffee production with the focus of a laboratory chemist. The ratios of coffee and water, and the grind of the beans must be precise. And he was damn good at it.

Gene looked up as the two stumbled from their tent and smiled. "Morning. Smells good, doesn't it?"

Daniel stretched his arms high into the damp morning air. The sky was still a slate gray with the sun not quite over the horizon yet. "It sure does, Gene," he replied.

Christy was dragging her sleeping bag with her and wrapped herself up in it once she sat down. Closing her eyes, she took a deep breath. "It smells so good, Gene."

Gene was hovering over the pot, closely watching the glass perk on top. "It's almost ready. Another minute."

Daniel took a seat and stretched his feet out towards the fire to warm them. From where he sat, across the fire and out towards the woods, he could see the two men from the day before. While in the gray morning they were nothing more than an indiscernible lump, he knew what the lump was. He averted his eyes to look down into the fire. Bush TV was certainly a more preferable sight to wake up to.

Gene started pouring cups and handing them out. It wasn't long before everyone was up, Bob and Teague joining them around the fire. While they drank their coffee, Gene went back to the van and returned with a box of Entenmann's Danishes. He'd smuggled them out of Bob's house with full intention of hiding them for himself. But he was really beginning to connect with these people, and he couldn't bring himself to do it.

Opening the box, he held it out in front of Christy. She saw the box and immediately reached for one. "Oh..., where did we get these?"

"From Bob's house," Gene replied.

He went around the fire, offering everyone a Danish. Daniel waved it off. "Thanks, Gene. But if I eat that this early, my stomach won't be right for the rest of the day."

The corners of Gene's mustache curled up. "More for me then."

With breakfast taken care of, they began to break camp. While the guys loaded the van, Christy checked Bob's legs. With her constant care, the wounds were already closing nicely. They were now fully scabbed over and only bled occasionally if Bob bent his knees to the extreme. Christy admonished him to take it easy and let them heal.

Bob smiled. "Thank you, Christy. Don't know what we'd do without you."

She patted his leg as she stood up. "Someone has to be the voice of reason around here."

They were on the road just as the sun was coming up. The day was clear and bright and lending it a positive vibe. Half an hour later, they were passing the white cliffs of the Tombigbee River near Epes, Alabama. As they crossed the old trestle bridge, Christy looked back at the towering limestone cliffs falling into the river.

"That is so pretty," she said, craning her neck to see it.

From his seat in the rear of the van, Teague had a prefect view. "Sure is. This country still has some beautiful, unspoiled places left."

It took considerable navigational skills on Bob's part to keep them away from Meridian, Mississippi. The wandering, winding route they were taking was adding considerable miles to the trip, but it was keeping them away from population centers, and that was the most important thing.

Approaching Chunky, Mississippi, Daniel looked at the fuel gauge. "I don't think we're going to have enough fuel to make it. The way we're going, we're burning too much."

Bob nodded and looked at the map. After a moment, he folded it into his lap and pointed up the road. "We're coming into a small place called Chunky." Christy laughed and snorted at the mention of the name.

"Are you serious?" She asked.

Nodding, Bob said, "Oh yeah," and pointed to a sign on the side of the road announcing their arrival. "Let's see if we can find fuel. We need to start keeping our eyes open and try to pick some up." He spun around in his seat. "Everyone pass up whatever cash you have."

Teague passed up the forty-seven dollars he had. Christy emptied her wallet. But like many young people today, she didn't carry much cash. She only had eleven dollars and some change. Gene passed up a thick bank envelope. Bob felt it, then looked back at Gene. "How much is in here?"

Gene shrugged. "About twenty-seven hundred."

Christy looked at him wide-eyed. "Why in the world do you have so much cash on you?"

"I don't like banks. When all this started, I went to the window at the bank and closed one of my accounts. Figured it might come to this."

Bob smiled and shook his head. "You are an interesting cat, Gene."

Again, Gene shrugged. He took the comb from his pocket and ran it through his mustache.

But there was no fuel in Chunky, or much of anything else for that matter. They saw few people even as they passed through the small hamlet. It wasn't until they arrived in

Newton that they found a station that, to their surprise, had the sign lit up.

"Two oh nine a gallon." Daniel said when he saw the green neon displaying the price of diesel.

"Interesting they have power." Bob said. "Let's go see what they have."

Daniel steered the van into the Marathon station, stopping at the green handle of the diesel pump. The store had several people milling about in front of it and the van was quite the oddity for them.

"Daniel, let's me and you go in and see if we can get some fuel," Bob said. "Gene, you guys watch the van." Before getting out, Bob pulled four hundred dollar bills from the envelope Gene had given him and tucked them into his pocket. Then he put the envelope into the glove box.

"I'm coming too," Christy said as she pulled the side door open.

She came around the driver's side and gripped Daniel's hand. He leaned over and kissed her on the head and smiled. Bob walked stiffly towards the store, the people there parting as they approached, offering a nod as a greeting. Bob smiled and nodded back as they went into the store.

Behind the counter was a middle-aged man of Indian or Pakistani descent. He sat on a stool talking to a man across the counter. He looked up as they came in.

"Morning," Bob said. The man nodded in reply as the other half of his conversation stepped aside. "You have any diesel fuel?"

With a hint of an accent, he replied. "Cash money only. Ten dollars a gallon."

Christy pointed towards the sign out in front of the

store. "But the sign says...." Daniel pushed her arm down. She looked at him and could see in his eyes he was telling her to hush.

Bob pulled just enough cash out of his back pocket to pay for the gas, being careful not to expose just how much money he actually had on him. "Can he go out and fill up while I wait here to pay you?"

The man behind the counter leaned forward and looked at the bills. Holding out a hand, he said. "Let me see one of those?" Bob slipped a crisp one-hundred-dollar bill out and handed it over. The man held it up to the light and inspected it. Satisfied, he looked at it and nodded. "Go fill up."

Christy said she was going to look around the store as Daniel headed out the door. Daniel quickly went to the van and stuck the nozzle in and got the fuel flowing. As the pump filled the van, an older man in overalls and a plaid shirt walked up. Pushing his Redman hat high up on his head, he said, "That's a heck of a rig."

Daniel smiled at him. "Thanks." He looked at the van. It certainly looked a lot different. "We were stuck in Atlanta and had to make some modifications."

The old man laughed, wiping at his nose as he did. "I'd say so. Looks like something out of a movie." After looking the van over, he asked, "Where you folks headed?"

"West," Daniel replied, trying not to offer too much.

The old man nodded. "I hear west is good. Hear there's places out there where the power is still on."

Daniel kicked the pump. "How do you guys have power here?"

The man spat at the ground. "This is the only place in

town with any power. Ole' Hajji there, that's what we calls him, has a big generator. It's nice to have a place with some power. Someplace you can go that seems normal."

Daniel smiled. "Yeah. Someplace normal would be nice."

The old man shook his head. "I just wish these damn politicians would get their heads out of their asses!"

"Ain't that the truth." Daniel then had an idea. "Have you seen any military trucks?"

"Military trucks? No, ain't seen no military trucks. Why, have you?"

"We saw some last night. Big line of them. Was just curious if they came through here."

The old man laughed. "Why in the world would the military come to Newton? Nobody comes to Newton. Lots of people leave Newton though. I was born and raised here. Lived my whole life here."

The nozzle clicked and Daniel looked at the pump. The van took thirty-two gallons. As he was reaching to turn the pump off, his hand was slapped away. He looked up at Gene.

"Let's refill this drum too while we can," Gene said. He had the empty blue drum waiting with the lid off.

"How long have you been there?" Daniel asked.

The corners of Gene's mustache rose up. "The whole time."

"What are you, some kind of chubby ninja?"

Gene shrugged. "Call me what you want. You didn't know I was here." Gene grabbed the nozzle out of his hand and filled the drum before hanging it up.

The old man watched and finally asked, "Hard to find fuel?"

Tipping the drum over slightly, Gene started to roll it to the back of the van. "There's none. No one has power, so we take it where we find it."

The old man nodded and stepped aside as Gene and Daniel hefted the drum and shoved it onto the rack. Gene had to climb up onto the ladder to help; once it was in the air and Daniel was stretching, Gene could no longer touch it. He continued up onto the rack and strapped the drum in place.

Daniel waited at the van. It wasn't long before Bob and Christy came out of the store. She was carrying a plastic bag in each hand. Once everyone was onboard, Daniel started the van and headed out. Christy began passing snacks and cold drinks out.

"Sorry, the selection was pretty slim," she said as she handed Daniel a diet coke.

He shrugged. "Hey, it's cold."

Gene looked at the one she handed him. "What, no beer?"

"No, Gene. The beer cooler was empty. Sorry, buddy," Bob said.

Gene looked at the coke and wrinkled his nose before dropping it back into the bag.

By late afternoon, they were crossing the Pearl River at Byram. It took a while to get there trying to avoid primary roads. It was decided this was the best alternative south of Jackson, Mississippi, and they certainly didn't want to go through there. Running alongside the bridge on the Florence-Byram Road was the old swinging bridge just downstream. It was one of the oldest crossings of the river still in place, built in 1905.

Byram itself wasn't much to speak of. If it weren't for the fact that I-55 ran through it, it probably wouldn't even still exist. But I-55 was there and, as they crossed over it, they were surprised to see it virtually empty. There were very few cars moving either direction.

"That just looks weird," Daniel said as he looked down at the nearly lifeless road running beneath him.

"Maybe. But we haven't passed many cars lately either," Bob replied.

Looking at the windshield, Daniel nodded. "You're right." Looking over at Bob, he added, "We haven't, have we?"

"Think about it. It's been days since this all started. People are running out of cash. They probably used what they had on hand to buy food, maybe some fuel. But they're out of it now. Not to mention that with the power going off, you can't really buy it anyway. That place in Newton was one of only a few that was even selling it."

"Why haven't we seen any response from the government?" Christy asked.

Bob chuckled. "Response to what? What are they supposed to respond to?"

Christy thought for a minute. "I guess I see your point. There's nothing going on."

Bob lit a smoke and blew it at the roof. "Exactly." He looked back at Christy. "We sure saw it in Atlanta, didn't we?"

"No shit." Daniel chuckled.

They continued to drive out of Byram, finding themselves on Owens Road. It was a rural road with few houses on it. Bob suggested they find a place to camp for the night while there was still light. Seeing several promising spots, they were thwarted each time by a fence. Here, the gas and power line right-of-ways were fenced off at the road. It forced them to keep going, looking for a place to pull off. But they needed a place out of view of any homes as well, which only added to the difficulty. You'd think it would be easy enough. During normal times, you wouldn't think twice about some of the places they had passed. But these weren't normal times. And after last night's events, they wanted to make sure no one would find them. At least as sure as they could be.

They finally came to a stretch of road that had no houses on it. Bob told Daniel to stop when he saw a gate on what appeared to be a rarely used dirt road going into a stand of planted pine. Gene hopped out with a large pair of bolt cutters and quickly opened the gate. Daniel drove through it and Gene closed the gate behind them. He took a minute to hang the chain so it looked as though it were still locked.

Daniel drove down the narrow road as limbs scraped and scratched down the side of the van. Just a week or so before, he would have cringed at the thought of driving the van through a place like this. Much had happened in a couple of weeks. The road opened up a little and they saw a small pond off to the left. Daniel stopped the van on the road and looked around.

"What do you guys think about this? Looks pretty good to me."

"Let me hop out and look around. I want to make sure there isn't a house or something at the end of this road. We don't need any surprises tonight," Teague said as he climbed out of the van, carbine in hand.

Christy opened her door. "I'm getting out."

Opening his door, Bob said, "I think we could all stretch our legs."

They all got out as Teague disappeared down the small trail. Gene was leaning against the van, cradling the shotgun under one arm. He looked down the small road and said, "I don't think there are any houses down there." He looked down at the trail and kicked away some of the thick carpet of pine needles covering it. "It doesn't look like there's been anything down here in a long time."

Bob lit a cigarette. "You're probably right, but better safe than sorry. Let Cousin take a look."

Daniel walked out towards the small pond. This was more his speed. Being out in the woods. He looked around and noticed a few things that brought a smile to his face. A small trail ran through the tall grass surrounding the pond. A dragonfly was dipping the water's surface, and a lone cicada was somewhere on the other side grating out its call. He always felt more at home in the woods. If it weren't for the carbine hanging over his shoulder, this could be like any other trip to wilder places for him.

Christy walked up beside him and took his hand. He looked at her and smiled. "Hey, sexy."

She smiled and laid her head on his shoulder. Closing her eyes, she took a deep breath. "Smells good out here."

"Yeah. I was just thinking how nice it was."

She looked out over the pond with him for a moment. "What do you think is going to happen?"

Daniel let out a long breath. "I don't know. We don't even know what's really going on out there."

Christy reached into her back pocket and took her phone out. She clicked the internet icon and waited. It wasn't long before a *page failed to load* message came up. Shaking her head, she said, "Why did they turn off our cell phones?"

He snorted. "Why in the hell did they turn off the power? Or kill the internet? They want us in the dark, both figuratively and literally."

Christy sighed. "You know, I used to hear those people talk about how the government was going to do this or that, how they were bad and not actually looking out for us. I never believed any of it." She pulled his hand up and closed both of hers around his. "But I guess they were right. Do you think they were right?"

Daniel shrugged. He was torn over the idea. *Maybe they were just trying to solve the current issue. Maybe they were actually working on it. That wouldn't explain why they killed everything though. You might be able to explain away the shutdown of the internet that way. Maybe justify killing the cellphones, though that would really be a stretch. But the power? None of this could explain that.*

After thinking about it, he said, "I don't really know, babe. All I know is we've got to look out for one another. No one else is going to do that."

She nodded. "At least we have the guys, too. It's nice that we're not alone in all this." She pulled away and looked at him. "Teague is still an asshole though."

Daniel smiled. "Yeah, he is. But he's got our back. That I know for certain. He's on our side. Come on, let's go back."

They walked back to the van holding hands. The grass was knee high and he smiled as he thought of the first trip into the woods with Christy. She wouldn't leave the trail. If she couldn't see the ground, she wouldn't' walk on it. Now she was in knee-deep grass and not saying a word about it.

When they got back to the van, they could see Teague walking casually down the trail towards them. Getting back to the van, Bob asked, "What's the word?"

"This trail ties into a paved road a couple hundred meters up there. I don't think it's the same one we were on. I didn't see any houses or people."

Bob looked around. "So we're good for the night here then, but to be on the safe side, I say no fire."

"I was going to say the same thing," Teague replied.

"Let's all try and get some sleep and leave early in the morning," Bob said.

"I'll make sandwiches," Christy offered.

As they sat around eating their sandwiches, their cell phones began to emit the emergency alert tone. Daniel went to the van and pulled his phone off the charger.

Due to the ongoing crisis, relief centers are being activated in the following cities.

A list of nearly every city of any size in all states was listed. It was long and detailed.

Additionally, price controls are being put in place to prevent price gouging. All prices of commodities shall remain at the price as of the first day of the crisis. If you find prices that have been artificially inflated, text the item, its price and business name and location to 99999.

In an effort to relieve the financial burden on people, the *relief centers will begin distributing cash. While credit and debit cards are not working, cash will be distributed in the amount of $200 per adult and $100 per child. Bring your ID to the relief center and all applicable documents for children to collect your disbursement.*

The curfew remains in effect. Anyone caught out after four PM daily will be arrested and held until the resolution of the current situation. Also, the possession of firearms is still illegal. Anyone caught with a firearm will be arrested immediately. To this end, if you know of someone in possession of a firearm, regardless of type, text their name and address to 77777. Upon a successful arrest, you will be eligible for a cash reward.

The government continues to work diligently to resolve the crisis and asks for your continued cooperation.

Daniel finished reading the message and dropped the phone in his lap. "Well, isn't that lovely."

Teague held out his hand, "Let me see it." Daniel tossed the phone to him.

Bob was thinking. He lit a smoke and watched the glow of the cherry. Gene read the message and dropped his phone into his lap with little or no care. Teague, however, had a lot to say.

"What a bunch of horse shit! Of course they'll give you a reward to rat on people with guns. And now that they've taken out everyone's debit cards, they'll start giving out a little bit of cash. Now everyone is totally dependent on the Feds! This is getting more and more ridiculous."

"Well, it doesn't mean anything to us. None of this changes our plans," Bob finally said.

"It's really weird that they're giving away cash," Christy said.

"Yeah. That kind of worries me. They want you to come into some *relief center* where they will just *give* you cash," Daniel said.

"The real point to consider here is the fact there are roughly 350 million people in this country. Without getting into ratios of adults to kids, we can say they are willing to give an average of one hundred fifty dollars per person. If only half of the people in the country show up to collect, that's twenty-six and a quarter billion dollars. And it only goes up from there, the more people that show up." Gene paused for a moment as everyone stared at him. He continued, "Now think about the complexities of distributing that much cash around the country. How long have they had this plan in place?"

Bob twirled a finger by his ear. "You uh, just did all that math in your head there, Gene?"

"How do you know all that?" Christy asked.

"I read a lot. Think about this. One billion in cash is ten pallets stacked three feet tall of hundred dollar bills So we're talking like two hundred sixty-three pallets of cash."

Teague shook his head. "Who the hell knows this kind of shit?"

With a straight face, Gene asked, "Who doesn't?"

"I don't!" Daniel said. "That's a shit ton of cash."

Gene pointed at him. "Exactly. Think about the logistics of getting that much cash and staging it. I mean, this isn't something you can do in a couple of days."

Teague snorted. "They just used some of those pallets of the trillion they *lost* in Iraq."

Gene smiled and pointed at him. "Now you're thinking. I mean, how do you lose a trillion dollars? You don't, that's how."

Christy shook her head. "This is more than I can think about right now. I'm going to bed." She sat down in the tent and kicked her shoes off.

Daniel told Teague to get some sleep, he'd take the first watch. Teague jumped up. "Thanks. I'm pretty tired." He moved towards the tent and stuck his head in. Christy pushed his head out with her foot.

"Don't even think about it!" She shouted. She suddenly squealed, jerking her foot back. "Eww, did you lick my foot? You sicko!" Her foot shot back out and connected with Teague's nose.

He fell back, holding his face. "Shit, Christy! I think you broke my nose!"

"Serves you right, you weirdo! That was nasty!"

Teague sat up. "I was only playing. I wasn't trying to go in with you. Jeez, calm down." He took his hands away and saw all the blood. "Dammit, my nose is bleeding."

Daniel went to the van and grabbed a handful of napkins, handing them to Teague. "You really need to leave her alone. She's going to hurt you."

With his head tilted back and the napkins pressed to his nose, he replied, "She already did."

"Should have learned sooner," Bob offered.

"I think I've got it now."

"Good!" Christy shouted from the tent.

Teague retired to the van to nurse his nose. Bob bid a good night and went to the van with Gene, who helped him get up into his reclined seat. Daniel settled into one of the camp chairs for a long night on watch. But staying awake wasn't hard, as there was a lot on his mind. Not to mention, the chorus of frogs from the pond was in full crescendo. After a couple of hours, he got up and walked over to the edge of the pond. He stood listening to the ruckus the frogs were calling out in all their number.

He watched the stars as they moved overhead. With the power out, the nation was dark, and celestial formations he'd only previously seen while in the mountains were clearly visible tonight, as well as others he'd never seen. Daniel stood for a long time just looking up into the sky. His mind drifted back to the physics classes in college and the explanation of the universe and the fact it was supposedly still expanding. The thought of all that vastness out there made him feel small and insignificant. The troubles here on this small part of this one small planet seemed so infinitesimal.

But that thought actually gave him heart in some strange way. The fact that, as big as the problems facing them seemed, they wouldn't even warrant a footnote in the history of the universe. *How many other worlds are out there right now?* he thought. He remembered reading somewhere once that everything that happened here on Earth had already happened on another planet and would still happen on others in the future.

He was about to return to the van when there was a change in things. He more felt it than anything, and it took him a few minutes to figure out what it was. Light. *Where the hell is that coming from?* He asked himself as he looked around. It wasn't a direct source, but suddenly there was light. Walking out to the edge of the pond, he looked around. Off to the north there was a very definite glow in the sky. *What the hell?*

"Teague, wake up." Daniel said as he gently shook his cousin.

After the second rousing, Teague bolted up, fumbling for his carbine. "What? What is it?"

Daniel held a finger to his lips. "Shhh, come here. I want to show you something."

Teague collected his carbine and pulled his boots on. "What is it?"

"Just come on. You'll see."

Teague followed him out to the pond. Daniel stopped near the edge of the small waterhole and looked at Teague as if to say, *see?* Teague looked around, "What? What am I supposed to see?"

Daniel pointed up at the northern horizon. "See the light."

Teague was scratching his head. "Yeah. I do now." He yawned big and asked, "What's that way?"

"I think Jackson, Mississippi is over there."

"You got your phone?" Teague asked.

Daniel pulled it out of his back pocket. "Yeah, why?"

Teague pointed at the phone. "See if Jackson is on that list of relief cities."

Daniel scrolled through the long list of cities on the message from earlier. After a moment, he said. "Yeah, here it is."

Teague nodded. "Makes sense then. They're turning the power back on to those cities."

"But why did they kill it in the first place?"

Rubbing his face, Teague said. "Well, after three days, any fresh food in people's fridges has gone bad. They've also probably run out of cash, and the stores are certainly empty. So they swoop in to save the day. Save everyone from the crisis they created."

Daniel thought about it for a moment. "I see what you're saying. But I don't think the government did this."

"Of course you don't. You suffer from normalcy bias. You don't want to see it. Don't want to see what's right in front of you."

"I don't suffer from anything. I just don't think the government would do this kind of thing."

Teague laughed as he stretched. "Why wouldn't they? Do you keep track of Treasury auctions?" Daniel shook his head. "Of course you don't."

"And I suppose you do?" Daniel shot back.

"I know you think I'm a dumbass, but yes, I do. The recent auctions have had very little demand. If they can't sell bonds, they can't create money out of thin air. If they can't create money, they can't spend it. Just the interest on the debt is almost everything the Treasury was collecting. So it's kind of convenient that this happens now."

Daniel's wheels were turning now. "They could declare the debt null and void because of this."

Teague pointed at him. "Winner, winner chicken dinner! And that will cause issues all over the world. How much do you want to bet that the cash they're handing out in those relief centers is some *new* dollar."

The thought shocked Daniel. He hadn't even considered the possibility of a new dollar. "That would also mean all the money everyone has is worthless."

"Starting to see the big picture now?"

"Wow. I never really thought about it all like this, the big picture, you know."

Teague slung his carbine over his shoulder. "I have been for years. I've been expecting it. Was really curious why it took so long. We saw the writing on the wall."

Daniel raised an eyebrow. "Is that the same *we* that carried out that action in Michigan?"

Without skipping a beat, Teague replied, "Yes. Same ones. We've been planning for this for a long time. The thing in Michigan wasn't really part of the plan though. It was just an opportunity that presented itself. We had to make a statement at that time. And I'm paying the price now. We were set up and ready. Now I'm here, with you, with nothing."

"It just seems so surreal."

Teague patted Daniel on the back. "Go get some sleep, buddy. I'll stay up the rest of the night."

Daniel went to the tent. Christy was sleeping softly and he tried not to disturb her. Getting into his sleeping bag, Daniel lay there for some time. His mind was spinning. There was so much to think about. But eventually the fatigue of the day overcame him and he nodded off.

Once again, Daniel woke to the aroma of coffee. He was surprised not to see Christy. She was already up. He pulled on his boots and climbed out of the tent. Everyone was up as he rubbed the sleep from his eyes.

"Why didn't you guys wake me up?" He asked.

Christy smiled. "You needed the sleep."

Gene was sitting by the small folding table. Its top was covered with canned food and other assorted food items. Daniel flopped into a chair as Christy handed him a cup.

"We have a problem." Bob said.

"What?" Daniel asked.

Bob pointed at the table. "That's all the food we have left. Plus, we're nearly out of water."

Daniel looked at the table. "Well, water isn't a problem. I have a filter. We can refill the jugs we have. But I don't know what to do about the food."

"We can hunt," Teague suggested.

"We don't have that kind of time," Bob replied.

"So what do we do?" Christy asked.

"One meal a day. We're not too far away. We'll just have to make it work," Daniel said.

"I don't like to be hungry," Gene said with a frown.

Bob laughed. "Tighten your belt, ole friend." Gene wrinkled his nose at the statement. "All we have to do is get across Louisiana and we're there. We're almost out of Mississippi. We could be there today."

Gene looked at the table of food. "We better be."

Christy got up and went to the table. "Don't worry, Gene. I'll fix us something before we get on the road."

That offered Gene a little relief. He sat back and smiled. "Thanks."

"I'll go fill our water jugs," Daniel said.

"I'll help," Teague offered as Daniel collected the empty one gallon jugs.

Daniel looked at him. "Dude, you look like shit."

Teague glared at Christy. "Yeah, well someone gave me two black eyes."

Christy was working a can opener on a can and didn't look up to reply. "Bet you don't stick your nose in places it shouldn't be anymore."

Teague reached up and touched his very tender nose, but said nothing in reply. Instead he collected a couple of jugs and followed Daniel.

They went out to the pond and looked for a place where they could get to the water. Finding it, Daniel knelt down with his Katadyn Hiker Pro filter and dropped the intake into the brown water. It bobbed in the grass-filled water as he unwrapped the discharge tube. He'd replaced the original one with a longer piece. The one that came with it was ridiculously short.

Teague held the discharge tube in the jug as Daniel pumped. It didn't take long to fill the first one. Teague capped it and held it up. The water was a light brown in color. Teague's face contorted. "That looks like shit."

Daniel laughed as he uncapped the next jug. "It'll be alright. There's tannic acid in the water. It won't hurt you."

"Acid?" Teague asked.

"Comes from decaying vegetation."

"And you can drink it?"

Daniel nodded. "Yeah. But if you drink lots of it, I mean like a steady diet, it can turn your hair and fingernails yellow."

"What?"

Daniel laughed. "You're not going to drink that much. I promise. Besides, when you make coffee it turns the water brown."

"Yeah, but that's coffee! Not rotted shit!"

They filled the rest of the jugs and headed back to the group. Christy had a pot sitting on Daniel's Whisper Lite stove. He'd selected it because it was multi-fuel and could burn any of several different fuels. It was a little heavier than others, and not as efficient as say a Jet Boil, but he felt the versatility was a worthy tradeoff.

Bob, being a bachelor, lived on quick and easy-to-prepare foods. To that end, he'd stocked his pantry with things like Dinty Moore Beef Stew and Sweet Sue chicken and dumplings. There were three cans of each of these, and the group had saved them. But as today was hopefully the last day on the road, Christy was heating the chicken and dumplings.

Daniel looked into the pot that was ridiculously large compared to the small stove. "Man, that smells good."

Gene was sitting at the small table with a bowl in front of him and spoon in his hand. "Yes it does. Is it ready yet?"

Christy laughed. "Hang on, Gene. It'll be better if it's hot."

Gene nodded. "Make it so, Number One."

Daniel chuckled. "You a Star Trek fan, Gene?"

"Star Trek, Star Wars, Star Gate, Hitchhiker's Guide to the Galaxy. Love them all."

Christy smiled. "You're just full of surprises, Gene." She held out her hand. "Give me your bowl." He quickly handed it over and she spooned some out for him, then served the rest of the group.

After their unconventional breakfast, they loaded the van and got back on the road. While waiting for Gene to close the gate behind them, Daniel looked at Bob. "Alright, which way?"

Bob had the atlas in his lap. "Well, we have the Mississippi River in front of us. There aren't that many bridges, and most of them are in larger cities. I just don't think that's a good idea. The closest one to us, not in a major city, is in Greenville, which is north/north-west of here. If we cross there, then we'll be in Arkansas, which might actually be a good thing."

"Lead the way," Daniel said. Bob pointed left and Daniel pulled out.

The trip to Greenville was a long and winding trip. It took them through small towns with names like Bovina, Redwood and Foote. It was also surprisingly uneventful.

"You guys notice how many more cars on the road today?" Teague shouted from the rear of the van.

"Yeah," Daniel shouted back. "And it looks like all of them are headed to Jackson, or at least that direction."

"Makes sense." Bob said. "They're all headed out to get themselves some government stash money."

Christy climbed up between the front seats. "You know, I'm really surprised we've done this as easily as we have."

Bob shook out a smoke and lit it, more to annoy her than anything else. That and the fact that a cigarette in his hand was his natural state. "You forgetting about the two dead men?" he asked.

Christy scowled at him. "No, I'm not. But we've really not had that much trouble considering how far we've gone. I really didn't expect to make it this far. When we started, it seemed like so far to go."

"We ain't there yet." Bob said. He asked for one of the water jugs. Christy handed one up to him. Bob looked at the off-color water, then at Daniel. "What the hell did you do, piss in these?"

Daniel smiled. "No. Just yours."

Bob eyed the jug with no small degree of suspicion. "This looks like shit."

Daniel laughed. "That's what's wrong with our country. Everyone is so used to everything being perfect. It ain't going to hurt you. Drink it."

Bob spun the cap off and held the jug out to Daniel. "You drink it."

He took the jug, turned it up and took a long pull. With his cheeks full of water that dripped down his chin, he looked at Bob and swished it around before swallowing. "See, it ain't going to hurt you," and handed it back.

Bob looked down into the opening and gritted his teeth. He took a cautionary sip at first, smacking his lips to taste the brown-tinted water. Deciding it was safe, or maybe that he was just thirsty, he took a long drink. After capping the jug and handing it back to Christy, he said, "That has an odd taste. If I get the shits, it's your ass."

Daniel howled and slapped the steering wheel. "It's surface water. You get the shits and it's *your* ass, Bob!"

At the Swiftwater Baptist Church, Bob told Daniel to take a left. The bridge was just down the road now. If they could make it over the river, they would be home free. There were no other large obstacles in their way. On either side of the road was empty farm land they could see all the way across. Bob was getting worried, the bridge was a natural choke point and he just knew there would be a roadblock and possibly vehicle searches. He told Daniel to pull over.

"Why?" Daniel asked.

"Just pull over."

Daniel slowed the van to a stop on the shoulder of the road along a dusty field. Bob got out, so Daniel killed the engine and climbed out with everyone else.

"What's up, Bob?" Gene asked.

Bob leaned against the front of the van and pointed at the causeway leading up to the bridge. "I'm worried about that bridge. Perfect place to stop and search vehicles."

"Wish we had some binoculars." Daniel said.

"We have something a little better." Gene said as he opened the driver's door and leaned in. He came back out with the laptop they had brought along from Bob's house. "I spent some time the other night messing with this while everyone was asleep. It took a while, but I found the camera utility on one of my thumb drives and installed it." He opened the laptop and clicked on an icon.

A window opened on the screen, and after a moment, the image of the road in front of them filled it. Using the mouse pad, Gene manipulated some buttons in the screen and the image began to move. "I put this together in case we had to drive in the dark. But these cameras have a 30x optical zoom, plus some digital. We should be able to see if there is anything up there."

As the image moved around on the screen, Bob smiled. "God I love you, Gene."

Without looking up from the computer, Gene replied, "The answer is still no."

"Oh, I have my spotting scope too!" Daniel shouted as he returned to the van.

The group crowded around as Gene moved the camera view to the bridge, then started to zoom in. As the magnification grew, the bridge came into much closer view. There was a line of cars, maybe a dozen, on the bridge. Then they saw the black MRAP with its blue lights flashing.

"Shit. That's what I was afraid of. If we get searched, we're screwed," Bob lamented.

"Is there anywhere we can hide the guns?" Christy asked, knowing as they all did what the issue was.

Bob looked at Gene and raised an eyebrow. Gene looked into the open side door of the van. Gene rubbed his whiskers. "I don't know. There isn't much in the way of options."

Daniel had set the scope up on a tripod. He was looking at the bridge when he replied, "Yeah there is," as he went to the rear of the van. He took out the small tool kit he stored in the pocket in one of the doors and walked around to the front. Kneeling down, he opened the kit. "You remember how I told you I didn't have my guns anymore?"

Bob smiled. "Yes. And I knew you were lying."

Christy looked at him, confused. "What do you mean? You said you sold them."

Taking out a small Allen wrench, he looked up at her. "That's what I told you. But there was no way I was selling my guns." He took a small screw out from the bottom of one of the caps on the end of his bumper. Reaching up into the large steel square tube he pulled out a piece of tightly wrapped foam. Setting it on the ground, he carefully untied it and unrolled the foam to reveal a disassembled AR and a Glock pistol.

Bob laughed. "That's a hell of an idea, kid."

Gene was immediately at the bumper. He pulled a small tape measurer from his pocket and measured the bumper and the one disassembled rifle. After a moment, he said. "We can get four rifles in there if we take them apart like this."

"What are we going to do with the others?" Teague asked.

Daniel nodded at the rear of the van. "There's another bumper back there."

Gene smiled, "We can fit them all."

"What about the ammo?" Daniel asked.

"We should be able to stuff it all into the rear bumper," Gene said. "We don't have that many rifles. But we're going to have to pitch the shotguns from the other night."

"We don't need them," Bob said.

Gene, Daniel and Teague got to work taking the weapons apart. To fit them into the bumper, they had to remove the pistol grips as well. Fortunately, Daniel kept the proper tools in the van for the job.

While they were working on the guns, Christy had Bob sit down so she could look at his wounds.

Christy finished going over Bob's wounds about the time the guys finished storing the guns. Daniel was about to put the cap on when Bob walked up. "Let's put our IDs in there too."

"Why?" Daniel asked.

"Couple of reasons. One, you and I were supposed to talk to the FBI. They could be looking for us. Two, if we need to do some creative talking, I don't want them to have anything they can pin us down with."

The explanation seemed logical, so everyone placed their wallets in and the cap was secured to the bumper.

"What if they ask for our names?" Christy asked.

Daniel shrugged. "I guess we'll wing it."

The approach to the bridge was long and elevated. Once on it, there was no turning around. Daniel gripped the wheel a little tighter as he watched the crest of the road ahead of him, waiting to see the large armored trucks appear.

Bob turned in his seat. "Gene, you're my brother. The rest of you are my kids."

"Like hell!" Teague shouted.

"Shut up and listen. We need a story. We're heading to my mom's place in Hot Springs. If we're questioned, we need a decent story."

Gene started to laugh. "Over the bridge and through the woods to Grandma's house we'll go!"

Christy started to laugh, but stopped when Daniel spoke.

"There's the truck." he said. Then he corrected himself, "I mean trucks!"

Bob looked up. "Oh shit."

Ahead of them was a proper roadblock with several MRAPs and many men. They had the bridge blocked at its center.

"Yep. They're looking to catch people out here. Once you're on this, there's no way to turn around," Bob said.

"They're searching every car," Daniel said.

"Just remember what I said." Bob reminded them.

As they approached the roadblock, a man waved for them to slow down. Daniel did as instructed, and rolled to a stop. Several men approached the van and ordered everyone out and demanded their IDs. These were what you'd expect of the modern militarized federal tactical ninjas. They wore black uniforms, kitted out with all manner of MOLLE pouches, thigh holsters and tactical vests that read POLICE in white letters on the back. The black balaclavas covering their faces topped the ensemble off.

Christy quickly said, "We don't have our IDs. We were robbed."

When Bob opened his door, the man standing there looked at his leg. "What happened to you?"

Bob shook his head. "We had a hard time getting out of Atlanta. And like she said, we were robbed. A couple of times."

The uniformed man looked at the van. "That why you did all this?"

Bob nodded and made a pained expression as he tried to exit the van. The man held out a hand. "You can stay in your seat."

The rest of the group got out as the men manning the roadblock began searching the van's interior. The man standing beside Bob asked, "Where are you headed?"

"To my mom's place in Hot Springs. We figured it was better than Atlanta. I was able to get my sons and daughter rounded up, and picked up my brother on the way out as we headed west."

The man nodded and asked. "Any weapons in the van?"

Bob shook his head. "No sir, no weapons in the van at all." He smiled inside at the fact and irony of the statement.

Another uniformed man asked Teague. "What happened to your face?"

Christy quickly threw an arm around Teague, which startled him. "We were robbed. He fought with them and my brother is the only reason we still have the van."

Teague nodded. "We've had a hard time."

The search ended up being rather cursory at best. The uniformed men gathered and spoke quietly. Daniel started to get worried and began biting his fingernails. Christy saw this and took his hand. He looked at her and she smiled, mouthing the word, *relax*.

After a moment, one of the men returned and said, "You can go. Just remember there is a curfew. You do not want to be caught out after dark."

Bob smiled and nodded. "Indeed. We'll be off the road by then. Thank you."

The group quickly got back in the van and continued across the bridge. Daniel was drumming the wheel with this thumbs. "I nearly shit myself."

Bob laughed. "Wasn't anything to it. No big deal."

"Because we were able to hide those guns," Gene said.

Teague grunted. "Let's hurry up and stop somewhere so we can put them back together. I feel totally naked."

Bob looked at his watch. "Let's roll for a couple of hours. We've got a little time before we need to be off the road."

In Lake Village Arkansas they turned west and drove through neat farm fields flat as a pool table. They passed through a couple of small towns that Norman Rockwell would have seen as sparse. They seemed totally devoid of life. There was no one out at all. That changed when they reached the town of Hamburg.

Hamburg is a small town nestled in a grove of hardwoods. Just outside of town, beside a sign announcing the annual armadillo festival, was a roadblock. As Daniel slowed the van, he said. "We were so close."

Teague leapt up between the seats to look. "I told you we should have put the guns back together!"

"I just can't believe it," Bob said.

"I know. What are we going to do?" Daniel asked.

"Only in Arkansas could you have a damn festival for something as nasty as a damn armadillo," Bob said.

Daniel looked at him. "What?"

Bob pointed out the windshield at the sign, "You don't see that damn billboard with a giant rat in the armor suit on it?"

"Screw the sign! What about those guys?" Daniel shouted.

The roadblock consisted of a couple of sheriff department cars and several civilian vehicles. Behind these stood many armed men of uncertain intent. Much like the last group, these too were kitted out in tactical of the day, save one major difference. No two of them were alike. All had various camo patterns, and their personal kit varied from man to man.

Bob held a hand out behind him. "Give me your 'kerchief, Gene."

Gene pulled a white handkerchief out of his hip pocket and handed it forward. Bob shook it out. Rolling down his window he held it out as high as he could through the gun port. "Drive forward real slow."

Daniel started to sweat. He didn't know why. Maybe it was all those men pointing guns at him. But he did what Bob said. He'd gotten them this far. They rolled slowly forward as the men behind the barricade held their positions. When they were about thirty meters from the barricade, the PA from one of the sheriff cars crackled to life.

"Stop! Everyone get out of the vehicle! Keep your hands where we can see them!"

"Alright, everyone. Real slow, get out," Bob said.

They all slowly got out, holding their hands high over their heads.

"Step in front of the vehicle and spread out on the road! The loudspeaker shouted."

"This is bullshit," Teague muttered.

"Daniel?" Christy said quietly.

"Just stay close, babe," he replied.

"Everyone, just stay calm," Bob said.

They spread out on the road as instructed and waited. Once they were all out on the road, several men came out from behind the barricade, walking towards them with weapons at low ready.

"Shit, shit, shit," Teague muttered.

"Be cool," Bob said. "These guys look different. I don't think they're feds."

As they got closer, details began to appear. Several of the men had a Velcro patch of the Texas flag on their chest. Some were bearded and at least one wore a cowboy hat. The deputies were in uniform, however.

"You're right, Bob. These look like my kind of people," Teague said.

The group of men spread out in front of them and stopped. One of the deputies stepped forward, his rifle at low ready, and he looked them over. "Where are you going?" He asked.

"We're headed to Texas," Bob replied.

One of the men with a beard and the Texas flag on his chest asked, "What for?"

"We heard it was the land of reason, that Texas told the feds to shove their Martial Law up their ass. That the power was still on and the grid was cut from the rest of the country."

The bearded man cocked his head to the side and asked. "And just how did you hear all that?"

Bob gestured with his head towards Gene. "He's a HAM guy and has a radio."

The group of men closed ranks, talking amongst themselves. After a moment, they broke up and the bearded man asked. "Texas ain't got room for any freeloaders. You got any weapons?"

"I thought we were in Arkansas," Bob said.

The man nodded. "You are."

"Then who are you guys?"

Pointing at the deputies, the man replied, "They're with the Ashley County Sheriff's Office." Then, thumping the Texas patch on his chest, added, "We're Texas militia."

Bob cracked a smile. "So the Texas militia invaded Arkansas?"

The militia members laughed. The joke made everyone relax as the men lowered their weapons. Bob lowered his hands, as did Teague and Gene. Daniel and Christy kept theirs up.

"No. We decided to create a bit of a buffer for ourselves," the bearded man replied.

"Plus, the federal government can kiss our ass!" One of the deputies shouted.

The bearded man pointed at Bob. "What happened to you?"

Bob looked down at his bare legs. "Bullet."

One of the deputies looked back over his shoulder and called out, "Hey, Doc!"

Another man appeared from behind the barricade and jogged up. The deputy pointed at Bob and told him to take a look. As the man walked over, Bob held a hand up. "I'm fine. We've got our own doc." And he pointed at Christy.

The man looked at her. "You a doctor?"

"No, I'm a critical care nurse. I was working in a pediatric center in Atlanta."

"Holy shit! You guys drove all the way from Atlanta?" The bearded man crowed.

Bob took a cigarette pack from his shirt pocket and shook a smoke out, lit it and blew out the smoke before replying, "Yep."

Seeing the cigarette, the bearded man licked his lips and rubbed his chin. "You got an extra one of those?"

Bob laughed and looked at the cigarette. "That's like asking if I got extra money." He paused for just a moment before pulling the pack out again and walking towards him, offering the smoke.

After lighting it with his own lighter, the man held out his hand. "Thanks, name's Mathew Ward. Call me Matt. We ran out yesterday and I'm about to lose my mind."

After shaking his hand, Bob offered him the pack. "Here, keep it. I've got a couple more. Call me Bob."

Matt smiled. "Thanks Bob, you're alright. Let's go meet the guys." He looked past Bob at Daniel and Christy. With a laugh, he said. "You guys can put your hands down."

CHAPTER 12

AFTER INTRODUCTIONS WERE MADE, DANIEL drove the van into town. Matt rode with them to the town square. He directed them to park across the street from an orange building. The sign over it read, Sawyer's Steak House.

"Figure you guys are probably hungry," Matt said as he got out of the van.

"Yes, we are," Gene replied.

Bob looked up at the gaudy orange building. "What's for dinner?"

Matt smiled. "Brisket."

Gene pushed past the two men, making for the open door of the restaurant shouting, "Make a hole! Make a hole!"

They went inside and took a seat. "You'll love the food," Matt said.

It wasn't long before a medium height pie-faced man with what appeared to be a perpetual smile walked up in a white apron tied around his waist. He was wiping his hands on a small towel. "Howdy, folks. Hope y'all are hungry. Today, we've got brisket, mashed potatoes and green beans."

Matt smiled. "This is Tommy. Really knows his way around a smoker."

"Wait," Christy said. "Tommy? Like Tom Sawyer?"

Tommy smiled. "Exactly like that. But everyone calls me Tommy."

Gene picked up a napkin and tucked it into the top of his shirt. "Sounds good to me, Tommy." Picking up a fork, Gene added, "Bring on the brisket."

Tommy laughed. "Sounds good, folks. I'll be right back. Sweet tea good for everyone?"

Bob nodded. "We're from Georgia, Tommy. There isn't any other kind." Tommy chuckled and disappeared.

"That's really funny. Tom Sawyer," Christy said with a big smile. Daniel laughed at her. "What?" She asked.

"You're funny."

Matt leaned in on the table. "Tommy is a really good man. He feeds anyone that needs it, no questions asked. He's been taking care of us since we came up."

Teague seized the opportunity to ask some questions. "What's your plan? What are you guys doing?"

Matt let out a breath. "We're just trying to keep a buffer between us and the feds. We're not sure what they're up to just yet."

Bob laughed. "Texas not big enough for you guys?"

Matt smiled. "You guys don't know, do you?"

"Know what?" Daniel asked.

"The Republic of Texas is a lot bigger now."

Bob leaned back in his seat. "I know you Texans like to call it a Republic. But I've got a feeling there's more to it now."

Smiling, Matt nodded. "Oh yes there is. The state legislature passed secession and the governor signed it. We are now *really* the Republic of Texas."

"You left the US?" Christy asked in surprise.

Matt nodded affirmatively.

"About damn time someone got the balls!" Teague added.

"You're not worried about what the government is going to do?" Daniel asked.

"Of course there's a concern. Plus, it's not going smoothly. But we're set on this path. It's the law of the Republic now."

"You said the Republic was bigger." Bob said.

Matt nodded. "New Mexico and Oklahoma joined us. Arizona is probably going to as well."

"What about all the federal assets? Texas has a lot of military bases. Not to mention the Border Patrol and other federal departments," Bob asked.

"We seized it all," Matt said. "Most of the personnel went along with it. Those that didn't were escorted to the border and released. We changed the logo on the Border Patrol equipment. Gave them new patches and issued new rules of engagement. Things are a little different down there now."

"And all that happened without issue?" Bob asked.

Matt shrugged. "Well, no. There was some trouble. Plus, there are a couple of DHS facilities that are holding out, but they've been told to surrender or a column of M1s is going to roll out of Fort Hood and turn their building into a pile of broken rock."

Tommy showed up with plates and served everyone. He then returned with glasses of tea. The talk paused while everyone ate. "Enjoy," Tommy said as he walked back to the kitchen.

"Oh wow, this is some damn good Brisket," Daniel said.

"Yeah it is," Christy added. "After the last few days, anything fresh is good."

With a forkful of potatoes, Matt said, "And it's all fresh. He makes these from scratch. Even the beans were grown locally."

"What do I have to do to join the militia?" Teague asked.

"You just have to sign up. We can get you kitted up if you need it," Matt replied.

"Why are you going to do that?" Daniel asked.

Teague dredged a bite of Brisket through a small bowl of sauce. "So I can kill as many of those federal fuckers as possible."

"So far, we've been lucky and haven't had any engagements," Matt replied.

"I'm ready for it. Done it once already," Teague replied.

Bob used a piece of meat to mop his plate. "You know they're sitting on the bridge over the Mississippi in Refuge, don't you?"

Matt nodded. "We know they're there. But they don't know we're here. We've been watching them since they showed up. But they haven't ventured to this side of the river. Not sure why."

"They had a lot of armor over there," Teague noted.

Pushing his plate away, Matt replied, "I know. But our rules of engagement are pretty clear. We are defensive only. We're not looking to start a shooting war with the Feds. But if they press us, we will defend ourselves."

Gene hadn't said anything, focusing instead on his meal. But he was done now. Pulling the napkin from his shirt, he dropped it on his plate. "You really think a militia with a few small arms can take on a column of MRAPs?"

Matt smiled and shook his head. "No. No I don't. It's not here yet, but we're moving armor closer to the border. A lot of the military sided with us, the ones here anyway. We've got fighters flying combat air patrols. And we've got naval vessels off the coast. We're doing what we can to protect ourselves."

"This is so weird," Christy said. "States leaving."

"We didn't leave it. It left us," Matt said. He waved a hand in the air. "This whole financial crisis is all BS. They shut everything down. Turned off cellphones and the internet. We didn't ask for any of that. They're not helping us."

"They're handing out money now," Daniel said.

Matt snorted, "Yeah, *new* money."

Surprised, Bob asked, "What?"

"Oh yeah. That money they're handing out. It's a new dollar. We think this was their plan the whole time. They did all this to introduce a new dollar."

"Have you seen it?" Daniel asked.

Matt pulled a cellphone from his tactical vest and pulled up a picture. It was a colorful piece of red currency with a man's portrait on it. "Yeah, they have Roosevelt on it. Not even one of the founders. I think they're sending a message."

Bob took the phone and looked at it. "Where'd you get this?"

"We politely asked the DHS to leave one of their facilities. They resisted at first, but gave up when they realized it was a no win for them. They wanted to take everything with them, but we made them walk out empty-handed. They burned most of their stuff. But we got some of it."

"So it was already here. Before all this started," Bob said.

Matt pointed at him, "Exactly."

"Can we get to Texas?" Daniel asked.

Matt sat back and tucked his hands into his vest. "I don't see why not. It shouldn't be an issue. Do you have someplace to go?"

Daniel shook his head. "No. We just thought it was better here. So we came."

"We're working out of Red River. We can take you there and see what we can do," Matt replied.

"When can we go?" Christy asked.

"We can go any time you want," Matt replied.

"I want to stay with you guys," Teague said.

Matt sat forward. "You'll have to go to Texarkana to enlist in the militia. It's a little more formal than just saying that you're in."

"Why are you going to do that?" Christy asked.

Teague shook his head. "I told you before, someone has to do it. Why shouldn't it be me?"

Matt stood up. "Let me go talk with some folks and I'll see what I can do about getting you guys down to Red River."

Tommy came out from the kitchen. "What'd you folks think of the food?"

"It was fantastic. I'm a fan," Gene said.

Bob nodded with a laugh. "And you can take that to the bank. If Gene likes it, it's pretty good."

Tommy smiled. "Well, I'm glad you folks enjoyed it."

They walked out to van. Matt told them to hang out

while he went and talked to some people. Bob leaned against the van and lit a smoke. Gene opened the side door and sat down. Looking up at Teague, he asked, "Were you touched by someone in uniform as a kid?"

Teague looked at him. "What?"

Deadpan Gene said, "You seem to have a lot of hate for folks in uniform. Just curious if you had a bad experience as a kid. You know, like someone touching you or something." Bob lowered his head to hide the fact he was smiling.

"Screw you, Gene!" Teague shouted.

Gene pointed at him. "See, so much hate. Takes a lot of hate to hide that much sadness."

Teague was fuming. "Fuck off!" He turned and walked away.

Gene laughed. "I think he's been buggered."

"That's just mean, Gene," Christy said.

Gene looked at her. "No it's not. He knows I'm just messing with him."

She looked at Teague. He was standing at the back of the van with his foot on the bumper. "I don't think he does. What's wrong with you guys? Why are you so mean to one another?"

Bob laughed. "Because we're guys. It's what we do."

Christy looked at Daniel. He shrugged and said, "Don't look at me. He's right. When Teague and I were kids, we were mean as hell to one another."

She shook her head. "But saying he was molested as a kid? That's really horrible."

Gene laughed. "That's what makes it so funny! Besides, he'll get over it."

Christy shook her head. "I do not, and never will, understand you guys."

Bob flicked his butt to the curb. "Well, if you ever figure it out, please let me know. I'd like some clarity."

Matt returned from his trip to the courthouse across the street. "We've got the nod to go. We can leave now if you want. I'll go with you guys too. Got some stuff to take care of down there."

Daniel smiled. "Cool. Let's go." Everyone loaded into the van for the last leg to the great state of Texas.

"How long is it going to take us to get there?" Daniel asked.

"About three hours or so," Matt replied.

"It's going to be dark before we get there," Christy said with an air of concern in her voice.

Matt laughed. "Don't worry about that. That curfew crap doesn't exist out here."

Even though the city of Texarkana straddles the border of two states, the entire city had power due to its connection to the Texas grid. They arrived about nine PM at the outskirts of the city, where they were stopped at a checkpoint manned by men wearing the same Texas state flag Matt wore.

Seeing the checkpoint, Daniel slowed. "What do we do?"

Matt waved him forward. "Just keep going."

Unlike the roadblock in Hamburg, no one pointed guns at them. Four men manned the checkpoint. And while they had tactical-style vests on with weapons, they were worn over Wranglers and checkered shirts. These men looked more like cowboys than soldiers.

Daniel rolled to a stop where Matt indicated. One of

the men walked up to the van as Bob rolled his window down. Matt leaned forward and said, "Hey, Jessie."

The man pushed a dusty, worn Stetson back on his head. "Hey, Matt. You guys got here quicker than I expected."

Matt nodded. "Yeah, this young feller here has a lead foot."

Jessie stepped back and looked at the van. "Hell of a contraption you got here."

"We started in Atlanta. It was a rough trip," Bob said.

Jessie looked at the door where Bob sat. "I'd say so." He looked back at Matt, "You heading to the depot?"

Matt nodded. "Yeah, got to see them before figuring out what to do with these guys."

Jessie waved. "Alright. See you later."

Matt patted Daniel's shoulder. "Go ahead."

Daniel pulled away, following Matt's directions. He told Daniel to get onto I-30. Daniel looked at him and asked, "Are you sure? We've been avoiding the interstates."

Matt smiled. "You're in Texas now. Things are different."

Christy leaned forward. "We're in Texas now? We made it?"

Daniel looked at her. "We made it."

Matt had him exit at Hooks and they pulled up to the very nondescript gate of the sprawling Red River Army Depot. As they approached it, Christy asked, "What is this place?"

They stopped at the gate, that was now manned by uniformed men wearing the Texas Republic flag. Matt showed his ID to the guard at the gate, who quickly waved them through. Bob noted that. Thinking it interesting they had already issued photo IDs to members of the militia.

"Its primary mission is the repair and maintenance of heavy equipment, tanks, MRAPs, that sort of thing," Matt said.

"So this place is full of armor?" Teague asked.

Matt turned and smiled at him. "Yeah it is. We've been getting some of it back into service. That's why I came down with you, to take one back."

"Look at the size of this place," Bob said as they drove through the massive complex of industrial-looking buildings.

Gene was looking out the window as they passed one of the sprawling buildings. The huge rolling doors were open and a hoist was moving an entire M1 Abrams tank through the air. "This looks like my kind of place."

Matt looked at him. "They could probably use the help. We lost some people here who didn't agree with the secession. So if you're mechanically inclined, they could use you."

Gene smiled. "I spent twenty-six years in the Navy. You could say I'm mechanically inclined."

Bob looked at Matt. "He's really good."

Matt pointed to a small brick building. "Pull up there."

Daniel turned into a parking spot and stopped, where they all got out. Daniel looked around at the massive facility that was very busy, even at nearly ten o'clock at night. Christy walked up to him and wrapped her arms around his waist. He smiled and leaned in and kissed her.

"Let me go in and check on some things. I'll see if I can find you guys a place to stay. Gene, you want to come in and see if you can help out here?"

Gene nodded. "Yes I do."

Looking at Teague, he asked, "You still want in the militia?"

"Damn right," he replied with a nod.

"We'll wait for you guys out here," Bob said.

Matt nodded and the three men went inside. Bob leaned against the van and lit a smoke.

"We're in Texas," Christy said with a smile.

"We're in Texas," Daniel repeated, then looked around. "Now what?"

Bob smiled and stood up. Nodding, he echoed Daniel's sentiment. "Now what, indeed."

Made in the USA
Coppell, TX
25 March 2025